THE GOD SQUAD

Reverend Lucas Holt—The pastor of St. Margaret's Episcopal Church in downtown Austin. After serving as a prison chaplain for twenty-five years, he remains friends with several former inmates, much to the aggravation of local church authorities.

Nikky Dorati—The Rev's right-hand man. They met in prison when Dorati was doing hard time for some hard crime. Although he's changed his ways, he's not above using his street smarts and old connections—especially if it helps the Rev catch killers.

Maxine Blackwell—The church secretary. While in prison, the former madame served as the Rev's inmate secretary. When he took over at St. Margaret's, he insisted that she come along as part of her parole.

Lieutenant Susan Granger—An old friend—and sometimes romantic interest—of Reverend Holt. As a member of the Austin Police Department, Susan doesn't like the God Squad getting involved in her business, even when they help her solve the crime.

Don't Miss the First Reverend Lucas Holt Mystery

The Saints of God Murders

The Reverend Lucas Holt's parish is troubled by a serial killer who c_____ lyrics of an old chur_____ according to the sc____

D0802684

MORE MYSTERIES FROM THE
BERKLEY PUBLISHING GROUP . . .

DOG LOVERS' MYSTERIES STARRING HOLLY WINTER: With her Alaskan malamute Rowdy, Holly dogs the trails of dangerous criminals. "A gifted and original writer." —Carolyn G. Hart

by Susan Conant

A NEW LEASH ON DEATH	A BITE OF DEATH
DEAD AND DOGGONE	PAWS BEFORE DYING

DOG LOVERS' MYSTERIES STARRING JACKIE WALSH: She's starting a new life with her son and an ex–police dog named Jake . . . teaching film classes and solving crimes!

by Melissa Cleary

A TAIL OF TWO MURDERS	FIRST PEDIGREE MURDER	THE MALTESE PUPPY
DOG COLLAR CRIME	SKULL AND DOG BONES	MURDER MOST BEASTLY
HOUNDED TO DEATH	DEAD AND BURIED	

CHARLOTTE GRAHAM MYSTERIES: She's an actress with a flair for dramatics—and an eye for detection. "You'll get hooked on Charlotte Graham!" —*Rave Reviews*

by Stefanie Matteson

MURDER AT THE SPA	MURDER ON THE SILK ROAD
MURDER AT TEATIME	MURDER AT THE FALLS
MURDER ON THE CLIFF	MURDER ON HIGH

BILL HAWLEY UNDERTAKINGS: Meet funeral director Bill Hawley—dead bodies are his business, and sleuthing is his passion . . .

by Leo Axler

FINAL VIEWING	DOUBLE PLOT
GRAVE MATTERS	

PEACHES DANN MYSTERIES: Peaches has never had a very good memory. But she's learned to cope with it over the years . . . Fortunately, though, when it comes to murder, this absentminded amateur sleuth doesn't forgive and forget!

by Elizabeth Daniels Squire

WHO KILLED WHAT'S-HER-NAME?	REMEMBER THE ALIBI
MEMORY CAN BE MURDER	

HEMLOCK FALLS MYSTERIES: The Quilliam sisters combine their culinary and business skills to run an inn in upstate New York. But when it comes to murder, their talent for detection takes over . . .

by Claudia Bishop

A TASTE FOR MURDER	A DASH OF DEATH
A PINCH OF POISON	

SAMANTHA HOLT MYSTERIES: Dogs, cats, and crooks are all part of a day's work for this veterinary technician . . . "Delightful!" —Melissa Cleary

by Karen Ann Wilson

EIGHT DOGS FLYING	COPY CAT CRIMES

FORREST EVERS MYSTERIES: A former race-car driver solves the high-speed crimes of world-class racing . . . "A Dick Francis on wheels!"—Jackie Stewart

by Bob Judd

BURN	SPIN
CURVE	

THE REVEREND LUCAS HOLT MYSTERIES: They call him "The Rev," a name he earned as pastor of a Texas prison. Now he solves crimes with a group of reformed ex-cons . . .

by Charles Meyer

THE SAINTS OF GOD MURDERS	BLESSED ARE THE MERCILESS

BLESSED
ARE
THE
MERCILESS

CHARLES MEYER

BERKLEY PRIME CRIME, NEW YORK

AUG 1 3 2002

BLESSED ARE THE MERCILESS

A Berkley Prime Crime Book / published by arrangement with the author

PRINTING HISTORY
Berkley Prime Crime edition / January 1996

ISBN: 0-425-15140-9

Berkley Prime Crime Books are published
by The Berkley Publishing Group,
200 Madison Avenue, New York, New York 10016.
The name BERKLEY PRIME CRIME and the BERKLEY PRIME CRIME
design are trademarks belonging to Berkley Publishing Corporation.

PRINTED IN THE UNITED STATES OF AMERICA

10 9 8 7 6 5 4 3 2 1

PS
3563
E8726 B64x
1996

FOR
Carl and Martha Meyer
Jack and Grace Faison
Dan and Dorothy Karrel

• Prologue •

The woman lounged on the soft white carpet by the fire that warmed her long bare legs. She draped the blue silk robe loosely over her strongly scented body when she heard the garage door open and close. She smiled with anticipation as a shiver of pleasure stirred deep within her. This was a night to celebrate, and, now that they were finally alone, they could.

"Everything go okay?" she said as the man entered the kitchen and tossed his car keys on the table.

"It went as usual," he replied. "She tried to make me feel guilty for not letting her live with us." He pulled a Fall Creek Cabernet Sauvignon from the wine rack.

"Upstairs or down?"

"What?" he said, rummaging through a drawer for a corkscrew. "I didn't hear you."

The woman raised her voice slightly. "Would your mother live upstairs, where she'd be totally isolated, or downstairs, where there's no bedroom or bath?"

"That's what I explained to her for the four hundredth time." He jerked out the cork. "She knows she's a lot safer and more independent out there than she would be with us." He picked up the bottle and two glasses. "Don't you look inviting?" her husband said as he placed the objects on the coffee table. He knelt down and opened her robe. "Besides, if she lived here, how could we do this?"

"Ah, ah, ah," she said, playfully pushing his hand away. "Look, but don't touch." She arched her back and pushed her breasts up toward him. "Not until you've showered off the smell of that nursing home."

"But I was barely inside five minutes!" He frowned and stuck out his lip in a pout. "I just walked her to her apartment."

"Long enough to smell like urine on wool pants."

"But—"

"That's right. Take your butt to the shower and we'll celebrate when you're clean, like me." She kissed him as she unbuttoned his shirt and twirled the curly hair on his chest, then pushed him away.

"Okay, okay," he said, reluctantly standing. "And here is yet another reason to detest my mother."

"Listen, I don't like her either, but—"

"No, really." The man pulled off his shirt and shoes. "She intrudes herself into my life even when she's not here."

"Well . . ." The woman lowered her voice and looked into the fire. "Someday she won't be."

"Not soon enough." He headed for the stairs. "You know—" He stopped. "Sometimes I think about—"

"Don't think at all tonight. Don't let her ruin another evening for us." She slipped her robe open more and raised her knee to her chin. "We have a lot to celebrate."

He came back and leaned over the couch to kiss her.

"You're right. What were we talking about?"

"About your butt in the shower. And yes, I will have a glass of wine while I'm waiting here all by my lonesome. Why don't you take one along, too?"

He poured the wine. "Don't move from that position," he said. "I'll be back in a flash."

She held the wine provocatively to her lips. "Just flash when you're back." She smiled.

As the shower ran, the woman slipped an envelope onto the table. It was the reason for celebrating tonight. The latest reason, anyway. There had been many like it in the last few years, but this was the largest. When they combined his bank's resources with her aggressive real estate company, businesses and buildings suddenly changed hands rapidly. Commissions on both ends mushroomed to five and six figures.

This was the first check with seven.

The shower stopped and she imagined him naked and wet. She

hoped the stench was gone. She didn't want any signs of his ancient mother and her constant interference.

The old lady expected to come to their house every Sunday, no
matter what plans they had. Holidays were marred by her obtru-
sive presence, her constant advice, her complaints about everything from the weather to her bowels. Today the old harpy had
arrived right after church full of venom and gossip. Insisting that
she could fix "her little boy" a dinner like she used to, she had left
the kitchen a disheveled mess for her little boy's wife to clean up.
There followed the obligatory retold stories they had heard a million times, the point of which was to indicate their ungratefulness
for her generosity to them. Finally, thank God, she had fallen
asleep in front of the TV. They had hoped she was dead.

Whatever they did was never enough, and her son, especially,
hated her for the relentless reminders of their shortcomings.
When they woke her to take her back, she had predictably resisted
going back to "the home," as she called it. Even though it was the
most luxurious such place in Austin, she described it as a dun-
geon that would make the state prison look preferable.

If only they could arrange that . . . The woman smiled as she
leaned toward the fire and sipped her wine. The good news was
the old lady was worse today, more forgetful, and her hands
shook more when she tried to hold her cup. With any luck, she
would not be an inconvenience much longer. It was a matter of
time.

Meanwhile, there was tonight. The woman stuck her finger in
the wine and licked it as the man returned to the living room
wearing only his black silk shorts. "Much better," she said, patting the floor beside her. "Come here, where it's warm."

He refilled their glasses and sat down. "You're right. I smell
better now that I've washed her off. God, what a pain. How do
you tolerate her?"

"It helps that she's not my mother."

"I wish she weren't mine."

The woman kissed his shoulder and bit him playfully. "Let's let
this wash her out of our heads—like the shower."

"Yes." He clicked his glass to hers and they drained the deep
red wine, laughing at his finishing last. He saw the envelope. "Is

that it?" he said, setting their glasses on the table. The cut crystal facets sparkled in the firelight.

She nodded, opened it, and handed him the check. "Let's drink to it." She undid her robe and moved her hand inside the black silk. "And celebrate the big one."

He reached for the bottle and nearly knocked it over. "Getting bigger all the time," he joked.

"The checks, too." She held out a glass to him, but as he poured the wine he missed, spilling some on her belly.

She laughed at the cool pool of red filling her navel. "Better get that before it slides to the carpet," she said enticingly, "or somewhere else."

"Good idea." He lowered his head to kiss her, then moved down. "Whoa," he said as he bent over her. "The wine and your perfume made me dizzy." He tried to straighten, but his arms were weak and his breathing hastened with his pulse.

His wife blinked hard to focus. "You sure it's not—the—smell of the check?" she said haltingly. "It's more intoxicating than the wine. I think it's making—my eyes blur." She laughed a little, and coughed, trying to fend off her sense of fear, telling herself the wine had simply acted too quickly. But she knew this was different.

The man put his lips to the wine on her skin but his trembling muscles would not hold him up.

"What—what the hell's going on?" He looked up at her, trying to smile. "Did you—put something—?" He collapsed, rolling onto her thighs. "I can't . . . I can't move. I—"

The tingling in her body changed suddenly to tightening knots of pain. Panicked, she tried to speak, tried to force words across her swollen tongue.

"Hurt!" she gasped as rolling spasms gripped her muscles like talons of a bird of prey, then dropped them, flaccid and useless. "Oh, God! Help us! Help!" Her wide, staring eyes barely saw the fading red-orange aura in the fireplace move farther and farther away from her, as she seemed to fall backward at increasing speed.

"No!" the man mumbled in disbelief. "Why—?" He used his waning strength to roll his head backward on her legs and look up at her. A thin white foam of saliva appeared at her lips just as the same drooled from his. Two wet streaks descended from her eyes. His body shook as he tried to lift a stiffening hand to her. His arm collapsed on her belly and dropped beside him onto the check.

The woman gazed down at the blurred form on her legs, heard a deep choking sound, then matched it with her own. The crystal goblet dropped from her hand and shattered against a table leg. She slumped over onto the broken glass but did not feel the deep gash in her shoulder.

White carpet strands swelled crimson; wine indistinguishable from blood. The fire grew cold like the bodies whose lives flickered out before it.

• One •

The man in black walked cautiously down the dimly lit hall-way, casting furtive glances through open doors. He found the room he wanted and nervously fingered the cold steel object in his pocket. He entered quickly, shut the door, and silently walked across the room, grateful for the carpet that dulled the thud of his boots. His five-foot-ten frame seemed to tower over the slight, re-cumbent form below him.

The figure in bed lay still. Vacant eyes stared at nothing. Dry, split lips formed a sunken *O*. A thin sheet covered the skeletal body of an old man, twice the age of the one standing. The sheet jerked as the mouth gasped and the wrinkled face grimaced; a shallow dry reflex forced a swollen tongue against his toothless gums. Then he stopped.

The man in black pulled out the steel object and cocked it open next to the old man's face. An oily thumb pressed the cold, damp flesh and made the sign of the Cross.

"May the angels in heaven receive you as you pass from this life to the next, from glory to glory, from strength to strength, through Jesus Christ our Lord. Amen."

The Rev. Lucas Holt anointed the dead man's head, hands, and feet with blessed oil from the stainless stock. He sat in the win-dowsill and read the Prayers for the Dead from the Episcopal Book of Common Prayer. In a few minutes he closed the book, removed his purple stole, and stayed by the bed.

At ninety-seven the old man had outlived his spouse and chil-dren. His grandchildren had no interest in him and seldom visited the hospital where he had lain for weeks in a coma.

Holt was glad to have arrived at the time of death. The old man was a sustainer of St. Margaret's Episcopal Church. As Rector of "Maggie Mae's," as the church was known, Lucas Holt represented an eternal family—the "great cloud of witnesses" that would forever be present with him in life and in death.

As the priest opened the curtains to let in the late afternoon sun, he saw his own reflection in the window. About to turn forty-three, he noticed the lines at the corners of his eyes and in his roundish face. His sandy brown hair had thinned and become interwoven with strands of gray, though friends told him it handsomely brought out the color of his blue-gray eyes. Those eyes were drawn to the dead man's image in the glass, perpendicular to his. The two figures reflected together like hands of a clock at a quarter to twelve.

Holt shuddered and turned to straighten the rumpled sheet, pulling it up to the lineless, peaceful face. Death made him want to *do* something to reassert the illusion of control; make the bed look more normal, like the person was "sleeping." Family members always wanted to close the dead person's eyes as they do in the movies. And he always had to instruct them that in *real* death the lids seldom stayed down and often flapped back open, as this man's did now—as his own father's had done.

Amazing, Holt thought as he shook his head, how memories hurled themselves into the present. In a flash of seconds each one a flaring scene of emotion, the dying face of Ben Holt was before him in the bedroom of their house, taking one last shallow breath into peaceful silence. Eight years of churning sadness brimmed over in tears for his father, for himself, for this man in the bed who all but the Church had abandoned. He snatched a tissue from a box on the bed and blew his nose, unceremoniously breaking the quiet, ending the memory.

Lucas Holt composed himself as he solemnly packed up the man's few belongings. He signed the Release of Body Form on the bedside table to designate a funeral home and used the room phone to dial an outside line.

"St. Margaret's Episcopal," the church secretary answered. "Can I help you?"

"Yo, Max," he said to Maxine Blackwell, the red-haired, former madam who had been his inmate secretary for most of his twenty-five years as a Texas prison chaplain. An embarrassment to the Diocese because of his theological and social outspokenness, Holt had been forced out of that job and into the dismally bankrupt St. Margaret's by Bishop Emilio Casas two years ago, hopefully to fail so the bishop might be rid of him. When Holt demanded she come along as part of her parole, the Vestry of the church, composed of elected parishioners, reluctantly agreed. It seems they couldn't turn down someone whose "house" many of them had visited; someone they secretly "knew"—in the biblical sense.

"Hey, Rev. You okay? You sound bad."

"How do you do that on the phone?"

"If you could hear your stuffy self on this sunny day, you'd ask the same question."

"I'll be fine. Thanks for asking."

"Been my job a long time, Rev. How's old Mr. Burnside?"

"Dead."

The secretary paused, held her smart-ass comment, and said instead, "Sorry to hear that."

"Why?" Holt replied. "He was old and demented and alone."

"Still, I liked how the old geezer looked at me when I took him flowers from the altar on Sundays."

"He's had dementia ever since you've known him, Max. How could you tell what he was thinking?"

"When you've been in the business as long as me, Rev, you can tell by the look in their eye. And darlin', that man had some eyes."

Holt pictured Max in her house on South Congress, and his mouth turned up in a smirk. He glanced at the glassy stare of the corpse in the bed. "Remind me to wear sunglasses around you from now on."

"Rev, I've known what you were thinking since your first day at the penitentiary," she teased. After years of surreptitious flirting they had once embraced and kissed in his prison office—only to realize their relationship was doomed to be friends. But no matter how much she mothered him, the attraction was—and always would be—still there. "And that's what makes my job here at the church so interesting."

"I'll mention that to Kristen."

"I already did."

"She called?"

"*State Representative* Kristen Wade called to say she can't have dinner with you tonight." Max paused. "Uh-gain. She's got another late committee meeting at the Capitol. Uh-gain. Said she'd call you when she got out. Uh-gain."

Holt frowned as Max reminded him it was the fourth time in three weeks Kristen had canceled. He patted the dead man on the shoulder. "It's just that life is short and getting a hell of a lot shorter."

"Careful, Rev, I'm ten ahead of you, you know."

"So what are *you* doing for entertainment tonight? And before you answer consider that—whatever it is—the alternative is having a superb dinner with me at the place of your choosing."

"I'm fixin' to go country-western dancin' with a bunch of friends tonight, but thanks anyway." She paused for a drink of coffee. "You want me to reserve a time for Mr. Burnside's funeral?"

"Yeah." Holt sighed. "Today's Wednesday. Make it Friday at eleven. We'll do a graveside afterward."

"I'll tell Cora Mae to alert the Altar Guild."

"Thanks." He looked out the large window into the park between wings of the hospital. "Any calls I need to know about?"

"Just one. Lieutenant Susan Granger from the Austin Police Department was here ten minutes ago looking for you with a scowl on her face and an unfriendly tone in her voice. Did you do something especially bad recently?"

"Not that I know of. But that's never been a requirement before."

"Well, watch out for her. I told her you were at San Jacinto Hospital with a dead parishioner."

"Great. Anything else?"

"Nothing that can't wait till tomorrow."

"Okay. But if you change your mind about dinner, I'll be on the pager."

"See you in the mornin', Rev."

Lucas Holt took a deep breath and hung up the bedside phone. A nurse knocked and peered around the door.

"Everything okay in here, Father?"

"Yes. I was just leaving, thanks."

The nurse walked in and emptied the patient's medications, toothbrush, and dentures into a plastic bag. "I wonder where he is now?" she said.

The Rev walked to the door as she placed the bag at the end of the bed to accompany the body to the funeral home. "Yeah. I wonder, too." He nodded at the corpse. "Bye, Mr. Burnside," he waved. "See you in church."

Holt saw the flashing red light and worried when he realized the police cruiser was parked behind his car in the Clergy space. His worry increased when he saw the look on the cop's face.

In other circumstances it would be a nice face, even pretty, he mused as he slowed his pace to think. Lieutenant Susan Granger scowled, giving her otherwise round eyes a critical narrowness. Her dark brown hair and full eyebrows framed her flushed cheeks and terse lips like an old schoolmarm, and Lucas Holt felt like he was on his way to the principal's office.

By the time he reached her, he had made up three great excuses for anything she could criticize.

"Hi, Susan," he said, holding up the oil stock for her to see. "Nice day to die."

"Nice day to haul your scrawny ass to jail, Father Holt." She grabbed his arm and turned him toward the hood of his car.

"What? What the hell are you doing?"

She pulled his other arm around and cuffed his wrists. "I have a warrant for your arrest issued by Judge Waller, for withholding evidence and obstructing justice." She threw the document on the hood in front of him.

"Wait a minute, wait a minute! What are you talking about?" He twisted around to face her, searching her hazel eyes for clues. "People looking out their windows up there will think you've lost your mind, arresting a priest. Which you have."

She opened the back door of the blue-and-white and pushed him down into the seat. "Watch your head, Father Holt."

"Susan! Stop! This is ridiculous!"

"No. What's ridiculous is you and your damned God Squad interfering in police business. I told you last time—with that 'Saints of God' case. Maybe now you'll believe me."

Holt's protestations were silenced by the slamming door. He watched her speak into her radio outside the car and hoped she'd smile at him, chalk up whatever she was so angry about to their long relationship, since college at U.T. Though they had been on opposite sides of every issue as students, there was the period when they lived together off campus. Their romantic involvement fell apart shortly before graduation, and they lost track of each other's careers until he was asked to give the invocation at a police cadet graduation. Surprised to find each other a priest and a cop, their lives reconnected upon Lucas Holt's return to Austin and St. Margaret's.

Now they attempted to keep their relationship arm's length and professional, though there were the occasional flashes of emotion on both sides, emotion that, like eighth graders caught in the maelstrom of hormones, wanted both distance and closeness. Susan Granger had warned him to keep out of police matters, it was true, during the "Saints of God" murders. But it was also true that he and his "God Squad"—the misfit collection of loyal excons who had followed him here from the pen—had solved the case for her in their own outside-the-law kind of way.

But that was over a year ago. Holt searched his mind for something they had done lately.

"Susan?" he said as calmly as he could.

"You have a right to remain silent. And I wish you would."

Lucas persisted. "Is this about that jewel thing?"

"When we get to the jail, you can read the warrant." She started the car. "All of you."

"*All* of us?" Lucas Holt said. "You're picking up *all* of us?" She must have caught hell from her superior, Captain Dixon, for the way the jewelry theft case was handled, and was rounding up "the usual suspects" to teach them a lesson. Holt had seen her in this non-negotiable mood before and knew he could only hang on for the ride. Besides, Judge Waller belonged to St. Margaret's and drank the same Scotch as the Rev.

With spinning lights and blaring siren, the APD cruiser lurched from the hospital lot, sped through stoplights, and rolled to a halt in front of the vintage Alamo Hotel. Built in the early twenties, the downtown landmark had become the subsidized home of transients and parolees.

Holt would try one more time, if not for himself, then for the person he knew was next to get picked up. "Listen. Susan. Can't we talk this out?"

Lieutenant Granger ignored the pleading from the backseat as she slammed her door and stormed into the Alamo. Minutes later she returned, and the Rev was joined by an equally outraged—and equally handcuffed—Nikky Dorati. She pushed him into the seat with her hand on his head, then reached in and wiped her hand on his shirt.

"Dammit, Dorati, will you quit using that greasy kid stuff? The worst thing about arresting you is I always get slimed."

"Yeah?" the black-haired, blue-eyed man replied. "Well it may surprise you to know I feel the same about you."

Nikky Dorati was no stranger to the backseat of a police car. The "Mafia Midget," as he was known in the pen, had done hard time for hard crime. Nobody messed with the meticulous hit man with a perfect possible on all his targets. Nobody except Lucas Holt.

When Holt came to the prison as chaplain, he purposely approached the inmate leaders most likely to hate him. If he could win even one of them over, he would fill the chapel and all of his groups. Surprisingly, a few responded, including Dorati, though most thought the con used the Rev for special favors such as phone calls and commissary. Over time, with many sparring rounds and the recognition of each other's "dark edge," Dorati and Holt crossed the line and became friends. Others approached and formed what became pejoratively known as the "God Squad"—men, and women from the female unit, who watched the Rev's back as he watched theirs, who listened to his unique brand of the Gospel, saw how it affected their lives, and wanted to know more.

When Lucas Holt came to Austin, Dorati had followed. When something happened to the Rev or his congregation, the God Squad responded swiftly, secretly, often to the chagrin of the police, and especially one Lieutenant Susan Granger, who was, once again, in the driver's seat.

"What the hell's goin' on here, Rev? What did you do?"

"What did *I* do?" Holt said incredulously. "What did *you* do?" He smiled at the five-foot-seven man beside him, like two boys caught playing hooky.

"Lieutenant?" Dorati yelled, pressing his feet on the hump in the floor to steady himself.

"What?" Granger said without turning around.

"Where's your car phone? Don't we have a right to call a lawyer or something constitutional like that?"

"Shut up, Dorati, or I'll add 'resisting arrest' to your fifty-pound rap sheet."

Dorati looked at Holt and mumbled: "Forty-nine."

"What did you say?" Granger barked.

"Nothin', your lieutenantship."

"Good. And you don't make any calls until I've got you all in tow and read your Miranda."

"All?" Dorati asked, his expression puzzled.

"That's what *I* said," the Rev replied, looking out the window to determine where they were going. The car was headed straight up Congress Avenue, the main street that intersected the city. "I guess it's the jewelry."

"Listen, Lieutenant," Dorati argued through the metal grate separating the front and rear seats, "I gave all that stuff up. Honest. Right after we located it. You didn't find anything missing, did you?"

Granger did not answer. She sped up Congress to the Capitol and screeched to a halt by the Sam Houston Office Building.

The Rev spoke to Nikky. "Like they said at the pen: 'You can beat the charge, but you can't beat the ride.' "

"You're not beating either one this time," Granger replied, checking her watch as she strode into the building.

Dorati laughed. "She must be takin' some kind of drugs to make her do this."

"No, she's only like this when she *doesn't* take her drugs."

Holt glanced up at the pink granite Texas State Capitol as the representative to the Texas House was escorted to the squad car in handcuffs.

"Omigawd—it's Kristen," Holt said, wondering what connection she had to the jewelry heist. To the best of his memory the God Squad had gotten involved because several of the robberies were at houses of St. Margaret's parishioners. In their usual underworld fashion, they had nailed the perp—who turned out to be a former cop selling security systems—and recovered the jewelry.

The door opened and a tall, auburn-haired woman joined them.

"Lucas?" she said in a puzzled tone of voice.

Kristen Wade had been Lucas Holt's "nearly significant other" ever since Susan Granger had introduced them at a fund-raiser two years ago. Their independent, noncommitted relationship served both of their purposes perfectly. As Holt's eyes met hers, he knew she wondered how personal this was. Though Kristen and Susan were old friends, Susan's feelings about her relationship with Lucas Holt varied from disinterest to ambivalence.

"Okay, guys," Kristen Wade said. "A joke's a joke. But there are people of the other party persuasion in there making videos to sell to Channel Twenty-four for the six o'clock news."

"At least we'll be on together," Holt added cheerily. "They got pictures of me getting cuffed at the hospital."

She looked at the two men seriously. "What did you get me into this time? Don't you realize I have a political career on the line here?"

"It's all a bad dream, Kristen," Holt tried. He had seen a lot less of her since the election. Maybe she'd be more available if her interest in politics waned with her popularity. "This isn't happening," he said. "In a few minutes we'll all wake up—"

Granger interrupted. "In the Travis County Jail on obstruction of justice charges."

"What?" the woman in the back said.

"You heard me, Ms. Representative—or should I say 'former' Representative, when the D.A. gets hold of this?"

"Have you taken leave of your senses, Susan?" Wade said.

"No more than you did when you conspired with these two— and the others—to withhold evidence in those jewel robberies last month."

"But, Susan," Holt began, "we busted that case wide open for you when you didn't have a clue about it." He was starting to feel defensive about what had happened. "Y'all never would have recovered the jewelry; it would have been fenced by the time you got around to catching that guy. We—"

"Dammit, Lucas!" Granger yelled. "You held back the information and didn't call me in until the very last."

"But—"

"Don't talk to me. I'm busy." Granger punched a button for the police radio. "This is Lieutenant Susan Granger to all cars on the God Squad Bust. Over?"

One by one they responded.

"Are all suspects on board?"

Three affirmatives radioed back.

"Rendezvous at base in three minutes. Over."

"Okay, Susan," Holt demanded, an edge of anger emerging in his voice. "What the hell are you doing? You've got a bunch of people rousted with no stated cause." Sometimes Susan pushed his

limits too far. She knew his basic distrust of authority, especially
armed and legally powerful authority. Harassing him—or Kristen
Wade—was one thing. Harassing people with little or no political
power to resist was quite another, particularly when they were his
friends, even more particularly when they were the God Squad.

Susan Granger answered in a way calculated to annoy him further. "Why not have your lawyer-honey back there protest for
you? Maybe represent you in court. But then who'll represent
Kristen Wade as an accomplice?"

"Accomplice? I didn't have anything to do with that case."

"When we found His Reverendship with the recovered jewelry,
he happened to be in your house in the Las Ventanas subdivision,
did he not?"

Lucas saw the Town Lake trail up ahead. "Susan—" Holt
began. They had just crossed the Colorado River on South Lamar.
APD Headquarters was at Eighth and IH35, north of the river.
Something was screwy here.

"Wait just a damn minute, Susan," Kristen Wade interrupted,
flushing.

"Just shut up till we get to the arraignment."

"Lieutenant?" Dorati winked at the Rev. "I'm ready to turn
State's on these two. What do you want to know?"

"Enough, Dorati. This bust will take you back to Huntsville for
the remainder of that quarter you were supposed to do before your
pal back there got you sprung."

Lucas worried that Susan was unrelenting. Already he was
thinking of strategies to counter her claims to the judge, the most
important of which was that some of the stolen jewelry belonged
to another member of St. Margaret's—*Mrs.* Waller, the judge's
wife. Holt watched the Casita Lobos Restaurant fly by. "Can I ask
the morally kind and socially just lieutenant to tell us why we're
going south of the river when APD is north?"

Granger fired back. "If the legally challenged Father Holt kept
up with the latest news, he would know that the substation where
we have to book all of you is on South Lamar. The warrant is
from there, so we have to book you there. I'm going to make sure
this bust sticks."

The car careened off Lamar and lurched to a halt, converging
with three other cruisers in front of the Broken Spoke Dance Hall.

The one-story, ramshackle building was an old house in the front with a barnlike dance hall tacked onto the back. It was the best known of Austin's authentic kicker joints. Rusty old tobacco and beer signs covered holes in the wood-slat siding. A handwritten sign tacked to the front post said OPEN.

"Everybody out, and I mean *now*," the lieutenant ordered.

Other officers took Dorati and Wade in tow. Along with six other prisoners in handcuffs, the two were led into the Spoke while Granger kept the Rev outside to read him his rights.

By now Holt questioned Susan's sanity. She had no case. She was harassing a state representative, not to mention some inno-cent—well, relatively innocent—ex-cons and himself, and using a lot of public funds to do it.

"As I mentioned, you have the right to remain silent," Granger continued. "I'm reading you these for everyone, because you're the only one I'm relatively sure can understand them." She took him by the arm and forcefully escorted him through the screen door into the dance hall of long tables with benches and pitchers of beer and margaritas. "Anything you say can and will be used against you."

"Let me remind you, Lieutenant," Holt said, stumbling in her grasp, "that the same goes for you, too."

"You have a right to an attorney."

As they passed the swinging doors into the dance hall, Susan Granger suddenly turned him around and kissed him on the mouth. "And you have a right to a Happy Birthday."

The Rev was stunned more by the kiss than the words. "What?"

They walked onto the wooden dance floor where they found the God Squad, Kristen Wade, and the Vestry of St. Margaret's Episcopal Church shouting: "HAPPY BIRTHDAY!" APD cops he knew, along with other friends from around Austin, were part of the crowed circle.

"Well, shitdamn!" The Rev smiled and shook his head.

The Five Card Stud band led by God Squad member Lisa En-right started the intro to a song.

"Y'all quiet down a second! Please!" Lisa Enright called from the stage microphone. She waited until the din receded. "Rev-erend Holt," she said with her Texas twang, "this is your night and you get to pick the songs we play—assuming they're all from our album, of course."

When the laughter and applause died down, she spoke again.

"We been smokin' Elgin sausage and barbecue all day, waitin' for you to get here. There's plenty of Shiner Bock and 'ritas for all you two-steppers." She winked her pretty blue eyes at the still-handcuffed Holt. "Don't worry, Rev," she said, "there's iced tea and sodas for us twelve-steppers."

More applause and cheers from the God Squad made the fettered priest want to clap, especially for Lisa Enright and her husband, Alan Greer. They were two of the few success stories of the penitentiary, coming out of severe drug backgrounds to make their marriage work and the Five Card Stud Band an up-and-coming hit. For Lucas Holt and the rest, the young and vibrant Lisa was the daughter in the God Squad family.

"We want you to have a happy forty-third birthday, Rev," Lisa continued. "But this is also our time to tell you what you've told all of us for so long. So we're gonna start the first dance with a tune that sort of summarizes our message to each other." She turned to her husband to begin the backbeat. "Everybody out on the floor now to remember that there's 'No Time to Kill.' "

Holt held up his hands to Granger. "Can I get out of these now, O Kind and Benevolent Sheriff of Nottingham?"

"In a minute, Robin," she quipped as she unlocked one of the handcuffs and shackled it to her own wrist.

"Since I went to all this trouble, I get the first dance."

Holt glanced at Nikky Dorati dancing with Kristen Wade.

"She'll wait, Lucas," Granger said. "Besides, she always gets the last one."

"You're on," Holt said, and pulled her into two-step position.

Lucas smiled at his friends as he and Susan worked the various routines. Each set of eyes he met meant something different, a story, history, times of sadness or joy. Maxine danced with Omar Dewan, white and black, prostitute and burglar, mixing with cops and the powerful governing body of St. Margaret's—the Vestry— all of whom had stories of their own. And Holt's life was tied to them all, in ways similar to the penitentiary but now richer than he thought it would be when he first came to the parish.

As Susan took the lead and Holt stepped backward, he flashed on the morning at the hospital, the dead reflection next to his in the window, the minute hand of death slowly moving up to meet him. This birthday was significant, the entrée to his mid-forties and beyond. So many forces seemed to be impinging on him all at once, so many things coming into focus with clarity he had never had before, so many decisions that pressed for resolution as he muddled through midlife crisis after crisis. The words of the song pounded into his consciousness with the strong country backbeat: "Do we keep on killin' time until—there's no time to kill?"

"Good dancer!" Holt heard a voice break into his thoughts.

"Huh?"

"I said you're a good dancer!" Susan Granger repeated. "You haven't forgotten a thing from the class I made you take with me in college."

"I also haven't forgotten that you made me pay for it." He laughed, turning her to the side so they danced hip to hip. The smells of barbecue and open pitchers of beer mixed with leather smells from boots and belts. It reminded Holt of his childhood in Smithville, going to places like this with his parents. "Thanks for arranging this, Susan. It means a lot."

"You're welcome." She grinned. "It's all my pleasure."

"Listen," Holt said seriously, "if you need help with the bill, I—"

"No problem," she replied, smiling. "Just remember to thank your Vestry, too. They're paying for it."

"Some things never change," Holt said to her as the music ended and people applauded one another.

The lieutenant pulled a tiny key from her pocket and unlocked the handcuff from his wrist.

"You're free to go now, Outlaw," she kidded.

Filled with gratitude and overwhelmed by the kindness of his friends, Lucas Holt quickly pulled her to him and kissed her.

"Thanks again," he said as the band started another song.

Kristen Wade grabbed his free hand and turned him around.

"Next!" she said, handing him a longneck.

As Holt danced the Texas waltz with Kristen, he was aware of the imprint of the handcuff on his wrist. Funny, he thought, that it had not so much felt binding as secure.

• TWO •

"I should be going soon, Marie," Cora Mae Hartwig said. She enjoyed these weekly visits to the sick and shut-in of St. Margaret's, especially when she had known the parishioner her whole life. Marie Wilkins sat in the dark wood rocker she had brought from her house, looking as faded as the pinkish-white satin that barely covered it.

"Oh, don't go yet," Marie Wilkins replied. "You've only just gotten here."

Cora Mae Hartwig smiled at her old friend. "You remind me of when we were girls and you didn't want me to go home for dinner. So my answer now will be the same as my answer then."

"Good. You're the only company I really enjoy."

In their heydays the two women had been inseparable pillars of the church, served on every committee, led the women's guild, ran the Vestry, ironed altar linens, and taught all levels of Sunday School. Together they had survived a string of clergy and seminarians who, according to Marie, they "no sooner trained to do it on the paper than they left." Though both women were now in their eighties, Cora Mae's mind and body were in better shape than her friend's, partly through diligent diet and exercise, partly through the luck of the genetic lottery.

Cora Mae picked up another sugar cookie from the large round tin. "These certainly are good. Where did you find them?"

"My new beau gave them to me, Cora. They're imported from Denmark, as you can see on the can." Marie Wilkins poured another cup of Darjeeling tea from the white bone china teapot. Along with the rocker, it was one of the few items she had been allowed to bring with her when she was moved to these three small rooms. Her thin, veiny hands shook slightly, but her dignity strengthened her grip and straightened the flow from the pot to the cup.

"I want to hear more about that beau, Marie. You've been very secretive about him." Cora Mae had never married. She had witnessed the succession of men in Marie's life since they were girls, commenting on them over the last eighty-some years with varying amounts of jealousy and amusement. Cora Mae could predict what he looked like. Gable-ish. Tall. Dark. Handsome. And bad for her. There was not one man Cora Mae could think of who had treated Marie well, including the man who was her son.

Marie Wilkins smiled, making her face a bed of wrinkles. "You know, Cora," she said, sitting back with a napkin and a cookie on her lap, "I always thought that once somebody got to be our age, well, that the—what shall I call it?"

"The 'urge to merge,' dear," her friend offered, biting into a cookie.

"Cora Mae Hartwig!" Marie Wilkins held her hands up to her reddening cheeks. "Where did you get that?"

"At the university, of course. The young people there are so fresh and full of what we used to call 'piss and vinegar.' "

"But not in front of our parents! We didn't talk about half the things children do today in front of their parents."

Cora Mae watched her gracefully sip the tea as the constant ticking of the old Regulator clock on the wall filled the momentary lapse into silence.

A look of recognition lit Marie's face. "Why, do you know that grandson of Mrs. Rumpke, next door to me—I believe he's a third grader—told her all he had learned in school last week about *condoms*!"

Cora Mae Hartwig laughed. "Just wait till your turn comes."

A black cloud covered Marie's face. "I don't think so, Cora. Erik and Janey are perfectly content to live without anyone, including me. They no more want a baby to interrupt their self-centered lives than they want me to spend every Sunday with them." The darkness was replaced by a flush of anger. "And after all I've done for that boy."

Cora Mae knew Marie's family and agreed with her. Marie's husband had died when their son, Erik Junior, was six, leaving her no insurance and a hefty mortgage. She remembered how hard it was when Marie took in laundry and cleaned houses until one of her laundry clients offered her a secretarial job. Thirty years later Marie retired as executive secretary with pension enough to be quite comfortable—but for her son.

The boy had always been greedy, or maybe it was needy, Cora Mae thought as she listened to Marie drone on about him. It was her own fault, really, having spoiled the boy to make up for lack of a father. Furthermore, Marie had refused Cora Mae's sage advice over the years to quit bailing him out of business failures. He had only escaped total ruin by marrying a smart business woman—and with the good fortune of his sinking bank being scooped up by a national chain practically as he was on the courthouse steps.

"No," Marie lamented, "I don't think I'll have grandchildren of my own. That's why I so enjoy it when other people's come to visit." She looked pensively at Cora Mae. "Do you ever regret not marrying?"

Cora Mae sighed and put down her cup. "Sometimes I do. It would be nice to have someone to grow old with." She smiled. "But I've already done that by myself, haven't I? Grown old, I mean. And it hasn't been entirely alone. I have good friends like you to talk with every week. And I do take on new things to keep me current. I'm halfway through my Ph.D. program, you know," she announced proudly.

"Don't change the subject, Cora Mae. You know perfectly well what I'm talking about."

"Marie," Cora Mae said, reaching for another cookie, "you and I have had this conversation forever. I love men. And I've always had a more than adequate sex life. You still remember our college days, don't you?" She pointed to the many framed photos on the walnut lamp table. "Those wonderful fraternity parties?"

Marie smiled and nodded.

"Well I do, too. And I've had wonderful relationships with men in my lifetime. I just never could find one that would put up with me for the long haul." Cora Mae smiled and propped her feet up on the small hassock in front of the chair. "But with all this typing I'm doing for my doctor's in English literature, I've attracted the daily interest of two really powerful fellows. Arthur tries to hold me back, but Ben always comes to my rescue."

The other woman smiled in agreement, knowing she meant "Arthur-itis" and "Ben-Gay."

"The youngsters at U.T. offer to carry my books and get me things." She shook her head. "They don't know the first thing about older people. They think we're all senile and decrepit."

"Look around this nursing home, Cora. Most of them are."

"Well, we're not. Not yet anyway."

"That's why I'm so glad you make these weekly visits. I can't drive any more with this Parkinson's, and there's hardly anyone around here to talk to—except for one person, I mean. Have another cookie."

"I believe I will." Cora Mae dunked it in her tea. "Easier on the choppers this way." She settled again in her chair. "Now tell me about the urge to merge with this fellow inmate."

Marie Wilkins flushed beneath the rouge on her powdered face. "I will tell you, Cora Mae, because we have been friends since Mathews Elementary School on West Lynn Street. But you must promise just as always between us, in your very heart of hearts, that you will not tell."

Cora Mae tapped the soft white crown of hair that perfectly framed her angular face and deep blue eyes. "I've got more secrets up here than I have skin folds, Marie. Why, if they ever put me on truth serum, half the population of Austin would have to move from embarrassment, and they'd implicate the other half!"

"Then fold this one down deep, dear." She lowered her voice and leaned forward. "I'm going to be leaving here soon."

Cora Mae looked as if someone had struck her in the face. Her blank, frightened stare conveyed her thoughts to her friend.

"No, no, I'm not *dying*, for goodness' sake!"

"Thank God! That's the first thing that comes to mind when someone our age says they're 'leaving.' " She took a deep breath. "I'm not ready for you to be gone in any sense of the word."

"Then you'll just have to *get* ready, Cora Mae, because my new beau may be able to take me away from here in a few weeks."

Cora Mae Hartwig put her cup down on the mahogany coffee table between them. "How shall I put this, Marie?"

"Carefully, if you value our friendship."

"Yes." Cora Mae thought a second, then cleared her throat. "Do you remember Jimmy Birsner?"

"Fifth-grade cloakroom."

"And Phillip Carter?"

"Junior high hayride."

"Bobby Gonzales and David Mitchell and Buddy Alford?"

"Wasn't college wonderful? But how *do* you remember all those names, Cora? You're older than I am!"

"And the late Kyle Winkler, Stanley Spillar and Bennett Parker, all three of whom you outlived here at the Center?"

"Women live longer than men," Marie managed coquettishly.

Cora Mae grinned. "I won't speculate on exactly what killed them, but rumor has it each one died with a smile on his face."

"Cora Mae Hartwig! You rude thing, you." Marie blushed.

Cora Mae thought it would be too bad if Marie let another man hurt her the way the others had. The succession of Romeos had relieved her not only of her loneliness, but also of varying amounts of her family money. The more abusive ones had battered several years from her life as well. That was partly the reason the woman lived in this center. Even her male offspring only wanted her for what she could provide, with no obligation to return financial support or losses.

"This one is nice and this time I guarantee he won't go before I do, Cora. This time he's younger."

"How much younger?"

"Younger enough," she demurred. "I can't give away *all* my secrets. But he's a very handsome man with worldly experience."

"That narrows the field here," Cora Mae commented.

"Did I say he lived in this center?"

"No, you didn't."

"Very well, then."

Cora Mae softened and she leaned toward her friend, taking her hand. "I just hate to see you hurt, Marie. You get your hopes up and they get let down. That's difficult at our age."

"That's exactly the point, Cora. Our age, I mean. It's exactly like this teapot. We never know when the last drop is going to be poured out and it's over." She patted Cora Mae's hand and slowly tilted the white teapot over their cups. "However, we *do* know there can't be much left in there, don't we? The question is whose will run out first—his, mine, or yours?"

She filled Cora's cup and began to fill her own. Black and green tea leaves splattered into the white china teacup.

"See what I mean? Life is short. What do the commercials say? 'You've got to go for the gusto.' Besides, what have I got to lose, Cora Mae? The truth is I'm an old lady with rapidly advancing Parkinson's whose kid barely tolerates her existence. Why shouldn't I take a few risks at this stage of the game?"

"Why indeed, Marie? I perfectly agree with you," Cora Mae replied, brushing cookie crumbs off her lap onto her napkin. "But I would appreciate it if you'd keep me posted on this. Who knows"—she winked—"maybe your beau will have a friend?"

"He's pretty much a loner, but you never know."

Cora Mae finished her tea and stood up. "I must be getting along now, Marie. Can I do anything before I go?"

"Yes, as a matter of fact you can, Cora." She pointed to the sink. "If you wouldn't mind taking this tea set to the kitchen there and bringing me back that little bottle of pills by the drainboard. I see I'm a little late with my afternoon medicine, and I seem to be fading a bit."

Cora Mae brought a glass of water as well.

Marie Wilkins downed the pills in a gulp. "There, that's better already. Thank you ever so much for coming so faithfully, Cora Mae. You are my oldest and dearest friend, you know." She stood, uncertainly, and reached for her cane. "We've shared each other's secrets for eighty years." Her eyes misted over. "And we'll have more of them to share as the days go by."

"I love you, too, Marie," Cora Mae replied, steadying her until she got her balance. She embraced her friend and said: "I'll see you next week at the same time. And *I'll* bring the cookies. I believe you like my homemade chocolate chip, right?"

"I'll look forward to it," Marie Wilkins said sweetly.

Cora Mae heard the door close and lock behind her as she walked down the carpeted hallway to the elevator. She could tell that Marie Wilkins would soon be moving, all right. But it would be from the independent section to the assisted-living section as the Parkinson's gradually stole her life from her. It might be a better place, as the rooms were nicer and there was more activity.

But what would happen to the beau, if in fact he existed anywhere outside Marie's quavering brain?

The bell rang as elevator doors parted to reveal a scruffily dressed Hispanic man in a wheelchair. Cora Mae assumed the man occupied one of the charity beds the center had to keep filled to maintain its government certification. She guessed the man in dirty jeans and stained sweatshirt was in his late forties, a disabled Vietnam veteran who was likely to be homeless. He carried a single rose in a bud vase in his lap.

"Could you hold the door, please?" he asked politely.

"Certainly." Cora Mae stood aside while he wheeled himself out into the hallway. There was something about him that caught her attention. What would Lucas Holt call it? His vibes?

"Thank you," he said, not looking at her. He turned and wheeled down the hall.

Cora Mae's body entered the elevator, but her mind stayed in the hall. What would the Rev tell her to do? He would say to follow her instincts. And Nikky would agree. So instead of pushing *G* she pushed *2*. Once there, she impatiently punched *3* again and again. When the excruciatingly slow elevator returned to the third floor, she peeked out just enough to see the man in the wheelchair enter the apartment of Marie Wilkins.

She shook her head and sighed deeply. She hoped Marie would not be too badly hurt this time.

Lucas Holt adjusted the sound on the headset as he started his second lap around the Town Lake Trail. Perhaps increasing the volume would take his mind off the fatigue of the second four miles. He had to complete eight to maintain his training schedule for the Austin Marathon. The October weather was typically hot and sunny, and his thin shirt clung to his sweaty body like a second skin.

Great timing, he thought, as he picked up his pace across MoPac Bridge and another country-western "cryin' and dyin' " song blared into his ears. As if he wasn't already in touch with his mortality, country music poured messages of lost love, loneliness, and death into his head for the hours of his long runs. By the time he finished he would be deluged with dead mothers, imprisoned fathers, partying daughters, no-count sons, and a corpse propped up beside the jukebox with a "stiff" drink in its hand.

Just like real life. At least it made him laugh, which tossed in another endorphin to counter the running pain.

Holt had decided to run the marathon when he realized his forty-third birthday was approaching. Even at the pen he had been concerned about maintaining a relatively healthy lifestyle. He ate vegetables and little red meat, didn't smoke or do drugs, and wore helmets, seat belts, and condoms, but not at the same time. His errors were too little sleep and too much Scotch, both of which he believed were offset by running. Nonetheless, lately he was especially conscious of his mortality.

At the penitentiary the mortality issues were of the more immediate kind. Inmates killed other inmates, some of them tried to kill him (and would have succeeded save for the God Squad); inmates died of AIDS or OD's, many died as soon as they hit the street from drugs or contracts for botched jobs. In his twenty years there he had handled the deaths, but never really related them to himself.

Here he had been hit in the face with the aging of his congregation. Every Sunday he looked out over a sea of faces that had more wrinkles and less agility. In the two years he'd been at St. Margaret's, he had done over thirty funerals. At first he thought he had just inherited an older congregation, but as he talked with other clergy around Austin, he realized he was dealing with the aging of the population in general.

He grimaced as an older man in Texas flag running shorts passed him. *He can't be running the* distance *I am,* Holt thought as the backbeat of the next song reminded him that "We're Only Here for a Little While."

Country-western music had recently discovered death. All the songwriters must have suddenly turned forty and realized they could see the bottom of the hill from there (often through the bottom of a glass). They were, like him, a part of the wave of aging baby boomers having mass anticipatory angst about what one local funeral home called "Life's Inevitable Certainty."

Holt hated the recent spate of movies that showed death as one more painless scene change, depicting afterlife as a permanent vacation in Northern California with all the beautiful people happily consuming even more health foods and Perrier. He had preached sermons on the way the movies and the New Agers never depicted the kind of death he'd witnessed at the hospital the other day, always showing death as clean, quick, and, most of all, temporary. There was never suffering, disability, slow deterioration, or indignity of incontinence, debility, or dementia.

Maybe that was what worried him as he turned forty-three, that he could see from this vantage point what lay ahead, and that it was not necessarily a pretty picture. Couple that with the aging of his congregation and the feeble attempt of popular culture to stave off the entire issue, and it was no wonder he was running—away from it all.

Enough of the country-western. He moved the dial on the headset to the oldies station. "Surfer Girl" swelled into his ears. Memory music. Thank God for the Beach Boys.

But his comfort level with nostalgia annoyed him. Like the C&W songs, the oldies were a good beat to run with, but they also were a way of running from the present to hide in the alleged comfort of the past, the familiar, the known, avoiding the certain uncertainty of the future. Still, he listened and sang along. He would take comfort wherever he could find it until he came to better terms with the aging all around and inside him.

He rounded the corner by Austin High School and saw the white stone marker for the end of the four-mile loop. It stood out in the midst of the fall colors on the heavily wooded path. Suddenly he heard his name blared out of nowhere, echoing under the bridge.

"REVEREND HOLT!" said the voice over the loudspeaker, like God screaming at him from a pigeon's nest in the overpass. "REPENT AND SIN NO MORE."

Other runners gawked as a blushing Lucas Holt turned and ran from the trail to the APD blue-and-white whose driver was laughing.

"God I've always wanted to do that to you." Susan Granger held her hand over her mouth and shook her head.

Holt leaned in the driver's window. "Well, I'm certainly glad you got it out of your system so you won't have to do it again." He smiled back at her and laughed at himself. "The echo was great. Under this headset I couldn't tell if you were God or the Great Oz."

"There's a difference?"

"God thinks there is. But She'll discuss that with you on Her own time." Holt pulled back from the car and took off his glasses and visor to better view her. In the two years since he'd been back in Austin, she seemed to have mellowed, or maybe it was matured, or maybe his attitude toward her had changed. When he first arrived, complete with God Squad, she had been stand-offish, kept her distance even in the midst of a murder investigation involving his church. But recently—did it have to do with his birthday?—she seemed more open, playful, almost like she had been in the best of their times together at U.T. He couldn't yet account for the difference. Was it because he was ensconced in a relationship with Kristen Wade and therefore unavailable? Was it a rekindling of her feelings from years past? Whatever it was he liked it, though he was aware she could revert to the straitlaced career cop at the drop of a corpse.

"I don't think you harassed me on your toy loudspeaker just to discuss theology—or did you?"

Susan Granger surveyed him. "You know, you've got great legs for a priest."

"I'll bet you say that to all the clergy." She was doing it again, making a personal comment that cut through their usual formality. "Come on, Susan. I'm sweating my brains out and I need a beer and a shower. What's up?"

"Okay—there's some bad news and some good news."

"Bad news first," Holt said, thankful she was playing cop.

"Bad news is that two of your parishioners are dead."

"What?" he said as though he had been blindsided with a ball-bat. His mind raced through the possibilities. "Who?"

Granger looked at the pad on the seat. "An Erik and Janey Bertrand. Lived in Westlake—before they were murdered."

"The *Bertrands*?" Holt said, shocked. This was a young couple. "Who the hell would want them dead?"

"That's the good news," she said, smiling sarcastically. "We got the killer."

"Why do I get the feeling there's more *bad* news?"

"Because you have great legs *and* great intuition."

Holt frowned at her. "I'm listening."

"Get in." She winked. "The perp's a friend of yours."

• Three •

The monolithic brown APD Headquarters stood like a huge wall facing east to the Interstate. As Lucas Holt and Susan Granger rounded the corner of Seventh Street, the building gave mixed messages: Welcome to Austin. Don't Mess with Us. Enjoy Yourself. Within Limits. Come In. Beware. Welcome. Go Home. He started to say something to the uniformed woman driving the cruiser, but didn't. He got the same messages from her.

The blue-and-white jerked to a halt in the parking spot reserved for the lieutenant.

"Can you wait just a second till I get my pants on?" Lucas Holt slammed the door of the police car and tried to pull his jogging trousers over his running shoes. He unzipped the lower legs and pulled them on easily, as two police officers sauntered by them.

"Must've been a nice afternoon for you, Lieutenant," the man smirked.

"Shut up, Campbell, or you'll walk a beat tonight and see what *real* police work is like."

"Great legs, Lieutenant," the woman said. "Where'd you find the stud muffin?"

"In church, Donna. He's a priest."

The woman blushed. "Oh! Sorry, Father." She and the man headed toward the station.

Holt smiled and spoke out loud. "Actually, Lieutenant, I had a wonderful time sweating in the car with you. If there are any stains on the seat—"

"Lucas!" Granger said as the officers laughed. "You won't think things are so damned funny when we get inside."

"Neither will you," Holt said, pointing to the short, greasy-haired man with the cigar at the door. "Look who's here."

"Yo! Rev!" Nikky Dorati opened the door for them. "What took you so long?"

"The police escort slowed me down." Holt smiled. "And I had to put on my pants."

"Way to go, Rev!"

"Shut up, Dorati," the lieutenant said with a scowl. "What are you doing here? Let me rephrase that. How well *do* you know the murderer? Enough to be an accomplice, I hope?"

"I know him good, Lieutenant. Brickhouse and I done a nickel together once."

"Brickhouse?" Holt exclaimed. "Jimmy Brickhouse? He's just a kid." The Rev remembered a buck-toothed, blond-haired black youth slouching into the Chapel at the pen, skinny as a rail, with round eyes that lit up his beaver smile. He was a likable kid, even when Holt knew he was getting conned out of his socks. "Wasn't he back in on another burglary bust?"

Dorati looked at him. "Rev, you got a long memory and a short attention span. As I started to tell the squeeze—"

"Dorati," Granger fumed, "I am *not* a squeeze or any other sexist expression your neanderthal brain can conjure up, and unless you have business in this police station, I'd suggest you get out of here before I squeeze you in there with Brickhouse."

"Calm down, Lieutenant," the Rev said as he peered at Dorati. He knew Nikky enjoyed the hell out of smart-mouthing her. There must have been something genetic that made him play with cops. He had once told Holt that even as a kid he had always been on the robber's side.

"Hey, I was just giggin' ya. It's just that three of your goons already tried to bust me when I walked in the door."

"Your reputation precedes you," Granger replied.

Lucas Holt cleared his throat. "Excuse me, you two, but could we take this fight someplace other than the lobby?" He pointed to bystanders watching. "Like your office, perhaps?"

"Sure, let's make it a party." Granger turned to the desk sergeant. "Get Brickhouse from the bull pen and bring him up."

"Gee, Lieutenant," Dorati began as they left the elevator and walked through the precinct room, "is this where it happens?"

"Dorati—" Granger looked over at him with annoyance.

"Nikky—enough."

"Yeah, okay. The only time I been this deep in a police department was when I was a guest of the establishment."

"Some coffee would take the edge off," Holt said.

"Around the corner." Granger pointed to Dorati as they entered her office. "Get us some, too."

Lucas Holt glanced around at the yellowed cop cartoons taped to the file cabinet and the old bumper stickers thumbtacked over the memos and papers on what must have been a bulletin board. "I see you've remodeled. The dust is down to half an inch."

"It's home. It's cozy. It's me."

"Your *house* is like this?" the Rev kidded, knowing her penchant for neatness at home, but absolute disorder at work.

"No," Granger replied, plopping down in her desk chair. "My house has neon beer signs on the walls."

Holt laughed and moved stacks of papers from three chairs. "Where should I put these?"

"I'll refrain from the obvious answer. Just pile them on the table over there."

"There's a table under that mess?" he said, dumping the stacks on the already paper-strewn top. "Has Missing Persons been in here lately? They could clear their list."

"Next time I'm at St. Margaret's, remind me to redecorate *your* office." She pointed to the door. "Look who's here."

A uniformed officer led a skinny, blond-haired black man to a chair. The prisoner's eyes looked down, and he did not speak.

"Cuffs on?" the officer said.

"For the time being," Granger replied. "That'll be all."

"Hey, Jimmy," Holt said.

"Hey, Rev," the man said, still looking at the floor. "What's happenin'?"

"I think that's what we're here to find out," Holt said.

Dorati returned, precariously holding three mugs of coffee.

"Nikky!" Brickhouse exclaimed. "You gotta tell 'em to let me out of here."

"I already tried that and they got me servin' cops coffee." He handed mugs to Holt and Granger and gave his to the man whose hands were cuffed in front. "You need this more than I do."

"No, here, he can have mine," the Rev said.

"You're a real piece of work, Dorati." Susan Granger sat back in her swivel chair. "And I don't believe you, Lucas, fawning over this creep who murdered two of your parishioners and ripped off their house."

Brickhouse shook his head in a way that, just for a moment, flashed Holt back to a penitentiary conversation with Nikky and Jimmy. Both were members of the "God Squad," the self-appointed group of inmates loyal only to then-Chaplain Holt and one another. Lucas had not encouraged the group, seeing it as one more prison gang to defend territory and garner power. He had, in fact, not even known who was in it until a guard was killed on the night shift and a member of the squad was blamed. Together Holt worked with them to uncover clues and find the real killer—another guard. From that time on the Rev had to admit they were a positive influence in a negative environment.

Brickhouse was the newer member, having been recruited by former hit man Nikky Dorati. Originally, Jimmy had hated anything to do with religion. But like Dorati, he was convinced not just by Holt's sincerity—sincerity was cheap in prison—but by his concrete way of interpreting Scripture in terms that prisoners could understand.

The God Squad dubbed it the "NBV," "The No Bullshit Version of the Bible." It made sense. It hit them hard. As Dorati said: "It grabbed them by the short hairs and got their attention." So Brickhouse had joined—and was sitting in front of the Rev in handcuffs again.

"I didn't do it, Rev. They just ain't picked up their quota of African-American males for this month yet, and—"

Granger laughed. "Our quota of *perps*, Brickhouse, who just happen to have in their possession a VCR and a camera with the murdered couple's Social Security numbers etched in them. You can go back to the bull pen. Start thinking about that little needle with bye-bye juice that will put you out of our misery."

"Before you start the IV, Lieutenant," Holt said, "I have a few questions."

"Shoot." Granger grinned. "Please shoot."

The Rev knew she enjoyed having him and his God Squad where she thought they belonged. She believed he could never reform these criminals, and here was proof positive his efforts were futile. She was gloating now. But it wasn't over yet, and "pride cometh before a fall."

"I thought you were doing two to ten for burglary, Jimmy."

"I was, Rev. But the joint got overcrowded, and they started paroling nonviolent types like me."

Granger mumbled: "You and Henry Lee Lucas."

Holt threw her a stern glance. "Where'd you get the stuff?"

Brickhouse pondered the question, then looked at Granger. "What're we talkin' here, Lieutenant?"

"Murder one, my main man."

"No bet, lady. You ain't got evidence for that and we all know it." He motioned around the room.

Lucas knew he was right, and they *did* all know it. From the time he entered the building, he had suspected that the reason Susan had dragged him into this was to use him to trick a confession out of the kid. Why else would she be so eager to bring him to the station to see this man? Normally she detested both his and the God Squad's interference with her job. Either she really had nothing on him and was using Lucas to get Jimmy to tell what he knew, or she had enough to indict but not convict and was hoping Brickhouse would break down in front of Holt. In either case she was using everybody, and Holt didn't like it.

"Susan, this is pretty low," Holt said, "even for a cop."

Granger came out of her chair. "That's the problem with you bleeding-heart liberal do-gooders. You want us to protect the innocent by catching the bad guys, and then when we do you demand we let them back on the street to do it again. Make up your damned mind, will you? Which one do you want?"

"What I want is—"

"I've told you before, Lucas, this is what comes from hanging out with creeps like these two. You eventually start to think like them, and you start to *act* like them." She sat on the side of her desk. "This is a prime example."

Even though he was angry at her for setting him up, the Rev couldn't decide whether she reminded him more of Mrs. Thomas, his third-grade teacher at Smithville Elementary, or his mother. There was something about Susan's schoolmarmish manner that was oddly attractive, if also amusing. It was that combination that

had interested him at U.T. twenty-five years ago and, along with
her strong hazel eyes and generous dark hair, still tugged at him.
He wondered momentarily about the stark contrast between her
and the auburn-haired Kristen Wade.

"So what's the deal, Lieutenant?" Brickhouse said. "All you
got me on is a meatball charge of possession of stolen property. I
coulda got that junk off a fence. You got no prints in the house,
you got no prints on the murder weapon."

Granger leaned forward and stared over her coffee cup. "How
do you know what the murder weapon was if you weren't there?"

"What he meant was—"

"Shut up, Dorati. You're not his mouthpiece."

"Perhaps some negotiation is in order," Holt began. "If Jimmy
had information that was helpful in finding the killer, wouldn't it
be worth your while to adjust the charge to a more appropriate
level?"

"Like manslaughter?" Granger offered.

Holt knew her decision to plea-bargain was a balance of how
much she thought Brickhouse knew and how much face she could
save in the deal. It was important not to make it look like she gave
away the farm from the jump. But what the hell, he'd try the low
ball first. "I had something like parole violation in mind."

Granger walked back around the desk and muttered under her
breath.

Holt knew she was posturing, trying to make the prisoner
sweat, knowing she didn't have to give at all since he was caught
with stolen goods. But the longer she took, the better the play.

The lieutenant sipped her coffee and glared at Brickhouse.
"You give it all up? Everything you know?"

Jimmy looked at the floor. "Cut the deal."

"B and E, possession—and the right to nail your ass to a capital
murder charge if I find out you had anything at all to do with this,
and I mean *anything*."

The Rev watched Jimmy Brickhouse stare at the floor. Just as
with the lieutenant, he knew exactly what was going through this
man's head. Taking the play meant going back to finish the bulk
of the ten-year sentence. Six more years. But at least it was a
play, and he'd get paroled the next time the joint filled up. If he
was smart, and Brickhouse was, he would take it.

Jimmy nodded his head. "You got it, Lieutenant."

Bingo, Holt said to himself.

" 'Cause I didn't have nothin' to do with it. Snuffin' ain't my thing, is it, Dorati?"

Nikky shook his head.

Granger sat down. "You were in the house?"

"Right." He looked at Holt. "Sorry, Rev. I needed cash and the house was my ATM." He shrugged his shoulders and took a drink of coffee. "Hell, let's face it, Father Holt, I'm a burglar. Actually, I'm a damned good burglar."

"So we see," Granger drawled.

"You know what I think of that, Jimmy," Holt said.

"You think it's a bullshit cop-out."

"In the words of Jesus, yes."

Susan Granger sighed. "Before you start passing out hankies, could we get back to the subject? What the hell did you see in the house?"

Holt was anxious to hear the answer. Brickhouse surely had clues to the murderer, and if he didn't spill to Susan Granger, he might later tell it to the Rev.

"Two dead bodies, Lieutenant." Brickhouse crossed his legs. He could relax now. He had the deal. "It made my job easier."

The Rev pressed him. "What else did you see there? Picture it as you walked in."

"Okay." He sipped the coffee slowly. "The fireplace was still warm. And there was a bottle of wine about three quarters full on the coffee table. Don't ask me what it was." He smiled. "I ain't that nosey. And, oh, yeah," he said, holding up a cut finger, "there was broken glass on the floor near the bodies."

"That's good, Brickhouse," Susan Granger said caustically. "When you get out of the joint you can be a P.I."

Holt ignored her. "Anything else?"

"I don't think so. At first I thought they were sleeping, but then the stink hit, and I saw the mess on the floor."

"What mess?" Holt asked.

"I don't know how you say this nice, but—"

Susan Granger spoke. "You say 'they lost bowel and bladder control.' "

"Yeah. The place smelled like shit."

Holt inwardly cringed. A horrible way to die, in your own feces. He hoped Erik and Janey Bertrand were unconscious. "And the murder weapon?" Dorati asked.

"There wasn't one, Nikky. That's how I know my prints ain't on it. You know me. I don't leave prints. But there wasn't anything obvious lyin' around that killed them. They were on the floor, no wounds, no bruises, no blood. Just piss and shit."

"So how did they die?" Holt asked no one in particular as he reviewed the possibilities in his head.

"Go ahead, Dorati," Granger said. "You're the expert."

"Poison, Rev," Dorati explained. "It goes down clean, but leaves a hell of a mess later. Relaxes all the muscles."

"So Erik and Janey Bertrand sat down in front of the fireplace and said 'Let's have a glass of eighty-three Hemlock?' " Holt shook his head. "I don't think so."

"Somebody poisoned them," Brickhouse said. "But not me."

Holt looked at Nikky. "How do you do that?"

"Yeah, Dorati," Granger echoed, "how do *you* do that?" Her jaw was set and her arms were folded over her chest.

"I've been *told*," the short man said as he stood to walk around the office, "there are lots of ways."

"Lethal injection is my personal favorite," Granger said under her breath.

"Let's say you wanted to be more subtle than that, Lieutenant," Dorati continued. "You could swish it around the glass and put the glass back on the shelf. When it dries and wine is added— bingo, they're dead. Then, of course, you can put it in the ice cubes, but that's too obvious. It's the first place I'd look." Dorati glanced at Granger. "You did check the fridge, right?"

"No, we didn't." Granger propped her feet on the desk. "But not many people, other than you and Brickhouse, of course, drink their two-hundred-dollar bottles of wine with ice cubes."

"True," Dorati said. "So it must have been by your method of preference, Lieutenant, *lethal injection*—into the bottle."

"But wouldn't that leave a hole in the screw cap?" Holt said seriously. "Just kidding. Wouldn't there be a needle hole in the foil around the top?"

"Not if you used a very small but sturdy needle, and smoothed over the foil when you were done." Dorati motioned with his hands.

Then it had to be somebody who had access to the bottles inside the house, Holt reasoned to himself. That should limit the suspects substantially.

"Why am I talking with you about this anyway? This is police business and not yours." She got up from the desk and waved her arms at them. "Y'all have served your purpose. Thanks for the help. Now get the hell out of here."

"Wait a second, Susan," Holt interrupted. He knew she didn't like the tables being turned. She had manipulated Lucas, and coincidentally Dorati, into the case to get information out of Brickhouse and now didn't like the fact that the two of them seemed to be taking over the investigation. "If you had experts from the lab here, you'd want to hear from them. Why not use these guys the same way? They didn't *do* it, but they might be able to *think* like whoever did. Right?"

Susan Granger finished her coffee and looked for an answer in the bottom of the stained Styrofoam. "It worries me when you start making sense, Lucas." She tossed the cup in the trash.

"Okay," she acquiesced, though Holt knew it was only for the moment. "But they *will* stay the hell out of this case."

Holt winked at Nikky and sat on the missing-persons table.

"The wine bottles might have been doctored in the house," Granger said, "but, as Mr. Dorati here will tell you from vast experience, this could be done in a matter of seconds by the carry-out kid in a supermarket. Or if they left the case of wine sitting in the car or on a counter when they bought it, someone could quickly make the move and be gone before they knew it.

"We're checking the liquor store the Bertrands bought from, including the supermarkets and the kids who carried their groceries—or who delivered to their house. We've gotten a list of names of housekeepers and grounds people, and we're checking to see if the Bertrands had any repairs done inside the house in the last three weeks. We found the cork in the kitchen and the lab is looking at it now." She looked at Dorati. "Anything I left out, Mr. Crime Consultant?"

Holt answered. "Not that I can think of right now."

"I was talking to the *other* sociopath," she said to him.

Dorati grinned. "If something comes to mind, I'll call you—and send you my bill."

"That it for me, Lieutenant?" Brickhouse said, relaxed. He looked like he'd just finished sex and needed a cigarette.

"Anything else you want to tell me? You've been Miranded."

"Yeah. I'll cop to bein' there and takin' the stuff. But it ain't quite right, the B and E."

"Why's that?" Granger asked, annoyed.

" 'Cause I really didn't 'break.' I just 'entered.' "

Lucas stood up. If that was true, somebody was there before he was. "You got a gate?" he asked.

"Yeah, Rev. A side door they probably never used much was unlocked. It led through a laundry area to the kitchen."

Dorati looked at Holt.

"Would you two like to be alone or do you want to fill me in?" Susan Granger stopped. "No, wait, you think that door was purposely left unlocked so someone could doctor the wine."

"It's possible." Lucas made a mental note to check to see if they dusted for prints. "The question is why anyone would want them dead?"

"You got anything to say about that, Brickhouse?" Granger asked, moving slowly toward him.

"Not a clue, Lieutenant." The smile left his face and he looked down again.

Susan Granger sat on the front of her desk. "Oh, I think you do." She lifted his chin with her hand. "Look at me. I think maybe you've got about a million motives for their deaths."

"What are you talking about?" Holt said, puzzled. There was a card she held close to the vest that she was now going to play. He hoped it wouldn't trump Brickhouse out of the game.

Granger let go of the man's head. "Ask him, Lucas. He knows what I mean."

Holt looked at the cuffed inmate. He had seen the look a thousand times at the pen. Why was it, when a man wanted to look innocent, a neon sigh flashed GUILTY across his forehead? But Brickhouse had never been a very good sociopath. He lied about as well as he stole. "Jimmy?"

"Don't know nothin' about that, Rev."

Susan Granger raised her dark eyebrows. "Deal's off, Brick. Back to murder one."

"Hey, Lieutenant," Nikky Dorati said. "That ain't by the book."

Granger's eyes narrowed at him. "Listen, Dorati. I got two dead bodies on my hands and I got a perp who has admitted being at the crime scene. But I got a million-dollar motive that this creep's willing to take back to the pen with him. That's not by the book, either."

Enough poker. Time to call. "Spill, Jimmy," Holt said.

"No. Let me." Granger turned to him. "There's a missing cashier's check for a million-dollar deal the Bertrands were celebrating. We found the envelope and the pink receipt for it." She looked again at Brickhouse. "And unless our man here gives it up, I'll make sure he takes it to his grave."

The Rev knew Jimmy Brickhouse didn't kill the Bertrands for the money. But it was a hell of a motive for somebody.

Jimmy looked at Holt. "Will she keep the deal?"

Granger answered for him. "You give up the check, I give up the B of the B and E."

"You been savin' that." Dorati smiled at her. "You're better than I thought."

"Don't forget it." She looked at Holt. "You, either."

"That the deal?" Brickhouse asked as Granger nodded. Jimmy looked at the Rev.

"She'll do it," Holt replied, hoping he was right. She honored the game, even if she kept aces up her dark blue sleeve.

"Okay. I need the cuffs off."

Granger removed them, and Jimmy untied a shoe lace.

"Got a knife, Lieutenant?" he asked.

"Why don't you tell me what you have in mind and let me do it?" said Holt, taking the shoe from Jimmy.

Dorati tossed the Rev a small red Swiss Army knife.

"Your area of experience, Rev," Brickhouse brightened with his buck-toothed smile. "It's in the sole."

Lucas Holt cut through the thinly glued layer of leather and opened the side of the shoe bottom. He remembered inmates at the pen could hide things in plain sight. He pulled back the flap and retrieved a dusty torn piece of paper. Opening it up, he handed it to Susan Granger.

"We could split it four ways, right?" the prisoner said.

"I didn't hear that, Brickhouse," the lieutenant responded, "because if I did I'd add another charge to your long list of accomplishments." She placed the paper in a plastic bag.

"Sounded good to me," the Rev replied. And it questioned the motive. If someone had killed for the money, why didn't they take it? A cashier's check could be cashed by anyone.

Dorati read Holt's mind. "Where'd you find that check?"

"That's what's weird," Jimmy said. "It was on the table next to the wine. Right out in the open."

Susan Granger waved her arms. "Enough." She motioned to an officer through the glass window of her office. "If we have more questions, Mr. Brickhouse, we know where to find you. Until then, Officer Klein will escort you back to the spacious accommodations provided for you by the City of Austin."

A tall, Germanic man with a beard entered the room.

"Book him on B and E—"

Holt and Dorati glared at her.

"My mistake." She smiled. "Make that unlawful entry and possession of stolen property. Notify his parole officer to schedule a hearing tomorrow."

"Thanks for the play, Lieutenant."

"Yeah. I'll be looking for a card the next six Christmases." Granger shook her head as they closed the door.

Holt knew there was more to be learned about the Bertrands and only one way to do it. "You got dinner plans?" he asked.

Dorati answered. "No, Rev, my whole evenin's free."

The Rev ignored him.

Granger said, "Is Kristen busy running the state again?"

She was either exhausted or angry about the case. Otherwise Lucas knew she would save her dislike of Kristen for the privacy of their own conversation. "As a matter of fact, she is."

"This is where I came in." Dorati started to leave. "You two want some advice from me?" he said, his hand on the doorknob.

They answered simultaneously: "No."

"Good, here it is." He turned around to face them. " 'Life is short.' " He opened the door. "Go to dinner."

. Holt and Granger watched Dorati unwrap a cigar as he sauntered through the line of desks in the office.

"You buying?" she said, picking up her purse.

"No. You are. My wallet's in my car by the trail."

"Great," she said seriously. "I'll drive you there."

•   •   •

A wiry old Hispanic man parked his faded white Chevy Impala across from the restaurant. He went around to the passenger side to help his equally elderly wife get out. His brown hands struggled to pull the heavy wheelchair from the backseat and unfold it by the front door. The stroke had paralyzed her left side, though she still had full use of her right extremities. He was pleased that his arms and back had actually gotten stronger now that he was doing her transfers by himself, without the help of the home health aide. He pulled her legs around and used the scooting technique he learned at the rehab center to position her into the chair.

Together they moved slowly but with dignity across the narrow asphalt street. Dressed to be seen, the man wore a black wool suit with a white shirt, a black and silver bolo and pointed black boots, shined to perfection. His wife, in her blue dress and turquoise jewelry, spoke haltingly and pointed to the neon sign that said Casita Lobos.

The two were greeted warmly by many of the people in line in the lobby. Others whispered the names of the old man and woman in nearly reverent tones.

In the adjacent bar a man in running warm-ups spoke to his companion. "Excuse me just a second," the Rev said to Susan Granger. "I have to say hello." He walked over to the entrance where the old couple basked in the limelight of their popularity.

"Señor y Señora Villalobos!" Lucas Holt embraced them. "You both look well. That country air in Elgin must agree with you."

"It is to be tolerated, Father Holt," the old man said dejectedly. "It is to be tolerated."

"We would be happy to have you to our *pequeño apartamento*, Father Holt," the woman in the wheelchair slurred. "After all you have done for our daughters, we welcome you at any time."

"Speaking of which," the Rev said, "here comes Serena." He stood back as a large round woman, like three circles piled on one another, grabbed the wheelchair from the old man.

"Hi, Father Holt." She pecked the Rev on the cheek. "Gotta keep the restaurant running. Catch you Sunday."

"Right." Lucas thought the interaction with her parents was abrupt at best. At worst, it was rude.

"Come on, Mama, I'll take you back to the kitchen to help with cutting. Papa"—she pointed to a small chair by the front entrance—"you sit over there and greet your old friends." She winked at the Rev. "We let him do that a few times a week. It makes him feel important."

Lucas Holt hurt for the old man. Jaime Villalobos had built the restaurant his daughters now owned from a storefront on Sixth and Congress to the most popular Mexican restaurant in Austin. In the process he had become, according to the God Squad, a major figure in the Austin syndicate of the forties and fifties. But now his cronies and connections were gone and all he had left were his two daughters, and the Rev knew the conflict that characterized their relationship. They treated him like a useless old man and their mother like a helpless child.

"Well you're important to me," Holt said, shaking the old man's hand. "And I don't see enough of you."

"*Muchas gracias,* Padre Holt."

"Gotta get going, Papa," Serena said as she ushered her father to his seat, barking an order for a margarita as she left him. Her mother was quickly wheeled behind the swinging kitchen doors as Lucas Holt returned to the bar.

"What was that all about?" Susan Granger asked.

"Don't you know who that is?"

"I assume the large woman is the owner, but the old couple?"

"You've lived in Austin longer than I have and you don't know Jaime Villalobos and his wife?"

"The boxer? Of course I know them." She turned to look again. "That's them? The last time I saw him—and her for that matter— must have been right before the old restaurant closed and they moved to this location." She stared at the old man. "God, he looks bad. He was a legend."

"Right. He still holds the record for welterweight wins."

"Is that why he's on his second margarita already?"

Lucas turned to see the empty glass being replaced. "Not unless his daughters are sedating him, which is possible."

"And what happened to her? How'd she end up in the chair?"

"Stroke. Took what was left of her dignity."

"She was an Olympic medalist who ran with Jesse Owens, didn't she?" She looked toward the kitchen. "Lousy way to go."

Here was the lead. "Much like the Bertrands," he said.

Susan Granger looked at him. Her hazel eyes sparkled green in the low light of the restaurant. Wrong timing.

"Lucas, I thought this was dinner. If you want Grilled Granger, I'm out of here."

"I'm sorry," he lied. Maybe after another drink.

"You get two chances unless I catch you the first time." Granger slurped the bottom of the glass. "These margaritas are right tasty."

"Good thing you're not on tonight."

"I'm almost on." She leaned toward him and winked. "Two more of these and you can drive me home and put me to bed."

"No soliciting in a public place."

"I meant 'alone.' "

"Oh, damn." For a second the Rev felt disappointed. He wrote it off to the margarita.

A skinny Hispanic woman approached them with a menu in hand.

"Father Holt?"

The Rev hugged her and turned to Susan Granger. "Susan, this is Blanca Villalobos, co-owner of this establishment."

"Nice to meet you, Lieutenant."

"Thank you." She shook the thin hand. "I used to frequent the old restaurant over on the access road right down from APD headquarters. I remember you had your parents' boxing and Olympic medals on the walls there. People used to come from all over the country to see those medals and meet her."

Blanca Villalobos smiled knowingly. "That was a long time ago, Lieutenant. Some people still remember them, people who have lived in Austin and know them from the old days. But most people now have never heard of them. My sister and I thought it best to keep the name but start over, with more modern ideas."

"I see." Susan Granger tried not to show her disapproval.

The younger Villalobos daughter pointed to a place by the window. "Your table is ready, Father Holt, with two gold margaritas and our homemade chips with our salsa especial."

"Thank you," the Rev said. He wondered why, with all the customers greeting her parents, the medals had been replaced with cheap Mexican decorations that made the place look like every other such restaurant in town? And he wondered, too, how Señor and Señora Villalobos felt about it.

The nearly anorexic Blanca led them across the crowded dining room. "For you the usual chalupa dinner, and I believe you mentioned to the bartender that the lady liked enchiladas? And tonight the dinner is on my family."

"I can't do that," Holt retorted, more sharply than he had meant. Perhaps with the Bertrands' deaths he was more sensitive than usual to taking relationships, and lives, for granted.

"Of course you can. Consider it a small bit of thanks for all you've done for my sister and me at St. Margaret's."

"You're too good to me," Holt said as he and Susan were escorted to the table.

Blanca kissed him on the forehead and nodded at the waiter. "Nice to meet you, Lieutenant," she said. "Come back anytime. We feed your local patrols here and they give us good service."

"Thank you. Glad we're doing our job." Susan Granger watched the thin woman walk away. "Lesbian, right?"

"Your skills overwhelm me sometimes. Yes, they're lesbian."

"And their parents are thrilled?"

"Their parents are appalled. They all hate each other."

Granger sipped her drink. "One big, happy, dysfunctional family."

"One big, happy, dysfunctional corporation. The women worked in the restaurant with their parents all their lives. But it wasn't till they managed to get Mom and Pop to turn the restaurant over to them that they let it be known they were gay."

"Their parents wouldn't have done it if they knew?"

"Are you kidding? They're rock-solid Catholic. The parents were furious. They made sure their parish church turned the daughters away, rejected them from the communion rail because of their sexual identity. They came to St. Margaret's because of the church's reputation for openness, but we lost some members because of them." Holt reached for a tortilla chip and loaded it with sauce. "They're adamantly open about their relationships."

"They sound manipulative as hell to me."

"Ambitious, maybe. They want to be twice as successful as their parents so they won't have to ask anybody for anything. They're resentful of how their parents rejected them, but they let the old folks come and greet people and work in the kitchen like they owned the place."

"Because it's good for business, no doubt."

"No doubt." Holt wondered if it was worth another try. "And speaking of business, why had the Bertrands just gotten a million-dollar check?"

"Lucas."

"And who benefits if it isn't cashed? Or does it become part of the estate? In which case we should be looking for a beneficiary, should we not?"

"Lucas." Susan Granger batted her long eyelashes across the table at him. "If it wasn't for this gold margarita, I'd get up and leave. Unfortunately, I don't think my legs are working."

"Perfect timing for me to ask you anything I want."

She pointed to the man nearing their table. "Wrong again."

A waiter placed two plates down in front of them and spoke to Susan Granger. "*Cuidado. El plato está muy caliente.*"

"*Gracias,*" she replied, grateful to be warned that the plate of enchiladas was very hot.

Holt's interest in the Bertrands was temporarily distracted by the sight, in the distance, of Serena putting another margarita in the old man's hand. He saw her make an offhand comment to another woman on her way back to the bar and laugh derisively as the proud man sat in his chair and smiled at incoming customers, like a cardboard dummy.

"That breaks my heart, to see him like that," Lucas said.

"Can't you talk to them? You're their priest."

"I have. They claim I don't understand their parents, that if the old man and woman didn't want to be here in the restaurant, they wouldn't be here. Nobody forces them to come. But maybe you're right. I'll get them after church this Sunday. If they've done anything, I don't know, wrong to their parents, we need to talk about it. I hate to be judgmental, but I also hate to see people used, especially old people."

Susan Granger lifted her glass. "Just like the old days. Storming the ramparts."

"Hey, it was *your* idea, you rabble rouser." Holt enjoyed this time with Susan, though he felt a little embarrassed about it. Still, he couldn't have this conversation with Kristen, who was nervous about gays, except of course as constituents, and her taste in restaurants had climbed with her social status. He couldn't remember the last time they'd had Mexican.

"Nice chalupas," Granger said.

"First it's my legs, now my chalupas. Pretty personal," Lucas joked. "You've got nice chalupas yourself, you know."

Their laughter was interrupted by a crash from the kitchen, followed by a horrific scream. Holt and Granger ran through the swinging doors to find the elderly woman on the floor, wailing, surrounded by broken plates of cheese and vegetables. Blanca and Serena yelled at her in Spanish as they roughly jerked her up, back into her chair. When they saw the Rev, they softened.

"She's okay, Lieutenant," Serena said. "She had a little accident with the hand that doesn't work so well anymore."

"The stroke," Blanca added. "She has no control, you know. We will have to completely dress her now, and change her diaper."

Holt watched Señora Villalobos stare silently into her lap, humiliated more by their words than by the fall.

"I'd be glad to help if I can," Susan Granger offered.

"No, thank you, Lieutenant. Go back to your dinner. We will see after Mama."

Lucas Holt spoke quietly to Blanca Villalobos. "I'd like to chat with you and your sister after church Sunday."

"Sure, Father Holt. We will make it a point to stay."

The Rev stooped by the elderly woman's chair. "Are you all right, Señora?"

"*Estoy bien,*" she replied, not looking at him. "*Muchas gracias.*"

Her daughter turned the chair abruptly and wheeled her away.

Holt and Granger silently left the kitchen.

"That was a nice thing for you to offer," Lucas said, genuinely taken with her willingness to help the woman. He had seen little of that side of her and felt a little surprised that it had surfaced so readily and publicly.

"I felt sorry for the old lady. It would also let me see if she had any bruises that Protective Services should know about."

"Always an ulterior motive." Holt was a little disappointed that his expectation of goodwill was tarnished by what he knew was police reality.

"As if you never had one in your life."

Lucas drained the melted green ice from the glass. She was right, of course. The one thing he learned at the penitentiary was that everyone, himself included, had an ulterior motive.

"I think I'm done here," he said, forgetting what his motive was for inviting Susan to dinner. "What about you?"

"More than done." She stood and stretched. "Nice to know adrenaline can overcome tequila and make my legs work again." She nodded toward the door. "Should we mention what happened to Señor Villalobos?"

Lucas Holt glanced at the statuelike figure. Though he had not moved during the commotion, the Rev knew the old man had heard it all. He watched as the former welterweight champ pulled out a rumpled handkerchief and pretended to blow his nose, while really wiping the dampness from his eyes.

"He knows," Holt said as they entered the lobby.

"Then I need to make a quick stop in the ladies' room."

"I'll wait for you here," Lucas said, getting his car keys out of his pocket. Preoccupied with the sad specter of Señor Villalobos, Holt turned abruptly and walked smack into the chest of a tall, older gentleman who had just entered.

"Excuse me!" the Rev said, grabbing the man to keep them both on balance. As he did, a key scratched the tall man's hand.

"No, no! Excuse *me*!" The older man laughed and held on to Holt to stay steady on his feet.

"You all right?" Holt pointed to the thin line of blood.

"Fine," the man said, grabbing a paper napkin. "A minor abrasion. Bleeding will stop quickly."

"I'm really sorry," Holt apologized again. "I obviously wasn't paying attention."

"No problem at all," the man replied, and walked past him into the dining area to meet someone. "Happens to the best of us. Really"—the man moved by him—"think nothing of it."

Lucas Holt took a seat in the wicker chair by the entrance window just as Susan Granger returned.

"That was fast," he said, pushing the door open as they walked out into the cool October night.

She hooked her arm into his and pulled him over to whisper. "I only had to go Number One, Daddy. How long should it take?"

"At least as long as it took you to drink the margaritas in the first place," Holt said, suspecting she had hoped to find Señora Villalobos in there. "Besides, don't you know the employees have their own rest room by the kitchen?"

She unhooked her arm and opened the car door. "Anybody ever tell you you're a smartass?"

"Other than my parents? No," Holt said, starting the car. "You're the only woman in twenty-five years who has had the audacity to say that."

"Good," Susan Granger mumbled, closing her eyes and slumping down in the seat.

What the hell did that mean? he wondered as he drove the slow back streets to her condo so as not to wake her. It was odd to see her sleep, as he had seen her so many years before. It was one of his favorite memories of her. For a moment she looked as she did in college, the stern lines of her face soft and relaxed, the wisp of dark hair out of place on her cheek. That image still attracted, stirred within him old feelings.

Holt stopped the car in front of her house and hesitated, his hand in midair. Both sides of what Kristen Wade called his "Libra personality" were in active conversation with each other, weighing out conflicting feelings, telling him opposite things.

He and Susan couldn't go back twenty-five years. But could he imagine going forward? Probably not. Too many differences and experiences separated their lives. Still it was interesting to fantasize, no matter how improbable the fantasy was. And, too, there was Kristen, whom he had to call as soon as he left here. But as Nikky said, life was short, he reasoned as he listened to Susan's soft breathing. Instead of safely nudging her shoulder, he touched her hand to wake her.

"Oh," she said, startled, pulling away. "Sorry."

"No problem."

Susan Granger got her key and yawned. "Thanks for dinner."

"Dinner was on the Villalobos family." Why didn't he just say "You're welcome" and accept her gratitude?

"Right." She closed the car door. "Thanks for the ride."

"Maybe we can talk more tomorrow about the Bertrands? Can I call you in the morning?"

"Sure," she responded sleepily. "We may know more from the crime scene by then."

Holt watched her enter the house and turn on a light before he drove away.

And later in his own sleep, long after he had dropped her off, after he had tried to call the absent Kristen and wound up coming to the safe familiarity of his own house, he tossed alone in bed, disturbed by vivid dreams of a young Hispanic boxer and a triumphal Olympic heroine whose bodies lay, covered with medals, motionless in front of a fireplace.

• Four •

The October sun nudged the temperature into the seventies, forcing the small gathering at Leander Cemetery to seek shelter under the green tent. Pungent perfume on sweaty clothes baked with fragrant floral sprays and the musty odor of the canvas.

Nikky Dorati watched with men from the funeral home and felt like a professional mourner, hired to take up space. He agreed to ride with the Rev, ostensibly to keep him company, but Nikky knew the real reason was to talk about the Bertrand murders.

Holt intoned a final blessing and tossed sand on the coffin. It was the worst part of the ceremony for Dorati, the most graphic, final, macabre, up in your face.

"Ashes to ashes. Dust to dust."

It was also, thank God, the cue for the end of the service. Dorati desperately wanted a cigar. He didn't like boneyards, though he had put more than a few people in them during his career. But every one of those slimeballs had deserved it. They had ripped someone, killed a Family member, or tried to power their own sect inside the Organization. This old man, according to the Rev, was just alone and forgotten by his family. Worse than forgotten. Ignored.

Neglect made Dorati angry. Nobody deserved that, especially old people. Maybe he should sidle up to that yuppie fortyish daughter and successful fiftyish son and hint that the old man had left money in his will for a hit, and they wouldn't know which one of them it was until it happened. He pursed his lisp as though he were smoking and grinned.

"Whatever it is you're thinking, don't." Lucas Holt folded up his stole and hit Dorati with it. "I've seen that look on your face before at the pen. It means somebody is in trouble."

"Like we say in the walls: 'Payback's a bitch.' "

"Right. But God's supposed to do the payback. Remember that bit about 'Vengeance is mine. I will repay'?"

"But God has to have somebody to get the job done, right? I mean God can't show up and slap somebody around." Dorati helped him put his alb in the long black bag. "So I figure you and I work for the same Boss, but in different departments."

"What?"

"You're sales"—Dorati grinned—"I'm enforcement."

Holt laughed. "I need you on the Pledge Committee."

They got into the black MX6 and turned onto a gravel two-lane Ranch Road, kicking up a trail of white dust behind them until they finally reached the main highway. Dorati was uncharacteristically quiet.

Holt wondered why and broke the ice. "The first time out here I got lost and nearly was late for the funeral."

"The first time?"

"Yeah. This is my third one in two months. It's sort of a trend. These old ranchers get to the point where they can't take care of themselves or their land, so they move in to nursing or retirement homes. In Burnside's case his family just moved him when they couldn't keep tabs on him anymore. He didn't answer the phone, forgot to eat most of the time, and the poor man's personal hygiene had deteriorated to a five on the Feinwell Scale."

Dorati laughed. "I forgot about Feinwell."

"How could you forget the Feinwell Smell?" Holt made a face and held his nose. He remembered David Feinwell as the inmate who had set the prison standard for personal repulsiveness. The man weighted 305, wouldn't use toilet paper, hoarded insect-infested fruit, and washed only when the goon squad dragged him into the showers or hosed him down on the basketball court. The Rev had intervened to get him paroled when an anonymous petition was sent to the judge implying that, if action was not taken soon, the health hazard would be "eliminated."

"Still," Holt continued, "old man Burnside could have stayed on that ranch a few more months where he was comfortable and familiar and we'd have found him dead three days after the event." He looked at Dorati. "Smelling like a Feinwell Ten."

Dorati patted the cigars in his shirt pocket and shifted nervously in his seat. "I can't smoke in here, right?"

Holt glared at him. Nikky knew how he felt about smoking. "Not just no, but hell no. What's eating you, Nikky? You've been edgy since you got in the car. You know something about the Bertrand murders you don't want to tell me? You think I'm going to make you captive in the car and grill you on them?"

Dorati settled back. "Nothin' you don't know, Rev, honest."

But Holt was not convinced. Nikky had something on his mind and was obviously ambivalent about blurting it out. "You sure?"

"Pretty sure, yeah. I been thinkin' about it, though, and I'm impressed how clean it was, like real professional, except that a professional would have done something about that check. It was too good to leave behind."

Lucas understood what he meant. If nothing was taken, the motives narrowed substantially, usually to revenge. A pro would have taken the check and a few items like jewelry or a VCR to throw investigators off track.

"But if that's true, what was the motive?" Holt asked.

"Beats hell out of me."

"Well, regardless of what we told Susan Granger, I want the Squad on the case."

"I knew you would, Rev." Dorati grinned. "I turned 'em loose last night."

Holt stopped at a light and looked at him. "So why do I think there's something else on your mind?"

Nikky frowned. "I don't know, Rev. It's been weird ever since your birthday. I been thinkin' about gettin' older, and your preachin' about it hasn't helped matters. I hit the big five-oh next month, so I'm sensitive to the issue. I mean, I never thought about gettin' old until lately. Fifty is startin' to look down the end of the dusty trail, ain't it?"

"Not necessarily, considering you've got another possible thirty years to do something with. Actually, older people in this country do quite well. The problem isn't that they're feeble, it's that they're forgotten, undervalued, discarded like paper cups. That's why Cora Mae is so refreshing. *She's* more the norm than the exception." He set the cruise control and steered. "The real problem, Nikky, isn't whether you're going to die. The Bertrands are a grim reminder of that. The problem is what're you going to do until then?"

"How old were your parents when they died?"

"What?" Holt asked, puzzled at the sudden directness of the question. "Why do you want to know?"

"Just askin', is all," Dorati said. "Thinkin' out loud."

The Rev was silent as pictures of his parents appeared in his mind. He never talked about them to anyone. He realized he seldom talked about anything really personal, not even with Kristen Wade. Maybe now was the time to start, with Nikky.

"Okay," he replied with a deep breath. "Mom died shortly after they moved back to Austin from Smithville. My dad pulled out of an election for county judge at the last minute. I never found out why. After that, my mother went downhill. They moved to Austin, in the house I live in now, and lived for a couple of years there while I was at U.T. Dad died a year after Mom of a heart attack, the way he wanted to go. Mom died on a respirator, hooked up to every tube known to medicine. I wouldn't let that happen today." He glanced at Dorati. "And don't let it happen to *me*, either."

"No prob, Rev," Nikky said. "I'll shoot you first."

Holt smiled. Nikky Dorati was the one person he could trust implicitly. At the penitentiary many people had thought it strange that a priest and a hit man could be so close, and told them both so at every opportunity. Inmates warned Dorati not to trust a preacher as often as guards warned Holt not to befriend a con. Initially each had been wary of the other, threatened by each other's influence and leadership in a system where everything depended on territory. Gradually testing, pushing, circling like animals evaluating the fight before starting, they came to respect each other's position. Ironically, they also discovered they were more alike than different.

"So," Holt shot back, "what about *your* parents?"

"My parents?" Nikky furrowed his brow. "You don't wanna hear about my parents."

"Right. That's why I asked." Holt remembered little about them from graveyard-shift discussions with Dorati in solitary confinement. Those conversations had cemented their friendship, especially when Holt smuggled cigars and smoked one himself as a cover. "Wasn't your dad a truck driver or something?"

"Dad drove a cement truck in New York. He was pretty high up with the Teamsters at that time. He died a long time ago, in my twenties." Dorati was silent a moment, remembering. "I heard bangin' on the front door, then a blast and my mother screamin'. I rushed out to protect her and saw my father's bloody body permanently embedded in the living room couch."

"My God"—Holt grimaced—"that's horrible. Who did it?"

"He was shotgunned by a rival union. I had been on the street a long time by then and had contacts of my own. I found out the two assholes that did it—and I did them."

Holt was not shocked by the revelation. It was the law of the street, of the Family. If left to the police, no arrests would have been made. It said more about the violent society than about the murderous abilities of the man sitting beside him.

"Then I found out who ordered it done," Dorati continued. "And there was a sudden vacancy in the leadership of that other union. You might say it was the way my dad launched my career."

Lucas Holt stared at the road. The odd part was that he had known Nikky Dorati for twenty years at the penitentiary and had never heard that story. The "Mafia Midget" had related many others about his family, but not how his father died. The Rev wondered if there was a lot more about Nikky he didn't know.

"And your mother?" Holt asked.

"I can't talk much about her."

"She's still alive, then?"

"I think so. I mean I assume she is. For both of our protections we had to cut off communication years ago. There are people with long memories who would off her to get at me. She's well covered now, though. The Family sees to her for me and I send her letters through a relative in New York sometimes. But I haven't actually laid eyes on her in about fifteen years."

"Think you'll ever meet her again?"

"Hell, I wouldn't know her if I did."

"Wouldn't you like to talk to her once before you get beneficiary papers in the mail?"

Dorati smiled. "That's assuming I'm the beneficiary. For all I know she could have gotten hooked up with some guy and left it to him." Nikky turned in his seat to face the Rev. "Which reminds me, there's something I been wantin' to ask you."

"Ask away—we've got twenty minutes before we hit town."

"I don't know how to be any way but blunt about this, Rev, so here it goes."

Holt straightened his arms on the steering wheel. "I'm bracing myself."

"Are you gonna get it on with Kristen Wade or Susan Granger and have some kids or what?"

Lucas Holt sputtered a laugh. "Ex-cuse me?"

"You heard me, Rev. Wade or Granger? Or is there another chick in there you haven't told me about? And when are the little Bubbas and Bubbettes comin' along? You ain't gettin' any younger, you know. If I'm ever gonna get to be a grandpa it's by you, so hurry the hell up and let me know what's happenin' here."

The Rev thought for a minute. Dorati had caught him off guard. He felt annoyed at Nikky for asking, probably because it raised the same questions Lucas was asking himself, and it meant dragging feelings out in the open that were better left buried.

"You're not old enough to be a grandpa, and I'm *too* old to be a father."

"I'm almost eight years older than you are. And don't round on me, Rev. Answer the question."

"Okay, but what makes you think Susan's a contender?"

"Gimme a break." Dorati smirked and put on his sunglasses. "You had a past. Why not a future? She actually ain't too bad." He made a sour face. "For a cop."

Holt's palms got sweaty on the wheel. He wasn't used to pressure from anyone, especially Nikky Dorati. In a way he appreciated the chance to talk; in another way he wished the car would blow a tire right now.

"It's precisely because of our past that we don't have a future. And my relationship with Kristen is fine."

"And the check's in the mail and a bear don't shit in the woods." Dorati took off his glasses. "Hell, Rev, you describe it like a contract."

"Describe what?" Holt said, sorry the conversation was going in this direction. Maybe talking was a mistake.

"You said you're happy with the 'relationship,' not with Kristen herself. Shoot, the Legislature sees more of her than you do. Come on, Rev. Handwriting's on the wall, to use a Bible reference you should get."

"Meaning?"

"Listen to me givin' the Rev advice for the lovelorn." He punched Holt on the arm. "Who'da thought it? Meaning that Kristen's goin' on with her political career, and sooner or later you won't fit into the plan."

Lucas Holt restrained his angry reaction. He felt defensive, knowing Nikky was right, having felt it for some time but not wanting to admit it. Kristen Wade was more arrangement than relationship. It was the tacit agreement to avoid a relationship that had brought them together in the first place.

From the beginning, when they were first introduced by Susan Granger, they had clearly admitted their need for companionship over commitment, for monogamy over sexual Russian roulette. It was fun but passionless, convenient but empty. They truly liked each other and enjoyed each other's company, but neither would risk feelings that could grow into love. Now that Kristen's career was on the upswing, headed utlimately toward Washington, there would be even less reason to let those feelings develop.

For his part, Lucas Holt felt content with what they had—until lately. Maybe it was this damned midlife stuff that kept coming at him from all directions, demanding that he assess where he had been and where he was going. Maybe it was the thought of losing Kristen that put him in touch with needs he had denied for years. Maybe, he thought as he steered the car through the increasing traffic of town, the image of Erik and Janey Bertrand dead in their prime had affected him more than he admitted.

"Yo, Rev. You still with me?"

"Yeah. I am, unfortunately. Did anybody ever tell you to mind your own business?"

"You minded my business for twenty years at the pen. I figure it's only fair I mess around yours the rest of your life."

"Dammit, Dorati! I don't know what the hell to do. I don't know what I want. I don't know anything about what Susan wants." Holt grasped the steering wheel tighter as his voice rose. "I just turned forty-three and I feel like a damned teenager."

"Well, don't take it out on the gas pedal, Rev. Being caught in a speeding car is a parole violation."

The Rev pulled his foot from the accelerator. "Shit, Nikky, why didn't you tell me I was that far over the speed limit?"

"I just did. Lighten up, Rev. Take a deep breath."

Holt slowed the car and pulled into a strip center parking lot. "What's going on here? Why is it so damned important to you? The Bertrands throw the fear of God into you, too?"

"They didn't help," Dorati said glumly. "Listen, you're not the only one in a midlife crisis. I'm thinkin' what to do with the rest of my life, too. I used to think in ten-year blocks, depending on if I got felonies or misdemeanors."

Holt laughed. "Life on the installment plan."

"Right. But where I am now, I see you and the God Squad as my family. Especially you, Rev."

"But you have a mother somewhere, and—"

"No, Rev. Pay attention here. I been talkin' a lot lately with Cora Mae Hartwig. All those old people she goes to visit every week, they all have famil*ies* somewhere who visit them once a year or less. But they also have family—the people close to you who care about you and check on you and, hell, I don't know, just plain damn *like* you. Not 'cause they have to, but because fate threw you together and you're stuck with each other."

"We're family because we're stuck with each other?"

"More than that. There's all you did for me and the Squad in the joint. Ain't no way I can ever repay you for that shit."

"I didn't do—"

"Like hell you didn't. And don't try to tell me you did it for some damn religious reason, either. You stepped between me and a shiv once, and you got the scar to prove it. Then there was that hostage deal, and the murders they tried to pin on the God Squad, not to mention saving my ass in the mess-hall riot."

"This is Texas," Holt said in his deepest voice. "One riot. One priest."

Dorati ignored him. "Anyway, here's the deal. It's not because I owe you a lot, including my short, dumpy life. It's because we're stuck with each other and we're family that I'm askin' these questions, and because, well, I made you the beneficiary of my will."

"Your *will*?" Holt looked seriously at his friend. "You get some bad medical news or something?"

"Shit, no, Rev. You'd be the first to know if I did. It's just Cora Mae and sermons got me thinkin' a lot lately about what would happen if I got offed or just up and croaked. And I want to know if some grandchildren are goin' to get some damn good out of my funds, that's all."

Lucas Holt shook his head. "You're a piece of work, Nikky, as Susan would say."

"She's the better bet, Rev. Higher up in the gene pool. Though it galls me to think my money's goin' to the cops."

"No guarantee of anything, Nikky. Not in this world, anyway. No guarantee you'll die before I do, or of me working anything out with Susan even if I wanted to. And there's no guarantee of kids, or that money's there when you do die. Maybe you'll spend it all first."

"Not my life insurance, Rev. I took out a big policy with old Harris Lambert's agency before he went nuts and killed all them people. So will my money go to good use or what?"

Holt started the car. "Truth is, you're my family, too. But what you do with your money is up to you." He pulled back onto Highway 183 toward Austin. "I can't make promises about the future. I am thinking about everything you said in great detail. For now, we aren't dead yet and the Bertrands are and I want to find who killed them. That's the latest news. Film at eleven."

"Cop at three."

"What?"

"Cop with radar at three o'clock, watch your speed."

"How do you spot them so fast?"

Nikky Dorati looked at Lucas Holt.

"Stupid question." Holt was about to be rude when a high-pitched chirp interrupted his thoughts. "What's that?"

"Your car phone. The one you never use."

"Don't mock the electronically challenged. Maybe Susan found something at the scene."

"Right," Dorati said. "As if the cops could find their ass with both hands."

Holt punched a button and the radio came on.

"Speaker button's the one next to it."

"I knew that," the Rev said. "Hello?" he yelled.

"Jesus, Rev!" a scratchy voice said.

"Fine language for a church secretary, Max," Holt said.

"I know you don't like me to call you on this thing because of the expense, but I thought you'd want to know this, and—"

"Cut to the chase, Max."

"Right. Where the hell is that slip? Shit. I just had it."

"Max!"

"Is someone else listening there, Rev?"

"No one but me, darlin' of my dreams," Dorati crooned.

"Where'd you pick up the stray, Rev?"

"Nikky can hear anything you need to tell me. Shoot."

"Some attorney called and wants you to stop by his office at One American Center. Darron Newell, of Newell, Calkins, and Bellomy? Card says 'Estate Law,' and I know what he wants."

"Then tell me and hang up." Holt slowed for a traffic light about to turn green.

"He said St. Margaret's was named as—" Her voice vanished as the car passed beneath the MoPac Highway overpass.

"So you'll want to see him right away."

"What? I couldn't hear you. What did you say, Max?"

The raspy voice raised in volume. "I said St. Margaret's is a beneficiary in the will of Erik and Janey Bertrand to the tune of five hundred thousand dollars!"

The tall, distinguished-looking man brushed his silver hair back over the balding areas before splashing on aftershave and straightening his tie. At seventy-five years of age, his six-foot-two frame was almost as straight as it had been when he stood over the operating table, poised to make the first cut.

Dr. Truman Reinhardt winced as the sweet-smelling lotion burned the tiny nicks from his razor. He was handsome for his age, and there was good reason for it. He exercised, ate appropriately, drank in moderation, and practiced safe sex every time he got the chance. He smiled in the mirror to see mostly his own teeth, capped though they were, reflected back at him. He was ready to make his entrance into the dining room.

As he left his townhome and walked down the sidewalk to the common area, the only noticeable imperfection in his appearance was what one of the old ranch ladies there called "a hitch in his giddy-up." Fifty years of standing over splayed bodies had taken a toll on his left hip. He knew he needed a replacement, and that, nowadays, it was a simple procedure with a quick recuperation. He just didn't know anyone he trusted to do it the way he would if he could operate on himself. So, for the present, he would tolerate a slight limp.

"Good evening, Vicki," he said to the hostess at the dining room.

"Good evening, Dr. Reinhardt. You're looking particularly well this evening. But then, you always do."

"Flattery will get you everywhere, my dear." He smiled and looked beyond her, scanning the dining room to see who he knew.

"I'm afraid I have some bad news, though."

"What's that?" His caterpillar eyebrows wrinkled and kissed.

"A new girl started training earlier tonight, and since I wasn't here to tell her, she seated someone else at your table."

The doctor glanced inside. "Who is it?"

"She's a new resident of the Center. Moved here about a month ago. A Mrs. Pelham, I believe."

The caterpillars relaxed. "There are two chairs at that table." Reinhardt smiled.

The woman hesitated, then returned his smile. "Why not?" She escorted him through the dining room, where he nodded or shook hands with most of the older ladies. At his table a striking woman with black hair and dark features turned to face them.

"Mrs. Pelham, this is Dr. Reinhardt, who actually had this table reserved."

"I was wondering," the tall gentleman spoke softly and in his deepest voice, "if it wouldn't be too much trouble, that is, if I might join you for the remainder of your dinner. The view of Barton Creek and the greenbelt is so nice from this window, and the sunset is particularly striking on these October evenings."

"I wouldn't mind at all, Dr. . . . ?"

"Reinhardt. Truman Reinhardt." He took a seat and the relieved hostess left.

"I'm Mrs. Nicholas Pelham." She paused. "Helen."

He shook her hand. "Truman." He signaled to the waiter, who delivered the waiting bottle of Fumé Blanc in a silver ice bucket. "I hope you will join me in a glass of this excellent white, crisp wine. It is my favorite and they have it for me regularly on Tuesday nights when fresh fish is the special."

She nodded and he poured two glasses.

"Welcome to Westlake Retirement Center, Mrs. Helen Pelham."

"Thank you, Dr. Reinhardt." Her red lipstick left a slight imprint on the glass, and a stronger one on the man observing it. "How did you know I was new?"

"Like any retirement facility, the grapevine is short around here. In the hospital, by the time I got to the patient's room, everyone knew the results of the surgery. It is the same here."

"Then you already know something about me?"

"Just that you've been here about a month." He sipped at the wine as the salad appeared with fresh ground pepper. "I know also that you smoke, and have for most of your life, which means there is little chance you'll quit now, that you had a minor bout with a melanoma which was surgically removed, that you are quite a creative person, and that you are from the Northeast, either New York or northern New Jersey."

The black-haired woman sat back in her chair and held the wineglass in front of her. "Pour me another, Dr. Reinhardt." She smiled, the red lips forming a perfect oval on her tanned face. "And tell me how the grapevine got all that information."

"Grapevine didn't," he said, filling their glasses. "Fifty-one years of medical practice did that." He took small bites of the salad and talked as he ate. "We are in the smoking section and the glass ashtray, though it has been emptied, still has traces of gray in it. Couple that with your raspy voice, and you get someone who's smoked a long time. Dedicated. Inveterate."

"Ready to die of lung cancer for the pleasure they give me," she said, lighting another off the butt of the first.

"A New York attitude with a slight accent to go with it."

"Larchmont. Born in Brooklyn and lived most of my life in Westchester, till I got tired of the pace and moved here."

Reinhardt watched her graceful movements and responded with

his own. He kept eye contact and showed interest as he turned on the charm. "Texas is quite a change of pace."

"You saw that scar from the surgery on my face?"

"People see the world from their peculiar point of interest. A thief sees your purse and your body size, an artist the contour of your face. Surgeons are alert to the work of their colleagues to evaluate whether they could have done better."

"Could you?"

"Not much. Whoever did that place on your cheek was either well trained or experienced." He wondered if she knew he was being polite about the scar, not ignorant of what a bullet wound looked like after a plastic man had covered it.

"And the creativity?" she replied, blowing smoke in the air. "I am very creative, both in my thinking and in my hobbies."

"Which are?"

"First, how did you draw the conclusion?"

"You are left-handed, are you not?" he said as the salad was replaced by broiled fish and vegetables, and glasses topped.

"Ambidextrous, actually."

"Even more to my point. Left-handed people—right brained, if you will—are consistently more creative than we left-brained, hard-working proletariat types."

She pointed out the window. "Oh! Look! The sunset."

He turned and held his glass to hers. "To the sunset, and the beginning of a friendship, I hope."

"Likewise, I'm sure."

"You know, there's a little Mexican restaurant out on the lake. It's a series of wooden decks built onto the side of a hill. Every night people drink margaritas as the sun sets, and when the last tip of the sun vanishes over the hill across the lake, they break into applause. It's an Austin tradition."

"It's a wonderful tradition—applauding the sunset." She let the waiter take her plate. "Whether it's the sunset of your career, or of your life. Every performance needs applause."

"People our age—or at least my age—can appreciate the meaning of that applause more than others, don't you think?" He liked this woman with the easy manner and quick wit. Her dark features attracted him, contrasting as they did with her red lipstick and green silk dress. He hoped she would make an excuse to go to the ladies' room so he could see her whole body in motion. He imagined still shapely legs and high heels shielding toes painted the same cherry red as her fingernails. He imagined them against the deep blue of his sheets.

"Our ages are not as far apart as you might imagine." She smiled from one corner of her mouth and puffed on a cigarette.

"So you know my age?" Reinhardt asked.

"Grapevines swing both ways." She added two sugars to her coffee and stirred, slowly. "You are five years older than I am, a former surgeon with a specialty in cardio-thoracic procedures. You need a hip replacement, but you don't trust anyone locally and won't go back to your friends at Mayo because you hate the weather up there along with the current administration."

Truman Reinhardt sat back in his chair with an FDR grin. He loved being known and talked about just as he had been in his practice years. But he wondered just how much this woman— through the gossips in the place—had actually unearthed.

"That's it?" he asked rhetorically, not looking at her.

"Depends on how personal you want to get." Her eyes narrowed playfully, and her thick mascaraed lashes flickered.

"You'd better tell me *all* the rumors so I can defend myself," Reinhardt said, emptying the bottle into their glasses.

She took a deep breath. "You moved here nine months ago from another facility where you and your late wife had retired. You couldn't bear to live in the same town up north without her, so you made a new start in Texas to live the rest of your life."

Reinhardt's smile vanished to somberness.

"I hope I didn't offend you. I only meant—"

The doctor sighed. "No." He looked down at the table. "No offense. Just surprised at the accuracy of the data."

"I'll stop if you wish."

"No." He sipped the wine. "Do continue. The sound of your voice is, if I may say so, fascinating."

"You may." She put aside her coffee and pulled the wine glass forward. "You are the most eligible bachelor in the Center, one of the few men with his wits still about him, not to mention his health." She chuckled. "All the old ladies around here say that your hip is the only thing about you that's limp."

"They're right, of course, and I'll drink to that."

"Me, too." She winked. She lifted the cigarette, inhaled deeply, and blew smoke toward the open window.

Reinhardt noted the red mark on the cigarette. This woman left her imprint on everything she touched. He wondered, with some titillation, what kind of imprint she would leave on him—and where?

"You wear expensive cologne, you don't color your hair, and you are causing every other woman in here to have cardiac dysrhythmias by spending so much time talking to me."

"Cardiac dysrhythmias?"

"I've done some hospital work in my time as well." She glanced at her watch. "But the most eligible bachelor is off the hook for the evening."

"A minute more while I finish my wine. And I'm not the only eligible male here." He cast his eyes on the well-dressed black man at a table for one. "There's Reverend Sparks."

"He's only eligible if you want to cash in on his insurance soon. The poor man strolls around here twitching his head and mumbling 'Vengeance is mine. I will repay, says the Lord.' "

"He seems to be very unhappy about something," Reinhardt commented. "I meant him no disrespect. He probably has senile dementia, though he's younger than both of us."

"Stroke five years ago, according to the illustrious grapevine. He was a prominent preacher in an East Austin church. Still goes back there occasionally." She watched as an older, gray-haired woman entered the dining room and took the seat across from Sparks. "Who's the woman with him now?"

"Local busybody," Reinhardt said disdainfully. "Cora Mae Hartwig. She's older than Methuselah and brings communion from St. Margaret's Episcopal Church downtown. Sticks her nose into everybody's life in the process."

"You don't much like her?"

"She's pleasant enough, I guess. I don't know. She reminds me of somebody from my practice I didn't trust." He finished the wine. "I suppose you have to give her points for spending time with old Sparks."

"I'd rather end up like her than like him, wouldn't you?"

"No question about that. Having Sparks around is a reminder of how short life is—like that sunset we were talking about."

"Perhaps," she said, pushing back her chair, "you could take me to that Mexican restaurant on the lake sometime?"

"Perhaps next week?" Truman Reinhardt quickly moved to assist her from her chair. "In the meantime, might I stop by for a nightcap?"

The woman put her hand on his. "Not tonight," she said softly. "But another time, soon."

"Very well, then. I think I'll go to the sitting room here and catch up on the news."

"I enjoyed our conversation, Truman, and I look forward to seeing you again."

They parted at the front door and went their separate ways. Later, as Dr. Truman Reinhardt read the *New York Times* in the Commons area, Mrs. Helen Pelham closed and locked the door to her townhome. She proceeded to the bedroom, where she took a .38 from her purse and slid it under her white satin pillow.

The two sisters thanked the officers for responding so quickly. Serena Sanchez and Blanca Villalobos only dialed 911 when they thought they couldn't handle it themselves. They closed up Casita Lobos alone every night and dealt with the usual drunks and homeless and street punks. More than once they had collared tough kids looking for a quick dip in the cash drawer and called the cops afterward.

But tonight was different. They were sure someone was hiding in the shadows behind the restaurant. The floodlight where they parked their car had been smashed two nights ago by vandals, and neither woman had taken the time to replace it.

After the kitchen was cleaned and the cash deposit dropped in the floor safe, Blanca had gone out the back door with shotgun in hand, ready for whatever or whoever was there. Serena had waited in the kitchen with the pistol. When Blanca returned, spooked, they called the police. After a thorough search, nothing was found.

Blanca checked the burners one last time, then turned off the lights as her younger sister set the alarm sequence and pulled the door shut behind them.

Blanca yawned as her sister pulled onto South Lamar and headed for IH 35, the north-south interstate on the east side of the city. "I just want to be home in the tub. I wish we didn't live way up in Georgetown. The drive is long, even together."

"You know we couldn't afford a house that big in Austin, not even with what we took from our parents' accounts." Serena sighed and patted her sister's hand. "Besides, it gives us a chance to wind down and talk."

But silence overtook them as neither woman spoke of her increased fatigue and decreasing ability to keep her eyes open. Blanca thought the heater was making them drowsy, so she turned the knob to provide an equal mix of hot and cold air. But even that did not affect their growing lethargy. The longer they drove, the weaker they seemed to get. Thirty minutes later they approached the sign for Route 29. "At last, we're here," she said sleepily as they turned at the Georgetown exit. "I thought for a minute back there that we wouldn't make it."

"To tell you the truth," Serena said, following the main street all the way to the end, "I fell asleep at the wheel a couple of times and had to bite my lip to stay awake."

She turned into the driveway of a beautifully restored Victorian house. Timers had turned on lights to make it look cozy and inviting. Serena punched the button on the visor and waited for the door to the detached garage to open. There seemed to be a long lag time between punching the button and the door rising, but her clouded mind ignored the discrepancy in her hurry to get inside.

"You can forget the bath," Blanca said. "I'll be dead when I hit that pillow." She listlessly reached for her purse, but dropped it on the floor of the car. "What's the matter with me? I'm so weak I can hardly speak."

"We'll be all right when we get in the house," Serena said, driving into the garage as the door closed behind her, though she had not pushed the button to make it close. "Let's hurry. I barely have enough strength to turn off the engine."

"Hurry?" her sister said, unable now to move from her seat. "That's a joke. Maybe we should just . . . sleep . . . here."

Serena tried to turn the key, but it would not budge. She moved her left hand to the switch for the electric windows and, panic throbbing in what was left of her waning consciousness, used her remaining strength to pull them back and open the two front windows.

She breathed deeply, expecting that somehow fresh air would

fill up her choking lungs, as if she were parked outside in the driveway or behind the restaurant. She heard herself gasping, as in a dream, and somewhere deep under the outer curtain of lethargy she realized they were suffocating. With her last alert bit of reason she forced her arm up to the visor and desperately squeezed the door opener. Hope surged with the glow of the tiny red light, but nothing happened. Her arm dropped to her side.

Serena coaxed her flaccid muscles to turn her head toward her sister. Through dulled eyes, she saw Blanca slumped in the seat with saliva drooling from her open mouth. If only she could touch her, move her hand to her sister. Tears welled and slid down her cheek as the signals from her brain to her hand went unheeded. And then she thought of it.

The horn.

The full weight of her heavy body surely would push the center of the steering wheel and call for help.

With her last ounce of will, Serena slumped her own bulk toward the steering wheel. She had calculated correctly. The center of the wheel depressed more than enough to set off the blaring noise that would awaken neighbors and call them to their garage. She relaxed and slept, confident she had saved their lives.

The last sound she heard was no sound at all.

• Five •

The crest of the sun inched like an orange balloon over Austin's northwest hills, chasing night shadows and October frost from the houses built neatly into wooded cliffs. In one secluded home the light fell through a large, curtainless window onto the face of a man who rolled his head away from the bright intrusion. As he did, he felt warm breath from the face on the pillow next to him and reached over to stroke her face and hair. When he touched her, a long wet tongue reached out and licked his lips and nose.

Lucas Holt's eyes jumped open.

"*Aspen!*" He pushed the golden retriever away. The large animal stood and licked him again. "Kristen! Call your dog," he hollered, pulling the pillow over his slobbery face, an action which Aspen read as a signal to play. She bit the pillow and shook it back and forth.

"Aspen!" the sing-songy voice called from the bathroom. "Food, girl!"

The dog dropped the pillow and stepped on the Rev as she bolted to the stairs. Holt heard her nails scrape across the Saltillo tile in the kitchen. "What time *is* it?" he mumbled from under a non-slimed pillow on Kristen's side of the bed.

" 'Five minutes past the hour' as they say on NPR."

"Which hour?"

"Six."

Holt peeked out from under the pillow to see Kristen neatly dressed in a red silk pant suit the same shade as her lipstick, running a comb through her curled auburn hair one last time.

"I've already had my third cup of coffee, so I'm nearly awake enough to drive." She leaned over the bed and pulled the pillow off his face to kiss him.

Holt grabbed her waist and rolled her back into the bed. She dropped her keys and shoes.

"Lucas!" she yelled, half playfully and half annoyed. "I'm dressed and I've *got* to get to the Capitol by quarter to seven."

"It's nine minutes past the hour," he mocked. "Takes you fifteen minutes to get there and park in the space ten feet from the Capitol held for you by old retired cowboys in lawn chairs who chase grackles and tourists. Gives us twenty minutes."

She protested, "I have to stop by the bank."

Holt nibbled her neck. "We'll have to act quick."

Kristen Wade held his face in her hand and kissed him deeply, then, withdrawing, licked his mouth and cheek. "That's to remember me and Aspen by until tonight," she said, pushing him back and getting up from the bed.

"Aspen's a pretty good kisser," he said. "And I see more of her lately."

Kristen ignored the comment as she smoothed out her trousers and ran the comb through her tangled hair. Holt raised up when she leaned over to pick up her keys and shoes.

"Of course, you have better cleavage."

Kristen threw a pillow at him. "Until she gets pregnant." She smiled and tossed him a kiss. "I gotta go or I'll be late."

Holt suddenly realized something. "On *Saturday*?"

"Yes, Lucas, on Saturday!" she said. "It was the only day we could get together to hammer out the compromise on this State healthcare bill. Maybe dinner," she said, heading for the bedroom door. "Call me around seven on my mobile phone."

Holt squinted in the brightening sunlight. "You're meeting for fifteen minutes?"

"Seven P.M., smartass."

"Kristen, wait a minute," Holt said as she looked at her watch. "No, really." He sat up in bed. "What's going on with us? I never see you."

"What was last night—a mirage?"

"No, no, of course not. I enjoyed the hell out of last night. That's the problem. It'll be the last night for two weeks if I don't impose myself into your schedule." Holt knew he was treading on thin ice here, calling their relationship into question. They never talked about it, taking for granted it would move along as it had for almost three years now—*not* moving along.

"Lucas, this is not the time to discuss this issue." She looked at her watch again. "I have to go and it's not fair of you to bring it up when I'm under pressure."

"I know that. I just feel like, I don't know, like you're having an affair with the Legislature."

"Wrong woman, Lucas. That's Max you're talking about."

"Ouch," Holt said, looking hurt. "Low blow."

"Well, I'm sorry, Lucas. I'm annoyed at your timing, is all. Cut me some slack here and we'll talk about it tonight."

"If tonight happens."

Kristen Wade turned and walked back to the bed. "Lucas, what do you want from me? I *am* having an affair with the Legislature. I'll never get the clout if I don't."

"But—"

"Listen to me. We're talking career here. I'm aiming for the State Senate race next year, and in the next five I plan to represent this State in the U.S. Senate."

The Rev knew she was watching his immobile face carefully. But he had learned well from the prisoners in twenty years at Huntsville State Prison. He could mask emotions as well as any sociopath who had none, and he did it now. It did no good to be upset. He would let her state her case and hope they could work it out later. If later came.

"This is not news to you, Lucas," she said, shaking her head so her tousled hair framed her face like an angel. "We've talked about my aspirations. No kids, no encumbrances. I'm even think- ing of getting rid of Aspen there." She pointed to the dog in the doorway with the leash in its mouth. "I don't have the time to take her out to dump."

"So what does this mean for us?"

"What do you mean, what does it mean? It means what it meant from the beginning, Lucas. It means this is what we've got and we've both agreed it's better than being alone all the time or playing stupid sex games with people we don't know." She took his hand. "What's wrong with it all of a sudden?"

Holt squeezed her hand. "It's like I told you last night about the

Bertrands. Their deaths blew me away. And they got me thinking about time passing."

"If any more of it passes, I won't get the first speaking slot in that committee meeting, and I need it for leverage." She kissed him on the cheek and hurried for the door. "Call me at seven. *Tonight*. And would you take Aspen out before you leave, please?" She vanished without waiting for an answer.

"Sure thing." Holt hid under the covers. "No problemo." He rolled over. "Love to," he grumbled. "In about a week."

He braced himself for the inevitable as sixty pounds of it leaped on the bed, dropped the leash, and barked.

"What's wrong with this picture?" the Rev thought as Aspen pawed at the covers and wagged her tail. Holt peeked out and yelled. "How can you be so *awake* at this hour on *Saturday*? Don't you know it's my only day to sleep *in* before that stupid clergy luncheon? Don't you know I have to work all day tomorrow?"

Aspen saw him and barked louder.

"Okay. Okay. Your bladder wins. Just let me empty mine first." He rolled out of bed, and the dog followed him into the bathroom. "No, get on out of here." He closed the door. "I wouldn't want to make you want to give up your boyfriend."

The dog laid down in front of the door and barked intermittently, like windshield wipers, until Holt emerged in a hooded sweatshirt, sweatpants, and loafers.

"Let's get this over with," he said, attaching the leash to her collar, "so you can go back to sleep and I can have some tea to support my well-earned grouch-hood all day." He had just opened the front door when the phone rang. The dog looked up at him, imploring him not to do it. He didn't.

"Come on," he said as they walked out into the brisk October air. "I don't want to talk to anybody who knows I'm here."

He held the leash loosely as Aspen sniffed objects on the street, looking for the perfect place.

How did he feel about Kristen? he wondered. Did he love her? Probably, but not as passionately as he imagined he would if he wanted to marry. And she likely felt the same about him. He knew from the experience of inmates and current parishioners that relationships of a lifetime were often built on a lot less.

But did he want to commit to a marriage, have a child, repeat the process his parents had repeated with him? Up until now he had had neither the time nor the inclination to think about a long-term relationship. It was partly his workaholic nature that had kept him busy at the penitentiary but also his independent rebelliousness that meant he enjoyed the single lifestyle—and had kept women who wanted more away from him.

And, he wondered as Aspen pulled at the leash, what about the scenario with the Bertrands? He knew from the prison that no one was immune. If he fell in love with someone, he risked losing her to accident, disease, or, like the Bertrands, murder. At least they died together; horribly, but together.

Aspen found the patch of grass she wanted in a neighbor's yard and squatted. Lucas unclipped the leash and let her run past the last few houses to Kristen's front door. Aspen sat on the doorstep with the morning paper in her mouth when he caught up with her. "Thank you," he said as he unlocked the door and opened the front page to read the headline on his way to the kitchen. He stopped in his tracks when the familiar name caught his attention:

VILLALOBOS WOMEN COMMIT DOUBLE SUICIDE

Holt read the description of a neighbor who had come home in the early morning to hear the car engine running in their garage. The same surge of anger rose in him that he felt when Susan told him about the Bertrands.

"No!" he yelled as he stormed into the kitchen and picked up the phone. It couldn't have happened! He and Susan had just seen them at the restaurant! "Damn it! No!" he yelled again, misdialing the number. Aspen disappeared with her tail between her legs as Lucas again punched in the number and noticed the blinking light on the answering machine. He hit the button.

"Lucas, if you're there, pick up. Oh, well, listen, I'm sorry about this morning. You're right, we do need to talk about this. Maybe it's time to—I don't know. I don't want to do this on a machine. I'll do my best to be free by eight tonight." There was a long silence as if she wanted to say something else, but couldn't. The machine beeped and clicked off.

"Shit!" Holt said.

"Hello?" the strong but elderly voice answered.

"Cora Mae?"

"Yes? Is this Lucas?"

"Cora Mae, is Nikky there?"

"You're very clever, Lucas! How did you know?"

Maxine had told him about the "little breakfast club" Cora Mae, Nikky, and a few others had started for themselves. They met at Cora Mae Hartwig's, ate at different restaurants, and walked around the lake. Dorati had lost two pounds, and Cora Mae's poker game improved dramatically. "Clergy knows everything, Cora Mae. Will you put him on?" Holt tried to control his voice, shaking from anger and shock, when Nikky came to the phone. "Have you seen this morning's paper?"

"Yeah, what about it?"

"The Villalobos women?"

"Them two lesbians owned that Meskin joint on South Lamar?"

"Blanca and Serena Villalobos." Holt sat down at the dinette table. "I just saw them a couple of nights ago. Susan and I ate at the restaurant. And now they're dead." Holt's heart was racing. "I can't believe this, Nikky. I mean, why would they do that now? Their business was booming." He flashed the old man with the margarita and the old woman in a heap on the floor. Mostly to himself he said: "Maybe they felt remorse."

Dorati interrupted. "Maybe they got their test results."

"What?" Holt said, returning to the present.

"Maybe they turned up positive. Like C Block."

Holt pictured the three-tiered maximum security unit with the big stone *C* over the entrance. He held separate Sunday services there for the men with HIV and AIDS. The most suicides were on that block. Inmates took the diagnosis as a death sentence, and many chose to hasten the event.

"God, I never thought of that." Lucas Holt was clearly shaken. The other night he thought their frail, dependent parents would die soon—and be better off for it, freed from the debilitating decline of their physical bodies as well as the humiliating treatment from their offspring. He had made up his mind to speak to the women, and now it was too late. It was one more regret to add to the "too late" pile.

"You never know what's in somebody else's mind, Rev, just

like the pen. Who knows what they felt sorry about, that made them want to kill themselves?" Dorati paused to see if Holt was listening. "My first bet is they had AIDS and wanted out."

Holt stood to look out the kitchen window. "Too easy, Nikky. These were tough women. They wouldn't do that right off the bat. They would have fought it, or at least talked with me about it." He felt himself calming down, his logic returning as did Aspen from the living room. He patted her as he wandered around the kitchen, thinking.

"You there, Rev?"

"I'm here." He put water on for tea. "You know what I think?" Holt said without waiting for a reply. "I think that, somehow, these deaths are connected with the Bertrands."

Dorati grunted on the other end of the line.

"No! Listen to me," Holt said, excitement showing through the calm. "Remember Saints of God? Nobody but you and I thought they were connected at first, either. Well, one connection is that the Bertrands and the Villalobos women went to St. Margaret's."

"It's a large church, Rev. How many other deaths have you had this month?"

"None under forty. Except these four." Holt was convincing himself as he talked. "I need to call Susan. This changes what we look for in the Bertrand case."

"Lucas, dear?"

"Yes?" The Rev thought mixing Nikky Dorati and Cora Mae Hartwig was like buttermilk and orange juice, motor oil and milk.

"I've been standing right next to Nicholas, so I couldn't help but hear you talk about the two situations, Lucas, and I have some distressing news of my own to add to the horror of those two nice girls."

"There's more bad news?" Holt frowned as he poured boiling water into the small pot with an Earl Grey tea bag.

"Not necessarily bad, Lucas, but it is curious, especially in light of your thinking the deaths are connected," Cora Mae continued. "Do you remember me mentioning Marie Wilkins last week? How she said a new beau was going to spirit her away? It was when I reported my nursing home visits in staff meeting."

Holt vaguely remembered something about it. "Go ahead."

"Well, I stopped by yesterday to see her—and Marie Wilkins is gone."

"Are you sure she's not just visiting a relative?" Holt asked, not seeing the tie.

"That's just the point, Lucas!"

The Rev poured the tea, hoping it would swish the remaining cobwebs from his brain. "What?"

"The point is that Marie is the mother of Erik Bertrand!"

The Rev's mind spun wildly, bombarded with crises. The Bertrands, the talk with Kristen, two dead sisters, now the mother of one of the murder victims. They pooled together like lead in the pit of his stomach.

"You there, Lucas?"

Holt took a deep breath and cleared his throat. "Yes, Cora. What time is it now?" he said, a bit disoriented.

"It's seven-thirty."

He glanced at the clock on the microwave. "Right." Time to get moving. The longer they waited, the greater the possibility any existing clues would vanish, along with perpetrators. He would start with Cora Mae. "Will you make the altar guild arrangements for the Villalobos funerals?"

"Certainly, dear. Anything else?"

The Rev picked up a knotted sock from the floor and tossed it hard into the next room for Aspen to fetch. "Yeah." He stood and walked with the portable phone toward the stairs. "Meet me at the Westlake Retirement Center at ten."

"I'll be there, Lucas. Here's Nikky." Cora Mae Hartwig handed the phone to Dorati.

"I've worked my way past stunned to pissed," Holt said, his lips tightening.

"You're pissed 'cause two lesbians killed themselves?"

"No. I'm pissed because four members of St. Margaret's are dead and an old lady is missing—and not just any old lady."

Dorati countered: "Two were murdered, right? Two did themselves in because they were gonna die anyway, and from what Cora Mae tells me, the old lady ran off with her new boyfriend."

"Dorati!"

"Okay, okay. I admit it's beginning to look like you said. What do you want me to do?"

"Have Doors check the suicide scene." Holt swallowed some tea. "Do it this morning. And call me when he's got something."

"You sound sure there's something *to* get," Dorati said.

"Damned right I do," Holt replied. "I've been around you too long."

Lucas Holt parked beside the new red Celica in front of the Westlake Retirement Center and approached the woman sitting on a bench in the lawn. Their mutual smiles acknowledged their friendship. In the two years he had been at St. Margaret's, he and Cora Mae Hartwig had developed a closeness that was one part priest-parishioner and two parts mother-son. He trusted her wisdom and loved watching her break the stereotypes of aging others imposed on her.

"Isn't it difficult to get in and out of that sports car?"

"No, Lucas dear, it's not." Cora Mae stood and took him by the arm. "That's another myth about old people—that we're all stove up and need oiling like the Tin Man. Why, I do more daily exercise than the youth group at St. Margaret's." The red coupe chirped as she pressed the remote button to arm the security system. "That car's fun to drive." She winked at him as they walked into the entrance of the facility. "And I've met so many nice friends of Lieutenant Granger's with it."

"How many tickets have you gotten?"

"Not a one." She released his arm with a squeeze. "I play the 'harmless old lady' role well when I have to."

"No wonder Dorati likes you." He stopped and faced her in the lobby. "Listen, you know these people better than I do. I only know the residents from occasional Sunday services, and I know the staff even less. You take the lead here. We need to talk with the administrator about your friend."

"One harmless old lady, coming up," she said brightly, and turned toward the receptionist across the lobby.

"Can I help you?" the woman behind the glass window said.

"Good morning!" she replied in a relaxed manner. "Father Holt and I would like to talk with the administrator, if we may?" Cora Mae continued politely.

The woman barely looked up from her magazine. "I'm sorry. But you'll need to make an appointment to do that."

Cora Mae's countenance remained the same. "Then we'll be back in an hour with news cameras to talk to him abut the resident murdered here." She turned to leave.

"Wait a minute! Wait a minute!" The woman stood behind the glass and picked up a phone. "What are you talking about? No one was—Mr. Graves? Mr. Graves, there's a priest and an old woman out here claiming one of our residents was murdered."

Lucas whispered to Cora Mae. "On second thought stay away from Nikky. You're a bad influence on him."

"Mr. Graves will see you now," the flustered woman said. "His office is just around the corner to your right."

"Thank you ever so much," Cora Mae said, and led the way down the hall. As they turned the corner, she almost bumped into a tall man with glasses.

"Excuse me!" he said. "I'm terribly sorry."

"All my fault," Cora Mae said. "I was in too big a hurry for my own good."

"Hello." The Rev looked at him curiously. "Don't you remember me?"

"I'm afraid I don't. Should I know you?"

"Not necessarily. But you and I had the same accident a couple of nights ago at Casita Lobos. You were coming in to meet someone, and I was leaving and I bumped—"

"I'm afraid you're mistaken, Father—"

"Holt. Lucas Holt. And this is Cora Mae Hartwig."

"Truman Reinhardt." He shook hands with them both. "Pleased to meet you. But two nights ago I retired early with a stomach virus. I can assure you I would not have been eating Mexican food under those circumstances."

From the time they shook hands, the Rev knew the man was lying. Two flesh-colored strips on the back of the left hand covered the scratch inflicted by Holt's key at Casita Lobos. But why would he lie about a chance meeting?

"In any case, Mr. Reinhardt," Holt continued, making a mental note to ask Cora Mae about the man, "we're looking for Mr. Graves's office."

The gray-haired gentleman turned and pointed behind them.

"Thank you very much." Cora Mae knocked on the door.

"Hope to see you again, Mr. Reinhardt," the Rev said as the man strode off down the hallway.

"Strange man, don't you think?" Cora Mae whispered.

"I think he's got Mexheimer's," Holt replied.

Cora Mae squinted at him. "What?"

"Makes you forget the last time you ate Mexican food. I have it, too. That's why I keep going back for margaritas."

The door opened and a man in his early forties greeted them.

"Come in, please. I'm Jason Graves, the administrator here. Can I get you some coffee? A soft drink perhaps?"

"Nothing for me, thank you," Cora Mae said.

Lucas Holt shook his head. "No, thanks." He instinctively did not like this prematurely balding man with smoker's cough, nor did he care for the expensively furnished office in which the man hid. The room reeked of stale cigarettes. A feeble air cleaner machine purred like a sump pump in the background.

"I recognize you, Miss Hartwig, from your weekly visits here," Graves said. "And if the receptionist had said it was you, Father Holt, I would have dropped what I was doing to see you. The services you do here are so appreciated by the residents." The man cleared his throat repeatedly. "So what is this about someone being murdered?"

"We're not certain she's been murdered, Mr. Graves," Cora Mae started.

Lucas Holt spoke up. "It seems a life-long friend of Miss Hartwig's and a parishioner of mine at St. Margaret's is missing from your facility."

"And who would that be?" the administrator said, smiling.

"Marie Wilkins," Holt replied.

"Marie Wilkins," Graves said. "Yes, I do remember something about her. Let me see, here." He turned to the computer at his desk and punched in a number.

The Rev wondered how he knew the number so quickly. With nearly two hundred residents in the facility, it would be normal to have to look it up.

"Yes, here it is. I remember her because of the recent notification of a death in her family. A son, I believe it was?"

"Son and daughter-in-law," Holt replied. That could account

for his knowing her number. "Both murdered." He studied the man's face for a response. It was blank.

"Oh, yes. The Westlake couple," Graves said, staring at the computer. "Hmmm." He looked back at them. "I'm afraid all I can really tell you is that she no longer lives here." He switched off the screen. "We highly guard the privacy of all our residents."

Especially if you had something to do with their disappearance, Holt thought. The man was too nervous under that smiling, bland exterior and kept reaching for and putting down the pack of cigarettes on the desk.

"I understand that, Mr. Graves," Cora Mae said. "But this is my best friend we're talking about."

"Then you'd think she would have contacted you if she wanted you to know where she went, wouldn't you, Miss Hartwig?"

The Rev didn't like the tone of the question. He pushed back. "Unless something happened to her and she couldn't contact us. In which case you and your facility might be negligent in your duties."

"I can assure you, Reverend Holt, that the staff and management of this center are most diligent in our care."

It was like pushing a marshmallow. The man was unctuous to a fault. "Is her room still intact?" the Rev asked, wondering why this man seemed like he had something to hide. Graves had a name like a horror movie, and acted like he dismembered the woman for a price.

"It is," the administrator answered. "And I can tell you that her rent is paid for the next two months, at which time she has chosen the option to terminate her residence here." He stood to indicate the meeting was over. "My guess is Mrs. Wilkins went to look for another place to live. Or perhaps she just decided to take a long trip and didn't want anyone to know about it."

"It's possible," the Rev said, standing. "Miss Hartwig and I will check with you later. In the meantime, if you hear from her, we would be most grateful if you would let one of us know." He noted that Jason Graves was noncommittal.

Cora Mae Hartwig stood and walked to a large board on the wall. "What are these bands for?" she asked, handling one of the slim metallic objects.

"Please put that back, Miss Hartwig," Graves said, hurrying to the board and replacing the band on the rack. "Those are a brand-new system we have just installed to monitor our more forgetful residents."

"Electric handcuffs?" Holt picked one up to annoy him.

"We prefer to call them 'care-guards,'" he said, putting it back. "Most of our residents wear them for safety purposes. We can monitor their movements anywhere in the facility. If someone has a degree of dementia, for instance, and mistakenly tries to leave the building at three in the morning, the band is identified by a sensor in every doorway, an alarm is sounded in security, and we very possibly save a life."

Jason Graves escorted them to the door. He opened it just as a man in a wheelchair was about to knock.

"Oh, excuse me, Mr. Graves," the long-haired Hispanic man said. "I didn't know you had anyone in there."

"That's fine, Tomas. *Está bien. Gracias.*"

The man reached into the saddlebag attached to his chair.

"This is for you," he said, handing Graves a package with a foreign postmark. "It was delivered FedEx this morning."

Graves tossed the package on a chair in his office. "More of the monitor bands from Germany." He turned to Lucas Holt. "Mr. Perez, here, is the facility delivery service."

"Is that so?" Cora Mae said. "Then can you tell me, Mr. Perez, if you delivered a rose to Marie Wilkins a few days ago?"

Graves interrupted. "Again, Miss Hartwig, I must insist we keep the business of our residents within this facility." He turned to the man in the chair. "Be about your rounds, Tomas."

"*Hasta,* y'all," Perez said as he wheeled away.

"Good day to you both." Graves closed the door abruptly.

Lucas Holt waited to speak until they were back to their cars. "If that place was any friendlier, they could rent it out to zombies."

"Maybe they're retired CIA or something," Cora Mae retorted. "With the exception of Marie Wilkins."

A red, white, and blue cab pulled up behind their cars and the young woman driver yelled out the window.

"Would you all know if this is the Westbank Retirement Center?"

"We would and it is," Cora Mae said.

"Thanks," the driver replied and parked her cab by the front ramp just as Tomas Perez wheeled out of the facility.

Lucas Holt ran over to him as Perez transferred himself from the chair to the backseat of the cab.

"Excuse me, Mr. Perez, but can you answer the lady's question now that Mr. Graves isn't around?"

The woman collapsed the chair and put it in the trunk.

"You don't understand, mister. Graves is *always* around. Don't turn and look, but he's watching us from his office window right now through the shades."

"But—"

"All I can tell you is old lady Wilkins got a rose a week from another resident here. I also happen to know she came into a whole load of money recently and a lot of people would like to get their greasy hands on it, if you get my drift. I don't know where she went. Now leave me alone. If Graves thinks I'm ratting I could be the next one to, uh, end up leaving."

What the hell did that mean? Holt wondered as he closed the cab door. And where had Marie Wilkins gone with the sudden wealth? "Thanks," he said, and returned to Cora Mae.

"Call me later, Lucas dear. That wonderful Mr. Graves is peering through the slats, pretending not to watch us."

The Rev watched her slip into the red Celica. He closed the door and leaned into the cockpit-like driver's seat. Another stereotype shot to hell. Maybe that was the problem with these deaths. Maybe he was looking at them too stereotypically. Maybe, like Cora Mae's car, he should blow off the usual views and motives and look for something different? But what?

"Wanna race?" Cora Mae said, buckling her belt.

"You'd win."

"Why do you think I asked?"

One place to start looking for an unusual motive would be in Marie Wilkins's possessions. "You going to see Nikky in the morning?" Holt asked.

"Omelletry West Café at six. Walk the lake at seven."

"Good. Tell him I want you to get into Marie's room."

"Not a problem, since I have a key and need to visit a few other parishioners anyway."

"Fine, but I don't want to take any chances. We need you wired."

"Lucas, dear, I'm always wired after a few cups of Omelletry coffee and their gingerbread pancakes."

As she started the engine, the Rev stood up and winked at her. "That's not the kind of wired I mean."

The sign over the Gruene Dance Hall proclaimed it "The Oldest Dance Hall in Texas." One glance confirmed the claim. The walls of old barn siding were split and bent, rusty metal signs advertised brands of gas, oil, and soft drinks that were extinct decades ago. Plywood panels on the sides were raised and hooked to the upper walls so a cross breeze blew through the large screens that served as windows.

Inside, the ceiling fans helped cool the sweaty "kickers" who would come to hear local bands, drink Lone Star and Shiner, down "shooters," and do the Cotton-Eyed Joe with their partners. The chipped green doors of the Gruene Dance Hall opened every day at noon to locals and tourists who stopped to have a beer or iced tea and listen to the band practice for that evening.

Two men sat at a table in the corner. The short, greasy-haired one chewed a cigar and poured Shiner Bock into a small glass. The fair-haired, lanky one held the huge plastic glass of iced tea and dropped a second lemon into it.

"I wish the rest of the Squad could've made it," Eddie Shelton said. "The band is really good."

"They'll come tonight," Nikky Dorati replied. "But I thought it'd be good to be here while Lisa and Alan rehearse. Make them feel more at ease with family around."

"I didn't know you even liked kicker music."

Dorati looked at him. "I don't."

"Not even that last one? 'Red Queen's Wild' is the title from their new album. It's gonna be a hit on the C and W charts. Maybe even a crossover."

"Good for them. I hope they make a zillion bucks. Just so I don't have to listen to it, is all."

"What kind of music *do* you like, Dorati?"

"Oldies."

"Oldies?"

"Yeah, Eddie. Oldies." Dorati flashed a smile at the band and frowned at his friend. "You got a problem with that?"

"No." Eddie Shelton quietly stirred his tea and added another pack of sugar.

"What?"

"Nothin'. Really. I was just wonderin' *how old*?"

Before Dorati could answer, their attention was drawn to a couple slowly wandering through the front door.

The round old man and wrinkled old woman stopped and waited for their eyes to adjust. Because it was more difficult to move from the bright outside light to the dark interior, Dorati assumed they had had cataract operations. Decreasing eyesight was one more infirmity in a seemingly unending list of body parts and systems that performed less and less reliably as you got older. He squinted and wondered when he'd need one.

The lone woman on the stage, Lisa Enright, had her back to the door, talking to the band. Dorati saw her husband, Alan, tap her on the shoulder and point. Nikky and Eddie exchanged glances as they listened to the conversation.

"Mama!" Lisa yelled, and ran over to hug the old woman. "And Papa! You came, too! I'm so glad to see you."

"It's just hard for us to get out at night anymore, what with driving and everything," the mother said, "and these kicker joints ain't too good on your father's emphysema, you know."

"Can't breathe worth a damn, honey. All those years of cigarettes. Shit, if I knew then—"

"J. D. Enright, hug your daughter." His wife nudged him.

"Oh, sure, honey. Come here."

The daughter was engulfed in the huge arms of her father. Dorati thought he looked just as Lisa had always described him, as if he were made of balloons. His tight balloon head had tufts of closely cropped hair encircling his bald top, and was covered with a sweaty gimme cap with BURLESON'S FEEDS on the front. His balloon chest was barely held in by the bulging buttons on his red and green flannel shirt. Balloon legs had gray Sears work pants tightly cinched around them, their seams crying for relief. Lisa told Nikky she was always afraid that if she hugged her father too tight he would pop.

Her mother also matched her daughter's description. The woman was as saggy as the man was tight. Large flaps of skin swayed from her upper arms and wrinkles layered her friendly, hound dog face. Her gray-brown hair was meticulously permed, and her blue-and-white dress seemed a size too big for her.

Their daughter escorted them to a table and ordered iced tea as her husband continued to work with the band. Nikky Dorati couldn't believe Lisa's parents had actually come to hear them play. They had been so dramatically opposed to her relationship with Alan from the beginning. Their blue collar pride wanted her to marry higher, not lower, and someone with security, not a songwriter who hung out all night in honky-tonks and reeked of smoke and liquor.

Unfortunately, as Dorati remembered the story, they had been right. She followed him straight down into the maelstrom of drugs and alcohol. Bars and clubs were where deals were done, and there was always a little extra for the band. But that was before the bust.

"Did you know Alan Greer in the joint?" Dorati said out of nowhere to Eddie Shelton.

"Funny you should say that. I was just thinkin' that Alan and her parents weren't on speakin' terms. Didn't the old man try to shoot him?"

"Correct on all counts." Nikky remembered that Alan hadn't joined the Squad till he got short on his sentence, nine months to go, and got a 'get your shit together or forget me' letter from Lisa. Faced with losing his girl and his recording contract, he went to Lucas Holt for help. The Rev called in big-time chits to get him into the toughest Twelve-Step Program in the joint, but it took. Six months after release, they were both clean, employed and, much to the disappointment of her furious parents, married by Lucas Holt.

"Her father showed up at their trailer house with a shotgun," Dorati said, mostly to himself. "If he hadn't been drunk, Alan and Lisa would've been splattered all over the walls." He lifted his glass to them and smiled as they returned the sign.

"So what is this? Change of heart?" Eddie asked.

"Change of wallet." People weren't crazy, and Dorati knew it. Anybody who did time knew it. People did things for reasons. With the Five Card Stud Band growing in popularity with a wider following, they'd be into big money soon.

"They came back for the money?"

"Wouldn't you?"

"They can just flip their feelings over like that?"

"No, but they can act like it." Nikky Dorati leaned closer. "Money makes you feel a whole lot better about your drug-dealin', booze-drinkin' kids who you are sure are still using."

"But they hated those two."

"Of course they did." Nikky recalled conversations with Lisa, who saw him as an adviser and father figure. She had cried when her parents accused them of stealing every dime the old folks ever had, using up all the parents' money for jail and lawyer costs only to end up doing time, and then, to kick them in the mouth for their help—getting married. It was true that the old man and old lady ended up having to let the house get repossessed and move into a rickety South Austin so-called "retirement center," where their pets were rats and roaches. He pointed to the table. "But hey, they're bosom buddies now. All her father had to do was be nice to Lisa, and she's back fawning over him like her daddy's dead and rose again."

Eddie shook his head. "And you think all they want's the money?"

"No. I think they came down here to express extreme remorse for their hateful behavior and reconcile with their beloved daughter and son-in-law and live happily ever after." Dorati emptied the glass of beer. "What do *you* think?"

"I see your point."

"Listen to 'em." Dorati poured another small glass as they turned their attention to the conversation two tables away.

"Can you stay and hear us play, Mama?"

"I'll last as long as this iced tea does, but you'll have to tell me where the ladies' room is. And Papa will go to sleep if the music ain't his style, no matter how loud it is."

Lisa Enright returned to the stage and spoke to her husband. Alan walked over and shook hands. Nikky Dorati instinctively followed him. He had done this scene before and wanted to be able to intercede if necessary. *When* necessary.

"Glad you both could be here," Alan said. "How'd you know we were playing Gruene?"

"Saw a poster in the nursing home." Mrs. Enright fiddled with the straw in her tea.

"It's a retirement center, isn't it?" Al Greer said.

"Call it what you might," her husband intoned, staring at the table. "It ain't the ranch we'd still have if it weren't for court and lawyer fees."

Nikky watched Alan's face flush and knew anger pushed the blood there. He also saw the clenched fists at Alan's side.

"Hi!" Dorati said, putting his hand out to J. D. Enright. "I'm Nikky Dorati. I recognize you from Lisa's description." Old, fat, and mean, he thought. "That's another friend of ours over there waving his beer glass and smiling, Eddie Shelton."

"Pleased to meet you both," Marlane said. "Any friend of Lisa and Al's is a friend of ours."

Not if we don't have money, Dorati thought. If these two weren't playin' straight with these kids, he'd deal with the old farts himself.

Alan Greer started to open his mouth to respond, then took a step backward. "I hope you'll stick around this afternoon. We have an announcement we'd like to let you in on a little later." He turned and walked back to the stage with Nikky Dorati.

"Sorry about the intrusion," Dorati said.

"Glad you did," Alan responded, gratefully patting him on the back. "I find it hard to be polite to the bastard who tried to kill me."

Lisa Enright joined them. "How'd it go?"

"Bad as usual. They're still convinced I'm doing drugs and you're drinkin' your brains out because of me. We'll never convince them otherwise."

Lisa Enright joined them. "Maybe we ought to tell them now? Maybe they'd be happy for our success."

"I'm not sure they'd call it 'success,' Lisa." Alan saw her father look at the watch that would barely strap over the taut balloon wrist. "Let's better play something before they leave."

"Great stuff, you two." Dorati patted Alan on the back. "Know any oldies?" He smirked. "Just kidding. The whole Squad will be here tonight to listen. We're behind you all the way."

"I'm glad somebody is," Alan responded. "Let's do it."

For the next hour the band regaled the growing audience with songs Alan and Lisa had written. By the time they had finished, Nikky Dorati was emptying his third beer into the tiny glass.

Lisa Enright announced a ten-minute break, and Dorati stood to head for the men's room. He stopped at the table to speak to the parents as the couple came over.

"They're really good, aren't they?" Dorati started. "Got a hell of a career in front of them."

Marlane Enright was about to answer him when her husband stood and embraced Lisa. "That was wonderful, honey," her father said. He wrapped his hammy fingers around her slight hand. "I'm right proud of you. We both are, ain't we, Marlane?"

"Yes." Marlane took Alan's hand in hers. "J.D. and I been talkin' and we decided we been too hard on you two. We'd like to make it up somehow and let you know how proud we are you pulled yourselves up by your own bootstraps and kicked your habits."

"Marlane's tryin' to say we'd like to be a family again and have you come visit us at the nursing home. Maybe we could come out the house sometime and have dinner."

Alan Greer was stunned for words. "I don't know what to say."

Don't say nothin', Dorati thought in the background. And keep one hand on your wallet.

"Don't say nothin'," J.D. said. "Just be grateful the good Lord makes us forgive others."

Dorati hoped the good Lord forgave J.D. for the shit coming out of his mouth.

Lisa cried openly and held her mother's other hand. "Can you stay through the next set, Mama?"

"I think so, honey," Marlane Enright intoned. "We'll leave out of here when we think we have to because of the light. J.D. planned to take me to dinner on Sixth Street tonight, as it's close to the home there on South First."

Lisa hugged them both. Alan shook his father-in-law's hand and kissed Lisa's mother on the cheek.

Dorati hurried to the john before he burst at both ends.

"I almost threw up in there," he said to Eddie Shelton when he returned to the table. "Did you hear that shit?"

"I kept waiting for Mr. Greenjeans to pop up from the bar."

Dorati wondered if Lisa and Al really fell for the line. He felt protective of them but didn't want to kill their hopes, either. What if it wasn't a line? What if he was just jaded and cynical from too much prison time?

"I wouldn't trust that old man as far as I could throw him," Nikky announced. "And the old lady is as phony as that ten-buck knock-off Rolex she's wearin'."

"You going to say anything to Lisa and Al?"

"Nope. But I'm gonna watch what happens real, real close. I ain't never had kids and I ain't likely to now," Dorati said as Alan

Greer introduced their new song, "Three of a Kind." "So I want these two to do good."

Lisa Enright stood up to the microphone, and before giving the band the signal to start, she spoke.

"Al and I would like to dedicate this next song to my parents, J. D. and Marlane Enright of Austin."

The crowd applauded as the band began the intro, but when Lisa Enright looked over the dance hall, she saw that their table was empty. As she turned to find Nikky and Eddie, Dorati could see the faint shimmer of tears in her eyes. He was unsure if they were tears of joy, sadness, or confusion, but he was certain J.D. and Marlane would cry all the way to the bank.

It was 4 P.M. when Lucas Holt had finished his run. He pulled in the church parking lot behind St. Margaret's and parked the black MX6 in the space marked RECTOR. After a year, unlike his counterpart at First Baptist, the Vestry still refused to put his name on the space. It was the source of constant kidding.

Travis Layton had told him at the last Vestry meeting, "Your predecessor was here twelve years, Lucas, and we were just fixing to put his name there when he up and died of a heart attack."

"That's probably why," Holt had replied, though in truth he liked the old black-and-white porcelain Rector sign that had been attached to the brick for decades. It reminded him of the cathedrals of Europe where generations of clergy lived and ministered, nameless in the flood of people and history washing over the ancient stones. The Church, like this old sign, was the one constant in the ever-changing sea of faces and ideas, the one thing that endured politics, plagues, and wars to witness to the ongoing constancy of God's presence.

Maybe that was what was behind the spiritual search of so many his age, he thought as he got out of the car. Maybe when you hit your forties, you started to have the perspective your parents had when you thought they knew nothing about anything, the perspective that has seen enough to know that trends come and go—and to realize that you will, too. Once that learning sets in, one begins to wonder what, if anything, is reliable, constant, able to be counted on for more than the next sound bite. And to wonder where you fit into it.

Holt opened the back door to the church and entered with a

sense of purpose. That was the challenge, for himself and his congregation, to show how the Bible not only *had* meaning, but *was* the meaning they all sought. It was just like the penitentiary—with one major difference—he thought as he walked down the main hall. The penitentiary had fewer deaths.

"Yo, Rev." Maxine Blackwell made a face when he entered his office. "I could smell you coming. How many you run today?"

"Ten. I was going to do six, but that clergy luncheon stressed me out so much I had to do four extra. The food was enough to snap your arteries shut and the pious conversation put me in a coma. Hell, we've all got problems in common to solve if we'd just cooperate instead of trying to one-up each other and be so damned religious all the time. Sometimes I hate church."

"Me, too, boss."

"Then to top it all off my damned headset went out at mile seven. I had to do the last three with no tunes." He handed the sweaty headset to Maxine. "Would you see if you can get this repaired for me?"

"Sure thing, Rev." She wrinkled her nose and, with two fingers, gently placed the headset on the floor. "I know a little place on North Loop that'll get it back in a couple days."

"Great. Thanks. Hard to do long mileage with no tunes."

"Right. I used to have the same problem." Maxine looked up at him and smiled. "So right now, honey, you got a stack of messages from people wantin' a piece of that skinny butt of yours." She picked up his cup from her desk. "Teatime, is it?"

"How'd you guess? And would you get me Susan Granger on the phone? I heard something at the meeting that she and I need to talk about. Which reminds me, did Nikky call?"

"He said he'd catch up with you later, that he had to check a couple things out first."

"It always worries me when he does that."

"It should, Rev," Max said, disappearing into the pantry to pour from the pot of Earl Grey. "One cop coming up."

Holt entered his office and tossed his running bag on the chair. He flipped through the pink slips and yelled to Maxine.

"What did Travis Layton want?"

"Same thing they all want. Talk to you. Call him back. He said it had to do with money, so put it on top of the pile."

"Yes, madam, I'll get right on it."

"Don't make fun of my former profession," Maxine said. "Heat on line two."

Lucas picked up on Susan Granger in midsentence. "Hello?"

"And I still cannot believe you keep that woman employed as your church secretary. Do you know what she called me?"

" 'The heat'?"

"That's right."

"That's because 'Fuzz' went out with *Hawaii Five-O*. She's the only woman who understands me and loves me all the same. I may have to marry her."

From the outer office, Max said, "Why didn't you ask me twenty years ago when you had the chance?"

"Because you eavesdropped even worse back then." Holt made a face at her and closed the door.

"Did you call to tell me about marrying Maxine or is there other good news you'd like to share?"

The Rev plopped down in his desk chair and propped his running shoes up on the windowsill overlooking Sixth Street. "I called for two things. First, any update on Erik and Janey Bertrand?"

"Not that it's any of your business, but we haven't got a damned thing. We checked their liquor stores and supermarket. Lab report on the cork says it did have a minute hole in it, so we know how the poison got in the wine."

"While it was in the house?"

"Not necessarily. It could have been done at the store. We're still checking outlets. So far, nothing."

"Like Brickhouse said."

"He's already been released, by the way. We R.O.R.'d him and threatened him with parole violations if he farted upwind."

"You have such a way with words." Nikky was right, Holt thought. Kristen Wade would never use that expression. Maybe Susan was more down to earth and honest. "I'm glad he's out."

"We'll bust him again. We always do with that type."

"Remind me to argue with you about that later." Holt sipped his tea. "Anything else on the Bertrands?"

"Not really."

Holt knew she was holding something back. "Listen, Susan, these are my parishioners here."

"Okay, okay. Here's the scoop. We found out that they had some kind of instant-pay rider on their insurance policy."

Holt wrinkled his forehead. With an aging parish he was familiar with the practice. "That's where the beneficiary might need the money before the thirty-day waiting period. It's used with older parents who need nursing home payments."

"Sometimes you amaze me, Father Holt."

"I do more funerals than you. So, since you'll remember St. Margaret's is one of the beneficiaries, who are the others?"

"Just one." Granger shuffled through notes on her desk. "Here it is. The only living relative is Erik's mother—a Marie Wilkins. She lives at the Westbank Retirement Center."

Lucas Holt gulped audibly. "Not any more she doesn't."

"What? Where'd she go? Don't tell me she's dead, too?"

"Hold on a minute. I talked with the administrator there today, and he's tighter-lipped than a mule with lockjaw. He claims not to have a forwarding address, unless of course he's got her locked in the basement. I don't like him and I don't trust him. Oh, and according to another resident, Marie Wilkins came into a lot of money recently and split."

"The insurance money?"

"Could be. Or could be from somewhere else. An annuity maybe? In either case, I don't like it."

"Don't like what?"

"I don't know. At this clergy luncheon today I talked to that new minister at University Methodist, Sharon Simmons?"

"And?"

"And she told me about a young couple from her old parish in Cincinnati. They were murdered and left some money to the church, but the bulk went to their elderly parents, who spent the rest of their healthy years traveling."

"So what? That's going to happen all over the country now, don't you think? With a higher population of much older people we're going to see more of them with aging adult children dying from one thing or another. Add in the younger population putting off begetting for careers and you easily have cases where elders are beneficiaries. That's not unusual. It's a social trend."

Lucas Holt gazed out the window at the darkening shadows on Sixth Street. "You're probably right. I'm getting paranoid in my old age." He turned around and drank the tea. "But like I told Dorati, I've got a lot of dead parishioners here lately."

"You *do*, don't you?" Granger said pensively, and Holt didn't like the implication in her voice. He jumped back at her.

"Yes, Susan. We needed more money after the 'Saints of God' caper, so I've been busy out making house calls to bump off wealthy parishioners. Do we still get paid if it's a suicide? In that case I screwed up and lost the Villalobos money. There goes my annual increment." On second thought Dorati was wrong about her. She was too critical, too demanding. Kristen Wade accepted him unconditionally, although lately it was infrequently.

"All right, smartass. I just got concerned about all this loss for you. I know how you feel about your people there and—"

The Rev noted the pause with curiosity. Was she having trouble saying something? That would be unusual for her.

"And if you need to talk about it, I'm sort of available."

Holt smiled. He liked the "sort of." He sighed deeply. He suddenly felt tired of lots of things. "Okay, if you're serious, I'd like to walk the lake tomorrow."

"Time?"

"I have to do a short run around one o'clock, so I'd like to meet you at three at the Gazebo and walk." He looked outside at the darkening clouds. "If it's raining meet me at the Waterloo Fitness Center. I have two more passes there and I'll leave one for you."

"See you at three. I'll be the unfashionable one dressed like your grandmother."

"I hope you'll look better than that. She's dead." Holt hung up the phone and stared out the window. Couples walked hand in hand down Sixth, looking in shop windows, making small talk and smiling at each other, secretly squeezing a hand or arm. Clearly there was something going on with him about his last birthday that was fundamentally changing his perspective on life. *Weltanschauung* was the word from seminary. World view. How you saw the universe and your place in it. Suddenly that place shifted; the ground rules changed.

He looked at the Cross over the door. Maybe he'd have to search inside to find new rules. And maybe that search would be helpful to his congregation as well.

But why did he resist it so much? What made it so scary? What was so frightening about the prospect of ending up like those couples he viewed from his window? He could do a lot worse. He could end up murdered like the Bertrands or sink to the despair and suicidal ideation of the Villalobos women. His rumination was interrupted by Max on the speaker.

"Yo, Rev. You prayin' in there? It's awful quiet."

"I was thinking about getting old and dying alone."

"Well, you can't do it this afternoon. You just got a call from Chaplain Barthel's secretary at San Jacinto Hospital. She's down with cedar fever and wants you to fill in for her at the hospital Auxiliary banquet this afternoon."

"What time?"

"They eat early. You have to be at the Headliner's Club in an hour. They'll feed you a great dinner in return for saying the blessing."

"So instead of a nice intimate dinner with Kristen, I get to eat with two hundred blue-haired ladies."

"Hey, Rev, at least you know they'll be there."

Lucas Holt shook his head. What he really wanted to do was go home, shower, and sleep. Maybe then he could work out the connections in these deaths. He was about to turn down the request when he realized that, given the age of attendees, it was possible they would know something about Marie Wilkins or the Villalobos family. Any data was better than no data at all.

"Tell her I'll do it only if I'm seated by the president of the Auxiliary. She knows more dirty jokes than you do."

The woman with perfectly coiffed hair put her bejeweled hand on Lucas Holt's arm as he leaned close to listen.

"So there's this old man and old woman sitting on the porch of the nursing home, and she says to him: 'If you take off all your clothes, I can tell you exactly how old you are.'

" 'You can not,' the old man says.

" 'Take them off and I'll prove it,' she says. So the old man takes off all his clothes, and he's standing there on the porch buck naked, and the old woman's looking him over and she says: 'You're eighty-seven years old.'

" 'That's amazing!' says the old man. 'How'd you know that?'

"The old lady says: 'You told me yesterday.' "

The Rev laughed. "Where do you get these?"

"At the retirement complex, where else? What do we have to do all day but sit around and tell each other jokes? I hate the place, even if it is the most luxurious one in town. Bunch of old fogies out there wandering around in their good clothes with diapers underneath. Half of them need to be taken out and shot except that their money keeps the place afloat."

"We haven't figured out yet, as a culture, how to deal with aging, have we?"

"Sure we have. Dump us in warehouses with poorly paid uneducated people to clean up after us." Agnes Gottig waved to the waiter holding the wine. "I'll have the white, please, and don't skimp." She looked at Lucas. "You know, it's a myth that our bodies are rotting and out of shape. I was kidding earlier. Most of the old people where I live are in pretty good shape for being so old. We have a lot to contribute—that's why I'm involved in the Auxiliary, you know." She scanned the room. "That's why we're all here."

Lucas Holt sat at the head table on the twenty-fourth floor of the old American Bank Building at Sixth and Lavaca. No matter how many times the name changed, it would always be the American Bank Building to him. He understood how really old people refused to update their points of reference in Austin.

The Headliner's Club was well known for celebrities. Members included former Congressman "Jake" Pickle, former President Lyndon Johnson and Lady Bird, former mayors, and former famous journalists. As the Rev looked around, he thought the walls contained more pictures and autographs from former people than live persons eating dinner in the place.

"You have to be a former Somebody to count anymore," Holt said as he passed the salad dressing to the blue-haired lady in the dark green dress next to him. "Don't you think, Miz Gottig?" Lucas knew it was polite Southern manners always to call women who were your elders "Miss" so that it came out sounding like "Miz." Only if you were on quite personal terms with them could you use their first name.

"It helps," Agnes Gottig replied, "but it doesn't always get you in. There are lots of people in this very room who are former Somebodies and very few of them belong to this club." She nudged him with her elbow. "I was a Somebody once, you know. I wrote for *Forbes* back in the forties. I have a great story I could tell you about uncovering a lead that makes Watergate look like a nursery rhyme." Her faded blue eyes sparkled as she winked at him. "Just to whet your appetite, I'll tell you the punch line—it was the Manhattan Project."

"I can't wait to hear it."

"That's more than I can say for my son, Father Holt. It's amazing to me how that boy is thirty-six years old and still mooching off of me. The little shit, you should excuse the expression, but that's what he is and we both know it, never listens to my advice, just hangs out with those 'revolving door hussies,' I call them. Not one has the brains God gave geese, and they only like him when he has money—*my* money, mind you—and then they dump him and he's back in my rent property again free of charge. I swear I don't know where I went wrong with him."

"Maybe nowhere."

"No, I must have done something terrible for him to end up such a—please excuse my expression at dinner, Father Holt—a slimeball, as all my friends say he is. He'll be the death of me or put me in the poorhouse, one." She leaned closer. "I can tell you I've just about had it with the little leech."

Lucas Holt listened politely as he looked out over the sea of blue-gray hair and balding male pates, porcelain plates among Brillo pads. What would his generation be like thirty years from now when they reached this age?

The thought of a room full of seventy-six-year-old baby boomers made him grin. Instead of chicken and broccoli, would they serve tofu and wheat bread? Instead of "Pennsylvania Four Five Thousand," would they play the tape from *The Big Chill*?

"Like you said, everyone seems to be enjoying themselves, even pitching a little whoopee there at the back table."

"It's 'pitching woo' and 'making whoopee,' Father Holt. And why shouldn't we? We're old, not dead. If we close our eyes, we see ourselves twenty years younger than we are. That's another reason we volunteer, to be around each other instead of our insipid, selfish, greedy though occasionally successful children who have written us off and are waiting around to collect the inheritance which we should be out spending."

This lady was beyond anger, Holt thought. She was on her way to revenge. "So tell me about your wonderful son," the Rev felt it his ministerial duty to ask. "Sounds like he did you wrong?"

"Thought you'd never ask. What are clergy good for, anyway?" Agnes Gottig nodded to pour another glass of Texas Chardonnay. "The little shit—he's thirty-six, did I mention that? Took forever to get his college degree. Kept changing majors as often as he did schools and bimbos. His father, God rest his Texaco-oil-baron soul, left a huge sum of money in trust for the boy's education. Little detail he left out by not designating it for a specific degree, so William Gottig, Jr., shot the whole wad in twelve years at eight colleges across the country. Then he came home to live here and leech everything out of me. What am I supposed to do? Toss his lazy hiney out in the street? I'm telling you, Father Holt, I'm about ready to do it."

"Has he ever sought counseling?"

Agnes Gottig rolled her eyes. "Says he doesn't need it. Claims a six-pack a day isn't unusual for his generation." She leaned closer and whispered. "I know this is a terrible thing to say, but it would serve him right if he died first. I just hate to see everything my husband and I worked for go to support his selfish, irresponsible lifestyle."

The Rev was distracted by a couple at a back table. An older man was holding the hand of a black-haired woman, clearly smitten with her and she with him. They were the only two at the table and seemed to happily ignore their surroundings to focus only on each other. From a distance, the man looked familiar.

Was that how he wanted to end up? With someone there in his retirement and old age? It seemed like he had never thought about what he would do later, after retirement. Maybe that's what this birthday thing was partly about, thinking for the first time not about how you were going to spend the next few years, but what you were going to do until you died. Because for the first time, especially looking over this crowd, death seemed a closer possibility than ever before. He wondered if Erik and Janey Bertrand had planned for their old age. Did the Villalobos sisters not want to end up like their parents?

"Who is that back there?" Holt asked. "Back table on the right. The older gentleman and the black-haired woman. He looks like a man I met this morning at the Westlake Retirement Center."

Agnes Gottig put on her glasses. "That's where he's from, all

he found Corinne Spellman seated in the dining room with
lunch tray in front of her, talking to no one in particular.
"Hello, Corinne."

"Why, hello, Martha! How are you?"

"I'm not your sister Martha, dear," Cora Mae said, sitting be-
he her and taking her hand. "I'm your old friend—and I mean
ld' friend—Cora Mae Hartwig from St. Margaret's Church,
here you and your family have attended for fifty years. I come
o see you every week, and today I'm going to help you with your
unch and then maybe we'll take a little walk outside."

"I'd like that very much. It is so hard for me to get out of the
house anymore."

"You're in the Westlake Retirement Center, Corinne."

"Yes, of course. I knew that. I don't know where my mind
goes, Cora. One minute I'm fine and I know what day it is and
where I am and who you are, and the next I'm in 1954 and you're
my long-lost—and dead—sister Martha. Sorry for the inconvenience." She stared ahead for a moment, then shook off whatever
thought had intruded itself into her mind.

"It's no problem for me, and I'm sure it's no problem for
Martha, Corinne." She smiled.

"He's such a nice man."

"Who is?" Cora Mae asked, not minding the change in topic.

"That tall man over there helping those people eat who have
ost their minds." She pointed across the activity room to a well-
ressed gentleman serving trays and joking with the residents. "If
ly they could find where they misplaced them."

Cora Mae looked up to see Truman Reinhardt nod his head in
eeting. She smiled back and continued speaking to Corinne.

"Do you know him?" Cora Mae said, lowering her head toward
chest to whisper something under her breath. She wanted Do-
to know it was Truman Reinhardt.

don't know." She paused, forcing thoughts up from the
y convolutions of her brain. "Wait. Yes, I do. He's a doctor
me kind. I see him around a lot, doing all kinds of things, ac-
." Corinne Spellman frowned and pursed her lips. "I remem-
mething about him that I don't like much, I think."

rhaps we should go for a little walk, Corinne, and talk about
e lowered her head again.

right. He's Truman Reinhardt, a former doctor, I think, and he's
been a real boon to this Auxiliary. One of the few men, you
know, though their numbers are increasing." She took off her
glasses and winked at Holt. "And eligible, too."

"Doesn't look like he's *too* eligible."

"I don't exactly know who that lady is. Could be someone he
brought tonight. We encourage that to get new members." Agnes
Gottig shook her head and picked up her wineglass. "It'll never
last, though. The woman isn't his type. She wears too much
makeup. And she holds that cigarette like she's dying to smoke it.
No pun intended of course. Nope. She'll be a flash in the pan and
gone. Believe me, I know women, Father Holt. I've seen that same
type snuggle up to my son's money until he got tired of them, or
they figured he didn't have as much as he lied and said he did. I
don't think Dr. Reinhardt will fall for that phoniness. And if he
does, just like my stupid son, he'll deserve exactly what he gets."

In two hours the banquet was over, speeches had been delivered congratulating outgoing and incoming officers, awards conferred, and flowers bestowed. Holt had watched the entire
proceedings with surprising interest. It was fascinating to see
these people continuing to be who they had always been in their
earlier years—active, funny, critical, sexy, flirtatious—and enjoying themselves immensely now that they were spending time out
of choice rather than the obligation of work or family.

As the Rev walked by the reception desk toward the elevators,
the man from the back table approached him.

"Wonderful invocation, Father Holt," Truman Reinhardt said,
shaking his hand.

"Funny to see you so soon, Dr. Reinhardt. Austin really is a
small town, you know."

"That's truer than I imagined. I was surprised to see how many
of the people from the Center belong to the Auxiliary."

"And the lady who was with you? I don't see her now." The
Rev noted a faint blush appear on the doctor's cheeks. Was it
anger or embarrassment?

"Yes, she—I mean—that she's a friend from the Center. Her
name is Helen Pelham and she's only recently moved there. I
thought she could meet people and get connected here tonight."

"I'm sure it was helpful." Holt stepped closer to ask him a

question as the elevator bell rang. "Oh, and I was wondering if you knew a resident out there by the name of Marie Wilkins?"

Reinhardt ignored the query. "There's your car, Father Holt. You go on. I must wait for Mrs. Pelham." He moved out of the way so Holt could pass him. "Hope to see you again when you come out for services."

"Yes," the Rev replied, stepping into the crowded elevator. "See you then. And bring Mrs. Pelham." He wondered if she knew Marie Wilkins.

Holt smiled at the initial drop from the twenty-fourth floor. As he emerged into the lobby, he saw an APD blue-and-white parked at the entrance to the bank building, and a familiar face come through the door. He was not certain he was glad to see her. Her sudden appearance always meant bad news.

"Hey, Lucas," Lieutenant Granger said. "Glad you're here. Can you stick around a few minutes?" She scanned people coming off other elevators.

"What's going on?"

"Do you know which one is Agnes Gottig?"

"Sure." He pointed to the woman carrying a bouquet of pink roses. "That's her with the flowers right over there."

"Then help me get her, and find us a place to talk."

"What happened?" Holt said as they walked toward the Auxiliary president. The Rev took the flowers from Agnes Gottig as Susan Granger asked to speak with her for a moment.

"I'm terribly sorry to have to tell you this, Miss Gottig," Granger said when they were out of range of the crowd, "but your son was murdered tonight."

Agnes Gottig looked at Lucas Holt with horror on her face. He knew it was the recognition that her wish had come true. "No," she said softly. Then a louder "No!" Finally she raised her clenched fists and cried out: "No! I didn't mean it! I didn't mean it!"

Holt and Granger caught her limp body as she fainted to the ground. Lucas gently placed his jacket over the old woman, as Susan checked vitals and radioed for EMS.

The body count rises, he thought. Another child of another elderly parent. What the hell was going on here? He heard movement behind him and looked up to see a blur of black hair and red lipstick turn, then quickly leave on the arm of Truman Reinhardt.

• Six •

"Remember what the Rev said," Nikky Dorati reminded Mae Hartwig as he stopped the car in front of the Westbank tirement Center. "We're just fishing here. Do your regular v then try to get into the room."

"I hope I don't tangle the reel," Cora Mae said, adjusting her clothes.

"Can't happen. That mike you got on is foolproof."

"I recall that's what they said about the *Titanic,* dear."

"Pick you up in an hour," Dorati said as she exited the bla BMW coupe. "And be careful."

"How do you think I've lived so long?" the old woman in purple jogging suit and pink running shoes replied. She wa into the lobby and spoke to the volunteer at the desk.

"I'm here to see Corinne Spellman, please?" she asked.

"Just a minute, please." The older woman punched th into the computer. "Here it is. She's been moved to the Care unit. I'm sure she'll be glad for a visitor. Her family but forgotten her." She shook her head. "I hope I neve far along with 'old-timer's' disease. I hope someb know—does me in first."

"I hope you get your wish, dear," Cora Mae Hartwi as she looked for the signs directing her to Speci knew "Special Care" was the Center's euphemism with patients who were no longer mentally or phy of caring for themselves, patients with Alzhein (Lou Gehrig's Disease), or who had had "a little s gently degenerating into complete dementia.

"Let's walk to my room." Corinne Spellman stared at her. "Can you bring the food with you? I'd like to eat it in there."

"Certainly." She motioned to the attendant, who shrugged her shoulders as if it didn't matter to her. And it didn't.

Corinne Spellman's dyed red hair shook as she walked down the corridor to her room with Cora Mae Hartwig. "I could tell you some interesting things about that man," she said, "if I could remember what they are." She stopped in front of the door to her room and concentrated on how to open it. "I hate this. They make opening the door so simple a two-year-old could do it and then don't supply the two-year-old. Why don't they just put a knob on the thing? What's this bar across the door for?"

"I believe you push it and the door opens."

Corinne pushed. "I resent this. I'm senile, not crippled."

Hartwig helped her to her chair and put the tray in front of her. As Corinne sat down, a slim band was barely noticeable at her ankle. Cora Mae pointed to it.

"Do you know what this is? This little band here?"

"Sure I do, Martha. It keeps the animals in the zoo."

Cora Mae smiled and kissed her on the cheek. She liked Corinne's spunk. "You just keep growling, Corinne," she said. "Lets them know you're alive."

"About that doctor?" Corinne Spellman stopped. "But then, who would believe me?"

"Oh, I would. You just rattie on, and I'll make us some nice tea to go with your lunch there on the table." She lowered her head to her chest and hoped Dorati was getting it. Here was a chance to get inside info on Reinhardt, and maybe on Marie, if Corinne's brain cells would only cooperate.

"That would be lovely. But would you answer me one question while you're fixing the tea?"

"Certainly, Corinne," Cora Mae said, going around the corner into the tiny kitchenette area.

"Why the hell are you talking to your bosoms?"

Unseen, Cora Mae squinted up her face and thought fast. "Oh, well, um, I'm just stretching my neck, dear. My doctor said to do that several times every hour to keep from getting stiff." To her bosoms and Nikky Dorati she whispered "Oopsy."

"Thank God. I thought I was hallucinating again. I thought any minute they would answer you back. I like the kind in the green canister."

Cora Mae rolled her eyes at her own inexperience and put two cups of water in the microwave. She opened the green canister and popped the tea bags in the cups. "You were starting to tell me about that nice doctor."

"To begin with he knows everybody's business here. He volunteers for everything and gets to know everyone but hardly tells you anything about himself." Corinne smiled at Cora Mae as the tea was brought to her chair. "But I know some things about him he wished I didn't know."

"Very interesting already, dear," Cora Mae said, sitting opposite her on the overstuffed sofa. "Like what?"

"Like he's got a sweetheart outside this place, that's what. I saw him last week when my sister took me out for the day."

"Your sister's been dead for twenty years, Corinne."

"Well, damn it, *somebody* took me out! Maybe my daughter. I don't know. But I *do* know it was him I saw in a little Italian place over on Guadalupe talking to a lady about his age. And he was doing a lot more than talking to her, I can tell you." Corinne Spellman nibbled her food and picked up the teacup. "You know, it's funny. I could have sworn that woman was the same one who recently moved in here, but when I asked him about it, he got all huffy like and . . . I know you'll think this is my stroke talking now . . . but he sort of, I don't know, threatened me."

"He threatened you? How did that happen?" Maybe it had some bearing on Marie as well.

"When I asked him about it—it was one time he was helping me eat lunch out there—he got real quiet and whispered in my ear." She pointed to the hearing aid. "As you know I can't hear half of nothing, so I asked him to repeat it a little slower and a little louder—so he did."

"And what did he say?"

"He said if I didn't mind my own business and stay the hell out of his, I wouldn't have to worry about losing my mind."

"My word, Corinne, are you certain about this?"

"As certain as someone in my condition can be, Martha."

"I'm Cora, dear," she said, patting a veiny hand, wondering if the threat had happened.

"Right. I knew that. Thank you. He's spent time in San Antonio, you know. I overheard him say that he was there during the war—the Big One, you know—and that he's always wanted to come back to Texas. He's been here about ten years now."

"I doubt it's been that long, Corinne."

"What did I say?"

"Ten years."

"No, it couldn't be that long, Martha. It must be only a year or so. I lose track of time so easily, you know. I think he must have lived here in the Center only about a year or more." She shook her head and closed her eyes. "But I can tell you in the utmost confidence that he's got a honey around here, and the two of them are in cahoots."

"About what?" Maybe a motive would show itself now.

"About the jewelry, of course. They all want my jewelry, don't you know? But I won't let them have it. I have it buried in a safe where nobody can find it." She picked up her sandwich and took a bite. "But I'll tell you someday where it is, Martha, because you come to see me every week and I want you to have it."

"Thank you, Corinne," Cora Mae said, standing to leave. She felt sad for this shell of a body leaking its soul, drip by drip. "Anything else I can get you before I go?"

Corinne Spellman looked around the room. The few objects she recognized as hers spun her memory through a wave of the past and deposited her on the beach of her current island of loneliness and fear. "You can get me the hell out of here."

Cora Mae Hartwig went to the chair and hugged her. "I wish I could, Corinne. I sincerely wish I could." She walked to the door. "I'll be back next week to see you again."

"If I'm not here next week, don't worry about me. I may have found a new place by then." She finished the tea. "It's always good to see you, Martha."

Cora Mae closed the door behind her and nodded to a stick of a man going the opposite direction down the hall with the help of a walker. She wondered what she'd do when her time came? Would she move to such a center when she couldn't manage her house? Would she take in a boarder? Or would she make use of all that medication she'd been hoarding all these years?

She put her hand in her pocket and touched the key Marie

Wilkins had given her in case of emergency five years ago. Cora Mae hoped it still opened her room. She walked down the carpeted corridor to the nursing station on the Tulip Wing, thinking she could pass unnoticed.

"Can I help you, ma'am?" the heavyset nurse demanded.

"I was wondering if Reverend Sparks was still on this wing?"

"I don't hardly think so, since this is a female corridor. We don't let these old people mix too much 'cause they get ideas, you know?"

Cora Mae got an idea about knocking the woman in the head.

"And crazy old Reverend Sparks got transferred with that wacko Vietnam vet day before yesterday. They make a great pair, G.I. Joe and Sparky. Finally got sent where they belong. They were just here 'cause there was no place else for them to go. Medicaid makes us hold people like that till there's an opening in some fleabag joint. Anyway, they're both gone now."

"And the veteran, I need to visit him from St. Margaret's, but his name somehow got left off my list."

"It was, uh, wait a minute, now. Some Mexican name I think. Yeah. It was Gomez, or Rodriguez, or Mendez. No, that wasn't it." The large nurse closed her eyes. "I got it. It was Perez. Tommy Perez. That was it. I knew it was one of them *z* names."

Cora Mae hoped the tape was rolling, and that this blowhard lady would later choke on it. "And the nursing home?"

"Sweet Jesus, lady, you want me to remember everything?" The nurse put down the bag of potato chips and picked up a sheet of paper. "Here it is. The Willow Branch Nursing Home. Over on East Seventeenth."

"I wonder why they always name things for old people after trees and flowers?" Cora Mae mused to her bosoms and Nikky.

The nurse nudged the male attendant next to her and laughed. "Old Reverend Sparks's daughter said we ought to name these units after *vegetables,* since that's who we're takin' care of here."

The attendant laughed. "Yeah, we ought to have the Carrot Wing and the Tomato Wing and the Squash Wing and the Okra Wing."

Cora Mae Hartwig did not smile. She hated the insensitivity in these "warehouses for the old." They might as well be dealing with inanimate boxes stacked on shelves who had no feelings, no past, no accomplishments; who had made no difference in anyone's life. Her only consolation was, as Nikky Dorati and Father Holt always said, "What goes around comes around." She hoped she'd be there to see it with this lady. Cora Mae turned to leave.

"Just where the hell do you think you're going?" the woman in the white uniform said menacingly.

"I'm going to visit another friend in your carrot patch, dear." Cora Mae wondered how long it would take Nikky to pry her hands off this woman's throat. "I don't know what your problem is, but I intend to report your behavior to the administrator."

"Go ahead. You won't be the first or the last. He can't get my kind of help for what he's payin' around here." The nurse snickered and shooed her away. "So go on and visit who you want, as long as you're out of my sight. I don't care if you strangle the lot of them. Save me doing diaper care all afternoon."

"Thank you for your kindness," Cora Mae said, taking a deep breath. She whispered to her chest as she walked down the hall. "I hope you're getting all this, Nicholas. Perhaps we should ask Father Holt to drop a copy in the administrator's office on his way to the State Department of Human Services? Oh, yes, and make a copy for that nice legislator of ours, Kristen Wade. Maybe it will change her opposition to that long-term care bill."

A resident walked past, noticed her mumbling at her chest, and quickened his pace. In the middle of the next wing, a high-functioning unit of the Center, Cora Mae Hartwig pushed the key into the door handle lock of Room 317 and turned.

It worked.

She entered the room, quickly closed the door, then stood still and looked around at the fully furnished apartment. It was as though Marie Wilkins had taken a walk or left for a few days' vacation. Just as Jason Graves had said, everything was still intact as though she was coming back. But Cora Mae knew she wasn't, not after the conversation they'd had the week before.

She thumbed through the message pad next to the phone in the living room, but found nothing. And there was no mail in the tall walnut secretary, no unpaid bills or telling letters. No, she thought as she wandered through the spotless kitchenette. She'd left for good. Or maybe for bad.

"Nothing in the living room or kitchen. Bedroom is next," Cora Mae whispered. "There is a strong odor of perfume here."

The old woman stopped in the hallway. She had first noticed the scent in the living room, increasing in strength toward the bedroom. It was not the brand of Chanel that Marie had used for thirty years.

Cora Mae knew this was a younger fragrance, not as spicy as those used by older people whose diminished olfactory senses required stronger, deeper scents. She smiled at the well-worn stereotypes of old ladies: violet water and lavender lotion. Today, older women like herself often went for newer perfumes like Lauren or Opium, something that sounded not just young, but daring, risky, even sexy. This scent was one she had tried herself: Jil Sander. She would know it anywhere.

Cautiously she pushed open the partly closed bedroom door and walked to the dresser bureau. She pulled out a center drawer filled with nightgowns and carefully laid it on the patchwork quilt covering the double bed. Reaching back under the second drawer in the bureau, she peeled off strips of silver duct tape holding a manila envelope to the plywood bottom. She opened the envelope and retrieved a small slip of paper.

"Yes, indeed," she said, then caught herself, realizing Dorati would wonder what in the world she was doing. "Oh, darn," she added, stuffing the paper into her pocket. "I thought I'd found an address book, but it's nothing. I'm on my way out." As quickly as she could, she replaced the nightgowns and softly pushed the drawer back in place.

Taking one last look around the bedroom, she caught a glimpse of something shiny through a slat in the louvered closet door. Probably a hanger, she thought as she picked up a framed picture of herself with Marie Wilkins taken at Sea World last summer. She put the picture in the manila envelope and walked quickly back to the living room. If anyone asked what she had been doing in Marie Wilkins's room, that would be her alibi.

She stopped again to inhale the pleasant smell of Jil Sander perfume, and wondered who had been there before her—and why? Then she peeked out the door and slipped into the hallway.

As the door clicked shut, so did the gun in the bedroom closet in the hand of Helen Pelham.

right. He's Truman Reinhardt, a former doctor, I think, and he's been a real boon to this Auxiliary. One of the few men, you know, though their numbers are increasing." She took off her glasses and winked at Holt. "And eligible, too."

"Doesn't look like he's *too* eligible."

"I don't exactly know who that lady is. Could be someone he brought tonight. We encourage that to get new members." Agnes Gottig shook her head and picked up her wineglass. "It'll never last, though. The woman isn't his type. She wears too much makeup. And she holds that cigarette like she's dying to smoke it. No pun intended of course. Nope. She'll be a flash in the pan and gone. Believe me, I know women, Father Holt. I've seen that same type snuggle up to my son's money until he got tired of them, or they figured he didn't have as much as he lied and said he did. I don't think Dr. Reinhardt will fall for that phoniness. And if he does, just like my stupid son, he'll deserve exactly what he gets."

In two hours the banquet was over, speeches had been delivered congratulating outgoing and incoming officers, awards conferred, and flowers bestowed. Holt had watched the entire proceedings with surprising interest. It was fascinating to see these people continuing to be who they had always been in their earlier years—active, funny, critical, sexy, flirtatious—and enjoying themselves immensely now that they were spending time out of choice rather than the obligation of work or family.

As the Rev walked by the reception desk toward the elevators, the man from the back table approached him.

"Wonderful invocation, Father Holt," Truman Reinhardt said, shaking his hand.

"Funny to see you so soon, Dr. Reinhardt. Austin really is a small town, you know."

"That's truer than I imagined. I was surprised to see how many of the people from the Center belong to the Auxiliary."

"And the lady who was with you? I don't see her now." The Rev noted a faint blush appear on the doctor's cheeks. Was it anger or embarrassment?

"Yes, she—I mean—that she's a friend from the Center. Her name is Helen Pelham and she's only recently moved there. I thought she could meet people and get connected here tonight."

"I'm sure it was helpful." Holt stepped closer to ask him a

question as the elevator bell rang. "Oh, and I was wondering if you knew a resident out there by the name of Marie Wilkins?"

Reinhardt ignored the query. "There's your car, Father Holt. You go on. I must wait for Mrs. Pelham." He moved out of the way so Holt could pass him. "Hope to see you again when you come out for services."

"Yes," the Rev replied, stepping into the crowded elevator. "See you then. And bring Mrs. Pelham." He wondered if she knew Marie Wilkins.

Holt smiled at the initial drop from the twenty-fourth floor. As he emerged into the lobby, he saw an APD blue-and-white parked at the entrance to the bank building, and a familiar face come through the door. He was not certain he was glad to see her. Her sudden appearance always meant bad news.

"Hey, Lucas," Lieutenant Granger said. "Glad you're here. Can you stick around a few minutes?" She scanned people coming off other elevators.

"What's going on?"

"Do you know which one is Agnes Gottig?"

"Sure." He pointed to the woman carrying a bouquet of pink roses. "That's her with the flowers right over there."

"Then help me get her, and find us a place to talk."

"What happened?" Holt said as they walked toward the Auxiliary president. The Rev took the flowers from Agnes Gottig as Susan Granger asked to speak with her for a moment.

"I'm terribly sorry to have to tell you this, Miss Gottig," Granger said when they were out of range of the crowd, "but your son was murdered tonight."

Agnes Gottig looked at Lucas Holt with horror on her face. He knew it was the recognition that her wish had come true. "No," she said softly. Then a louder "No!" Finally she raised her clenched fists and cried out: "No! I didn't mean it! I didn't mean it!"

Holt and Granger caught her limp body as she fainted to the ground. Lucas gently placed his jacket over the old woman, as Susan checked vitals and radioed for EMS.

The body count rises, he thought. Another child of another elderly parent. What the hell was going on here? He heard movement behind him and looked up to see a blur of black hair and red lipstick turn, then quickly leave on the arm of Truman Reinhardt.

• Six •

"Remember what the Rev said," Nikky Dorati reminded Cora Mae Hartwig as he stopped the car in front of the Westbank Retirement Center. "We're just fishing here. Do your regular visit, then try to get into the room."

"I hope I don't tangle the reel," Cora Mae said, adjusting her clothes.

"Can't happen. That mike you got on is foolproof."

"I recall that's what they said about the *Titanic,* dear."

"Pick you up in an hour," Dorati said as she exited the black BMW coupe. "And be careful."

"How do you think I've lived so long?" the old woman in the purple jogging suit and pink running shoes replied. She walked into the lobby and spoke to the volunteer at the desk.

"I'm here to see Corinne Spellman, please?" she asked.

"Just a minute, please." The older woman punched the name into the computer. "Here it is. She's been moved to the Special Care unit. I'm sure she'll be glad for a visitor. Her family have all but forgotten her." She shook her head. "I hope I never get that far along with 'old-timer's' disease. I hope somebody—you know—does me in first."

"I hope you get your wish, dear," Cora Mae Hartwig whispered as she looked for the signs directing her to Special Care. She knew "Special Care" was the Center's euphemism for the area with patients who were no longer mentally or physically capable of caring for themselves, patients with Alzheimer's and ALS (Lou Gehrig's Disease), or who had had "a little stroke" and were gently degenerating into complete dementia.

She found Corinne Spellman seated in the dining room with her lunch tray in front of her, talking to no one in particular.

"Hello, Corinne."

"Why, hello, Martha! How are you?"

"I'm not your sister Martha, dear," Cora Mae said, sitting beside her and taking her hand. "I'm your old friend—and I mean 'old' friend—Cora Mae Hartwig from St. Margaret's Church, where you and your family have attended for fifty years. I come to see you every week, and today I'm going to help you with your lunch and then maybe we'll take a little walk outside."

"I'd like that very much. It is so hard for me to get out of the house anymore."

"You're in the Westlake Retirement Center, Corinne."

"Yes, of course. I knew that. I don't know where my mind goes, Cora. One minute I'm fine and I know what day it is and where I am and who you are, and the next I'm in 1954 and you're my long-lost—and dead—sister Martha. Sorry for the inconvenience." She stared ahead for a moment, then shook off whatever thought had intruded itself into her mind.

"It's no problem for me, and I'm sure it's no problem for Martha, Corinne." She smiled.

"He's such a nice man."

"Who is?" Cora Mae asked, not minding the change in topic.

"That tall man over there helping those people eat who have lost their minds." She pointed across the activity room to a well-dressed gentleman serving trays and joking with the residents. "If only they could find where they misplaced them."

Cora Mae looked up to see Truman Reinhardt nod his head in greeting. She smiled back and continued speaking to Corinne.

"Do you know him?" Cora Mae said, lowering her head toward her chest to whisper something under her breath. She wanted Dorati to know it was Truman Reinhardt.

"I don't know." She paused, forcing thoughts up from the murky convolutions of her brain. "Wait. Yes, I do. He's a doctor of some kind. I see him around a lot, doing all kinds of things, actually." Corinne Spellman frowned and pursed her lips. "I remember something about him that I don't like much, I think."

"Perhaps we should go for a little walk, Corinne, and talk about it?" She lowered her head again.

"Let's walk to my room." Corinne Spellman stared at her. "Can you bring the food with you? I'd like to eat it in there."

"Certainly." She motioned to the attendant, who shrugged her shoulders as if it didn't matter to her. And it didn't.

Corinne Spellman's dyed red hair shook as she walked down the corridor to her room with Cora Mae Hartwig. "I could tell you some interesting things about that man," she said, "if I could remember what they are." She stopped in front of the door to her room and concentrated on how to open it. "I hate this. They make opening the door so simple a two-year-old could do it and then don't supply the two-year-old. Why don't they just put a knob on the thing? What's this bar across the door for?"

"I believe you push it and the door opens."

Corinne pushed. "I resent this. I'm senile, not crippled."

Hartwig helped her to her chair and put the tray in front of her. As Corinne sat down, a slim band was barely noticeable at her ankle. Cora Mae pointed to it.

"Do you know what this is? This little band here?"

"Sure I do, Martha. It keeps the animals in the zoo."

Cora Mae smiled and kissed her on the cheek. She liked Corinne's spunk. "You just keep growling, Corinne," she said. "Lets them know you're alive."

"About that doctor?" Corinne Spellman stopped. "But then, who would believe me?"

"Oh, I would. You just rattle on, and I'll make us some nice tea to go with your lunch there on the table." She lowered her head to her chest and hoped Dorati was getting it. Here was a chance to get inside info on Reinhardt, and maybe on Marie, if Corinne's brain cells would only cooperate.

"That would be lovely. But would you answer me one question while you're fixing the tea?"

"Certainly, Corinne," Cora Mae said, going around the corner into the tiny kitchenette area.

"Why the hell are you talking to your bosoms?"

Unseen, Cora Mae squinted up her face and thought fast. "Oh, well, um, I'm just stretching my neck, dear. My doctor said to do that several times every hour to keep from getting stiff." To her bosoms and Nikky Dorati she whispered "Oopsy."

"Thank God. I thought I was hallucinating again. I thought any minute they would answer you back. I like the kind in the green canister."

Cora Mae rolled her eyes at her own inexperience and put two cups of water in the microwave. She opened the green canister and popped the tea bags in the cups. "You were starting to tell me about that nice doctor."

"To begin with he knows everybody's business here. He volunteers for everything and gets to know everyone but hardly tells you anything about himself." Corinne smiled at Cora Mae as the tea was brought to her chair. "But I know some things about him he wished I didn't know."

"Very interesting already, dear," Cora Mae said, sitting opposite her on the overstuffed sofa. "Like what?"

"Like he's got a sweetheart outside this place, that's what. I saw him last week when my sister took me out for the day."

"Your sister's been dead for twenty years, Corinne."

"Well, damn it, *somebody* took me out! Maybe my daughter. I don't know. But I *do* know it was him I saw in a little Italian place over on Guadalupe talking to a lady about his age. And he was doing a lot more than talking to her, I can tell you." Corinne Spellman nibbled her food and picked up the teacup. "You know, it's funny. I could have sworn that woman was the same one who recently moved in here, but when I asked him about it, he got all huffy like and . . . I know you'll think this is my stroke talking now . . . but he sort of, I don't know, threatened me."

"He threatened you? How did that happen?" Maybe it had some bearing on Marie as well.

"When I asked him about it—it was one time he was helping me eat lunch out there—he got real quiet and whispered in my ear." She pointed to the hearing aid. "As you know I can't hear half of nothing, so I asked him to repeat it a little slower and a little louder—so he did."

"And what did he say?"

"He said if I didn't mind my own business and stay the hell out of his, I wouldn't have to worry about losing my mind."

"My word, Corinne, are you certain about this?"

"As certain as someone in my condition can be, Martha."

"I'm Cora, dear," she said, patting a veiny hand, wondering if the threat had happened.

"Right. I knew that. Thank you. He's spent time in San Antonio, you know. I overheard him say that he was there during the war—the Big One, you know—and that he's always wanted to come back to Texas. He's been here about ten years now."

"I doubt it's been that long, Corinne."

"What did I say?"

"Ten years."

"No, it couldn't be that long, Martha. It must be only a year or so. I lose track of time so easily, you know. I think he must have lived here in the Center only about a year or more." She shook her head and closed her eyes. "But I can tell you in the utmost confidence that he's got a honey around here, and the two of them are in cahoots."

"About what?" Maybe a motive would show itself now.

"About the jewelry, of course. They all want my jewelry, don't you know? But I won't let them have it. I have it buried in a safe where nobody can find it." She picked up her sandwich and took a bite. "But I'll tell you someday where it is, Martha, because you come to see me every week and I want you to have it."

"Thank you, Corinne," Cora Mae said, standing to leave. She felt sad for this shell of a body leaking its soul, drip by drip. "Anything else I can get you before I go?"

Corinne Spellman looked around the room. The few objects she recognized as hers spun her memory through a wave of the past and deposited her on the beach of her current island of loneliness and fear. "You can get me the hell out of here."

Cora Mae Hartwig went to the chair and hugged her. "I wish I could, Corinne. I sincerely wish I could." She walked to the door. "I'll be back next week to see you again."

"If I'm not here next week, don't worry about me. I may have found a new place by then." She finished the tea. "It's always good to see you, Martha."

Cora Mae closed the door behind her and nodded to a stick of a man going the opposite direction down the hall with the help of a walker. She wondered what she'd do when her time came? Would she move to such a center when she couldn't manage her house? Would she take in a boarder? Or would she make use of all that medication she'd been hoarding all these years?

She put her hand in her pocket and touched the key Marie

Wilkins had given her in case of emergency five years ago. Cora Mae hoped it still opened her room. She walked down the carpeted corridor to the nursing station on the Tulip Wing, thinking she could pass unnoticed.

"Can I help you, ma'am?" the heavyset nurse demanded.

"I was wondering if Reverend Sparks was still on this wing?"

"I don't hardly think so, since this is a female corridor. We don't let these old people mix too much 'cause they get ideas, you know?"

Cora Mae got an idea about knocking the woman in the head.

"And crazy old Reverend Sparks got transferred with that wacko Vietnam vet day before yesterday. They make a great pair, G.I. Joe and Sparky. Finally got sent where they belong. They were just here 'cause there was no place else for them to go. Medicaid makes us hold people like that till there's an opening in some fleabag joint. Anyway, they're both gone now."

"And the veteran, I need to visit him from St. Margaret's, but his name somehow got left off my list."

"It was, uh, wait a minute, now. Some Mexican name I think. Yeah. It was Gomez, or Rodriguez, or Mendez. No, that wasn't it." The large nurse closed her eyes. "I got it. It was Perez. Tommy Perez. That was it. I knew it was one of them z names."

Cora Mae hoped the tape was rolling, and that this blowhard lady would later choke on it. "And the nursing home?"

"Sweet Jesus, lady, you want me to remember everything?" The nurse put down the bag of potato chips and picked up a sheet of paper. "Here it is. The Willow Branch Nursing Home. Over on East Seventeenth."

"I wonder why they always name things for old people after trees and flowers?" Cora Mae mused to her bosoms and Nikky.

The nurse nudged the male attendant next to her and laughed. "Old Reverend Sparks's daughter said we ought to name these units after *vegetables,* since that's who we're takin' care of here."

The attendant laughed. "Yeah, we ought to have the Carrot Wing and the Tomato Wing and the Squash Wing and the Okra Wing."

Cora Mae Hartwig did not smile. She hated the insensitivity in these "warehouses for the old." They might as well be dealing with inanimate boxes stacked on shelves who had no feelings, no past, no accomplishments; who had made no difference in any-one's life. Her only consolation was, as Nikky Dorati and Father Holt always said, "What goes around comes around." She hoped she'd be there to see it with this lady. Cora Mae turned to leave.

"Just where the hell do you think you're going?" the woman in the white uniform said menacingly.

"I'm going to visit another friend in your carrot patch, dear." Cora Mae wondered how long it would take Nikky to pry her hands off this woman's throat. "I don't know what your problem is, but I intend to report your behavior to the administrator."

"Go ahead. You won't be the first or the last. He can't get my kind of help for what he's payin' around here." The nurse snick-ered and shooed her away. "So go on and visit who you want, as long as you're out of my sight. I don't care if you strangle the lot of them. Save me doing diaper care all afternoon."

"Thank you for your kindness," Cora Mae said, taking a deep breath. She whispered to her chest as she walked down the hall. "I hope you're getting all this, Nicholas. Perhaps we should ask Fa-ther Holt to drop a copy in the administrator's office on his way to the State Department of Human Services? Oh, yes, and make a copy for that nice legislator of ours, Kristen Wade. Maybe it will change her opposition to that long-term care bill."

A resident walked past, noticed her mumbling at her chest, and quickened his pace. In the middle of the next wing, a high-functioning unit of the Center, Cora Mae Hartwig pushed the key into the door handle lock of Room 317 and turned.

It worked.

She entered the room, quickly closed the door, then stood still and looked around at the fully furnished apartment. It was as though Marie Wilkins had taken a walk or left for a few days' va-cation. Just as Jason Graves had said, everything was still intact as though she was coming back. But Cora Mae knew she wasn't, not after the conversation they'd had the week before.

She thumbed through the message pad next to the phone in the living room, but found nothing. And there was no mail in the tall walnut secretary, no unpaid bills or telling letters. No, she thought as she wandered through the spotless kitchenette. She'd left for good. Or maybe for bad.

"Nothing in the living room or kitchen. Bedroom is next," Cora Mae whispered. "There is a strong odor of perfume here."

The old woman stopped in the hallway. She had first noticed the scent in the living room, increasing in strength toward the bedroom. It was not the brand of Chanel that Marie had used for thirty years.

Cora Mae knew this was a younger fragrance, not as spicy as those used by older people whose diminished olfactory senses required stronger, deeper scents. She smiled at the well-worn stereotypes of old ladies: violet water and lavender lotion. Today, older women like herself often went for newer perfumes like Lauren or Opium, something that sounded not just young, but daring, risky, even sexy. This scent was one she had tried herself: Jil Sander. She would know it anywhere.

Cautiously she pushed open the partly closed bedroom door and walked to the dresser bureau. She pulled out a center drawer filled with nightgowns and carefully laid it on the patchwork quilt covering the double bed. Reaching back under the second drawer in the bureau, she peeled off strips of silver duct tape holding a manila envelope to the plywood bottom. She opened the envelope and retrieved a small slip of paper.

"Yes, indeed," she said, then caught herself, realizing Dorati would wonder what in the world she was doing. "Oh, darn," she added, stuffing the paper into her pocket. "I thought I'd found an address book, but it's nothing. I'm on my way out." As quickly as she could, she replaced the nightgowns and softly pushed the drawer back in place.

Taking one last look around the bedroom, she caught a glimpse of something shiny through a slat in the louvered closet door. Probably a hanger, she thought as she picked up a framed picture of herself with Marie Wilkins taken at Sea World last summer. She put the picture in the manila envelope and walked quickly back to the living room. If anyone asked what she had been doing in Marie Wilkins's room, that would be her alibi.

She stopped again to inhale the pleasant smell of Jil Sander perfume, and wondered who had been there before her—and why? Then she peeked out the door and slipped into the hallway.

As the door clicked shut, so did the gun in the bedroom closet in the hand of Helen Pelham.

• • •

The Austin Special Transit bus pulled to the curb at First and Congress. The doors swung open and the steel platform lowered the stringy-haired man in a wheelchair to the street. He wheeled himself around to the Pulse machine in the courtyard of the twenty-four-story Franklin Federal Building.

Dressed in combat boots, dirty jeans, and a black-and-red Harley T-shirt covered by a flak jacket, Tomas Perez removed his wallet from the saddlebag slung over the side of the chair.

Across the street, from the second level of the Radisson Hotel parking garage, Nikky Dorati focused a small pair of high-powered binoculars on the ATM keypad. The Rev and Cora Mae had thought tailing him might lead to information about Marie Wilkins. So far, they were wrong.

"Eight-six-two-six," Dorati said, smiling. "I shoulda known." He moved the binocs slightly and watched Eddie Shelton nervously approach the man from behind.

"Could you hurry it up there, buddy?" Shelton said to the man in the wheelchair. "I gotta meet my girl in fifteen minutes and I'm outta dough."

Perez looked at him, expressionless. He turned, punched more buttons, and waited for the machine to spit out a small stack of twenty-dollar bills.

"Listen, if you want to share any of that, I'd be glad to help you get rid of it," Shelton said behind him.

The man took the cash and the plastic card and stuffed them in his flak pocket. With his left hand he reached into the saddlebag while his right hand quickly wheeled the chair around.

"Look, asshole," Perez said, holding a serrated black military knife to Shelton's belly. "I was a medic in Nam, so I know where to cut. I could dump your guts on the sidewalk right now and you'd never know it."

"I was . . . kidding," Shelton said somberly, promising himself to kill Nikky Dorati if he lived to hold a gun again.

"I've done a hell of a lot worse with less provocation."

"I meant . . . nothing by it."

"Turn around."

"What?"

"You heard me, turn around."

Shelton hoped Dorati would appear to save him before this Vietnam psychopath cut his heart out from the back. "But—"

"*DO IT!*"

Eddie Shelton turned around, scanning the broad plaza for signs of Nikky, finding none. He felt a tug at his belt and knew it had been severed, as had the seam of his pants.

"Now haul ass out of my way," the voice behind him said, "or I'll core it for you."

Shelton ran forward, feeling light swipes on each cheek as he did. He turned the corner and saw Nikky exiting the Beemer.

"Where the hell were you when I needed you?"

"Your butt's hanging out of your pants and you've got little red lines on it."

"Thanks for the info, Dorati," Shelton said, twisting around to see the damage. "You owe me big for this one."

"Here, wrap this towel around you," Nikky said, reaching into the trunk and handing his friend a dark blue beach blanket. "We need to get back to that teller machine."

"I feel like Carmen Miranda."

"Without the hat," Dorati replied as they approached the ATM. "Good work distracting him. He left the receipt." Nikky hoped it would tell them more than they could get at gunpoint. If you want to know more about a person's illegal activities, check their bank account.

"Shit," Dorati said. "It doesn't give the available balance. We'll have to cheat." He handed Eddie Shelton a white plastic blank.

"This will work?"

"First put your Carmen Miranda skirt over the top panel. Inserting the card activates the camera."

"But my ass'll hang out."

"Not for long."

"Okay, okay."

Dorati held up the towel and Shelton slipped the blank card in the slot.

"Punch in the letters V-N-A-M.".

"You're kidding."

"Do it."

Shelton punched 8-6-2-6. "Welcome Tomas Perez" appeared on the screen.

"Please, please let me take out money for pants."

"How much?"

"A thousand dollars."

Dorati shook his head. "Fifty. He owes you that."

Eddie Shelton gleefully received the fifty dollars cash.

"Now ask for the balance."

Shelton punched the numbers.

"That can't be right," Dorati said. "Do it again."

Eddie did. "It's right, Nikky. All six figures."

"The boy must make some big deposits."

Eddie squinted at the numbers. "Even I know you don't keep $426,327 in a *checking* account, for God's sake. Why doesn't he invest it in something?"

Dorati wondered less about the veteran's investments than why he lived in a nursing home and dressed like a homeless person. "Exit the machine," he said to Shelton.

"Can I just get a couple hundred for spending money? He'll never miss it."

Dorati glared at him. "I think Maxine needs a new chair."

"Five hundred?"

"Take an even grand. You got blood on my towel."

"Right." He retrieved the cash, withdrew the card, and took the receipt.

"Get away from the machine," Dorati ordered, "like around the corner."

"Naw," Shelton said, smiling. "You go around the corner."

"But the camera is still on for fifteen seconds after the transaction."

Shelton grinned. "I know."

Dorati walked away from the direct line of view. He watched from a safe distance as Eddie Shelton pulled the towel over his face and bent over as he walked away from the machine.

"I love to moon those security cameras," he said as they approached Dorati's car. "It was even more fun in the joint."

"I remember they had more mug shots of your ass than they did your face."

"And they were better lookin', too."

Dorati laughed. "We'll get you some jeans and then we'll hunt up Mr. Perez. The Rev wants you to tail him."

"Let me tell you how excited I am about chasing a Nam medic around town. Even in a wheelchair that sucker's dangerous."

"Right. Keep tabs on him for a few hours and see if he leads you to this woman." He handed Shelton the framed photo Cora Mae Hartwig had removed from the apartment earlier.

"Ain't that the old lady from the church?"

"Not Cora Mae. The other one."

"What's her name?"

"Marie Wilkins. And it would be nice to find her alive."

Lisa Enright stepped out of the shower and dried her short red hair with a thick emerald towel. She flipped on the exhaust fan to clear the steam and took a sip of ice water she'd brought from the kitchen. She hoped it would help clear the swirling inside her head as well.

It was odd, she thought as she dried off her freckled body, that the coffee that woman had brought them had had the opposite effect and made them both so drowsy. Neither she nor Al had thought much about it when she offered it as the Five Card Stud band broke down their equipment and carried it to the Blazer.

"South Austin's a long drive home, even from Gruene," the woman had said. "Y'all drink this. We wouldn't want all this singing talent to be found in a cattle culvert tomorrow morning."

They had reluctantly agreed and taken the coffee from her. A mist had set down on the hill country roads. Visibility would be bad, not to mention dodging deer and armadillos.

Lisa ran a comb through her hair as she blew it dry, sitting naked on the padded stool in front of her vanity. She loved this house they had built with their savings from work and the band. She especially liked this special area all her own just off the bath, where she could primp and paint and polish herself silly—all out of earshot of the bedroom where Al could watch TV or sleep undisturbed, as he was doing now.

Her parents complained that she and Al had not paid back the carefully tracked amounts the old couple had spent over the years getting them out of jail and into one program after another. But what they didn't know was, if things worked out, she and Al would offer her parents to come live with them in that house.

She looked out the bathroom window to the back addition. The reason it was there was eventually to have one or both of the older folks live there, take care of things while she and Al were on the road with the band. That was part of what they would have told her parents today had they stayed long enough to hear.

Lisa opened the door and listened to Al snoring. He always pooped out before she did, poor guy. He worked so hard and had such high hopes for them. She smiled as she dabbed perfume from the tip of her finger to her neck. Maybe he would awaken when she came in, she thought. No. She touched the perfume to her inner thighs, and stroked it slowly under her firm breasts. She would make sure he woke up.

But her own rising desire was suddenly quelled by a drowsy weakness. She had felt it first on the way home. They both had and took turns talking to each other to stay awake. As soon as they made it home, Al had taken a quick shower and literally dropped into bed naked. Lisa had gotten her usual second wind but now was fading again. She looked up at the crystal clock on the vanity window.

No wonder, she thought. It was nearly four. But there was something unusual about this drowsiness. It reminded her of her drug days when she and Al mixed crack with uppers and downers to maintain their wake-sleep cycles. This was more than lethargy, it was a leaden feeling all over, as though her veins were filled with sludge.

She took a long drink of ice water to rouse her. Standing in front of the mirror she put her hands on her belly, below her navel. She turned sideways and, holding her arms straight out to the side, looked at her profile. She was still flat. But wasn't there just the slightest bulge there?

She slouched down, still looking at her profile, to see if she could predict how her swollen belly would appear in a few months. As she did, her legs weakened and she lost her balance. She grabbed the top of the vanity but knocked the glass of water onto the carpet.

Enough for one night, she thought, tossing the towel on the

water. She told herself she needed to quit fighting sleep. There
would be plenty of sleepless nights come summer.

Lisa Enright turned off the exhaust fan and the bathroom light.
She walked softly to the bed where Alan pushed the blanket up
with his steady breathing. Her head spun with drowsiness now as
she slipped her cool legs down next to him. She placed his hand
with hers on her belly, kissed his shoulder, and fell deep into
sleep beside him.

Twenty minutes later a figure ejected the classical disc in a car
three houses down from the Greer House in Tanglewood Acres.
He glanced at the rearview mirror and quickly lay down on the
seat until he heard the heavy blue-and-white slowly lumber past.
When he raised up, the cruiser was gone.

After first turning off the interior light, the man opened the car
door and walked to the darkened rear of the house. He pulled on
tight latex gloves, took the key he had been given, and opened the
back door to the kitchen. The sound he heard stopped him cold. It
was the crying of a child.

But that could not be. There were no children in this household,
unless they were sitting for a friend. But that wasn't possible.
They had just gotten home from Gruene Hall.

The man reached into his coat pocket and pulled out a small
spray canister. The noise drew him through the kitchen into the
dining room, where he found its source. A huge Siamese with
bright blue eyes opened wide at him in the dark. It crouched de-
fensively on the dining room table, where it whined and spit, raising its child-sounding voice louder as he approached.

To be certain not to miss, the man extended the canister toward
the face of the large cat, but the cat swiped at his hand, stabbing
her needlelike claws through the latex to his skin. The bottle clat-
tered to the hardwood floor and the man, fearing the noise had
awakened the couple upstairs, grabbed the canister and sprayed
indiscriminately in the cat's direction.

The animal squealed and tried to jump from the table but the
man caught it by the tail and held it upside down as he sprayed
the burning liquid anaesthetic at the drooling, gaping mouth. The
struggling stopped and the cat hung limp in his hand. He dumped
it in the kitchen sink, then twisted its neck until he heard the

crack. The dead animal would have to go with him, and all signs of its struggle must be washed down the drain later.

The delay had cost him precious time. He had to be out of the neighborhood before the sky began to lighten. Thank Ben Franklin for providing an extra hour of darkness, he thought, as he moved back to the stairs and climbed to the landing that led to the bedrooms. The drugged coffee had an increasing effect, causing near coma in three hours. Just in case, he readied the spray container. Alan Greer would be first.

The man moved to the side of the bed and pulled the sheet down to expose a bare arm. He removed a small syringe, uncapped the needle, and laid it in front of the sleeping man's hand. Carefully he placed a rubber tourniquet just above the elbow and tied it tight. Alan Greer moved his uncomfortable shoulder and grimaced, then settled back down.

The tall man knelt by the bed and slowly inserted the needle under Greer's middle fingernail. The hand at first recoiled, but the man gripped it and injected the contents of the syringe, then quickly loosened and removed the tourniquet.

The man watched as, even under heavy sedation, Alan Greer sensed the burning in his arm, opened his eyes and tried to raise up—but could not move his leaden body. And the gaping mouth could not warn the woman next to him. The staring eyes teared up, then closed forever.

The figure moved to the other side of the bed and tied the tourniquet on the woman. She rolled from her side to her back out from under the covers, exposing her naked body to the glow from the dim nightlight in the wall. Taking time to look at her, the man thought her breasts too large for her small frame, her nipples too red for someone of her coloring. He touched her forehead and knelt by her. He uncapped the needle and inserted it beneath the left ring fingernail.

She jerked her hand back with a force unanticipated by her attacker, and he injected it again. Suddenly Lisa Enright opened her eyes and forced herself up in bed. She stared at him wide-eyed and tried to scream, but the constricting muscles in her throat choked out all but the vaguest guttural gasp.

The man stood back as she grasped the clammy body of her husband and placed her burning hand on her belly. The bulging veins in her neck made her face the color of her hair as her mouth forced a final sound from her oval lips. A barely audible "Noooo" broke the silence and caused the man to step back against the wall until she dropped onto the pillow. Her open wet eyes stared at nothing as her hand slid to the sheet.

Quickly the man placed her limp fingers around the syringe he had used on her husband and the husband's fingers on the one that had been injected into her, dropping the needles where they would lay if the couple had injected each other.

He pressed his hands against their jugulars and, noting no movement, left the room for the hallway stairs. From this angle he could see into the room at the opposite end of the hall, where a large box sat on the floor. He glanced at it peripherally as he descended the stairs, barely making out the word *Carseat* in the dark. In the kitchen he found a plastic grocery sack into which he dumped the body of the Siamese. He rinsed out the sink to dispose of saliva and cat hair, and took the bag with him as he locked the back door of the house.

He tossed the sack on the floor when he entered the car and started the ignition. At the first stop sign, the man paused. His mind flashed on the woman's bare body and her fight against the inevitable. His breath vanished as he groped at the buttons to roll down the windows, but still he could not gulp enough air to fill his tightening lungs.

He knew who the carseat was for.

• Seven •

At eight in the morning Lucas Holt pulled his black MX6 into a Clergy Parking spot in front of Archbishop McCard Hospital, known to locals as "Archie Mac's," in East Austin. He checked in the visor mirror to make sure no traces of Kristen conveyed where he had spent the night. Given the late hour, his upset over the Gottig murder, and her annoyance about the proposed long-term care bill, they had decided not to talk about their relationship as they had planned. Comfort, not confrontation, was the order of the night. And there had been plenty of that—until the pager jump-started him from her side this morning.

He took one last sip of tea and half-ran to the hospital entrance past two nuns who motioned to him to slow down. If there was a gene for giving orders, nuns had it.

Slow down. Maybe it was a warning. He felt slower, worn down by the loss of control he felt until he could make some headway in finding the killer. But there was no time for that now. The call from the head nurse to hurry to ICU at Archie Mac's was an emergency in reverse. Where once there had been an imperative to rush to intervene and save life at all costs, now his mission was to do the exact opposite—to rush to intervene in the prolonging process of high-tech death.

Ignoring the elevators, Holt bounded up the stairs and followed the familiar corridor to ICU. He took a deep breath and pushed through the electronic doors marked RESTRICTED VISITING. The flurry of activity drew him to Bed 9. As he approached, two interns barked orders around the bed of Verdie Tyler, a seventy-four-year-old parishioner whom Holt had visited only yesterday. She had been admitted complaining of "a little flu." Her doctor had given her IV fluids to get her ready to return to the nursing home. She had been content to have nothing further done.

"Stop the code!" Holt yelled into the ICU cubicle.

All heads turned in his direction, incredulous.

"Who the hell are you?" a short intern asked angrily, continuing to pump on the old woman's chest. An audible snap meant a fragile rib cracked under the pressure.

"No!" Holt replied as he elbowed his way into the small, cramped room. "Who the hell are *you?*"

"Resume the code," the tall, blond-haired intern yelled. "And get this clown out of here."

"Stop the code! And get *these* two clowns out of here," Holt replied. "This lady was a Comfort Only Category. She was not to have CPR, much less have her heart shocked."

"Call Security." The short intern waved at the nurse, who rolled her eyes. "We can't just let the patient die."

"That's exactly what you will do," Holt demanded, raising his voice. "I have her power of attorney, and if you don't stop right now I'll sue you for assault and battery and, if she lives, for wrongful life."

Both interns looked up. God put the fear of attorneys in them rather than the other way around, Holt thought.

"Call the code," the blond woman said. She looked at the Rev. "I hope you know this woman's death is on your conscience."

"I hope you know that the way she was brutally battered with her final wishes totally ignored is entirely on yours." He and the charge nurse watched the two interns leave the unit shaking their heads at the stupidity of allowing a senseless death. He held the old lady's hand as the line on the monitor flattened, emitting a monotone beep from the machine.

"She's expired," the nurse said routinely as she pulled the leads from the woman's naked torso.

"God, if I'd known she was going to expire I'd have put another quarter in her," Holt said. "Credit cards expire. Parking meters expire. Verdie Tyler died." Holt removed the small round stock from his pocket and pressed his thumb into the oily cotton. "But not the way she wanted to. She had known a lot of insult and abuse in her life." He made the sign of the cross on her forehead. "From her parents because she was number eight and that was one too many." Then her hands. "From her society because of her skin color." And her feet. "From her church because she had the audacity to think and challenge." Finally he touched the place over her heart where the electric paddles had shocked her, searing her skin. "And lastly from those she trusted to care for her." He pulled the sheet to her neck and leaned down to kiss her sunken cheek. "May you know peace at last and be welcomed by angels into eternity."

The charge nurse took his arm as he walked from the cubicle.

"Sorry, Father Holt. I called you as soon as I could. We tried to stop them." She shook her head. "We did everything but refuse to follow their orders."

"Maybe you need to do that a few times to get their attention," Holt replied, patting her shoulder.

"Maybe we do."

The Rev left ICU and headed for the nearest rest room. He locked the door and stood over the sink, holding the basin with both hands. Anger and revulsion swept over him; anger that an old lady was denied her final wish and battered on her way to death; revulsion at the method of undeserved suffering inflicted on her. But there was something at a deeper level.

Holt splashed cold water on his face and watched in the mirror as it dripped down off his chin like a stream of tears that would not come from inside of him, but wanted to. He saw his mother lying in the bed he now slept in, taking her last breath; his father lying on the floor in urine and vomit as Lucas called 911, beginning the three-day assault that ended in the same ICU cubicle from which he had just come.

He imagined the Bertrands dead in their living room and the Villalobos women bloated from carbon monoxide poisoning in their car. At least Verdie Tyler knew her assailants—the eager interns in the ICU.

Finally he saw himself, not in his bed or on the floor of his house or even in the ICU, but lying in some darkened room, an old man withered and alone. He grabbed a paper towel and wiped his face, forcing his vision back to the present. The question was what would he do in the meantime? That was the issue he struggled with now that he was forty-three, that kept nagging at him to resolve before there was no time left to resolve it.

Holt took a deep breath and returned to the corridor. The only thing worse than a bad death was a senseless one. The deaths of the Bertrands and the Villalobos sisters terrified him more than the one he had just witnessed for that very reason—seeming senselessness that ended otherwise meaningful lives.

A bell rang and the elevator doors opened.

"Hey, Lucas!" the light-skinned black man said, holding out a hand. "How you doing? Come on in to my elevator."

"I'm okay, Garvin," Holt replied to the hospital's CEO, Garvin Davis. "Verdie Tyler just died in ICU, though."

"Yeah, I heard a few minutes ago." Davis frowned. He was a handsome man with his full black beard and shiny bald head, as though gravity had pulled all the hair from his slippery pate down to his face. His deep voice matched his hefty appearance and provided a formidable countenance for negotiations with doctors and other players in the health-care game. Lucas had come to know Garvin and his wife Lavelle from both church and the hospital. He instinctively liked Garvin from the beginning, and thought Lavelle to be the most beautiful woman in town.

"You know everything that happens here?" the Rev asked.

"Pretty much so. Gotta stay on top these days."

"So how *is* business? Looks like your rooms are full."

The doors opened on Two, but no one got on.

"That's because a Norther blew in last week. Hospital administrators thank God for bad weather, allergies, and flu because it fills our beds with easy to treat—and reimbursable—people on Medicare." The old elevator bounced to a stop, and Garvin Davis held the door for them to exit into the lobby.

"So the aging of the population should keep you in business a long time, right?" Holt added.

"Not necessarily. Our census is good now, but the whole system is going to outpatient. In five years the only place you'll find an acute care hospital like this is in the basement of the Smithsonian with the mastodons."

"So what do you do?"

"We change, like everybody else. The good news for us is that Archie Mac is being looked at by Lutheran Healthcare. They'd like to own a hospital doing our kind of indigent work. The Catholic Daughters have got three facilities in Austin already and would be glad to hand this one over—for the right price, of course." Davis walked out to the car with the Rev.

Holt pushed the button that opened the door locks. "Would they keep you on? An old Baptist like you?"

"I'm not old and since we joined St. Margaret's I've learned a lot of hymns that the Lutherans wrote. That's probably why their offer is better than just keeping me on, Lucas." Garvin Davis looked over his shoulder before continuing, and lowered his voice. "They'd bump me up to the head office in Minneapolis."

"Minnesota?" Holt replied, smiling. "Do you know they've got funny white stuff that falls from the sky and piles up taller than your okra plants and buries your car and your house and your neighbors and the only way out is to run naked through a sauna?"

Garvin Davis smiled. "We'll love it. It'll be different."

"They'll figure out that you're not Norwegian, Garvin, probably as you're taking leave of your senses in one of those ice huts over a lake."

"Lucas—"

"So you might as well divorce Lavelle before you go, because it's only a matter of time till she comes to decry the cold and wish she was in Austin. And when you do let me know because I may soon be in the market for someone to run the lake with and I've always admired her from afar."

By now Davis was laughing out loud. "I'll tell my wife she has other options."

"And besides, what about her father? You going to let old Reverend Sparks sit in that crummy nursing home?"

Garvin Davis clouded up like a storm in the western sky. "Yes, we are. She and I both have careers. She's a full partner in the ad agency and she can transfer to their northern branch." He knit his brow and shook his head. "As for the old man, he's on the verge of extinction—and good riddance."

Lucas saw lightning flash in his friend's eyes. "I knew you didn't like him, but—"

"*Like?* That mean-spirited, self-righteous son of a bitch?"

"Don't hold back, Garvin. Tell me how you really feel."

"Not funny, Lucas," Davis replied with a scowl. "I've always hated that old man even more than Lavelle does. Him and his pompous strict Baptist ways. He beat her silly for doing normal kid things, especially as a teenager—and I mean we're talking broken bones here."

Holt listened as Garvin Davis gesticulated wildly. He had seen this depth of hostility before. In less acculturated men, men without the internal restraints Davis had, the feelings led directly to actions ranging from verbal abuse to murder.

"And here in the wonderful South none of the authorities did anything because it was a nigger kid and they didn't mess with them any more than with Mexicans. Plus old man Sparks thought he was setting an example for that ragtag church of his." Davis cursed. "Lavelle even took her mother's maiden name—Wright— so she wouldn't be connected with him. Hell, she wouldn't hardly marry me for fear of me turning out like her old man."

Holt was surprised but not shocked. He knew that most people showed well on the surface, but scratch them a little below that and experiences of incredible pain, tragedy, and endurance surfaced. "I didn't know any of this."

"Course you didn't, Lucas. We've been friends for a short time. And Lavelle and me, we keep pretty much to ourselves when it comes to her old man. You can see how this promotion is great for both of us. As for old Reverend Sparks, he deserves all the shit he gets, and I hope the senile old bastard gets worse and suffers the way he made Lavelle and her mother suffer."

"What goes around comes around?"

"Not good enough unless I get to see it," Garvin Davis said. "Or be part of it. The sooner I hear that man's dead, the better. And it isn't for the insurance, either. I don't know or care how much he's got. I do know he's saved every dime he's ever had and he lives off welfare. He just sits in that nursing home blaming his daughter and me for everything ever happened to him when he's the cause of it all his own damned self, him and his damned—and I mean 'damned'—fundamentalist theology." Garvin Davis calmed down as the storm blew itself out. "Sorry, Lucas, but where Lavelle is concerned I get worked up."

"It's okay. You love her. And life isn't fair." The Rev put an arm around his shoulder. If life were fair there wouldn't be four corpses from St. Margaret's in the city morgue. "So what's the time frame here, and does Reverend Sparks know anything about it?"

"He's so in and out of la-la-land he wouldn't know if we wrote it out to remind him. We haven't told him, but that gossipy flock of his spreads news like the flu. He knows."

"I thought he was out of that church now."

"He got them to call him 'Pastor Emeritus' and give him an office like he's still boss over the young preacher that took it over. That's so he can still get a piece of the take. The part of the old bastard's brain with dollar signs on it still works."

Lucas smiled, though inside he was surprised at the depth of Garvin's feelings. In the two years he had known the man, he had seen his compassionate side come out in situations in the church and at the hospital. Now Holt was reminded that the capacity to love was often matched in the same person by an equal capacity to hate. He had seen the same, only in reverse, at the prison. The depths of hate often masked incredible abilities to love and sacrifice in people society otherwise wanted to banish.

Davis continued. "Our house is on the market now that the hospital deal looks serious. If it's approved in the next two weeks, we'll be out of here." He punched Holt playfully. "Hey, you can come up and run *that* lake with us, man. In the snow!"

"There's not enough love or money in the world to get me north of Dallas in winter and you know it."

"Healthy Norwegian blondes, Lucas. Running naked in and out of saunas. Skiing down slopes."

"Forget it. I can't catch someone who's running in and out of the Texas Statehouse." Holt threw his arms around the larger man and hugged him. "I'll miss the hell out of you. You're one of the sane voices in this hospital, not to mention the church. You're not afraid to pull tubes and let people die. And you've never been afraid to voice your opinions on the Vestry, either."

"I'll miss you too, my man."

The Rev got in the car and rolled down the window. "Call me before you go and we'll do a final run, with the beer on me at one of the new microbreweries downtown."

"Deal, Lucas," Davis replied. "I'll call you the end of next week. Take care."

Holt backed from the space and watched Garvin Davis lope into the hospital. Perhaps it was the grotesque image of Verdie Tyler still vivid in his mind, or the wave of deaths deluging him with life's uncertainty, but as he pulled out into traffic, the Rev wondered if he and Garvin Davis would ever drink that beer.

The intrusive buzz of the car phone startled him.

"Hello?" he answered loudly.

"Yo, Rev. Max." Her voice was shaking.

"What's wrong?" Holt slowed for a red light at Comal.

"Susan Granger just called. She said to tell you now."

"Tell me what?" Holt's heart quickened.

Maxine paused. "I'm sorry, Rev," she said, starting to cry. "Lisa and Al are dead."

"Come on, Dorati, pick it up," Eddie Shelton mumbled nervously into the mobile phone as he sat parked in the huge lot at Manor Downs Race Track. "I used the signal, now pick it *up.*"

"Yeah?" a groggy voice finally answered.

"Nikky. Eddie."

"You sound like friggin' Tarzan. Where the hell are you?"

"You sound like you just woke up."

"I did. What time is it?"

"Noon, Baby Face. And I'm at the track."

Nikky Dorati paused to get his bearings. "Wait a second. We got a bad connection and it's in my head."

Shelton heard the clink of bottle to glass and knew it was a shot of rye. After an audible swallow, the voice returned.

"Now I can hear you. I coulda sworn you said you were at the track. I thought the Rev and I sent you out to follow Perez."

"That's exactly what I been doin' since yesterday. And he didn't do nothin' but shop. I gained ten pounds eatin' crap while I waited. He's a little slow in that wheelchair."

"How long did it take to wheel himself to the track?"

"Not long. Let me tell you what happened."

There was a pause while Dorati took another shot and gasped at the burn. "I'm all ears."

"This morning around eight I parked a block away from the nursing home in time to catch the night shift leaving. They all looked like rejects from NarcAnon. I mean they were messed up."

Dorati interrupted. "You ever let me get put in a place like that, and if I can remember it I'll kill you."

"Me, too. So half an hour later this cab pulls up and Perez is pushed out by old Reverend Sparks."

"The dumb leading the blind."

"Right. So I follow the cab to this fancy garage downtown, and old man Sparks waits on the corner while No Legs disappears into an elevator. Five minutes later up drives this van with disabled plates and Perez at the hand controls and in pops Sparks, big as you please."

"And they went to the track?"

"Hold up a minute. No, they drove around town till Perez dropped Sparks at a storefront attorney on South First and waited for him over an hour. I got heartburn from the fried chicken I ate while he was in there."

"I'm sorry to hear it."

"Thanks for your sympathy," Eddie said sarcastically. "No Legs smoked a pack of Camels and made four phone calls, one of them a long and heated one. Finally the old man came out with a manila folder in his hand and handed it to Perez."

"His will?"

"Hell, it could have been a real estate deal for all I know. I got the attorney's name."

"Now the track?"

"Not yet. They went to a bank drive-up teller, and I quit counting at thirty bills. I don't know what size they were, but it took them twenty minutes and people started beeping and backin' out of line behind them and the guard had to come and reroute cars till they got through."

"I wonder whose account they drained?" Dorati asked.

"The Mexican's."

"How do you know?"

"He did all the signing and smilin' and old Sparks just sat there babblin' and spittin' like he was preachin' at somebody."

"Then the track?"

"Nope. One more stop. They went to Zilker Rose Garden."

"Because it's too small to be followed without being seen."

"You got that right. I had to drive around the back and walk up the rear entrance all the way across the gardens and up to the lot." Eddie Shelton moved the phone to his other hand. If the thing gave him brain tumors, he wanted them symmetrical. "So I get up there, pantin' my lungs out. I gotta stop those damned cigars you been givin' me. And there's this older—I'd say about sixty something—broad with black hair. All I can see is her backside 'cause she's talkin' to Sparks through the window and she's holdin' the manila envelope from the lawyer's."

"Was she wearin' a dress or slacks?"

"Dress. A bright green thing with big flowers on it."

"Shit. And I'll bet you're gonna tell me Sparks handed her a plastic bag with the bank envelope inside."

"You got it, Nikky. Payoff time." Shelton squinted at the phone. "You know this chick?"

"Did she have red lipstick, or could you see?"

"Damn, Dorati! Were you lookin' over my shoulder or what?" Eddie Shelton made a mental note never, ever to mess with Nikky.

"I got my sources." Another glass sound. "Now the track?"

"Right. I ran back to my car and caught 'em at IH 35. They drove to Elgin Downs and bet the ponies for two hours."

"How'd you do?" Dorati said.

Nikky knew him too well. Never miss an opportunity for a buck. "Great! I made the same bets they did. Always to Show except for when they put down big bucks to Win. But it's funny. Sparks puts up the money and No Legs collects the bets. Like he's payin' him back or somethin'. Why else would that preacher break every rule in his Bible by bettin'? He must owe Perez a bundle. Not anymore, of course, the way they're winnin' today."

"It's time to get your ass out of there. Meet me here in an hour. You can buy lunch."

"Glad to. But there's two more races I want to see."

"You should take the money and run, Eddie. Come back and let's talk before they make you watchin' them."

"I gotta go make a pit stop. So I'll give 'em one more look and maybe put a few bucks on whatever they bet on."

Dorati sighed. "See you when you get here."

"Right." Eddie Shelton walked across the lot to find Reverend Sparks and Tomas Perez where he'd left them. Sparks handed Perez money, which the latter took to the betting window. Eddie immediately laid down a hundred dollars on the same horse to Win, and noticed that Perez was headed to the men's rest room.

Eddie followed at a distance. Once inside the crowded, smoky lavatory, he made his way past the line of men spitting and pissing into a common urinal. It reminded him of the penitentiary where CROSS STREAMS AND DIE was cut into the wood above the trough. He looked up and saw the door close behind a wheelchair in the larger accessible stall, just as a man came out of the stall next to it.

Shelton bolted the door closed, dropped his pants, and sat on the throne. To his right he should have heard a wheelchair clank against the hand rails as No Legs lifted and positioned himself.

But no sound came. Either Perez was already situated or he hadn't made it to the toilet. Eddie had to know. He leaned way over, nearly to the floor and looked under the stall—right into the barrel of a gun and the grin of Tomas Perez.

"Let's shoot the shit, man." Perez smiled and cocked the trigger. "What do you say?"

"I already did," Eddie Shelton replied as two pairs of large feet appeared in front of his stall door and waited.

Lucas Holt got off the elevator on the top floor of One Congress Plaza with his running bag in hand. He felt out of place in this ostentatious art deco building, as though his presence endorsed the values it represented. He passed well-groomed yuppies in the hallway and grinned at the fact that the place was known locally as "One Taco Plaza." The best taco stand in Austin had been replaced by a steel-and-glass structure that was home to the typical downtown infestation of bankers, lawyers, accountants, and pigeons. He walked through a green marble arch into the Waterloo Fitness Center and thought he'd have preferred the tacos. At least money changed hands in the right direction.

It would be his last visit, he decided as he got a key and checked into the locker room. A parishioner who officed at One Taco suggested he try the Center, since St. Margaret's was only four blocks away. If he liked it, the man's firm would donate a membership to the church. But Holt didn't like the lifestyle of "the young and the rested" who played at fitness because it was part of the image of success. He had returned today because a Norther had blown rain into Central Texas, making the running trail too soggy to walk with Susan Granger. He preferred the rain. Given his depressed mood, it would have felt better.

The Rev left the locker room and picked an empty spot on the stretching rail. The view from the floor-to-ceiling windows made it seem as though he could fall over the edge into the Colorado. Right now it sounded like a good idea.

Lisa and Al dead. He couldn't get Max's words out of his mind. It didn't fit. Why would they overdose at this point in their career? But then why would the Villalobos sisters kill themselves just as their business was taking off?

Holt shook his head as he bent to touch his nose to his knee. He needed distraction, time to get perspective and pull himself together. The workout would help. The view of the rain outside falling across the lake was distracting. So was the view inside the Center.

He crossed his legs and bent to touch his palms to the floor to stretch his hamstrings. From this upside-down perspective he saw two women in their late twenties wearing color-coordinated mid-calf leg tights under bike pants under wind shorts. Their tight sport bras bobbed beneath off-the-shoulder tank tops.

Who cared what you looked like when your main purpose was to sweat? The men didn't. They looked like a drawer of mismatched socks. The women looked like a new box of Crayola 88's. He switched legs. Sweating was clearly not the main purpose here.

Holt stretched his quads, then turned on the treadmill, wondering if Susan Granger would attack this last vestige of sexism in his otherwise fairly nonchauvinist psyche. She would have to concede he had a point. What you wore communicated why you were there, and Holt's white Asics, blue-topped socks, green shorts, and red Oatmeal Run T-shirt said he was there to do six at a rate of speed high enough to run off his angry cynicism—and to dull the pain of the loss.

Ten minutes into his run Susan Granger emerged from the dressing room wearing a blue and white Austin City Limits shirt and gray sweatpants; her hair was tied back in a ponytail.

"How you doing?" she said.

"Some days life sucks," he replied, looking ahead.

Susan Granger looked down and pursed her lips. "Sorry about Lisa and Al, Lucas."

"No shit. Me, too." Holt realized he was taking out on her what he meant to pound into the treadmill. He glanced at her as she mounted the stationary bike facing him. "Nice outfit," he said. "I mean, you won't make the cover of *Elle* this month, but you might actually get some exercise."

"Yeah," Susan replied, setting the timer. "The colorful nubile cuties with the perfect hair and makeup are date bait."

"No comment."

"Right approach," she replied. "If *you* make a comment you're sexist. If *I* make one I'm observant."

Holt smiled in spite of himself. He shook his head as he watched her pedal with her feet and pull with her arms. She already had a fit body under those wonderfully nonmatching clothes. He wondered how much that body had changed in the twenty-five years since they had been a pair at the university.

Granger laughed. "I know that look, Lucas," she said, startling him. "You'd better turn up the pace on that thing—the treadmill I mean. And spend more time with Kristen."

"Maybe I need to run for office so I can find her."

Susan Granger closed her eyes and pulled harder on the handlebars, pedaling faster. Lucas knew she was ignoring the comment. Whatever they had meant to each other in the past, she would not interfere with his relationship with Kristen Wade. Maybe Susan actually wanted that connection to continue. If Lucas was occupied, there was no need to think about his availability, to raise the issues they had laid to rest so many years ago. But she was thinking about it now, or thinking about something that made her push the bike to its limit.

"Slow down or you'll never make your full time," he said. "You already hit a reading of six there." He nodded.

"Thanks, I don't know what I was thinking."

But Lucas thought he knew, because he had the same conflict. Their impossible attraction and equally impossible differences once again had reared like a horse on hind legs, powerful, adamant, whinnying against the inevitable. They both were opinionated on opposite sides of every issue from gun control to capital punishment. And still there was this pull.

He saw her glance sideways at him. "I know that look, Susan," Holt said, surprising her.

"No, you don't." She laughed. "And don't tell me to spend more time with my vibrator. How do you know I'm not dating a wonderful man who thinks I hung the moon?"

"Because you're too involved with your job to have room for anything else than credits toward making captain."

She ignored him and changed the subject. "This aging thing is getting to you," she said, pedaling harder.

"And it's not getting to you?"

"Cops know better. You live. You die. Though I do hear more aging jokes around the station lately."

"Jokes? You?"

"Yeah, jokes. Me." She looked over at him smugly. "In fact I'll tell you one. Maybe it'll cheer you up."

"You don't tell jokes."

"What do you call your birthday bash at the Spoke?"

Holt grimaced. "Yeah, that was a surprise, too."

"So watch your assumptions about me. I have, in the intervening years, developed the ability to tell jokes exceptionally well. Come to think of it, that's probably why."

"I'm listening. But hurry," he said with a straight face. "I don't hear after mile three. Endorphines kick in and I bliss out." He hoped they would kick in soon. Despite the pleasant talk with Susan, the knot of anger was in his stomach again.

"Okay. It's a cop version of an old person's joke." Susan Granger slowed her pace to get her breath. "These four old men in four separate cars meet at a local bar and get pretty drunk. And there's this cop outside the bar who is just waiting for them to come out so he can pop them, no pun intended, for DWI."

Holt smirked at her.

"A few hours later the cop sees the first guy come out and watches him stumble to the car, get in, and drive down the road, weaving from side to side. He lets him go a few hundred feet, hits the siren and races after him to pull him over."

Holt nodded at her to continue.

"The old man stops and the cop gets him out of the car. 'Good evening, Officer,' the old guy says. 'You got a license and insurance?' the cop says. 'You bet I do, Officer,' the man says, taking time fumbling with the glove compartment and his wallet. The cop looks at them and hands them back. 'Walk this line,' the cop says, drawing a line in the dirt with his boot. And the old man walks it perfectly. 'Now blow into this breathalyzer.' And the man takes his time doing it. The cop looks at the machine and says, 'You've been in that bar all night and you haven't had one drink. What are you—the designated driver?' 'No, sir,' the old man replies with a smile on his face. 'I'm the designated *decoy!'* "

Lucas laughed half at the joke and half at the satisfied look on Susan Granger's face. "Very good, Susan. Thank you. That'll preach." Funny what age does to you, he thought. He wondered what else she did now that she didn't do back then. "Speaking of cops, anything from the Bureau of Criminal Identification on Erik and Janey Bertrand?"

"No." She pedaled and moved her arms back and forth in a rapid rhythmic motion. "BCI says there's nothing. I had to call someone I know there personally even to get a response."

"They have any suggestions?"

"Sure. They suggested I stay the hell out of it."

Holt finished mile four and slowed his pace. "What? Why would they say that?"

"They didn't in so many words. But I know that tone of voice like they're not really interested, which of course means that they're too interested."

"That's why I always like cops. Your communications are so honest and direct. What the hell does *that* mean?"

"It means that they must be doing their own investigation, and they'll keep me at bay so I don't intrude on their deal. They must be on to something bigger that they think we local yokels will screw up."

"Would you do that?"

"I wouldn't. But you and your gaggle of bozos would."

Lucas Holt considered the remark. "So are you by any chance asking here, Lieutenant Granger, for the kind assistance of my former prison parishioners in areas where you are officially unable to get cooperation from your own colleagues?"

"I wouldn't go that far," Granger replied. "But if you came across anything, I would be grateful to hear about it."

"You're pissed at BCI and want the God Squad to help."

"Nope. I know you well enough to know you're probably up to your ass in information. I just want in on what you know."

"Okay," he said, finally. "But turnabout's fair play. Start with the lab."

"On which one?"

A wave of anger splashed over him. He could not start with Lisa. "Villalobos."

"Easy. It looks like carbon monoxide poisoning."

"But you don't believe it?"

"I'd like to," Granger said. "And I would if BCI hadn't been so closed-mouthed to me. Hell, I'd have written it off to a couple of depressed lesbians distraught over their life if we hadn't just eaten at their place and they seemed fine." She slowed the bike. "My guts don't like it."

"Did the lab run an HIV test? Dorati thought if they were positive, it could be another motive for suicide."

"Always thinking, that boy," Granger mumbled. "But they weren't."

"So much for that," Holt said, wondering what Dorati had found at their house. He would wait to tell Susan about that until after he had the information. "What about the young William Gottig? Did you check out his mother with BCI?"

Susan Granger hit the timer on her running watch, and kept the speedometer on a cool-down pace. "You think it's his own mother?" She winked at him. "You are too jaded, Reverend Holt."

Lucas couldn't tell whether or not she was kidding. "Not jaded. Realistic. All she talked about at that dinner was her lousy money-grubbing son. She even said she wished he was dead." He pressed the buttons to increase speed. "Half mile to go."

"And you speed up?"

"Good finish," Holt said. "Like a fine wine."

"Like William Gottig. I'm afraid his death reeked of your dear friend the psychopathic killer, Mr. Dorati."

"You think Gottig was a hit?"

"It looks like it from where I sit."

Holt looked over at her. He liked where she sat but didn't say it. "He didn't fit the pattern," he said, under his breath.

Susan Granger scowled. "What did you say? What pattern?"

Lucas decided to trot it out in the open. He had thought it for a while. He would see how it looked in daylight. "The pattern of the murders."

"The Bertrands?"

"Not just the Bertrands, Susan," Holt said, panting as he

reached the end of his run. "You said yourself something else is going on here. I think all of these deaths are murders."

"I'll get back to you when you finish running, Lucas. The endorphins have obviously flooded your brain."

Lucas hit the five-mile mark and pushed the buttons to slow the machine to a walk. "No, listen to me. You think it, too. You just haven't put it all together."

"Lucas, the Villalobos women killed themselves, and, sorry as I am to say it, Al and Lisa did, too." She wiped her sweaty forehead on her shirtsleeve. "Gottig, on the other hand, was different. The others have been peaceful deaths, gently done, as though they were going to sleep."

"Maybe the murderer's a veterinarian," Holt said nastily.

"Except for Gottig," Granger said, ignoring him. "He was severely beaten—and slowly. They knew what to hit and where. The last thing to be ruptured were his spleen and liver, with a final blow to break his sternum and puncture his heart."

"No head trauma?" Lucas asked, knowing that meant a professional job.

"None. And no evidence of drugs. They wanted him as alert as possible. So I don't think his blue-haired mama offed him, not that she didn't pay somebody to do it."

"Scratch that, too. According to the last hit menu I saw, she doesn't have the kind of money to do it. Maybe the killer was trying to throw us off?"

"The only killer out there is the one who did the Bertrands, Lucas." Granger shook her head. "Unless—I don't know. Now you're making me paranoid." She slowed the bike to a halt just as Holt stopped the treadmill.

"Okay." He took a deep breath. "I feel like I can ask now."

"Lisa Enright?" Granger got off the bike and grabbed a towel for her face. "I glanced at the summary on my way here. Doc says it was street coke, shot up under their fingernails."

"The man's middle finger and the woman's ring finger?"

"I'm glad to see you acquired some useful knowledge at the penitentiary."

"But why would they OD now?"

"Beats hell out of me, Lucas. Maybe some bizarre sense of appropriateness? Live by the needle, die by the needle?"

Holt stepped off the treadmill. "Throw me a towel, will you?" He wiped the sweat off his face and looked puzzled.

"What is it?"

"Bear with me just a minute, Susan," he said. "I wonder if the deaths have been somehow—what was your word—*appropriate?*"

"The Bertrands were killed with wine and the Villalobos women suffocated," Granger said. "How are those appropriate?"

"Wine was the symbol of Erik and Janey's lifestyle. Isn't it interesting that it was also the means of their death?"

"Then Blanca and Serena Villalobos should have died of an enchilada overdose."

"No. Their slow suffocation had to do with being lesbian."

"This should be an interesting explanation."

"No, Susan. Listen. A lot of people see homosexuality as a sin that has slowly, insidiously infected the whole society."

"Like fumes pervading a car and killing its passengers."

"Exactly. And the way to end it is to contain it. Lock the doors and windows and shut off the horn. Quarantine it and let it die in its own poisonous atmosphere."

"I hate to admit it, Lucas, but that's not bad. Lisa and Al Enright fit right in there, given their past history of drug abuse. If you're right, somebody has a strong sense of irony."

"Or of punishment." Holt stepped off the treadmill. "Like Dante fitting eternal torments to earthly sins."

"Look, I still think you're wrong. It's an interesting idea, but there's absolutely no evidence of it in either case." Susan Granger stretched by the window. "But I'll look in the murder direction for you. And I'd appreciate it if you would keep me informed for a change if you and that Squad find anything."

"Done," Holt said, still noticeably troubled. He could not believe Al and Lisa killed themselves for any reason.

"Thanks for the treat to the Center," Granger said. "I'm going to the whirlpool and sauna and home."

"Shower and Vestry meeting for me." He thought about asking her to have dinner but remembered his rescheduled meeting with Kristen at seven—if she showed. "Listen." Lucas grabbed her elbow. "I, uh, may have a change of plans later and wondered if you might want to get something to eat?"

Granger smiled at him and shook her head. "Translated, that means if Kristen stands you up, I'm Plan B."

"That's the unreliable emended translation from the Greek. The original Aramaic reads: There's a shitload of stuff going on in my life, and I'd like to talk to a friend about it."

"How about you call me and if I'm hungry and not asleep or curled up with a good book or otherwise occupied with another caller—I'll consider it."

"Deal." Holt released her arm, then took it again. "How'd you get that scratch there? It's seeping blood."

"There's a rough spot on the handlebars on that one bike." She dabbed at it with her shirt. "And that reminds me"—she paused— "though I hesitate to tell you this because it supports your theory. There was blood on the carpet at Lisa Enright's house—and the cat was missing."

"Cat blood?"

"Don't know yet. If you're right and it was an intruder, let's hope the cat *drew* the blood before it vanished. We're running a DNA now. Should know in a day or so."

"Let me know," Holt said dejectedly, the despair setting in like the rain over Austin. He touched her hand. "This Lisa and Al thing was the last straw, Susan. Something stinks big time in these deaths, and I am by God or by God Squad going to find out what it is."

"Just don't go off on some holy tangent and get your runner's ass into a crack those cons can't get you out of." She swatted his butt. "I'd miss watching you run."

The two split to their separate dressing rooms. As Lucas Holt showered he was aware of hoping the Vestry meeting ended early and Kristen had to work late. He wondered if, on the other side of the wall, Susan Granger was hoping the same thing, or if she was deciding whether or not to answer the phone if it rang.

She was startled but not surprised when he called. She had earlier decided to skip dinner tonight and was just out of the bath when the phone intruded into her solitude. His persistence had won her over, though she insisted on meeting him rather than being picked up on the way.

Dinner had been unremarkable, save that he consumed more wine than usual and filled her glass repeatedly so that a second bottle of the Sauvignon Blanc was brought to the table—and finished after a lingering dessert.

Though at first she demurred, she let him talk her into stopping at his place for a nightcap. The crisp night, the fire softly burning in the fireplace, and the second glass had turned her expectant face to his.

Now, two hours later, Helen Pelham and Truman Reinhardt lay under black silk sheets in his king-size bed. The bright light of the nearly full moon shone through the floor-to-ceiling windows. He moved in his sleep and something damp touched her leg. She reached down to retrieve the spent condom and dropped it over the side of the bed. He had not wanted to use one. She had had to supply it and insist, playfully, that she could provide the extra attention needed to put it on.

Sex at this age was different; slower, but more passionate than even ten years ago in her fifties. He had turned out to be a good lover, and she had learned more about him in the last two hours than she had in the last two weeks of their acquaintance. He had slept, though not immediately. She had dozed, and now was about to get dressed and go to her own condo.

As she put one foot out from the sheets, she felt a hand on her breast. She turned and kissed him.

"Give me a minute in the bathroom," she whispered.

"Don't be long." Reinhardt touched her shoulder. "Do you have another?"

"In my purse."

"Bring it."

She returned from the bathroom and stopped suddenly at the window. "I could have sworn I saw someone out there."

"They're selling tickets to prove old people have sex. Come here right now."

She opened the package and threw back the sheets to find him ready for her attention.

He pushed up on one elbow, and she nudged him back down.

"I'll do the moving this time." Helen Pelham kissed his lips and his chest and ran her tongue around his navel and below. Her loose black hair and deep red lips contrasted with her white skin in the translucent moonlight. She hovered over him like a mask in the shadows.

They swayed and closed their eyes and did not see the figure of a woman outside the bedroom window peering in through angry tears. She knew she should leave but could not move her leaden feet till she had watched them end and fall asleep together. She pressed her bright red lips against the outside doorframe to make a perfect imprint he would never know was there.

The kiss of death.

She tossed her thick black hair from her face and vowed not to cry for him again.

Ever.

• Eight •

Lucas Holt stopped the car outside the back entrance to the church and sat behind the steering wheel, immobile. He imagined Maxine Blackwell looking up from her desk when she heard the engine quit. He thought it strange that she knew him better than anyone; knew his moods, his dreams, the strength of his integrity, and the depth of his weaknesses. He knew she would gauge his mood by the amount of time he took to exit the car and enter the church. If the engine stopped and the car door slammed immediately, he would throw open the church door, do his usual speed walk down the hall to his office, and greet her in a positive frame of mind. Variations on that standard baseline signaled moods ranging from high stress to depression. The longer the time, the worse the mood. He looked at his watch.

Ten. Eleven. Twelve. Slam.

Thirteen seconds. She would know the graveside had not gone well. The door opened and Lucas Holt paced slowly down the hall.

"Tough funeral?" Maxine came out to greet him.

"It sucked." He tossed his Prayer Book and stole on a chair and put his arms around her, letting her hold him. "And I've got Lisa and Al's to do in an hour." He closed his eyes and put his head on her shoulder. Her comforting embrace released his tears, as it had so many times before.

"Yep," Maxine replied, hugging him to her pillowlike bosom. "Just like Jesus said."

Lucas Holt lifted his head. "Jesus said 'It sucked'?"

Maxine frowned at him, her own eyes wet. She kissed him on the cheek. "If he didn't, he meant to."

The Rev grinned as she pulled tissues from the box on her

desk. This was why he wanted this woman around. She and the other God Squad members brought him back to earth.

"Blow your nose."

"Yes, ma'am." Holt did as ordered. "I love you, Max."

"Me too you, Rev." She returned to her chair and handed him a stack of pink slips. "And I hate to do this to you, but you better answer the one from Boom-Boom at the God Box."

Holt looked at the scribbled message. "The bishop called?"

"And he wasn't in a very good mood."

"How unusual. Maybe he found out about the insurance bequest. He only calls for bad news or money."

"He wanted to talk to you about lesbians in the church."

"Why?" Holt headed toward his office. "Is he thinking of becoming one?"

Maxine grabbed the pink slip from his hand. "On second thought, don't call him back. This will wait." She handed him a cup of tea. "Like a month."

"Thank you," the Rev said. Max was right. His anger at the deaths contaminated everything else. This was no time to mess with a bishop who wasn't fond of his style of ministry in the first place. "We ready for the funeral? Altar guild, organist?"

Maxine looked at her watch. "All set. T-minus forty-five and counting." She looked at him curiously. "I don't know how you're doing this, Rev. The Villalobos graveside this morning, now Al and Lisa's service in the church, and then you've got to do the weekly nursing home service with Cora Mae this afternoon?"

Holt nodded and put his hand on the doorknob. "Maybe I need something stronger than tea."

Maxine stopped him. "You'll find it behind that door." She whispered. "I forgot to mention your senior warden is here."

"Travis Layton's in my office?"

"Stopped by thirty minutes ago. I told him you were out at the graveside and you had another one and shouldn't be disturbed." She raised her hands in the air. "What can I say? He insisted on waiting, and I've already brought him two cups of rotgut coffee Ricardo made this morning. I know the old alky's spiking it with whiskey from his briefcase."

Holt tossed a tissue wad at her. "You're bad."

"No badder'n you." She grimaced as she picked it up between

two red pincer fingernails to drop it in the trash. "Shootin' your wad in the office."

The Rev scowled at her and opened the door. Travis Layton sat on the couch with his briefcase open on the coffee table.

"Shitdamn, boy," the old attorney said, looking at his watch. "I thought you'd never get here. I know you got another funeral to do—hell, I'm the layreader—but I wanted to show you this bid for the new roof before the Vestry meeting Sunday."

"Glad to see you, too, Travis."

The two shook hands and Holt caught the familiar smells of Bugler and Jack Daniel's. It reminded him of his father, just as everything else about Travis Layton reminded him of his father: the black pointed toe boots, the gray yoked western suit, the wiry white hair.

"You want some coffee? Or you just want a straight shot of Jack?" Layton offered his cup. "You look like you sure as hell could use something."

Holt got a glass from the tray on his desk and handed it to Layton. "Straight Jack. That graveside was gut-wrenching."

The lawyer poured from a silver flask. "Maybe this'll unwrench 'em long enough to get through the next one."

"Here's to you." Holt knocked back the shot. The bourbon burned his throat, distracting him momentarily.

"And to Maxine. Yeah, buddy, that's one hunk of woman out there." He squinted his eyes and grinned at the Rev. "Maybe you could help me with her. I know she hates my drinkin', but hell, everybody hates my drinkin'." He poured whiskey into his coffee. "Even I hate it. But a man's got to do something to cope with all the shit in his life. That's what I do. And before you get on me about it again, I'm seventy-two and not going to change."

"I had no idea you felt this way about Max."

"I didn't either, boy, till right now. Been thinkin' about her a long time, though. Ever since you brought her here. Before that, actually. I used to run into her and her girls at the courthouse in her jailin' years. Hell, maybe it's the whiskey talkin' or maybe I'm just gettin' old and thinkin' about all these damned funerals you're doin'."

Holt squinted one eye closed, partly in thought and partly in response to the whiskey. "Have you asked her out?"

"Got to be sober to do that, son. Maybe if I catch her of a

mornin', on a court day, when I have a client that's payin' me particularly well, and it ain't facin' a weekend."

The office door opened.

"What about next Wednesday, you old coot?" Maxine brought a fresh cup of hot tea to the Rev. "I'm off at five, so pick me up at seven and take me to dinner at the Paggi House."

A red faced Travis Layton stammered. "By God—I'll do it."

"I only have two conditions."

"Shitdamn. Forget it. I ain't stoppin' drinkin'."

"That's not one of them." She stepped over to him and brushed his cheek. "Course that could affect how lucky you get later. In the meantime, shave and put on a clean shirt."

"Hell, I'll buy a shirt."

"Good, then you'll have two." Maxine patted Lucas on the head as she left the room. "You boys have a good talk, now," she said seductively, and closed the door.

"God," Layton said, pouring more bourbon in his coffee. "I need a drink after that."

Lucas held out his glass. "So do I." He had never paired the two together, but there was symmetry about them. It was a pleasant thought in contrast to the rest of the day.

Layton looked at his watch and stood to leave. "I got to go get suited up and so do you." He handed him a manila envelope. "Read this roofing bid and let me know what you think."

"I've got something for you, too." Lucas pulled a letter from his coat pocket. "This is the part of the Villalobos will that establishes an endowment fund to help women start small businesses. They want St. Margaret's to administer it. Would you set it up? You'll need to be in touch with their attorney."

"Good people, them girls, even if they were lezzies. Interesting trend, though." Layton opened the door and hollered at Maxine. "Honey, would you call my office? I forgot to tell them I'm layreadin' this funeral."

She smiled and batted her eyes. "I'm not your honey, and you can call your own damned office."

Travis Layton closed the door and smiled. "I like a woman like that. Hell, they're used to my bein' late anyway."

Holt wanted him to finish his sentence. "You were going to tell me about some trend?"

"Right." The white-haired man finished his coffee, shut the briefcase, and continued. "At Rotary last week and three of us at the table had helped draw up wills that left a substantial portion to a certain foundation. Some weird-ass thing. Just a minute." He pulled his glasses from his vest pocket and glanced at his calendar, as Ben Holt would have done. "I wrote the damned thing down. Here it is. 'The Mandala Foundation.' "

Odd name, Holt thought. Sounded Indian, or Californian. "Out of where?"

He replaced the glasses and book and headed to the door. "It's out of, of all the damned places, Liechtenstein."

"Liechtenstein, as in the country? Why there?" And why was Layton telling him this? What triggered the thought? Was it something about the Villalobos estate?

"Because they have no rules governing the activities of such foundations coupled with the strictest confidentiality of anybody in the world."

"I thought the Swiss were known for that." The Rev opened a closet and removed an alb for the service.

"Son, these people make the Swiss look like blabbermouths."

Holt watched him leave the room and lean over Max's desk.

"I'll see you Wednesday, ma'am, if I make enough money between now and then to afford dinner at that place."

"You will." Max smiled. "Don't forget about the shirt."

"Hey, Travis." The Rev appeared with his alb half buttoned, hanging on one shoulder, as a question mark hung on his face. "About that foundation?" He would push Layton further. "Can you tell me who those people were that left money to it?"

Layton looked indignant. "Course not, boy. A lawyer's got to keep confidence." He turned to Max. "But, honey, their initials are Wilkins and Villalobos."

Holt dropped his alb. Marie Wilkins and the Villalobos family? These connections had to be more than coincidental. "Who was the third one? You said there were three."

"Did I?" Travis Layton screwed up his mouth to one side and thought. "Damned if I know. If I think of it later I'll tell you. Hurry up or you'll be late for this thing."

They watched him amble down the hall.

"Will he be all right to read?" Maxine said.

"He'll be fine." Holt grinned at her. "You surprise me a little more every day I know you. I had no idea—

"No idea what? You've known me twenty years, my dear, and you know what my basic philosophy is."

Indeed he did. It was one of many things he had learned from her. "Life is short? Go for the gusto? You only go around once? And the Nike ad."

"Just DO it?"

"Like Jesus said, Max."

"Jesus said, 'Just DO it'?"

"If he didn't, he meant to." Holt smiled.

"Get upstairs and give them a good funeral."

Lucas Holt stood at the altar facing the congregation. The first part of the Service for the Burial of the Dead was the hardest and it was over. He had slowly processed down the long aisle preceded by the crucifer and followed by two palled caskets. He had conducted the service gazing down on them, side by side, filling the entire aisle like sarcophagi in an ancient cathedral. He had stood in the pulpit and struggled to maintain his composure while talking about two people he had known well and even loved, lamenting the unfairness of their deaths as he affirmed the fragility of life.

Now, with Lavelle Davis serving as acolyte and chalice bearer, he prepared the altar for Communion. As she handed him the elements, her hand squeezed his for support. She looked like an African angel, smooth dark skin against the bleached white cotta and tight-fitting cassock. Her quiet presence and graceful manner calmed him as she slowly poured the water over his fingers and offered him the linen towel on her arm.

When he finished setting the table, he took a seat and waited for the anthem to be sung. The top two numbers from the Red Queen's Wild album were to be played by the Five Card Stud band with their backup singers.

Electric guitars bounced the steady country beat off the old wood-and-stained-glass building as Lucas Holt scanned the congregation. J. D. and Marlane Enright sat in the second pew, unmoved by the music, stoic as American Gothic. Strangely enough, he thought they looked more annoyed than sad. Holt knew they were angry that Alan and Lisa had made arrangements for cremation, a decision her parents thought un-Christian at best. They would really be pissed when he told them about the grand Albert had given the Rev to hold for a party for the God Squad if anything happened to them while they were on the road.

Alan Greer had no living relatives, but his family was here, Holt mused. The God Squad sat scattered through the congregation, like biblical leaven, and the Rev made eye contact with each of them. Dorati had his arm around Max, who winked and blew her nose. Cora Mae Hartwig's small frame was sandwiched between two stout women with hats, regular funeral-goers from the church who would undoubtedly be on the phone to the bishop about this vulgar musical display as soon as the service was over.

The Rev smirked. As they said at the pen: "TFB."

Omar Dewan had a red handkerchief wrapped around his hand and occasionally lifted it to his face. Lucas remembered the time Omar stepped into a fight to defend Alan. Two pews over from him was Frankie Colovas, looking like he wanted to hit something.

The band started the second song, a slow rendition of "Raise and Call," and the Rev's attention was drawn to a different group. Three rows over from J.D. and Marlane sat Señor and Señora Villalobos. Odd that, having not gone to their own children's service, they would come to this one. Lucas had been told by another family member this morning that the parents felt doubly disgraced by their lesbian daughters' suicides and refused to attend the only service the women had wanted—a simple graveside. Maybe this was the closest thing to the traditional church service they expected and needed to put their children to rest—a vicarious funeral.

On the other side of the aisle Garvin Davis had somehow left a vacant spot next to him on the far end of the pew. Strange that it was the seat formerly taken in years past by Marie Wilkins, as though she were sitting there now.

Holt barely heard the music end. They were all there, the living and the dead, what was called "the community of saints" or the "great cloud of witnesses." But witnesses to *what?* What was the connection between all of them? Why were they lumped together in his brain like Van Gogh faces screaming at him to get it?

But he didn't get it. Not all of it. Not yet, anyway. He did get the murder part, he thought, because neither the Villalobos women nor Lisa and Al would commit suicide. And he got the age issue; his own, his congregation's, the people out there staring at the altar. He needed more time to think. Like two lemons on a slot machine, his mind raced to find the third.

Distracted by his thoughts, it took Lavelle Davis clearing her throat to get his attention. Red-faced, he stood to continue the service. Twenty minutes later he had escorted the caskets back down the aisle and outside to the twin black pickup trucks in which the band would carry them to the crematory.

"Damned good service," Travis Layton said as they hung their vestments in the Sacristy. "I want a send-off like that one."

Before the Rev could respond, Lavelle Davis poked her head in the door. "See you, Lucas. You be careful, Mr. Layton."

"Sure thing, darlin'," Travis responded.

"Thanks for serving," Lucas said, going to her. "And thanks for the support." He kissed her cheek.

"Garvin told me what you said." She winked. "If things don't work out in Minneapolis, I'll call you."

Lucas watched her walk out through the chancel and hold her husband's hand as they left the church together.

"Nice couple, don't you think?" Holt said.

"Reminds me, Lucas," Travis Layton said. "That third person you asked about that left money to the Mandala Foundation?"

Like falling through a time warp, Holt's mind slammed back to their conversation before the funeral. "Yes?"

"It was Lavelle's daddy." He motioned through the door.

"Reverend Sparks?" Holt said absently, dizzy from the juxtaposition of events. He blinked and stared down the hall at Garvin and Lavelle Davis. "Really?" he said. But something had just happened. The third lemon appeared on his mind's slot machine and the payoff spewed into consciousness.

"You okay, Lucas? I know this has been a strain."

"No. I mean yes. I mean I don't know what I mean." He stared blankly out the Sacristy window at people getting into their cars, just as Nikky Dorati walked in.

"Yo, Rev. Good service."

Holt turned around and scowled. "Shit. That's it."

"What's it?" Dorati looked at the lawyer. "What happened?"

"Beat's hell out of me," Travis Layton said. "He got weird all of a sudden."

"How could you tell?"

"Shut up, both of you," Holt ordered. If what he thought was true, he had to confirm it before the next death. "Nikky, run down and get J. D. Enright before he gets into his car. Bring him to my office."

"And if he has other plans for the afternoon of his daughter's funeral, Rev?" Dorati said sarcastically.

Holt grabbed him by the shoulders. "Don't take no for an answer."

"In that case," Dorati said as he disappeared out the door, "Omar goes with me."

"What the hell are you doing, Lucas?"

"Giving orders." Holt tossed his stole in the closet. "And yours are to trace that foundation you told me about. I want everything you can get on it."

"Won't be much." Layton stroked his white five o'clock shadow as he left. "But I'll call you."

"Lucas, dear?" Cora Mae Hartwig met the Rev in the hallway. "What time are we leaving for the nursing home service?"

"Soon as you're finished setting up the altar for Sunday."

"Already done, Lucas."

The Rev looked past her at J. D. Enright coming down the hall with a God Squad escort.

"Then call and tell them we'll be late."

"Wait outside," Lucas Holt said to Nikky and Omar in his office. "Tell Max to take the afternoon off." He nodded to the two God Squad men. "This is a warden's talk."

Without speaking they left and closed the door, knowing to enter the office only if they heard the Rev in trouble. Any other noises were to be ignored, like an inmate going in to talk to the warden and coming out to the Infirmary.

"What the hell is this all about, Father Holt?" the baggy man said, standing with his hammy hands on his huge hips.

"Sit down, J.D.," the Rev said, his teeth clenched. "It's confession time." He would see what he could get voluntarily. Otherwise he'd use Warden's Rules.

"What?" Enright headed for the door. "You can't hold me here. You're full of shit doin' this at my daughter's funeral."

"Open the door and Dorati will put your fat ass in that chair. The only reason he's not here now is out of respect for Lisa and Al."

J.D. hesitated, then turned and sat.

"Better." Holt paced nervously behind his desk, glaring at the man. If what he thought was true, he would have to be very careful in eliciting the information, or there would be no evidence to present to Lieutenant Granger. "I'm going to ask you some questions, J.D., and I want the right answers the first time. You got that? Because the second time they will be asked by Mr. Dorati, with sound effects."

The man glared back, surly. "You can't do this, Father Holt. You ain't the cops. You got no right. This is America. I got a right to a lawyer."

Holt exploded inside. He strode over to Enright and got in his face. His slow, even tone telegraphed volcanic emotion ready to erupt. "Listen to me, J.D.," Holt said through tightened lips. "I hate greed. I despise unfairness. And right now you smell like a shitload of both to me."

"I don't know what you're talkin' about." The big man pushed himself back in the chair, away from the Rev.

"Sure you do, J.D. You want to tell me how Alan and Lisa had no right to a lawyer, either, how they died with you playing cop and judge and executioner?" Holt pulled back and stood. "You make me want to puke."

Enright snorted. "You're the one that's off here, Father." He started to push up from his seat. "I ain't done nothin' and you can't prove otherwise."

The Rev wanted more than anything to kick the man back into the chair. "You sure about that? What if I know otherwise?"

J.D. stopped. "What are you talkin' about?"

Holt backed away, feeling like he had the upper hand. He looked out the window. "You first. Then I'll answer questions."

"Like what?"

"Let's start with an easy one. Where did Marlane go?"

J.D. frowned and stood. "None of your damned business."

"Nikky!"

Dorati plunged through the door, his hand under his coat.

"I think this man had something to do with Lisa and Al's death," he announced to Dorati.

"No shit?" Nikky frowned, and moved in front of the man to block his movement.

"No shit." Holt nodded. "I would like you to ask Mr. Enright where his wife is. Ask him like Warden O'Neil would."

In one swift move Nikky stuck the barrel of his chrome .38 against J.D.'s nose. "Where's the little lady?"

"Buck chew," Enright mumbled, unable to breathe.

Dorati rammed a hard left deep into Enright's gut, collapsing him into the chair.

The big man sputtered out an answer.

"He said she went home to take her medicine," Dorati announced.

"Buck chew," Enright snarled again.

" 'Buck chew'?" Dorati repeated, his eyes wide. "The man says 'Buck chew'?" He grabbed J.D. by the hair and pulled his head back over the chair, leaning an elbow into his throat. "Listen, mofo. You seem to need a program here. The next blow breaks your nose. The one after that is your jaw, and the third ruptures your spleen. You won't be able to count to four. Now stuff the 'buck chew' and answer the man."

"Okay. Okay," Enright choked.

Holt nodded and Dorati backed off. "I'll be outside, Rev."

Lucas waited until the door was closed. "The second question has to do with you and Lisa. Dorati told me about your conversation at Gruene. Did you mean that or was it bullshit?"

"Bull." He coughed. "Bullshit."

"So you and Marlane, correct me if I'm wrong about this, the two of you still hated Lisa and Alan, blamed them for your problems, despised them for your ending up in that residence instead of your own house?"

J. D. Enright blew his nose into a rumpled handkerchief. "Right," he finally said, catching his breath. He sat back in the chair and stared at Holt. "The little shits—I'm glad they're dead. Marlane and me had a good life before Lisa come along. Oh, she was sweet as a little kid, but then she got wild, went boy crazy and drug crazy, did the opposite of everything we said. But she still expected us to bail her out of all the trouble she got into. Well, hell, her mother fell for it every time and spent all our savings."

"And you figured out a way to get it all back."

The big man looked at the floor.

"Let me put that in the form of a question, J.D.," the Rev said, staying behind his desk for fear of leaping on the man himself. "Did you figure out a way to get all your money back?"

Enright swallowed hard. "My wife and I was raised Catholics, you know."

"This has a point?" Holt said, though he knew what it was.

"Yeah, it does. And you, you're sorta like a priest, right? So if I say anything in here and it's like a confession, you can't tell it, right?"

Check and checkmate, the Rev thought. J.D. knew damned well it was right. If the man invoked the seal of the confessional, Lucas Holt could not reveal the content of the priest-penitent conversation. Unless, of course, Holt thought he wasn't really being penitent but coercive, flaunting the sanctity of the sacrament as a shield for heinous crimes. In that case, the Rev would have a decision to make. "I'm listening," Holt said.

"Then this is confession and I want absolution when I'm done."

"Right." Holt took a deep breath. Maybe he'd have Dorati administer it. "Did you find a way to make back the money?"

"Yes," Enright said darkly.

Lucas stared into his eyes. "What was it?"

J. D. Enright composed himself and sat straight up. "I can't tell you that much even in confession, Father Holt," he said. "Honest to God, I can't. You can bring that guy in and beat me to a pulp, but it won't be nothin' to what will happen if I tell. My wife, Marlane, is already having second thoughts about what we did. She left here talking about killing herself. It would be easy to do, she's on so much medication for her diabetes."

The Rev leaned against the desk, rage and pity vying within him, as Enright's voice changed to a whiny pitch.

"I admit it was my idea and I talked her into it when I found out what to do. Shit, Father, those kids took all our money and stuffed it up their damned nose or shot it in their arms. Now they were doing better, but there was nothing to say they wouldn't go back again when they hit the road. We had to act while we still could. The idea was presented to us and we bought it. I confess to you that I had a hand in their deaths and right at this very moment I feel sorry as hell about it."

"You're not very convincing," the Rev muttered.

"You didn't live it, Father. You didn't see everything you

worked for your whole life wasted, thrown away like slop to hogs. I said I'm sorry I did it and I want absolution for it."

"My God, Enright," Holt shot back at him, "she was your daughter—he was her husband."

The big man looked up at him. "It's worse than that, Father." His demeanor softened, weakened. "There's one thing that makes me sorry for Marlane."

Holt looked puzzled. "What?"

"I said it's worse than that." He took a deep breath and continued. "Before we left home today for the funeral, we got a call from the coroner." He mumbled something into his hand.

The Rev stood and leaned closer. "I didn't hear you."

"I'm sorry," J.D. repeated, a hint of dampness in his eyes. "It's hard to say it." He paused and the Rev tried to think of the worst possibility. "Lisa, well . . ." J.D. looked away and blurted it out: "They said she was pregnant." Quickly he added: "Now we didn't know nothin' about that or of course we wouldn't have gone through with what we did."

Lucas Holt sat in his own chair behind the desk, teetering between fury and despair. He didn't know whether to call in Dorati or simply bash the man in the face with a paperweight and finish it. He was caught between the duty of his office and his feelings of wanting to kill the bastard. Ultimately he had to trust that God would work it out, though Holt desperately wanted to have a literal hand in it right now.

"I know we done an awful thing, Father, but the good Lord forgives all sinners, don't he?"

The Rev walked around to the front of the desk, a few feet in front of the man. "Too cheap, J.D."

"Huh?"

"I said, God's easy but not cheap."

"What the hell's that mean? Do I get absolution or not?"

The Rev lowered his voice and clenched his fists. "I'd like to absolve your ass right into the carpet, J.D., but as a priest I have to tell you God forgives you, even if I don't. Personally, I hope your fat ass fries in hell." He held his fist out to the man's face, as if to strike him. Unclenching it, he made the sign of the cross. "Having confessed your sin and repented, I pronounce that you are forgiven in the name of the Father, the Son, and the Holy Spirit. Amen."

"Amen." J. D. Enright stood from the chair, and the Rev knocked him back down.

"Not yet, asshole."

The man looked up at him, stunned. "You ain't like no priest I ever saw."

"Shut up and listen." Holt backed away to keep out of striking distance—his own. He turned and folded his arms across his chest. "You've asked for and received absolution for your actions. Done. But now you've got two options."

"About what?" Enright said smugly. "You don't know what exactly we done, and the part you do know you can't tell nobody."

Holt ignored him. "Your two options are these: You can go home and turn yourselves in to the police."

"Right, sure thing."

"Or my friends and I can come looking for you."

J. D. Enright hesitantly pushed his huge frame up from the chair. "You don't know how I feel about this, Father," he said angrily. "You think you do but you don't. It was one thing for Lisa and that scumball husband of hers to die." He hitched up his sagging pants to his waist. "But it's another damned thing to kill Marlane's grandbaby." He walked to the office door. "So there's a third option, Father. And that's the one I aim to do."

"I never pictured you for suicide, Enright."

"Who the hell's talkin' suicide?" He opened the door and turned around. "I'm gonna take care of a certain party before the police or you find out any more about it."

"Enough people have died, J.D."

"Not hardly," the big man replied. "Not hardly at all."

Omar Dewan stood in the opening. Holt blinked to let him through. "One more question before you go, J.D.," the Rev said. "Does the Mandala Foundation have anything to do with this?"

Enright looked startled, but walked away.

Holt nodded. Dorati smashed the gun across the man's face.

Blood gushed from J.D.'s nose and mouth, and he wiped it on the sleeve of his jacket. "Buck chew," he mumbled.

Dorati reared back, but Lucas shook his head to stop. "Let him go. He's his own worst punishment."

"This ain't over yet, Father," Enright replied, glaring at Holt. "You ain't so safe either, collar or no collar."

"None of us are, J.D.," Holt said solemnly, waving at an anxious Nikky Dorati to back off.

When the door closed at the end of the corridor, Omar Dewan looked at the Rev. "You want us to watch him?"

"No, he's not going to stray far from a wife who needs her medication. Not right away, anyway." The Rev walked back in his office and pulled a card from his desk with an address on it. He was back on the comment Travis Layton had made in the sacristy. "But I do want you and somebody else to stake out the Davis house up on Mount Bonnell. This address."

"You think somethin's gonna happen to them?" Dorati said.

That was exactly what he thought. He was certain of it.

"What are we looking for?" Dewan asked.

"Prowlers," Holt replied.

"And if we see any?"

"Stop them," the Rev said. "Any way you can."

The small electric organ in the Westbank Retirement Center chapel spewed cotton candy hymns as the residents walked, rolled, and shuffled to their seats. Lucas Holt and Cora Mae Hartwig had arrived late, but in time for him to take his place in the front as the guest preacher. Cora Mae was to introduce him but had not entered the chapel yet. The Rev had sent her on a mission that would determine how much of a suspect old Reverend Sparks really was, now that Travis Layton provided a connection between him and the missing Marie Wilkins and the old Villalobos couple. It would be impossible to interview them the way he had done J. D. Enright. With any luck he wouldn't have to.

The organ swayed from "Rock of Ages" to "How Great Thou Art," the favorite hymn of nursing homes and funeral homes, which Holt thought were remarkably interchangeable. He remembered one funeral, looking at the corpse's nose while this hymn was played, thinking the title appropriate—How Great The Wart.

He looked over the gathering crowd of people dressed in their Sunday finest, some frail and some hearty people who had taken hours to get ready. It was no small task to bathe, shave, or put on makeup and get your hair right, force your stiff limbs into uncooperative clothes, and make your body go the distance from your room to the chapel with a walker, wheelchair, cane, or entirely on

its own. Lucas could see the satisfaction in their faces as they
completed their journey and plopped down in one of the well-
padded folding chairs.

Most were fully mobile, though many leaned on friends for stability. Some showed telltale shaking of Parkinson's, others the
rigidity of strokes, and a few the wig or bandanna badges of cancer. Holt was surprised to see how many wore the thin wire band
around a wrist or ankle. "Elopement risks" they were called, as
though they were going to run off and get married.

He scanned the wrinkled faces borne of lifetimes of deep joy
and profound sadness. Scratch below the proud surface of anyone
there, and you would find family stories of birth, death, marriage,
divorce, war, economic hardship, heroic strength in the face of
debility, terror in the face of ultimate loneliness. There were lives
well lived and lives of regret and sorrow, all etched indelibly into
the creases of their eyes and cheeks.

They were all here for their version of church, to hear familiar
hymns and scriptures that would remind them that, whatever their
disability, whatever their past mistakes, whatever their families
thought about them, there was a loving Jesus who would rock
them in his bosom as they marched to Zion beneath the old
rugged cross in the garden alone when they gathered at the river
to be washed in the blood of the lamb. The Latin term *religio*
meant "to bind," and it bound them to their history and to the
greater history of something larger, outside themselves, universal,
transcendent beyond their present situation.

The Rev heard the strains of "Holy Spirit Breathe On Me"
quiver from the organ. He wondered what his generation would do
for church when they sat in these chapel seats? The pastoral im-
ages of hymn and scripture were anachronistic in an age of high
technology. The metaphors were timeless, but there would have to
be new theology to address modern events more directly, or his
generation and their children would simply not be interested.

Children, he remembered. How many of these people hated
their children like the Enrights hated theirs? How many of these
old people were abused by their kids, humiliated like the elder Villalobos couple? How many of their grown kids visited or wrote?

Maybe children started out as a distraction to focus you not on
your own inevitable decline, but on their inevitable growth and

blossoming, something to put the balance back in perspective. Life goes on, even if it's not yours. But what if relationships turned sour, were tainted by greed, abuse, or neglect? Could you come to hate your offspring, detest them beyond all reasoning?

Mesmerized by his inner thoughts, the Rev blinked to see Cora Mae Hartwig sit down beside him.

"I love this place," she whispered. "You get the best jokes here."

"Don't tell me now, I've got to do this service. The organist is on the last song."

"I have to tell you this one."

"No. Tell me what you found out first."

"I couldn't get any info from the nurse on the unit. We had a small run-in before, and she didn't want to see me, much less tell me about specific dates. We'll have to see our friend Mr. Graves as soon as we're through. He's coming to the service." She rolled her eyes. "Can you believe they let a man with that name run a nursing home? It gives me chills."

"Last verse. Get ready."

Cora Mae leaned closer as if to ask him something about the service. "So this doctor says, 'I've got two really bad things to tell you.' And the guy says, 'What are they?' And the doc says, 'Well, first, you've got really bad cancer.' 'Good heavens,' the guy says. 'What's the second thing?' 'The second thing is you've got Alzheimer's.' 'What a relief,' the guy says. 'At least I don't have cancer.'"

The hymn abruptly ended. Lucas stifled his laughter with a cough, and Cora Mae stood up to the podium to announce the hymn: "I Was Sinking Deep in Sin."

"You certainly are," he muttered.

An hour later they sat in the well-furnished office of the administrator of the Westlake Retirement Center.

"I cannot believe you are asking me for this kind of personal information about the reverend," Graves said from behind his desk. He sounded a little too outraged to Lucas Holt. "I told you the last time, we value highly the privacy of our people." The lanky man eyed the box of cigarettes on his desk.

"I do understand that, Mr. Graves," Holt replied. The man was calculating, watched his words, avoided eye contact. "And this may be a wild-goose chase. On the other hand, if it's possible, we would like to know if your nursing chart shows anything unusual for Reverend Sparks on the nights in question."

Cora Mae Hartwig responded. "I asked the nurse and the aid on his unit, who both said there was no record that he had been checked on. But they swore Sparks was here all night because either the nurse or the security guard would have known."

"That much I am certain is correct," Graves said, intertwining his fingers as though he had a cigarette in them.

The more Graves protested the obvious, the more it looked like he had something to hide. The Rev sat forward on his chair. He couldn't tell if this man was just an obstinate asshole or if he really was somehow trying to withhold information. In either case it was time to pull out the stops, as he and Cora Mae had discussed on the way over. "Reverend Sparks had a mandatory bracelet monitor while he was here, did he not?"

"I'm not sure," Graves said nonchalantly.

"Can you look it up?" Holt requested in a stern tone.

The administrator sighed as though to do so would mean lifting a thousand-pound weight. He scanned a sheet hidden inside his top desk drawer. "Yes, as a matter of fact he did."

"So you could check the electronic record to see if he wandered out of any of the exits, could you not?"

"That is technically possible." He balked and shook his head. "But I'm sure you can understand the privacy issues."

At a glance from the Rev, Cora Mae Hartwig took a cassette from her purse. "And it is technically possible for me to drop this tape of my conversation with your less-than-friendly staff to the Department of Human Services Review Board, is it not?" Cora Mae spoke without smiling. "And perhaps to the *American-Statesman* for the front page tomorrow?"

Got him by the short hairs, Holt thought. "She's a very tenacious person, Mr. Graves. I'd take her seriously."

"What is this? I don't know that there's anything on that tape." He stood behind the desk as a signal for them to leave. "I think this interview is concluded."

Holt remained seated. It was gratifying to see the man flustered. Flustered people made mistakes. "If Sparks wasn't here on those nights, your facility could be named as a negligent accomplice in any lawsuits that might be filed." He nodded toward Cora

Mae. "I've listened to that tape. If it's played in court or on the news, this place will be empty tomorrow."

Jason Graves sat down and scowled. "This is blackmail. I won't let you get away with this."

"Calm down, sonny," Cora Mae replied. "And get that electronic record, or we stop at the *Statesman* on our way home."

"Shit," Graves mumbled as he pulled a printout from a stack on the file cabinet. "This is the time period you want." He tossed it on his desk. "Look for yourselves. I didn't see you. We're only supposed to give them to the police with a warrant."

The Rev and Cora Mae scanned the sheets.

"We'll have to take this with us—or run us a copy now."

"Why?" Graves came around the desk to look.

"Because"—Holt pointed to the green paper—"contrary to your staff, Sparks left by the rear doors on the dates of the deaths—and returned around five in the morning each time."

"But the aide and security guard would have seen this and reported it," Graves protested.

"Not if they were playing Hide the Salami in an empty room," Cora Mae commented.

Holt glanced at her and wondered where she got the phrase. He also wondered where Sparks had spent the nights he had escaped from the Center. If he was as demented as everyone said, there was no way he could have caused the deaths. But what if dementia was a cover? Or the setup for an insanity defense?

Cora Mae continued. "They probably thought the residents were drugged out for the night. Sparks tongued his pills and waited for the staff to disappear so he could." Cora Mae sat back down. "Maybe you've got the bands on the wrong people."

Jason Graves picked up the phone. "Get the Tulip Wing staff to my office immediately." He slammed down the receiver and grabbed the printout. His tone became deeply formal. "I will address the situation with my staff immediately, and there will be no further incidents of this type." Graves stood and opened the door with his hand out to Cora Mae. "Thank you for stopping by. May I have that little item now?"

"Thank you for your kind cooperation," Cora Mae Hartwig said unctuously as she dropped the tape in his hand on her way out.

"Come back soon, Reverend Holt. The residents always enjoy

your meddling—I mean message." The man turned beet red. "Good evening." He slammed the door behind them.

As they left the building, Cora Mae and Lucas heard yelling from the administrator's office.

"Certainly stirred that pot, didn't we, dear?" Cora Mae said as they got into his car.

"Needed stirring. And Susan will be interested in the info on Sparks. It doesn't mean he did anything, really. Just means he happened to be out for a midnight walk on the nights when all the deaths happened."

"Purely circumstantial, Lucas," Cora Mae responded. "But it does make things interesting." She looked out the window. "I'd be more worried about Graves. He must figure into this somehow."

"What if Graves used old Reverend Sparks in some way?"

Cora Mae shook her head. "Hard to believe Sparks could be made to do anything. He was recalcitrant when he was sane, and now that he's sort of in and out of reality, he couldn't take an order if you taped it for him."

The Rev heard her snicker. "What's that about?"

Cora Mae smiled in the darkness. "I was just thinking about Mr. Graves." She giggled. "I hope he likes the tape. It's a copy of my compact disc recording of the Bee Gees. I wouldn't take anything so valuable as the real tape out of my house, you know. Indeed not. It's well hidden there. But it will find its way to the appropriate people."

"You've been around Dorati too long."

Minutes later Holt pulled up in front of her Meadow Mountain condo.

"Good night, Lucas. Sleep tight."

He watched until she got inside and flashed the porch light, her signal that all was well.

He'd like to sleep tight, he thought. He'd like to sleep tightly wound around somebody who was in for the same long haul as the people at the retirement Center. As he pulled the car back onto the main road, the gallery of faces from the chapel flashed before him. But as he drove in the darkness, he saw interspersed the faces of the Bertrands, the Villaloboses, and Al and Lisa. The young dead among the old living. There was more to figure out than met the immobile eyes of those who stared at him. He suddenly felt the need to talk to Nikky. But first he had to see Kristen Wade.

• Nine •

Cora Mae Hartwig glanced at the kitchen clock as she poured steaming water into the china teapot she had gotten on a trip to England. She had to make the call at exactly seven minutes past eight or the window would close for twenty-four hours.

She put the pot on a tray and arranged her homemade sugar cookies on a plate beside it. Picking up a blanket and portable phone, she made two trips to the porch overlooking the greenbelt. The blanket would take the chill off the cool evening as the sun faded behind the gray clouds in the west, and the phone would be at hand when her digital watch turned to eight-zero-seven.

This was her second favorite time of day. The first was the early morning, when she sat out here in her nightgown and robe with hot tea, cinnamon toast, and the morning paper, listening to the sound of the birds and animals beginning to stir. The evening was what she called her relaxing time, when she imagined the same critters found safe haven for a cozy night, as she did. But tonight was not relaxing, she thought as she took the piece of paper from her sweater pocket. She sat in the padded porch chair and held the tea to her lips. Steam funneled into the air, obscuring her view. It was then that she heard the sound.

Having lived alone her entire life, not much frightened her anymore, but she had taken precautions should someone mistake her for a vulnerable old person. She glanced at the green light on the wall speaker. The voice-activated security system was on, programmed to her own tonal pattern, and would call 911 whenever she told it to. The jalapeño spray was accessible under the cloth that protected the cookies from stray insects.

As she seemed to reach for a cookie, she palmed the spray container, brought it to her lap, and held it while she raised the cup with her other hand. She was accustomed to the evening sounds of the greenbelt, and the snap of the twig beneath her porch was not one of them. With her feet propped on another chair and covered by the afghan, she could not see the two grimy hands reach up for the bottom of the railing. And she could not see them let go when she suddenly spoke.

"Cora Mae Hartwig," she said out loud, "lighten up! This phone call has got you spooked." She checked her watch. Five minutes to go. "Let's figure this out."

She opened the piece of paper she had retrieved from Marie Wilkins's room and looked at the numbers: 2110223102432103. It could have been almost anything: security code, bank account, computer password, plane ticket, hotel reservation. She smiled for a moment, remembering when they had established their contact system. As little girls, they planned that if either ran away from home the other would be able to find her. For as long as she could remember each had had an envelope taped under her second dresser drawer with a series of numbers on a slip of paper. As kids, the numbers were updated almost weekly; later they joked about changing them every New Year's day as they decided where to run away that year.

But this was no joke. Marie had done it. And now Cora Mae was going to call her. She remembered the code as if they had invented it yesterday. As girls they had made it simple so they wouldn't forget it in their old age. Delete the first and last numbers. Double every other digit and read backward.

She rewrote the numbers and, with thirty seconds to go, punched in the digits. At exactly seven minutes past eight the ringing stopped.

A cautious voice answered: "Cora?"

"Marie?" Cora Mae sat up in her chair. "Is that you?"

"Yes, Cora." The voice was relieved. "I knew you'd call."

"What happened?" Cora Mae asked in her most concerned tone. The connection sounded ominously scratchy, somewhere modern communications weren't so modern. "Where are you?"

"I'm far away where I can't be found. That's the reason for the bad connection."

Cora Mae did not like the tone of this conversation. It sounded as if they would never see each other again. "How can I help you, dear? Can I come get you?"

"No, Cora." The voice faltered, holding back tears. "Believe me, I wish you could. I wish we were girls again and you could join me at my grandmother's house and we could eat sugar cookies and milk. But those days are gone forever."

"But why?" Cora Mae asked, her heart beating wildly. Her friend sounded so alone, so sad. "Why did you leave?"

Marie's voice lowered. "I'm afraid I've done a terrible, terrible thing. So bad I'm certain I'll go to hell for it."

Instinctively Cora Mae looked around. "Are you sure you should tell me this on the phone?"

"Yes. It's all right. I'm moving from this number tomorrow, and I'll be unreachable then."

"But, Marie! How will I get in touch with you?"

"You won't, Cora." Marie Wilkins could not control her tears. "This is our last conversation." She wept.

Cora Mae Hartwig slumped in her seat, as if she had been punched in the stomach. "No, Marie!" She recovered her breath to ask the obvious question. "What have you done?"

Marie Wilkins tried to compose herself to speak. "Oh, I don't know why I did it, why I agreed to it. I feel like I got talked into it, but no jury in the world would believe that, given what I got out of it."

This wasn't making sense, even for Marie, the woman Cora Mae had supported through numerous crises and broken hearts. "What are you talking about, Marie? The last I heard, your beau was going to sweep you off to some exotic place."

"He swept me off, all right. *Brushed* me off is more like it. He swore he'd go away with me if I did what he said, did what—what I actually had wanted to do for a long, long time, God help me. You know how easily I've been duped by men all my life."

Cora Mae nodded at the truth, though this was not the time to say it. "Now, Marie—"

"No, we both know how I am. You've always been the sane one where men were concerned. But this time, Cora, this time is the worst. And there's no one to blame but myself."

Cora Mae leaned forward in the chair. "Perhaps you'd better tell me the whole story."

"I can't tell you much, certainly not names. I am okay but I won't be coming back, so I want you to have everything in my room at the Center. We have a lot of common memories in there, I know. Keep what you want and dispose of the rest. I've sent you legal papers to show to that horrible Jason Graves."

Cora Mae remembered her difficult encounters with the man. "Did he have anything to do with this, Marie?"

"I can't say, Cora. I can't stay on the line much longer. Just know that I'll be fine and I have enough money to last the rest of what may be a very short life, after what I've done."

Cora Mae's eyes filled with tears. "Don't talk like that, Marie. There must be something I can do."

"What I want you to do is to remember me and to remember that I love you, Cora," the trembling voice on the phone said. "You've been closer to me than a sister all my life."

This couldn't be happening! Marie was fading from her life at the end of a phone call. Like the sun fading from view in front of her, a darkness began to close in around Cora Mae. "Marie, you've got to let me help you!" she cried.

"The only way you can help me is to ask God to forgive me for what I did." The voice changed to anger. "Because, to tell you the truth, Cora, I feel bad but not all that bad about it. Take it all around, it was the right thing to do. The boy was selfish and ungrateful all his mean, irresponsible life, and he made me suffer miserably for it. Now I can live my remaining years in peace with every luxury he denied me."

Cora Mae's mind was spinning. Too much was happening. She blinked her disbelieving eyes and looked out at the final rays of the sunset. "Are you saying what I think you're saying, Marie?"

"Yes, Cora," Marie blurted. "I am responsible for Erik and Janey's deaths."

"What?" Cora Mae gasped. This was impossible! "How could that be? You were nowhere near them when they died. You were at the Center, weren't you?"

"If I answer your questions, I may be the cause of your own death, Cora, and I could never bear that burden." Marie Wilkins paused. "I will tell you I paid, and paid dearly, to have it done. Now I must go, Cora." She openly wept, saying good-bye.

"No, don't hang up yet, Marie." Cora Mae wept with her.

"Good-bye, Cora. And thank you. Thank you for being my life-long friend."

The line went dead.

Cora Mae clicked off the phone and wiped the tears from her face. She stared at the darkness that had overcome the sky, and tried to steady the teacup in her hand. A sudden shiver shook her body as if someone had grabbed her by the shoulders. This cold could not be warmed by her afghan; it made her heart ache and her soul mourn for the loss of her friend, a loss worse than death because she would never know what happened to her.

Night had crept over the greenbelt and engulfed the porch when she decided to go inside. She would need to call Lucas Holt right away, and Nikky Dorati, too. Together they would figure out what this meant and what to do about it. She stood and heard a rustling sound in the brush below her—and felt a strong hand grasp her ankle.

She screamed and grabbed the spray, but knocked it to the floor. She grasped the teapot and was about to bring it down on the head of her assailant when she heard her name being called.

"Miss Hartwig! Don't yell! It's *me,* Miss Hartwig."

Cora Mae gasped and tried to think. She had already had one shock. This second one pushed her from grief to fury. She held the teapot ready as she bent over to get the jalapeño spray.

"Who the hell are you?"

"It's *me,* Miss Hartwig! Eddie Shelton!"

"My dear man, you scared the living crap out of me!" She put the teapot down. "I should brain you here and now to teach you not to creep up on old ladies."

"I'm sorry, Miss Hartwig," he said, climbing over the railing. "I'm really sorry."

"And well you should be, young man." She took a deep breath and held her hand over her palpitating heart. She put the teapot down. "Haven't you ever heard of knocking at the front door?"

"I couldn't get around to that side of the condos, Miss Hartwig. And I gotta talk to Nikky, fast. I was followin' old man Sparks for the Rev when these guys, well they got hold of me in a tight situation, and once they got done grillin' me, they dumped me in the country and I had to hitchhike back this direction. I ended up at the greenbelt and I knew your place was on the other side. You're

the closest phone. I'm really sorry. I didn't mean to scare you. It
was dark and I was trying to get to the railing to yell up to you."

Cora Mae was starting to think straight again. Though still
shaken from the talk with Marie Wilkins, things were clearer and
she suddenly realized she was cold. "Help me gather up these
dishes and come inside, Eddie. We'll have something to drink and
make our phone calls." She led him into the kitchen. "A nice
blackberry brandy should warm us up."

Eddie made a sour face. "First I gotta get Nikky."

Cora Mae handed him the phone. "Punch star six."

Shelton raised his eyebrows and auto-dialed Nikky Dorati.

"Yo, Nikky? This is me, Eddie. We gotta talk with the Rev,
man. And soon, too." Shelton did not wait for Dorati to reply.
"I'm at Cora Mae's and it's too long a story to tell you on the
phone, so don't ask. But you know that No Legs guy in the
wheelchair? That Tomas Perez?" He looked at Cora Mae as if to
tell her and Nikky at the same time. "He's about as crippled as
those ponies he bet on all day."

Cora Mae took the phone. "Nikky, dear? I talked with Marie
Wilkins." She paused. "No, I talked with her from the grave." She
rolled her sparkling blue eyes at Eddie. "Of course she's alive,
Nicholas. But I don't know where she is. I thought we might have
a chat about that. In the meantime Eddie and I are on our way to
pick you up. While you're waiting, call Lucas and tell him to
meet us all downtown. Where would you recommend? Yes, the
Buffalo Barn Grille will be fine." She hung up the phone.

Eddie Shelton poured two blackberry brandies as Cora Mae
held up three fingers. "Whoever is behind this, Eddie?" Her eyes
again watered. "I want them bad."

Eddie Shelton clicked her glass. "We all do, Miss Hartwig."

Cora Mae emptied the glass and grabbed her keys. "Then let's
go get them."

It was nine-thirty when Lucas Holt punched the security code
on the keypad at Las Ventanas. As he waited for the huge metal
gate to swing open, he felt like it was a lot later. Three services,
the encounter with J. D. Enright, and the revelation that Lisa had
been pregnant left him staring at the car clock totally exhausted.
The only thing that had helped was the eight-mile run around the

lake, and that was difficult without his headset. He had missed the distraction of the music, especially tonight. He hoped Max had remembered to drop it off on her way home.

He punched the keypad again, as he punched elevator buttons repeatedly. He felt depleted and impatient and if the damned gate didn't hurry he would run straight through the stupid thing. No anger here, he thought as he drove through the narrow opening. No anger at the senseless deaths, the helplessness he felt in response to them, though he was beginning to put together a picture of how it worked. Right now, all he wanted was a cold glass of wine and a hot shower in Kristen's stadium of a bathroom. Then, after pleasantries about how each other's day went, he wanted a companion in bed. Other than Aspen.

Sex was not the issue. Another body was. It was the snuggling he wanted, the comfort of bumping butts in the middle of the night, the extra kiss when returning from the three A.M. bathroom call.

He turned on her street and relaxed when he saw the lights in the living room. Then the den went dark and he remembered the timers. Her car was not in the driveway, and he found himself hoping it would be in the garage when he pressed the opener.

The empty garage reflected the hollowness he felt tonight, the void he wanted to fill with her presence, her smell, her touch. He drove inside and pressed the button again. Holt always parked in the garage to avoid gossip in what was, for all of its sophistication, still a small town; and to avoid photographers in what was, above all, a town of tough Texas politics. The slamming car door and his preoccupation covered the sound of the phone buzzing on the dashboard.

Aspen growled and barked at him as he entered the kitchen and turned off the alarm system. He knelt down to ruffle her ears, and she licked his face as her nervous motor slapped her palmlike tail against everything in a two-foot radius. She watched him fix her a bowl of food and fresh water. He let her sniff the food before leading her to the front door.

"Go do your worst, Aspen girl. Just come back or your mother will kill me if she ever notices you're gone."

He ascended the stairs to the master bedroom. He turned on the shower, and the steaming water splashed on his cold skin, washing off the physical and emotional debris of the day. But as the outer layer vanished, his deeper feelings surfaced. Tears of loss and anger melted into the spray of water; loneliness washed over him like waves crashing on the shore of his soul.

In the din of the shower the ringing phone went unnoticed. No message was left, but another call came just as he finished. He grabbed a towel on the way to the phone. Dripping in the doorway, he heard the end of Kristen's message.

"—should be there in about half an hour or so. Bye."

Leaving a sluglike trail, he made his way back to the bathroom and put on the terrycloth robe that hung on the back of the door. Combing his hair, the Rev saw in the clearing mirror the initials monogrammed on the pocket of the robe. If she ever dumped him she could only date men with the initials L.H."

He heard Aspen bark outside.

Not entirely alone, he thought as he descended the stairs and lit the fireplace. Aspen impolitely called his attention to the front door to be let inside. She barked hello and ran to the kitchen for food. Lucas followed her and opened the Sauvignon Blanc. He picked two glasses and a small bowl from the cupboard.

Aspen followed him into the living room and sat on the floor, her big head on her paws with her back to the fire.

"I appreciate you welcoming me when I come in the door," he said to the dog.

Aspen blinked.

"I like the way you come home after you've been out taking a dump in the Legislature." He slowly drank the crisp white wine and poured a little in the bowl he had brought for the dog. "And the way you keep your dinner appointments is very thoughtful."

The golden retriever lapped up the wine and stared at him.

"But I especially enjoy it when you call me during the day. Do you think you could teach your mother to do that?"

Aspen circled the rug and then plopped herself down on it. She leaned her head over and laid it gently in his lap.

Lucas rubbed her head and patted her neck. The wine warmed him inside and the heat of the fire calmed him, wrapped him in a benevolent, quiet glow. It was the first time all day he began to relax. His heavy eyelids closed and his hand dropped to Aspen's paw. Twenty minutes later the Rev still did not stir at the sound of the garage door. Aspen knew the familiar noise but did not move, either.

Kristen Wade appeared in the doorway. She quietly put down her purse and bag, kicked off her shoes, and pulled off her clothes. Picking up her grandmother's quilt from the back of a chair, she draped it around her naked body and crawled onto the couch directly behind Lucas Holt.

Kristen smiled gratefully as she reached for her glass of wine and propped herself up to watch the embers of the fireplace burn themselves out. When she finished, she laid down beside Lucas, gently kissed his cheek, and closed her eyes.

The ringing phone startled all of them awake.

Aspen barked, Lucas slowly stirred, and Kristen bounded to the kitchen to pick it up.

"Probably for me," she said on the way.

The Rev followed her. "Who would call you this late?" He looked at the clock. "Oh," he said, "it's only ten-fifteen."

"Hello?" Kristen grimaced and handed Lucas the receiver. "It's for you."

The Rev listened without speaking as Kristen wrapped herself and the afghan around him.

"Right," he said finally. "Be there in a few minutes."

"You have to leave?" Kristen said as he hung up the phone. "Now? When we're finally here alone together at last?"

"Business," he said, heading upstairs to get dressed. "Just like you."

The Rev parked at St. Margaret's and walked down to the crowded sidewalks of Sixth Street. Passing the loud noise and bright neon of the numerous clubs, he came to the older, dimly lit part inhabited by locals and lost tourists. On one remaining turn-of-the-century stone building, a dim bulb lit the hand-carved insignia of an old sign: THE BUFFALO BARN GRILLE. It was the last vestige of old Austin on Sixth Street, the one place where cowboy culture and Hispanic music still mingled easily in thick smoke and cold longnecks. Holt sat at the bar.

"Evenin', Rev." The blond bartender with the red halter top and tight jeans winked at him. "What can I do for you?"

"Evenin', Jill." Holt winked back. "Cold one." She had worked

at Maxine's before the house closed. Holt got her the job at the
BBG. "Aren't you freezing in that thing?"

She put the bottle on the bar. "Honey, I'm hot no matter what
I'm wearin'. You know what I mean?"

The Rev looked at her. He certainly did. "Not a clue," he said,
laying a bill in front of her. "Upstairs?"

She nodded and pushed his money back. "Dorati's buyin'."

"Great." Holt walked through the kitchen to a hallway with
three doors. He knocked twice on the center one, then twice more
and heard the lock click. He opened the wooden door and climbed
the steep, narrow stairs. Nikky Dorati, Eddie Shelton, and Cora
Mae Hartwig sat around a large square domino table with cards in
their hands. Holt thought they looked like the old German pictures he remembered from his childhood of dogs playing cards.
Dorati was a bulldog, Shelton a shepherd, and Cora Mae a collie.
If he followed the alliteration, he would have to be a Lab.

"All hell's breaking loose and y'all are playing cards?" he
barked.

"Hello, Lucas dear," Cora Mae said. "We were just passing
time until you arrived."

"Good thing you got here, Rev," Dorati said, pushing his chair
back. "Cora Mae was about to wipe us out again." He tossed his
cards down and picked up the glass of rye.

"Hey, Rev," Eddie said as Holt pulled up the fourth chair.

"Hope I didn't interrupt anything," Dorati said, raising his eyebrows.

Lucas shrugged his shoulders. "Tell you what. It's late. I'm
tired and furious. It's been a shitty day, and the night isn't much
better, so can we get down to business?"

"I agree, Lucas," Cora Mae said. "We need to pool what we
know and see where to go from here."

"What we know is that I have buried six people in a week.
Let's take them two at a time." He put the Shiner longneck on the
table. "We know that Erik and Janey Bertrand were poisoned.
There was little attempt to cover that one up. Although—who
knows? The killer might have come back in after they were dead
and arranged a suicide note to cover it if Jimmy Brickhouse
hadn't gone shopping in their living room."

"Right." Dorati poured himself another shot of rye. "And we

know the Mes'can girls didn't suck fumes on their own. Doors went over their garage with a fine-tooth comb. He found three things," Dorati said. "The digital sequence on the door opener was off one digit from the hand clicker they had in the car."

"So they couldn't have opened or closed the garage door from their car?" Holt said, frowning. Holt imagined Blanca or Serena desperately trying to push the button, with no result. The thought of their helplessness, and that somebody had actually planned it that way, made him furious. "So, if I understand this correctly, somebody nearby made it look like they opened it?"

"Right," Eddie said. "Once they were inside they were trapped."

"My God." The Rev sighed and shook his head.

"How horrible," Cora Mae said.

"Worse than that," Dorati added. "Doors also found the car's electrical system messed with. The ignition couldn't be switched off and the horn wouldn't sound. Whoever it was knew they would instinctively open the windows for air, so that system was intact—making it look even more like a suicide."

"Murders three and four," Holt said. The next two would be hardest to dissect for all of them. "What about Lisa and Al?"

"Five and six," Dorati said. "But nothin' to go on."

"Maybe I do," Holt said, standing. "Susan Granger said they OD'd on street coke, injected under their fingernails."

"But why?" Dorati said. "Their careers were on the upswing. Plus they wouldn't do their fingernails; they'd mainline a hot shot and go out in a blaze of glory."

"There's another reason they wouldn't do it." Holt looked up at Dorati. "Lisa was twelve weeks pregnant."

"No!" Cora Mae cried.

"Shit," Eddie said. He stood and walked across the room. "We got to get these mofo's."

Nikky Dorati was noticeably silent. Lucas knew he was holding back something important. At the penitentiary Holt had learned to trust him when this happened, as it often did when Dorati had information he couldn't spill, just as the Rev couldn't break the seal of the confessional. In this situation, where people they cared about were involved, it was as hard for Nikky as it was for him to keep that seal closed. But they had to, each for different reasons. If either broke it, they would never be trusted with secrets again. Dorati had one priesthood, Holt another. But it was time for them to say what they could.

Nikky Dorati stared at the floor, then poured another rye. "Lousy damned deal," he said solemnly.

Holt spoke to him, hoping to break the impasse. "What's going on, Nikky? What are you thinking?"

Dorati looked up. "I think we've done enough screwin' around." He poured a second shot glass and handed it to Holt. "Bottom line, Rev. What do you know from J. D. Enright?" he said.

Lucas Holt reached across the table and flipped over a card from the deck. Queen of Hearts. "You show me your card. I'll show you mine," he said.

Dorati slid the second card from the deck and turned it over. "King of Diamonds," he said. "Ladies first."

Cora Mae Hartwig leaned forward. "Then perhaps that should be me," she said as Dorati and Holt turned to her. "You see, I talked with Marie Wilkins this afternoon."

Wild card, Holt thought. "Where is she?"

"Somewhere comfortable where she won't be found. I'm afraid I have to tell you she said she was responsible for her son and daughter-in-law's deaths, though she didn't say *how.*" Cora Mae became teary. "It is a terribly tragic thing, and she knows it."

The Rev drank the shot and leaned forward, looking at Nikky. He couldn't reveal the specifics, but he could confirm the pattern. "What Marie Wilkins said fits with Lisa and Al also."

"What about the Villalobos chicks?" Nikky asked.

Holt flashed the scene at the restaurant with Susan Granger. "The way I saw them treat their parents the other night at Casita Lobos and the fact that they cheated them out of the restaurant qualifies for the pattern."

"Which pattern, Lucas?" Cora Mae said, sipping her brandy.

Dorati answered, "The pattern of wealthy children being offed by greedy, resentful parents."

Lucas Holt thought Nikky answered too knowledgeably and too quickly, though he was relieved that Dorati had said it and not himself. He wondered what else Nikky knew.

"Oh, dear!" Cora Mae exclaimed. "How could parents think of such a thing? Those are their *children.*"

"Happens all the time, Cora Mae," the Rev replied, walking with his drink in hand. "Only usually they do it when the kids are small. The media treat it as though it's crazy or unusual. Truth is it happens over a thousand times every year."

"What would possess them?" she wondered aloud.

"The standard motives," Holt said. "Greed because demanding small children get in the way of pleasure. With adult kids, revenge for years of disrespect, or mistreatment and neglect."

Dorati breathed deeply. "Coupled with a way to do it that kept their dirty little hands nice and clean."

Holt looked at him. "Hits."

Eddie Shelton squinted. "If I get this right, you think these parents hired hits on their kids for the money?"

Dorati downed the shot and Holt nodded.

"Bizarre," Shelton said, sitting back down at the table.

"Quite biblical, if you follow some people's theology," the Rev replied. He felt angry and cynical at his helplessness to do anything about the deaths. "Abraham and Isaac. God and Jesus. Parents killing kids. Why should we be surprised?"

Nikky Dorati grinned. "That's the kind of shit the bishop hates you for, Rev. You make too damned much sense."

"So what are we gonna *do* about it?" Eddie Shelton raised his voice. "This is really pissing me off."

"I'm afraid I passed that point days ago," the Rev said.

"Shouldn't we let Susan in on this?" Cora Mae ventured.

"Sure," Dorati said. "You tell her. She won't arrest you."

"I'd be happy to if that would help," the old lady said.

"You're right, Cora," Holt interjected. "I know how to tell her." He would call Susan first thing tomorrow and meet her at the lake. She'd be less apt to scream at him outdoors.

Cora Mae looked at Nikky, who avoided her gaze. "What if we could find out how the hits were set up? And what if we would set up—what does Susan call it—a 'sting'?"

Eddie Shelton looked over at the Rev. "But that would mean one of us would have to be set up for a kill. Right?"

Lucas Holt suddenly got it. There was something he could do

about the murders. His sense of helplessness vanished in a surge of enthusiasm. "I can do this," he said.

"I had someone more like Omar in mind," Dorati replied.

Holt tossed the Queen of Hearts on top of the King of Diamonds. "You think I can't take care of myself?" Holt replied.

"I think I don't want you dead," Dorati said. He stood and took the shot glass with him. "We're expendable. You're not."

"Bullshit," Holt answered. "None of us is expendable. Erik and Janey Bertrand, Blanca and Serena, Al and Lisa, none of them was expendable, either." He brought Dorati back to the table. "What the hell, you guys won't let anything happen to me."

"All this is ridiculous anyway," Eddie Shelton said. "We don't know how to set it up."

The Rev looked at Dorati. That was it, he thought. That was what Nikky had been holding back. He did know. But how? "You want to say anything about that?"

Dorati emptied the contents of the bottle into his glass.

"I know how to do it," he said seriously. "Leave it to me."

• Ten •

Corinne Spellman squinted through the blurred bus window at corner street signs. Why were they so small? she wondered. With all the old people in Austin, the city council should have the sense to think of that. But none of them were even sixty.

She had caught the bus at Barton Creek Mall, where the van dropped off residents to shop. Corinne hated the mall stores and ventured downtown where she had known the elegance of shopping at Scarbrough's and Dillard's. The salesladies knew her sizes and tastes and called her when something came in. But they had not called in a long while. Maybe they didn't have her new number.

In her mind the stores still faced Congress Avenue where the streetcar went from the Capitol to the Colorado River and back. She hoped for lunch at the Woolworth's counter; grilled cheese and a Cherry Coke with a peanut. But when the bus turned from MoPac onto First Street, Corinne Spellman stared at the skyline in disbelief. She had the panicked feeling that she was heading into the wrong city.

She steadied herself and gaped out the window. There was the old City Power Plant with the original art deco lightning bolts. And there was no mistaking the Colorado River and the Carillon; she could hear the noon bells playing. The Crest Hotel was in its same place, but it had a different name. What was that huge building doing across the street from it? Where was her favorite taco stand?

The bus turned north on Congress, and she was comforted to see that no one had moved the Capitol. It still squatted firmly at the far end of the street. She would get off at the first stop and look for Woolworth's on Sixth.

"Hey, lady!" A young Hispanic man in a business suit called out to her and hurried down the aisle. Corinne hesitated, trying to get her bearings to think about where her feet were. An oncoming passenger bolstered her up.

"Whoa, ma'am." The bearded man wearing a huge leaf bag gently grabbed her arm. "Don't fall now."

"Here." The Hispanic man handed down her purse.

Puzzled, but knowing she should be grateful, Corinne smiled as she let the homeless man help her descend to the street. "Thank you both very much. You are most kind."

The men's eyes acknowledged each other like basketball players slapping hands.

Corinne Spellman straightened her dignity and as much of her mind as possible and turned toward Sixth and Congress. She strained her eyes for the familiar red and gold script sign, but Woolworth's two stories had been replaced by thirty-five boxes of yellow-brown stone stacked at right angles.

Bewildered, and not sure why she had come here, the old woman took a deep breath and forced her legs to move in the direction of her favorite clothing store. As she passed through the noontime aromas of restaurant after restaurant, the sensation in her stomach worked its way up through frayed internal wiring to her brain and leaned hard on the buzzer.

Hungry. The thought repeated itself, and she felt in control again. She glanced up and down the street and decided on Mexican. It had been off her list, or her doctor's list, for years. But this was starting to be fun, and the Mexican food she remembered was so good, especially with margaritas. If only her sister Martha had come. They would enjoy talking over lunch.

Corinne spotted Las Manitas across the street. She aimed her internal guidance system to cross at the light and had to pass several more eateries on the way. As she glanced into the second one, an Italian place with red checked tablecloths separated by black licorice-looking lattice work, she did a double-take, then walked on as her heart pounded wildly. She leaned against a building to get her bearings, caught her breath, and fanned herself with the bus schedule. Realizing she might call attention to herself, an old lady looking faint, she walked back by the window pretending to look at the menu.

It *was* them. It was Dr. Reinhardt and that black-haired woman Corinne had seen with him one other time when she had been— who cared where she had been? The woman looked like that new one from the retirement Center. What was her name? Helen something-or-other? She put on her cataract sunglasses so the black frames totally concealed her eyes from front and side. She opened the door and went in.

"Table for one, if you please," she said to the teenage hostess. "And, if you don't mind, I'd very much like to be seated at that table over there." Corinne pointed to the table on the other side of the latticework from Dr. Reinhardt and friend. "It's better for my eyes. A little darker, you know."

"No problem. Follow me." The girl seated her and gave her a menu. Corinne removed her sunglasses to read it. This would be great gossip at the Center. She couldn't wait to tell Cora Mae Hartwig the next time she and Martha came to visit.

"Anything to drink?" The waiter appeared in a red apron and white shirt with black bow tie.

She was about to answer when, somewhere in the recesses of her mind, a warning flare exploded. If she spoke, the doctor might recognize her voice. Corinne smiled as she held up a bony finger and pointed to the beverage list on the back of the menu.

"Iced tea?" he asked.

She nodded and mouthed the words "Thank you." Pointing to her throat, she mouthed the words "Can't talk."

"I get it, lady. No problem. We get a lot of you old folks in here, and I take care of all of 'em. I'll bring that right back, or do you want to order now?"

She smiled sweetly and mouthed "Now" to get rid of this jerk who she wished would have a heart attack at thirty for calling her old and dumping her in with everyone else. Pointing to *grilled cheese* with her single middle finger gave her some satisfaction. She shook her head no when he asked about a salad.

"I'll take care of you, sweetie," the waiter said, taking the menu and patting her arm.

Sarcastic words formed in her mouth, but she swallowed them to concentrate on listening to the other side of the lattice. Somehow this excitement had cleared her mind of the fuzziness she normally knew. Now if she would only be able to remember what she heard. No. She would write it down on the pad she always kept in her purse. Corinne positioned herself up against the lattice side of the booth with the paper to her right. The waiter brought her tea. He observed the pad and smiled.

"Letter," she mouthed, and winked at him. "Asshole," she mouthed, knowing he would think she said "Thank you."

She scrunched her body into the corner, assuming the couple could not see her over the booth wall and lattice on top of it. Though they would not expect anyone to be listening to them talk, they seemed suspiciously cautious, speaking in low, solemn tones, too low to be overheard in the next booth by anyone with normal ability. Corinne smiled. She could fix that.

She retrieved from her purse a small device that looked like a calculator. She hoped she could recall the proper buttons to push. There was some rhyme to it, she remembered, something that made it very logical. It had to do with colors and ears.

The waiter returned with the grilled cheese and put it on the table in front of her. She waited for him to vanish before she punched the red button three or four times. It worked! She smiled in amazement. Ruby Red was for the right ear. Lemon Lime for the left. She grinned and felt pleased with herself. Two more punches and she could have heard a fly fart across the room. She might as well have been sitting in their laps.

". . . mad at me for something, dear?" Truman Reinhardt said, as Corinne printed *DEAR* on the paper in capitals with an exclamation mark.

"Why should I be mad at you, Truman?"

"I don't know. You just seem—distant today."

"It's being separated from you for so long. A wife misses her husband, though that may not be as much of a problem for you, being surrounded by all those widows at the Center."

Corinne printed *HUSBAND!* and took a bite of sandwich.

"Those widows can't hold a candle to you, not after all these years."

Corinne frowned. This woman was nuts if she believed that crap. She scrawled *CRAP* and sipped her tea.

"It's just that it gets very—lonely—if you know what I mean,

Truman, all by myself in that rented apartment under a false name. I can't make friends or really speak with anyone."

"Believe me, I wish I could make a little communal visit to your place. But we're taking a chance being seen together. At least here it could be social, whereas at your apartment it would be different. In any case, like the monkey said when the train ran over his tail—it won't be long now."

"That's true. It won't be long now."

Corinne frowned again. Either she needed a new battery or the woman's tone of voice changed. She wrote *Uh-oh*.

The blinking yellow light on the control case caught her attention as she started missing parts of the conversation.

". . . down payment . . . Perez . . . Sparks," the woman continued. "Now all I have to do is figure out—"

Corinne Spellman cursed in her mind. What the hell was wrong here? She tapped the control case lightly, though she wanted to stomp it with her foot. The static was hurting her ears and she was missing the important parts, she was sure.

". . . Mt. Bonnell . . . ?"

"Right."

It came back on, though the light still flashed.

"Sparks told Perez they had a hard time getting natural gas up there. Everybody has electric but Garvin and Lavelle Davis."

"Seems appropriate to me, doesn't it to you?" Reinhardt said with a smile in his voice. "The children rejected *Sparks.*"

The woman paused, and Corinne Spellman held her breath. She should be able to make sense out of this, but it wasn't coming together at all. Why wouldn't her mind work when she wanted it to? She would just have to listen and write. She hoped Cora Mae or Martha could figure it out. She pictured her sister in a casket. Well, maybe not Martha.

"That's why I love you, Truman dear. 'Sparks.' It will be spectacular."

Corinne printed *SPARKS* in capitals. She knew the name meant something, or somebody, but she could not force her synapses to connect. And the connection in her ear was incomplete again. Static screeched so loud she had to punch the volume down.

"It . . . final . . . fireworks," Reinhardt said confidently.

Corinne wrote *FINAL* and turned up the volume. She had to get as much of the words as possible, even if it made her deaf.

"Assuming Perez . . ."

Reinhardt laughed. "For enough money, my dear, even you and I are reliable."

"Speak for yourself, Tru."

Corinne again printed *Uh-oh.* There was something in the woman's voice that Corinne associated with danger—for the man.

". . . plane arrangements?"

The red-lipped woman said something unintelligible as she rustled through her purse. Corinne could see her hand him a ticket. ". . . arranged payment . . . ?"

The voices were clear again.

"Done. Just as our scheme is . . . done. This . . . over our five million . . ."

Corinne wrote *5 Mil,* unsure of how many zeros to put.

"Unless we need more."

"More?" Reinhardt said with surprise in his voice.

"Nothing's perfect, Truman. That's the difference between us. That's why I provide . . . reality balance . . . You . . . should know . . . especially after those mistakes . . . operating table. The ones I bailed you out of, the ones . . . us started."

Corinne misspelled *MISTEAKES,* but she knew what she meant. Out of juice again. Come on, damn you, kick back in. She glanced through the lattice and saw puzzle pieces of the woman's face—enough, even with bad eyesight, to do a double-take. The woman had jet-black hair, and the tea glass Corinne could see on the table was smeared with bright red lipstick, like that new woman at the retirement Center. This woman held a cigarette in her hand as though it was an appendage. She couldn't smoke in the restaurant due to Austin's antismoking ordinances, but she could keep it ready. Corinne wrote *BLACK AND RED* in capitals. She hoped she would remember later what all these words meant.

Watching had distracted her from their conversation, so she was unprepared when Truman Reinhardt scooted out of the booth. As he stood, he casually glanced in her direction as she quickly reached for her black glasses and looked the other way.

Reinhardt sat down and spoke in tones so low they were inco-

herent even when the machine worked. She wrote down all the
words she caught.

Change. Plane. Tonight. Over. Leave.

"Anything else, ma'am?" The waiter startled her.

She mouthed "No" and made a sign for the check, which he
handed her. Corinne Spellman turned off her useless hearing aid
and pulled a bill from her purse. This was no time for plastic. Her
heart raced as she stuffed the notes in her purse and pushed her
body from the booth. Her confused mind knew she must leave,
get out in public where she would be seen and, hopefully, safe.
When she got to the door of the restaurant, she saw a head of
black hair rapidly move down the street and around the corner.

"Be careful out there, ma'am," the waiter said. He handed her a
wad of money. "You left me a fifty for your lunch. Here's your
change." He watched her fumble with her purse. "Would you like
me to call you a taxi? They have elder rates now, you know."

Taxi! Why didn't she think of that? This idiot waiter was good
for something after all. She could afford the ride and it would get
her back safe. Corinne started to nod her head when someone
took hold of her arm and squeezed it, menacingly.

"That's okay, son," the tall man said. "This lady's an old friend
of mine from the retirement Center. I'll see to it we both get
back." Reinhardt stuffed a twenty in the waiter's pocket and whispered: "She gets confused. You know how it is."

"Yes, I do, and thank you very much, sir!"

"But—" Corinne started to protest, and the waiter turned at the
unexpected sound of her voice.

"Come along now, Mrs. Spellman."

"Please," she said, looking plaintively at the waiter. "He's hurting me. Don't let him—"

The waiter winked back. "You go along now, ma'am, and let
this nice man take care of you."

Truman Reinhardt forced her out the door and onto the sidewalk. "We'll take a walk down to Second Street where you and I
can chat with a little privacy. I don't know how much you heard,
but I am sick and tired of your messing in my affairs."

"I heard it all, you miserable bastard," Corinne tried to threaten
him. She thought she had practiced what to do if anything like
this ever happened. Somewhere she had some kind of protectant.

Where was it? He was walking too fast for her. "Slow down or I'll have a heart attack right here on the pavement and you won't get the pleasure of killing me."

Reinhardt slowed a little, but kept his grip tight, pressing her on toward an alley off Second Street.

Corinne remembered a small black canister in her purse, attached to her keys, that Cora Mae Hartwig had given to her. She couldn't quite remember what exactly to do with it, but thought she might recall if she had it in her hand.

"I need a nitro pill from my purse," she insisted.

"You need mace from your purse, and I'm not letting you get it, you old bag." He pushed her into the alley and forced her back against a brick wall. "What did you hear in there?" he said, pulling off her sunglasses to see her terrified eyes.

Corinne's brain raced to find the right thing to do. Too scared to scream, she could only stare into the deep black pits of this man's eyes and watch his hands move up around her neck.

"Of course it doesn't really matter what you heard, since you'll never repeat it to anybody."

She felt his hands tighten. Still she could not think what to do. She choked, gasping for air. Martha. Martha would know what to do. The older sister knew. Why couldn't she think? Her purse? Was there something there? Her bulging eyes focused on a shape coming up behind her attacker. Martha? Was that Martha? But what was that in her hand?

Reinhardt saw her stare beyond him. "You can forget that old trick," he said, tightening his grip on her pulsing neck.

She felt the final pressure to her windpipe, a move she knew would crush out her life, when a gun butt smashed her attacker from behind, and he slumped into darkness on the cobblestones. Corinne Spellman coughed and choked till she caught her breath, held by the figure that had saved her life.

"Who—who are—?" she started to say. She stared and took a deep breath of astonishment. "You—you were in the restaurant!" she said to the black-haired woman before her.

"No. That wasn't me."

"But—but you look just like— No! You're—you live at the Center! I've seen you there." The black-haired woman with the bright red lips put her arm around Corinne Spellman's waist and helped her out of the alley into a car. "Just come with me." Her rescuer held the door and helped her into the car.

Corinne spoke to the woman who had saved her life. "Should we call the police?"

"Can I get you anything first?"

Corinne Spellman's adrenaline-surged brain cells conspired and delivered their decision immediately. "A margarita?"

"You're not as stroked out as everyone thinks," Helen Pelham said to her. "Now talk to me."

Omar Dewan sat behind the huge steering wheel of the green '84 Caddy, drinking his fifth cup of coffee from the local "Stop & Rob." He watched a few cars pass and wondered whether this stakeout would prevent him from going to the gym again tomorrow. Omar stretched in the driver's seat. He felt flabby after one missed day on the weights and hoped the Rev would call them off.

Dewan yawned and sipped the hot coffee. He had the previous night's watch, and it was Eddie Shelton's turn in a few hours. Right now Eddie was sound asleep in the backseat, getting ready.

Nothing had happened at the house of Garvin and Lavelle Davis. Except for the cars of tourists and teenagers going up to Mt. Bonnell for the view, their street had been relatively quiet. Omar wondered who would want to hurt this couple. They had it together in every way imaginable to him. House. Looks. Jobs. They were well known and respected in the community. The Rev was wrong on this one. He wasn't usually off track, and Omar had listened to him before at the pen. But this time it seemed like the regular routine here was boredom broken only by sleep.

Except for the van.

Shelton snored. Omar grinned and looked at the car clock. He hated daylight saving time. It was only six-thirty and already dark. He would wake Eddie in an hour and send him to get food. Later, Eddie would take the graveyard shift. He hoped it wouldn't turn out to be one.

Omar looked up as headlights flashed in the rearview mirror, momentarily blinding him. A van with wheelchair plates passed the Cadillac and turned right on Del Norte to go back down the hill. It was the same one Omar had noted two hours ago, before

Eddie had arrived. Same plates with mud making them unreadable. Same dude with shades, even in the dark.

Dewan smiled to himself. Who would have ever thought his Nam training in military intelligence would be put to use in Austin, Texas, guarding a brother? He sure never thought of that running point for search-and-destroy squads. He tensed his muscles and watched the van drive off, thinking he should wake Eddie. Hell, this wasn't Nam; there was no need to be paranoid about every movement. So he would wait, unless something happened.

Ten minutes later something did.

The van slowly came round the corner from Del Norte onto Mt. Bonnell with its bright lights on, passed the Cadillac and the Davis house, and parked on the opposite side of the street.

Charlie was here. Rock-and-roll time. "Eddie! Wake up!" Omar kept the van in sight in the left outside mirror and raised the .45 on the floor to his lap.

Eddie Shelton rubbed his eyes. "What's goin' on?"

"I don't know. But get up. The dude in the van came back and he's playin' with us. Drove by us once, turned around, and drove directly facing us and parked his ass down the street."

Shelton looked out the rear window. "I know that van! It's the one No Legs Perez uses." Eddie reached up and grabbed Omar's coffee. He drank half of it and turned to observe the van.

"Shit!" Omar exclaimed. "He's headin' for the house."

"Yeah, and you can see how much he needs a wheelchair from the way he's runnin'."

"The Rev said we were to stop whoever looked like an intruder." Omar opened the door. "Let's go."

Shelton tossed the cup in the street as he exited the car. "You're the expert here," he said. "How do we do this?"

"You go 'round one side. I take the other." Omar stopped. "You packin'?"

"You crazy?" Shelton removed a .38 from his waist holster. "These people are killers."

Omar watched the shadow of Perez disappear behind the Davis house. He didn't like the feeling in his gut. It reminded him too much of a sudden silence in the jungle, or the vacant halls in the pen right before something bad went down. Small live oaks and scrub cedar clogged the steep hill where the Garvin house was perched. Omar crouched low to the ground and stopped to listen for footsteps. With all the brush it would be easy to hear someone approach.

He heard a loud thud from where Eddie should have been. Omar ran around the back to the other side and saw his friend sprawled on the ground, not moving.

Instinct told him to rush in and help. Nam and street smarts told him to stay the hell where he was. Eddie, no matter how bad he was hurt, was like bait in a bear trap. The best chance of being alive to help him was to wait. He cocked the gun and slowly backed away, then stopped suddenly when a cold steel circle pressed against his neck.

"You can make this hard or easy," the voice behind him whispered. "You choose."

"Easy," Omar said. He tossed his gun toward Eddie.

"Smart man."

"What's the drill here, Perez?" Omar asked, buying time.

"Did Eddie tell you my name?" The voice sounded surprised.

"Didn't have to. We know who you are and what's going down." If his calculation was correct, the man stood about three feet behind him with his arm extended holding the gun.

"You don't know shit, man."

Perez was annoyed, Omar thought, nervous. That was good. "Lieutenant Granger knows about you, too." He would raise the anxiety a notch more. "We called her on Eddie's phone before we left the car. They're right behind us."

"Bullshit, man. You're bluffin'." Perez jammed the gun hard into Omar's neck, drawing blood.

Perfect, Dewan thought, calculating exactly where his attacker stood.

"But just in case, I need to hurry up what I'm doin' here."

"You know I can't let you hurt these people, Perez."

The voice laughed. "Like you got a choice, motha-fu—"

Omar turned fast, knocked the gun arm against the house and sent a rock-hard left to the man's jaw. The gun dropped and Perez fell back, rolled to his feet and crouched in a martial arts pose.

Omar swung and Perez dodged, grabbed his arm and dropped

backward to the ground. He lifted Omar with his feet, slamming him into a tree trunk.

Dazed, his mind whirling and his body numb, Omar vaguely saw a shadow coming toward him and tried to stand.

"Damn you," Perez said, with a final crushing blow to the chest. "The hard way makes me work more."

Lucas Holt parked in his driveway and took a deep breath. A bad day was about to get worse.

The meeting at the Buffalo Barn Grille had ended at three in the morning and Lucas had not gone back to Kristen's. Her worried and partly annoyed voice on his answering machine had awakened him just three hours later. By the time he was alert enough to get to the phone, she had hung up. More than slightly exhausted, he had plopped back in bed and slept until noon when Maxine called to tell him the little ladies in the St. Anne's Guild Bible Study Group were wondering just where the hell he was for their luncheon. He had shaved in the car and, with the help of high-test leaded coffee from Max, appeared in time for dessert with "Jesus and the Ten Lepers."

The whole afternoon he had vacillated between depression and anger about what he now surmised were well-planned murders. He had been only half attentive at the staff meeting to plan Sunday services, wondering if he could pull an old sermon from the pickle barrel and not have to write one. Finally, his twelve-mile run had been less than relaxing with no headset and overly tiring with not enough sleep from the night before.

He exited the car and stared momentarily in the dark at Dorati's black Beemer in front of Susan's blue-and-white: cop and robber freeze frame.

Lucas had changed his mind from last night when he felt bolder. He had decided, somewhere in the midst of pecan pie and lepers, that there was safety in numbers. He had Max set up this meeting at his house with Susan and hoped the presence of Cora Mae, who she liked, and Nikky, who she reluctantly tolerated, would defuse her anger at what he had to say.

Holt ascended the wooden steps to the wide front porch and hoped they had already told her. When Dorati welcomed him at the door, he knew they hadn't. They were still alive.

"How'd you get in?"

Dorati looked at him. "I got here first."

"Oh," the Rev said, remembering Nikky had taught him there was no such thing as a locked door, only one that he hadn't yet gone through.

Susan Granger sat next to Cora Mae Hartwig on the couch and looked more displeased than usual. Her normally stiff uniform was rumpled with pleats where there should be none. Holt saw she was here for business and wanted to get down to it. "Other than systematic torture of a police officer, what exactly is the purpose of this meeting, Lucas?"

Holt tossed his collar and briefcase on the dining room table and kicked off his shoes.

"The first thing is to get him a beer," Nikky Dorati said, disappearing to the kitchen and returning with a Shiner Bock.

"Thanks." Holt accepted the bottle. This was not going to be easy. "And the second thing is that, though you may not want to hear it, we have some information for you about the murders."

Susan Granger sat back and crossed her arms over her chest. "You know for certain they were murders?" she said, an air of defensiveness in her voice.

"Look, Susan. When we talked at the fitness center you asked me to keep you posted if the God Squad found anything. We have and I am."

"Go ahead," she said. "I'm all ears."

Holt looked at Cora Mae Hartwig. "Perhaps you should start," he said, hoping to lead with the least intrusive story on Marie Wilkins. Dorati went next with Doors's discoveries at the Villalobos house; finally, Lucas told her their theory of parents arranging hits on their wealthy children.

The Rev had watched Susan stare, unmoving, as each person talked. He wondered whether she would be grateful that they were helping solve the murders or furious that the God Squad again had overstepped what she surely thought were its bounds. It worried him that she asked no questions at all until they had stopped.

"That's it?" the lieutenant said, looking directly at Holt.

Lucas did not look at either Nikky or Cora Mae as he lied to Susan Granger. "That's everything." Everything he could tell her for now. If she knew of the sting they were setting up, she would go ballistic, whether it was helpful or not. So far, he thought, she was taking everything pretty much in stride, and it worried him. Knowing Susan as he did, she should be yelling.

"Thank you for the information," she said, standing, with no smile on her face. "It is extremely helpful." Susan Granger nonchalantly unholstered her gun.

"Susan—" Holt began. Maybe she was having a brain fart.

"Shut up, Lucas," she said, reaching for her handcuffs. "You have a right to remain silent. You have a right to an attorney. If you cannot afford an attorney—"

This was more like it, Holt thought.

"What the hell are you doing?" Nikky said.

"You of all people should know that, Dorati," Granger replied. "I'm placing you all under arrest." She glanced at Cora Mae Hartwig. "Sorry, Cora Mae, but you, too."

"On what charge?" Holt was getting heated. It was okay to be angry. It was another thing to lock up innocent people, or at least people who could, arguably, be presumed innocent.

"Gosh, Lucas," Susan said sarcastically. "Let me count the ways." She opened the cuffs and motioned for Dorati to turn around. "How about withholding information from the police, meddling in police affairs, interfering with an investigation, and intruding on a crime scene? And if Mr. Dorati doesn't give me his hands, I'll add resisting arrest to this laundry list."

"Don't do it, Nikky," Holt said angrily. His face was as red as Susan's. It was showdown time. "If you arrest us you have to arrest yourself, too. You asked us to help dig up information, if you will recall."

"Dammit, Lucas, I didn't ask you to invade the crime scene," Granger snapped. "I didn't ask you to withhold evidence from the police." Lucas watched her move toward Nikky. "You stepped over the line once too often. And it's the line my ass is on."

"No, Susan," the Rev said, moving between her and Dorati. "Your problem is you don't know where the hell the line is. We did what you asked. We told you what we know. You're just pissed that the police are too damned incompetent to come up with this shit themselves."

"Lucas, dear," Cora Mae said. "I think we can work things out a little more quietly than this, don't you agree, Susan?"

"No, I don't, Cora Mae," Granger barked. "You have got to learn I mean it when I say I want you the hell out of police business. Maybe the way to convince you is send the whole damned God Squad back to prison and end this shit once and for all."

"You don't want to know the person behind it?" Dorati said.

Lucas Holt and Cora Mae Hartwig turned to him.

"What are you saying?" the Rev asked, surprised and a little aggravated. It was one thing for them to withhold information from the police. It was another to withhold from one another, especially after he thought they had cleared the table. "You didn't tell me you knew that last night."

"What happened last night?" Granger said.

"Stay out of this," Holt told her. "Why didn't you say you knew who it was?" The Rev's righteous indignation was on the rise. He pictured the services with dual caskets and felt the rage all over again. He was pissed at Susan for her attitude and felt conned by Dorati, though his memory reminded him that Nikky didn't keep secrets without reasons, damned good reasons.

Susan Granger persisted. "What happened last—"

Dorati ignored Granger and spoke to Holt. "I didn't know last night. I swear it's true, Rev. And even this is second-hand, but an older couple were overheard making certain plans today that sound almost exactly like we figured."

Susan Granger raised her voice. "Dammit, you two! Pay attention! I've got a *gun* here!"

"And a very nice one it is, Susan," Cora Mae inserted, trying to relieve the tension.

"So who *is* it?" Holt said to Nikky.

Susan Granger holstered her gun and pushed herself between Holt and Dorati. "I don't know a damned thing about this and you people *drive me crazy!*" She turned to the Rev. "If any part of this is true, do you know what it means?"

"It means we've solved the case?" Cora Mae offered hopefully.

Holt knew Susan had reached her limit. She was yelling now.

"No, Cora Mae! It means I have to put out warrants for Marie Wilkins, the Villalobos couple, and Lisa Enright's parents! These are old, minority, working-class people that the community will not want to see the police mess with, much less put behind bars!"

Holt still ignored her. He wanted the name from Dorati. He saw again the pathetic look on J. D. Enright's face, admitting responsibility for the death of his and Marlane's grandchild. "Who the hell is it, Nikky?"

Dorati moved to the chair where Susan Granger had been. "An old doctor at the Westlake Retirement Center by the name of—"

"Truman Reinhardt?" Holt said, startled at the thought.

"Who the hell is Truman Reinhardt?" Granger yelled. "Cora Mae—help me out here." She plopped on the couch, exasperated.

"I wish I could, dear."

"Then we've got to get him right now, before something happens to Garvin and Lavelle," Holt said, pulling on his shoes.

"What are you people talking about?" Granger exclaimed.

Lucas calmed down enough to be civil. They would need her help if they were to stop another killing.

"We've got Omar and Eddie watching the Davis house up on Mt. Bonnell. We think Lavelle's father, Reverend Sparks, might have put out a contract on her and Garvin." Holt looked at Dorati. "I suppose through this Dr. Reinhardt somehow."

Nikky glanced down and mumbled. "Long story for later, Rev."

Lucas spoke to Susan. "Come on, Susan! Cut us some slack here till we fit it all together. Right now just let us get Reinhardt and check on Garvin and Lavelle."

"Okay. Okay. I give. Uncle. I promise to arrest you later." The lieutenant grabbed her radio. "Granger to Base. By?" In thirty seconds she learned that no calls had come in from Mt. Bonnell. She dispatched a car to check on the Davis house.

"I hope you're wrong about Reverend Sparks, Nikky," Cora Mae said. "I don't see how someone with his limited capacity—" Her voice was drowned out by a huge boom that shook the windows.

"What the hell—?" Susan Granger ran outside, followed by the others. From the street they saw a large plume of black smoke ascending from Mt. Bonnell.

"My God!" Holt exclaimed. "We're too late!"

"Shit!" Granger shouted at Holt. "I hate it when you're right."

She ran to her car. "Y'all stay put!" she yelled over her shoulder to the three figures on the front porch. As she turned on the siren, she knew she would be ignored.

The Rev spoke hurriedly to Nikky Dorati. "Have the Squad find Sparks. Credible or not, he's the only witness we have."

"You got it, Rev," Nikky said, running to the phone.

Holt turned to the old woman. "Cora Mae, I need you to come with us to the Westlake Retirement Center. It's a big place and we'll need all three of us to track down Reinhardt."

"Do you think we can catch him, Lucas?" Cora Mae asked.

"If we don't, I know who will," the Rev answered, heading for his car. "Somebody else wants him even more than we do."

Cora Mae looked puzzled. "Who's that?"

"Lisa Enright's father."

"Cop to the left, man," Jimmy Brickhouse said from the back-seat of the 1983 Chevette which he entirely occupied. The car slowed and got off IH 35 at the East Twelfth Street exit.

"That'd be a great bust for him," Frankie Colovas agreed from the passenger seat. "Three ex-cons on probation under the Rev's supervision."

"And me without my license." Ricardo Valdez smiled. The sexton of St. Margaret's was behind the wheel of the beat-up automobile he had bought with a small loan from the church. "R.V." had arrived in Austin on parole three days after the Rev, who hired him on the spot. Having been the head Trusty for maintenance at the pen, Valdez could fix anything that broke. After some difficult times and misunderstandings, he liked the job; the monastic nature of the church felt just like home.

"You got insurance on this heap, 'Dez?" Colovas asked.

"Sure, man." He patted his chest. "Protected by Smith and Wesson."

"Shit," Jimmy said. "If we're busted, we're cooked."

"Then let's don't get busted," Ricardo replied.

"Hard not to when we're riding onto East Eleventh and Comal," Doors said. "It's Coke and Hooker streets, man. And all we know is old man Sparks's church is in this 'hood. He's got to be there since he wasn't at the nursing home."

"He'll be here," Valdez confirmed. "He's here the same time of night every night, just like when he was the preacher there."

"I used to know where the church was," Jimmy said. "I knew old man Sparks a long time ago from the street. But I think he's moved his church since then."

"He has, but there's so many of those little storefronts, I guess we gotta ask directions," Valdez said, pulling over to a busy corner. A tall black woman in tight short-shorts and a blouse open to her navel came over to his window.

"Hey, baby," she said. "Whachu got in mind?"

"I just need some directions, is all," Valdez said, staring at her cleavage. The monastic life was getting boring.

"Sure thing, honey." She took his hand and placed it in her blouse. "This enough direction for you? Or you want it lower?"

Doors leaned over and pulled Ricky's hand back in the car. "Don't be doin' that shit, man. Just ask her where the church is."

"Church?" The woman laughed. "Baby, you had me fooled." She looked in the backseat and spotted Jimmy Brickhouse. "Honey, I'll go to whatever church he's goin' to."

Valdez caught his breath. "We want the Holiness Church of Jesus." Could God perhaps transport him there right this minute? Or maybe transport the two of them to the Bahamas?

"Old Reverend Sparks's church? What do you want with that crazy old man?"

"We think maybe he's in trouble," Doors said.

"If he's in the 'hood this time o' night, he's sure nuff in big trouble, baby." She pointed straight ahead and motioned as she spoke. "You go down two streets and turn left on Chicon. Center of the block. Little place. Hand-painted sign in front."

"Thanks," Valdez smiled. "For everything."

She pushed her head in the window and thrust her tongue in his ear. "When y'all are done prayin', c'mon back, baby. Just don't put all your money in the plate."

Valdez hit the gas and the three sped away from the corner.

Jimmy Brickhouse laughed in the backseat. "Ricky, you liked that shit, man. You one horny mofo."

"Not for that, man," Valdez replied. "She felt like a used pillow at Goodwill. She's too old to be turnin' tricks."

"You better get your ear looked at, man," Jimmy chuckled and poked Doors in the arm as they laughed at Valdez. "That chick had more bugs than Orkin."

St. Margaret's sexton wiped his ear with his shoulder. He slowed the car and pointed to a one-story building on the right. A hand-painted marquee stood sentry in front. In minutes, thanks to Doors, they were inside the dark church.

"I don't like this," Valdez whispered. He opened his coat and removed his gun. Shafts of white from the streetlights cut through the darkness, striping the old worn pews. R.V. thought the place smelled like St. Margaret's, that mixture of candle wax and mildew. But this was a poor, drafty version of Maggie Mae's. The floorboards creaked. One near the altar had just done so.

Jimmy Brickhouse spoke. "Somebody in here. Trust me."

Doors stood up. "You two weenies don't know what you're—"

A shot rang through the tiny church.

Doors collapsed backward. "Shit," he said. "Just my ego hurt, man. I dropped so hard I think I broke my butt."

Before Jimmy could speak, the lights came on and a voice roared: "Vengeance is *mine! I* will repay!"

The three fanned out behind the back pews.

"Get thee *behind* me, Satan!"

Valdez peeked over a pew to see a glassy-eyed Reverend Sparks standing in the center of the aisle waving a pistol. The bare bulbs hanging from the roof cast his shadow in all directions, like a hexagon.

"Stand up! Stand up for Jesus!" he shouted at them.

Jimmy stood slowly. "Yo! Reverend Sparks. It's me. Jimmy Brickhouse. You remember me? You helped me off the streets a long time ago." He carefully edged sideways across a pew to the center aisle. "I know I let you down, but you'll be glad to know I'm straight now. So you see what can happen when you help someone. Why don't you let me help you now?"

A bullet splintered the pew to his left.

Sparks shouted: "Mine help is in the name of the Lord, the Maker of Heaven and Earth."

Valdez had worked his way nearly to the front of the church. Two more pews and he'd have a straight shot at the old man. One to that right shoulder should take out the gun.

The pew in front of him exploded.

"Get back!" Sparks yelled as R.V. retreated. No sense getting killed here. He had been shot at before, and hit before, and he was in no hurry to repeat the pain.

"My house is a house of prayer, but ye have made it a den of thieves."

"Yessir." Frankie Colovas stood with his hands behind his head and walked down the center aisle. "You right about that, Reverend. We thieves—all of us here. Some of us is worse than that, like my man Jimmy here."

He came to the pew where Brickhouse stood. Jimmy saw the .38 stuffed down the back of his neck, inches from his hand.

"And my man Valdez down there on the floor."

R.V. moved into position as Doors distracted the preacher. Ten feet more and he'd have a shot.

"We all thieves and we all going to have to answer to that great Judge on the throne some day." He moved within two pews of the front. "Just like you are."

Two bullets ricocheted off the floor in front of him and he stopped.

"Judge not, lest ye be judged. For the measure ye give will be the measure ye get."

Valdez motioned to Brickhouse, who moved up behind Doors. R.V. saw the old man sweating now. But it was not the sweat of preaching, that glistening, dripping sweat of high emotion. This was the flat, sallow sweat of exhaustion, of remorse, the sweat of death. They had to stop him.

"You gotta listen to us, Reverend Sparks," Jimmy said.

The fog lifted for a fleeting moment, and the old man spoke in his normal tone of voice. "No. I don't have to listen to you or to anybody else ever again. I been too busy listenin' to the Devil and playin' the Devil's games and now I'm going to pay for my transgressions." He looked at the empty pews and commanded the three men to sit.

"Right there, in the second pew." He waved his gun at them. "All of you together. And throw your weapons here, on the floor in front of me."

Valdez stood. If he fired, the old man would nail Frankie Colovas and maybe get Jimmy, too. He tossed his gun and nodded at Brickhouse to do the same as they walked to a front pew.

"I'm unarmed, Reverend," Doors lied, edging his way into the pew between Jimmy and Ricky, whose weapons were now in the hands of Sparks. The three sat an arm's length apart.

"You want to know why I am here tonight?" Sparks began the singsong style. "Why I am here in church with a gun in my hand? Is that why you come into God's house to disturb one of his people?" He closed his eyes and wiped his face with the handkerchief at the pulpit. "I'll *tell* you why, my brothers. I'll tell you why I stand before you tonight with this weapon of violence. And with your weapons, also."

Valdez nudged Brickhouse. The old man's eyes were huge; his pupils looked drugged. R.V. knew if the man got any higher, he could hallucinate and kill them all.

"These guns are symbols, *symbols* of the evil in our world. They look so innocent." He held his gun to his head and cocked the hammer. "But a simple movement of one or two small muscles in my finger can put in motion a chain of events that ends in my death." He turned the gun toward them. "Or perhaps yours."

Shit, Valdez thought. "But wait a minute, Reverend—"

"Hush!" Sparks roared. "You must listen to me! Listen to me! It was just the same—a single, simple movement—that set into motion the chain of events that brings me here tonight."

"What was it, Reverend?" Brickhouse asked. "Preach on!"

Doors and Valdez glanced at him like he was out of his mind, egging on the emotion of the man with the gun on them.

"Yes, brother, I will. I will preach on. And you will listen and tell me whether I should ask mercy on my soul or go straight to the hell prepared for me and other sinners."

"This makes me very nervous," Valdez whispered to Doors, looking straight ahead. Very slowly, with unnoticeable movements, Ricky edged a few inches closer to Doors, so his hand on the back of the pew was now behind Frankie's neck, and close to the gun.

"Because," the sweating Sparks continued, closing his eyes and raising the fisted hand without the gun, "because my only child had rejected me after I had given her my life, my attention, my money, my love and affection, and everything I ever had—just as the world rejected Jesus Christ when he came and gave us everything he had—I conspired with others to have her slain. Like

Abraham our forefather I felt commanded by Almighty God to
take her to the mountaintop, and there to make a sacrifice of her
life, that she might be purified, washed in the blood of the Lamb,
forgiven for her sins against me and against Yahweh Elohim, God
of Thunder."

Valdez knew Sparks was pushing himself beyond the traditional frenzy, emphasizing words in syncopated rhythm. Still, like
Brick and Doors, he did not dare move. Between sentences the
old man glared at them, waving his gun and moving closer, down
from the altar to the aisle in front of them.

"But I could not do this by myself. I had to borrow the money
from a cripple who was sent to me as an angel of the Lord."

"Perez?" R.V. said, too loud for his own comfort.

"Yes! You know him, too! He is Cherubim and Seraphim combined, a very present help in time of trouble. He immediately
loaned me the money and then provided the means, sinful as it
was, to let me pay him back."

"Ponies?" Doors said, remembering a conversation with Eddie
Shelton.

"Sin money for sin money. Just as it shall be blood for blood,
an eye for an eye, and a tooth for a tooth. From then the die was
cast. And tonight, tonight it happened. My only daughter and her
husband, them who hated and rejected me, have gone on to their
final reward. But they deserved their fate. They were bad, evil
people."

"That's not true, Reverend, and you know it," Valdez said angrily as Brickhouse and Doors cast him hostile looks.

"What? What's that you say? How do you know the suffering
of my life?"

Ricky would have to make a lot of this up, putting together the
pieces from what the Rev had told him and what he guessed or
overheard. If Sparks was watching R.V.'s mouth, he wouldn't see
his hand reaching for the handle of the gun in Frankie's neck.

"The way I hear it you deserved everything you got, Reverend," Rikky said. "It's not that you were bad, but you were preoccupied with yourself and your work and you judged them and
rejected them. You hated seeing them succeed where you never
could, seeing your daughter climb out of this neighborhood and
leave you and your church behind. Seeing her get the things you

always wanted but could never let yourself have, the material comforts you always rejected, along with her."

"What the hell are you doing?" Frankie Colovas looked at him wide-eyed. "The old man's nuts enough without you juggin' at him!"

"Shut up and let's end this shit," Valdez said, edging his hand around the grip of the gun.

Sparks threw down the handkerchief like a gauntlet. "No! You are wrong! They deserved their fate for what they did to me and to God. Rejecting us both."

"Who the hell you think you are, Reverend Sparks?" Valdez continued. "You're a good man, but you sure as hell ain't God any more than I am."

"I am God's servant," Sparks said angrily. "God's messenger. I have lifted up his Holy Name in this church for forty years."

Suddenly the preacher's tone changed, as if another person was speaking. "But you are right. In the last few years my mind has not been what it was." His volume increased again. "I have been struck by the Devil who weakens me. I hear strange voices and see horrible things. And it was that—that which led me to the mountain to slay my daughter."

Ricky didn't like the tone of the confession. He'd heard it before, they all had, from inmates who left the pen feet first.

"I am two people divided," he railed. "And a house divided against itself cannot stand. I cannot serve both God and mammon, and I have served mammon, just as my daughter has, so I had to stop us both."

"He's losin' it, man." Valdez stretched and wrapped his hand firmly around the gun grip and placed his finger on the trigger. "The dude is about to crack."

"And you, you of all people, should know about that!" He pointed the gun at Jimmy. "To lose your mind to the devil and do things that will lead you to hell in the final days of your life. It's worse than the drugs you used, that took control of everything you did. I used no drugs and yet—and yet it is happening to me even as I stand here."

Sparks raised the gun and aimed it at Jimmy from four feet away. The point blank shot would blow open his chest.

"I can't stand any more!" the old man shouted. Sweat poured

from his face and soaked his black robe. "I must end it! God forgive me!"

Suddenly Sparks turned the gun on himself, placed it in his mouth, and pulled the trigger.

Valdez whipped out Frankie's gun as the old man went down in front of the pulpit where he had preached hellfire and damnation his whole life.

Jimmy ran to him and held his mangled head. Blood streamed from the preacher's mouth, literally embodying the words he had shouted all those Sundays. Bright red on white teeth; gray stubble on black skin.

There was a final gasp and his head dropped to the side.

"We're outta here, man!" Valdez shouted at the two of them. "You hear those sirens? They're comin' this way!"

"They don't ignore *that* many gunshots even in this neighborhood," Doors agreed.

"You two get in the wind. Now!" Jimmy said, still cradling the preacher's head. "Take my piece with you. I'll stay with the old man and take the heat. Just get to the Rev and tell him what happened. He's the only way out of this one."

"Right." Valdez and Doors ran to the car. Cordons would already be in place, so they could not go far. They rounded the block with no lights and parked in the driveway of an empty house. Blue-and-whites screeched to the church with flashing lights and blaring sirens.

"Shit, man. Jimmy ain't walkin' easy on this one. Do you see what I see?" Doors said, trying to hold down his voice. "Check the lead car, man! The tall black chick with the tight shorts and gun?"

"Awright!" Valdez grinned. "I had my hand on a cop's tit."

Frankie Colovas ducked down in the seat as a cruiser flashed its searchlight in their direction. But he couldn't restrain himself. He looked at the crouched Valdez and whispered:

"I bet that's the first police bust you enjoyed."

• Eleven •

As he approached the Westlake Retirement Center, Lucas Holt wished he had called Susan Granger for backup. She was so focused on the explosion, she had apparently relegated Reinhardt to a lower priority, to be dealt with after the body count at Mt. Bonnell. But Reinhardt was the cause of that body count that the Rev worried might include Omar Dewan and Eddie Shelton. He could not imagine that right now. The emotion of losing those two might propel him beyond capturing the killer to assisting God and a jury in determining what should be done with the bastard.

Speaking of bastards, Holt thought as Jason Graves came out to meet him, what if this slimeball was in it with Reinhardt? No. Graves wasn't that smart. Reinhardt might use him, paid him to cover tracks or do scut work, but nothing more. It would be an interesting twist, though, if it were the other way around, if Jason Graves was using his position to know of situations suitable for the scheme and forcing Reinhardt to carry out the murders on threat of exposure of some kind.

Graves shook his head in response to the Rev's question about Reinhardt's whereabouts.

"I don't know where he is. He's a high-functioning resident here. Doesn't wear the ankle wire because he doesn't need it. People need their privacy, you know. What do you want him for, anyway? Perhaps I can help?"

The administrator sounded defensive, like he was buying time. Stalling. Holt persisted. "When did you see him last?"

"Let me think. He was walking down the hall on the way to his room when you called from your car saying you were coming. He had a nasty fall downtown the other day, a bloody, messy head wound and all over his good clothes, too. Wouldn't let anybody touch him, of course. Doctored it himself. Been taking more exercise lately, that or he's been more nervous. I don't know which. Regardless of your request, I couldn't have detained him. You're not the police, you know. Anyway, he can't have gone far in fifteen minutes."

"I hope not." Holt trusted Jason Graves about as far as he could spit. "If he has escaped, Mr. Graves," the Rev threatened, "and if he is in any way involved with further harm being done to my parishioners, I will hold you responsible."

"I assure you, Reverend Holt," Graves responded with a smug, malicious smile, "that I had nothing to do with his leaving."

Holt lowered his voice inversely with the rise in his anger and moved closer to the man's face. "If you're in this with him, I will come for you. With assistance. Do you understand me?"

"I don't have a clue what you're talking about," Graves slimed assuredly.

Before Holt could respond, he saw Nikky Dorati and Cora Mae Hartwig return to the front of the building from opposite directions.

Nikky chewed a cigar. "Not here. Cora Mae and I checked the whole joint."

"Lots of people say they saw him within the last half hour," Cora Mae added. "In fact Corinne Spellman is certain she saw a woman with dark hair drive up and get him at the back entrance."

Jason Graves snickered. "Corinne Spellman is also certain she had dinner with her dead sister tonight."

Holt glared at Graves. It was looking more and more like a cover-up. "What kind of car did Corinne say it was?" If he had helped Reinhardt escape, he would share the pain.

"She said it was a light color, maybe white or beige. A large, new model." Cora Mae Hartwig pointed to the road. "Sort of like—that one there!"

A champagne-colored Lexus roared from the driveway with a tall, older male passenger. A dark-haired woman drove.

"Are you sure that's him?" Graves said as the three turned and ran to the car.

"Cora Mae, you'd better wait here!" the Rev suggested.

"And miss the fun?" the woman said, pulling the back door closed behind her. "Piffle on that! Let's go!"

Holt liked her spirit but worried about her getting hurt. Hell, she was nearly ninety, she could decide what risks she'd take. "Fine," he said as he started the engine.

"Hit 911!" Lucas yelled to Dorati and peeled out of the driveway.

"I should be drivin' this thing," Dorati said, punching the numbers. "You don't know getaways." He held on tight to the door. "That car's got more power. You'll never catch her."

"She's heading to 360 because it leads to the Interstate," Cora Mae said.

A voice blared on the speakerphone. "911. Can I help you?"

"This is Father Lucas Holt and I need you to patch me through to Lieutenant Granger immediately." The Rev's voice was sharp. His adrenaline surged at the possibility of catching the man who had killed Lisa Enright and the others. The other car was gaining ground, leaving them further behind. He had to get to Susan for backup. "Matter of life and death."

"Yeah." Dorati tightened his seat belt as the Rev floored the accelerator. "Ours."

"That is highly unusual, Father Holt. We can't tie up this line—"

"No," he demanded. "You don't understand. I need to talk to her right—"

"Listen, asshole!" Dorati yelled at the microphone. "Do you want to be the one to tell her you let two perps escape?"

"Patching now."

Dorati turned toward the backseat. "Sorry, Cora Mae."

"I've heard the word once or twice in my time, Nicholas."

"Granger here. By."

"Susan, this is Lucas."

"Lucas! What the hell are you—?"

"We're chasing Truman Reinhardt and a dark-haired woman presumed to be his accomplice down Bee Caves Road at ninety miles an hour." He hesitated as the car cornered on two wheels up the entrance to the Capitol of Texas Highway. Holt had driven fast on the Autobahn, a road designed for no speed limit, but it was all he could do to hold the MX6 to the road as the needle approached 100. "And now we're heading north on 360 with a Westlake trooper on our butt."

"You'll have more than that on your butt if you don't stop and leave this to us."

"Then get us some backup, Susan dear!" Cora Mae yelled from the back seat.

"You've got Cora Mae in the car with you, you idiot?"

"Me, too, Susan dear," Dorati trilled.

Holt laid on the horn as a green light turned yellow fifty yards ahead at the entrance to the Austin Country Club. The Lexus swished through as the light changed to red. Holt cursed and blinked his bright lights. He swerved left to miss the car turning in front of him.

Cora Mae and Nikky screamed as the MX6 skidded, then righted itself and sped up even faster.

"Shit!" Granger exclaimed. "Are you getting this, Central?"

"Got it all, Lieutenant. A big ten-four."

"Then dispatch cars up to 360 where it empties into IH 35. Call Round Rock and Georgetown and alert them to the chase." She raised her voice. "And you, Lucas!"

"What? Hurry the hell up, Susan! They're going to make it to the interstate before you can stop them." He watched the tachometer needle move to the red zone. Sweat poured from his face. His hands locked on to the steering wheel. The interstate turn ramp was a single lane overhead one hundred feet up. He hoped the tires would hold the road.

Susan Granger pleaded. "Lucas! Listen to me for a change! They can't outrun the radio. I need you here at the Davis house."

Holt saw an APD cruiser cross the median and scream past them. His mind flashed on Eddie and Omar and hoped Susan wasn't alluding to them—or the Davises—as the reason to return.

"Cavalry's here, Lucas dear. I think we can back off now."

"Thank you, Cora Mae," Granger said.

"Thank you, Cora Mae," Dorati echoed, his foot pressed hard to the floor where the brake would be.

"Okay. Okay," Holt said, slowing the car past the turnoff. He would have to trust that the police would get them. That was, after all, their business. His business was to attend to Garvin and Lavelle Davis and Omar and Eddie, assuming there was anything left to attend. He had to ask her about them. He had to know before he got there. "Have you found any, uh, bodies?"

"EMS is searching the area. We can't get in the house yet."

Holt thought her voice sounded pessimistic. The scene must be a mess. "We're on our way. Roger Wilco. Over and out."

At the next crossover he turned and raced for Mt. Bonnell.

Bulging canvas hoses disengorged torrents of water onto the burning black shell of the house, and still the flames licked high into the black sky.

"Got the damned gas turned off yet?" Susan Granger yelled at the fire chief.

"You'll know when the flames die down!" the chief yelled back. "The gas is feeding them. Main's at the bottom of the mountain—a special line. It's taking them longer to locate it. Should be any second, though." He pointed to the reduction in fire. "That's got it. Should be a lot easier to end now."

"How soon can we get into the house?"

"You mean for bodies?"

"Yes. Should be two of them. Maybe an animal, too. A dog."

"Check with me in ten minutes. We'll know if it's safe."

Susan Granger was about to thank him when she saw the black MX6 pull up to the periphery of the hoses. She was furious at Holt for not disclosing what he knew earlier. Maybe the disaster in front of her could have been prevented. But she also knew how distraught he felt about the four potential bodies in the blaze. If they were all dead, and it looked like they had to be, Holt would be an even bigger problem. He wouldn't rest until the perp was caught, and he and the rest of his cronies would be in her face until that time. She took a deep breath and radioed to the officer stopping them at the police line.

"Campbell, this is Granger. By."

"Go ahead, Lieutenant. Got Father Holt, a senior citizen, and a greasy ex-con here. By."

"Let them through. By."

"You got it, Lieutenant. Out."

In the background of white light she could see the cop's outline shake its head. As the trio approached, she overheard parts of their conversation.

"—senior citizen shit. I'll deck him for you."

"I'm quite capable of decking him myself, thank you." Cora Mae patted Nikky's arm. "You've been very helpful in that regard."

Holt squinted from the intense heat of the blaze as he walked toward Susan. He could see the tight-lipped frustration reflected in the orange light on her smoke-streaked face. Their eyes met and acknowledged the horror of the scene.

"Nobody could walk out of that," Holt said with resignation. "Found them yet?"

Dorati shielded his eyes from the blaze. "Only thing you'll find in that crematory is a few loose teeth."

"If we'd have been faster we could have prevented this," Granger snapped. "A neighbor smelled gas and had just reported it when the explosion happened. By the time the trucks got up the hill half the house was gone. They just shut the gas off a few minutes ago."

Holt felt the verbal punch from her. He wondered if she was right, if they could have prevented this, if he should have told her earlier what they knew.

"Probably too late to catch anybody in the cordon," Dorati said, looking around. "And any tire tracks are history in this water and mud."

"Campbell ordered a perimeter check but I haven't heard the result." She spoke into her radio. "Campbell? Granger. By."

"Okay, Lieutenant. By."

"Status on perimeter? By."

"Funny you should ask. Pardue just called in a van."

"What kind of van?" Holt said. Maybe Omar and Eddie had borrowed—or stolen—the thing to watch the house in?

The dispatch officer broke in. "Got a patch from the pursuit car, Lieutenant. Want it? By."

Lucas didn't want it. He wanted to know about the van. He shook his head and Susan ignored him.

"Yes. Sit tight, Campbell. By."

"Lieutenant Granger?" A slow drawl dripped through the radio like molasses through a sieve. "This is Ranger Kendall."

"We got the Texas Rangers on this?" Dorati rolled his eyes.

"Just one." Holt rolled his eyes.

Susan scowled at them. "Go ahead, Kendall. By."

"I happened to be in the area, ma'am, when I heard the pursuit call. They said the ve-hicle turned off IH 35 at the Walburg exit, so I pulled my cruiser across the center of the one-lane road that goes through the town."

"Just your cruiser? By."

"Well, I did commandeer three civilian cars from the local German restaurant. You know the Walburg Mercantile? They were glad to help. Then I just stood by the car and waited."

"He just stood there?" Cora Mae said in the background.

"Yes, ma'am," the drawl replied. "I just stood there with my shotgun slung over my arm. I knew they'd stop. They always do."

"So you got Truman Reinhardt and the woman? They're in your custody? By."

"Not exactly, ma'am."

Dorati shook his head. "The mofo shot 'em. I knew it."

"Shit," Holt said and turned away.

"No, sir," the deep, steady voice from the radio replied. "I didn't have to shoot 'em."

Holt turned back. What the hell was going on here? Something sounded very wrong.

"What happened? By."

"As soon as they saw the block across the road, they slowed and came to a stop right at my feet. I instructed them to exit the vehicle and they obeyed."

"You would, too, if a shotgun was in your face," Dorati whispered to Holt.

"I asked them their names and they showed me ID for a Mr. and Mrs. Wilhelm Krueger. I asked why they were traveling at a high rate of speed and they explained they had reservations for a restaurant and they were an hour late. They said they thought the police were chasing somebody ahead of them."

The Rev looked at Susan Granger. "Designated decoy."

She nodded and spoke to the Ranger. "Book them on suspicion of conspiracy to commit murder. By."

"Unless you have some connection with the original perps, ma'am, I don't think I'll do that. I checked their records, and of course they don't have nothing so much as a parking ticket. I think we'd save the State of Texas a lot of wasted court money if we just gave them a speeding ticket and sent them on to dinner."

"Shit," Granger said, unaware her finger was on the button.

"Hell," Holt said dejectedly. "Let 'em go. Reinhardt paid them off just like he paid off Justin Graves. And we'll never prove any of it now."

The Ranger spoke again. "Whoever that is, he's right, ma'am. I think you just plain got snookered on this one. Don't feel bad. Happens to the best of us. How could you know? By."

"Ticket them. Get all the usual information. We'll follow up when we catch the perps. By."

"Glad to help, ma'am. Anytime at all. Ay-di-os. Out."

"So much for that dead end," Holt said, looking back at the now smoldering fire. He was glad that Susan Granger looked as disgusted as he felt.

She started to speak. "How the hell will we find—"

"Lieutenant? By."

"Yes, Campbell. By."

Shit, Holt thought. He had already forgotten about the bodies. What was wrong with him? He was too distracted. He had to pull himself together if they were to find any leads. Stay on track. Pay attention. Keep your emotions at bay for the moment.

Campbell continued. "About that perimeter search? I started to tell you Pardue called in a report of a van. By."

"A wheelchair van?" Dorati mumbled as Holt threw him a puzzled look.

"A wheelchair van? By."

"Ten-four, Lieutenant. But the funniest thing about it—"

"The sliding door's open, but the wheelchair's sitting empty in the van," Dorati said to himself.

"The side door's open, but the wheelchair's sitting in the van," Campbell repeated, as if they were singing rounds. "And there were two men taped up in there. By."

Holt looked at Granger. "Omar and Eddie."

"One black. One white?" Granger said.

"How'd you know, Lieutenant? The black guy was hurt pretty bad. EMS sent them to Archie Mac's."

"We'll stop there on the way home," Holt said to Cora Mae. He was relieved they were alive. Now for Garvin and Lavelle.

Granger continued. "Registration on the van? By."

"Tomas Perez," Dorati said. "He's a Vietnam veteran."

"Checked to a Tomas Perez. DPS says Vietnam vet. By."

Susan Granger looked at Nikky. "Damn you, Dorati. Is there anything else I should know about this case you haven't yet deigned to reveal to me?"

Dorati held up his hands. "Just because you all are slow on the uptake, don't blame—"

"Stop it, you two," Cora Mae intervened. "We have bigger fish to fry here."

"Bad analogy," Dorati mumbled to the Rev, rolling his eyes at the fire.

"And I think I have an idea how we can do it, too." The old woman leaned against the lieutenant's car.

"How's that, Cora?" Holt asked.

"Follow the—"

Suddenly they heard a shout from behind the house.

"Lieutenant! Back here!"

The fire chief nodded his okay. "Go ahead. It's under control now. Just be careful."

The three circled the sizzling house through the dense woods, ignoring the mud and soot as they stumbled toward the voice of Officer Pardue. In the light of the flames they saw a mud-covered officer holding up the badly burned body of Tomas Perez. The smell of burnt flesh turned Holt's stomach, and he had to gulp hard not to vomit.

Holt saw two other bodies in torn garments propped against a tree just beyond. To his shock, Lucas Holt recognized them as the unmoving bodies of Garvin and Lavelle Davis. He looked at the cop. "Are they—?"

"No." Pardue nodded toward the couple. "The med-tech says they'll be all right. They must've gotten knocked out by the blast and inhaled too much smoke. Minor concussions, maybe a few burns. EMS is right behind you to pick 'em up."

Holt looked around to see four people in fluorescent jackets descending the slope with the help of ropes and lights from their trucks. He said a quick thanks to God. At least Reinhardt had failed at this one.

"This guy's another story," Pardue said, shaking his head. "His burns are bad," he said to Holt, grimly.

"Cold," Perez whispered.

Nikky Dorati took off his jacket and laid it over the man's chest. "We'll get you out of here, man."

"No," Perez coughed out. "Not going. Need—to talk—with Rev. No cops."

"I'm afraid I can't allow—" Susan Granger began.

"He's dying, Susan," Holt replied sternly. "This is my territory now, not yours." Cops were good at restoring order, but now that the scene was under control it was up to him to take charge of the uncontrollable—this man's death.

"My job is to know what happened, and EMS has to try to save him, if for nothing else than for me."

"Tell her—later." Perez squinted his eyes. "Now—you."

Holt frowned at Susan. They both knew from their separate backgrounds that Perez was dying. The Rev wanted it to happen quickly here, instead of in an E.R. after being pommeled by well-meaning rescuers and questioned by well-meaning cops. "Come on, Susan. Let me do this."

Granger stood and stepped away. "Right."

EMS techs applied oxygen to Garvin and Lavelle Davis and strapped them on body boards to carry them to waiting transports. Garvin Davis awoke to see Lucas Holt kneeling beside a badly burned man. He tried to speak under the mask. Cora Mae Heartwig heard his voice.

"What did he say?" she asked the tech.

"Something about 'saved lives' was what I got." The EMS woman looked at her partner. "One. Two. Lift," she said, and they carried him off. The other two followed with his wife.

"No—cops." Tomas Perez waved away the EMS tech trying to attend him. The woman shook her head and handed Holt a plastic squeeze bottle with a straw.

"Give him this when he asks for water," the tech said. "He's going."

Nikky Dorati waited for her to leave before he grabbed the bottle and dumped it out. He emptied the contents of a pocket flask into it and screwed the top back on. "We'll give him this when he asks for water. It'll kill the pain."

Cora Mae motioned to Officer Pardue. "I'll help here. You can join Lieutenant Granger." She cradled the dying man's head in her lap. The smell of sloughing skin from his face mixed with the charred remains of his hair. She couldn't help but cough. "Sorry, dear. I'll be still now."

Perez looked up at Dorati and Holt. Nikky put the plastic tip to the man's mouth and squeezed slightly. Perez swallowed, coughed and seemed to regain his senses.

"Thanks." He grimaced a smile. "One more—"

Dorati squeezed again.

"Absolution?" Holt offered.

"Don't—matter, Rev. Wait till I tell you—before—"

He coughed and Cora Mae lifted his head higher on her lap.

"Not much—time here, Rev. Okay to tell cops after. Just don't want them around now. No authority. Too much like Nam."

"What happened tonight?" Holt asked.

"First—first let me tell." He gasped as he shivered in pain. "Shit. First—after Nam. Used the chair to be left alone. If disabled, people ignore you. Hated people. Everybody. Money no problem—had disability and inheritance. Family wealthy. I didn't want—be around them, either." He looked up at Holt. "Tell them, my family, Rev. What I did."

"What did you do, Tomas?" Holt knew Perez had a few minutes left, nothing more. He wanted the man to say what he could while he could. "Go on."

"Made friends with no one. Till met Sparks. Nice old man. Crazy old man. Liked him. He wanted help with Tru—"

"Truman Reinhardt?" Holt said.

"Yeah. I—not trust him. Bad person. But Sparks thought he—had good idea. I drove Sparks around. Helped set it up. Not for money. For Sparks. Liked old man. I loaned him money."

Perez shivered and Dorati gave him another shot of whiskey.

"You took him to the track, didn't you?" Dorati said. "You wanted him to win back the money you loaned him so he could pay you back without losing face. You knew the boys at the track and told him which ponies would hit."

"Right," Perez said, his voice weakening. "But last minute—had second thoughts."

"You couldn't see people senselessly killed, could you?" the Rev said. "It was too much like—"

"Yeah. Too much like Nam. Stupid killing. Innocent people. Especially—" He painfully nodded his blackened head toward the house. "Especially—that."

"Fire?" Dorati asked, ready to squeeze again.

"Like napalm," Holt replied. He had talked with many vets in the pen, heard the horror stories that branded them for life. Fortunately the branding on this man had resulted in saved lives.

"Explosions!" Perez was wide-eyed. "Couldn't let it—happen—again."

"You came here to stop it," Cora Mae said, her eyes brimming. "Why didn't you just call the police?" she said. "They could have—"

"Hate—authorities." He shivered. "Cold."

Dorati gave him more whiskey. A larger shot this time.

Perez coughed. "Came here after Reinhardt left. Took out two dudes—nosin' around. Don't know who—"

"I know them," Holt said. "They're okay." Lucas was thankful the two were alive, and that he and Dorati wouldn't have to pay a return visit to Jason Graves.

"Broke in house after Reinhardt left. Saw explosive but couldn't—" Perez made the motions but seared glands would not let the tears come. "Couldn't stop it in time. Woke them up and forced them—"

"They didn't believe you?" Holt asked.

"No. They thought I—crazy. Forced them out—with gun. But too late."

"The explosion caught you as you left the house," Cora Mae whispered.

"Yes. They were ahead. I heard—noise. Dog. Turned around and—all—all red." His breathing seemed to change. "Just like Nam." He breathed out and relaxed beyond pain.

"Absolution?"

His mouth formed a silent "Yes."

Holt made the sign of the Cross over the dying man's body. "Your sins are forgiven in the name of the Father, the Son, and the Holy Spirit. Amen. Depart in peace, welcomed by angels."

"Tell—family." Tomas Perez shuddered a final time, saliva

drooling from his lips. "Cold," he whispered as his head fell limp on Cora Mae's lap.

She crossed herself, kissed her fingers, and placed them on his charred forehead.

Susan Granger returned with two EMS techs. "They'll take him to the morgue, Lucas," she said. "You and I need to talk."

"Shitty deal. Lousy death," Holt said sadly. Perez had been a good man who wanted to live in solitude, he thought. Whatever bad traits there had been were transfigured by the risk of his life tonight, and the painful loss of it by fire.

"Are there good deaths?" Granger asked.

He looked at her. "Some are a hell of a lot better than others. Better than this one," he said angrily. It was not enough that Garvin and Lavelle were saved. He was furious that Reinhardt had escaped, leaving one more dead body in his wake.

"We have to find that Dr. Reinhardt, Susan," Cora Mae said, giving Perez over to the EMS tech. Dorati helped her to her feet and guided her back up the slippery hill.

"We'll get him, Cora Mae," Dorati said when they had reached Granger's car.

"You're damned right we'll get him," Holt repeated.

"I don't like the way you said that," Granger said. "If you have any information the police need to catch this couple, I suggest you spill it now."

"This is one time I'd be glad to oblige you, Lieutenant," Dorati replied. "But I'm as stumped as you are." He looked at the Rev. "At least temporarily."

Granger growled at him. "Keep the God Squad out of this, Dorati, and that's an order."

"Where the hell else you going to look, Susan?" Holt asked sarcastically. He was going to rally the Squad to find Reinhardt tonight, regardless of what Susan said.

"I did have something to add on that, if you don't mind my intrusion," Cora Mae said delicately.

"What's that, Cora Mae?" Dorati asked.

"I think I have an idea where—or *how* to find him."

"How's that?" Granger said.

"The same way you find anyone, Susan, dear." Cora Mae

Hartwig smiled as if stating the most obvious thing in the world.

"Follow the money," she said.

They all sat nervously in the lieutenant's office as Susan Granger paced behind her desk. "It's eight-thirty, no banks are open. Any deposits were made with untraceable cashier's checks. No way can we know where they're headed."

"Susan?" the Rev said. "Do you think you could vacate your office a few minutes?" He knew he was pushing. He also knew she was to the point of taking help where she could get it.

"I should lock you all up and put you through polygraphs." She grabbed her purse and went to the door. "I'll pretend to get coffee. Just have something when I get back." She pulled the door closed.

"Turn on the radio by her desk," Holt said to Cora Mae. "Loud."

Dorati pulled a plug under the carpet by her chair. "Nice try, Lieutenant," he said, pointing to the speakerphone.

"Good," Holt said as they huddled in the center of the small office, close enough to hear each other over the country-western music. "How will we tell her we can trace the money?"

Cora Mae spoke. "Simple, Lucas. We'll tell her the truth."

The Rev shook his head. "Cora Mae, I don't think we can say you hired someone to kill me so the God Squad could catch him."

"And besides"—Dorati bit his lip—"the check didn't go to Reinhardt."

"What?" Holt said, his eyes wide. "I thought you said he was behind the whole deal."

"I did. But I knew Reinhardt wouldn't go for Cora Mae having you offed. He's seen her at the retirement center, and he knows how she feels about you. He'd never believe us."

"But you told me you set the whole thing up?" Holt said, puzzled. How had he done it without going to Reinhardt?

"What did you do with the check I gave you, Nicholas?" Cora Mae said in a worried voice.

"I arranged a drop with his accomplice."

"His *accomplice*? Reinhardt has an *accomplice*?" Holt was surprised by the revelation from Nikky. Is this what he had been holding back so long? And if so, how the hell did he know who it was? "Are you talking about Jason Graves here?"

"No, it's a woman," Dorati confessed sheepishly.

Holt stared at him. "How do you know this?" He had trusted Nikky at the pen, and he trusted him now. The Rev's anger was being overcome by curiosity. Nikky had a hole card somewhere, and he wasn't showing it, even yet.

Dorati took a deep breath. "Hold on, Rev. Lighten up here a minute, will ya?" He took out his cigar and chewed on it. "We don't have time to go into all that now. You got to trust me." He looked at Cora Mae. "I gave the check to his partner. And I guarantee you, if we find her, we'll find him."

"'Her' who?" Holt said, surprised again. Why was Nikky still holding back? "What's her name?" Holt knew there must be something big at stake for him to keep things this quiet.

"It doesn't matter right now, Rev."

"Maybe not to you," Holt began. Then he backed off. There was no time to argue this now. Susan Granger would be back and they needed a plan. He would press Dorati later in the privacy of the Buffalo Barn Grille. "You're right, Nikky. Later."

"What we need right now is a good lie," Cora Mae said, "as to how they got my check."

"No, we don't," Holt said. "We just tell her—"

Susan Granger opened the door with a cardboard box of coffees balanced in one hand. "Tell her what?" she said. "And turn that damned radio off, Dorati."

Nikky and Cora Mae looked at the Rev.

He furrowed his brow and tried to look truthful. "Tell you that Cora Mae wrote a check to—to the perpetrator, by mistake."

"You're full of shit, Lucas Holt," Granger said, passing the coffee cups. "But fortunately for you I don't have time to fight with you. I don't even want to hear the lie. I can press charges later. The question now is, how do we find it?"

Cora Mae spoke up. "I believe Lucas thinks that if we trace the flow of the check and see where it went, we should have some idea of where Dr. Reinhardt is headed, don't you think?"

Susan Granger took a deep breath before she exploded. "Dammit, Cora Mae. This man will lead you down the wrong path every time."

"Why don't we just try to find the check, Susan," Holt proposed. "You can be upset at us later if it doesn't pan out. And I promise we'll explain just as soon as we think of something plausible." The Rev walked by the open door as two officers escorted a prisoner through the adjoining room. "Right now we have to figure out how to get into the bank files after hours."

There was a loud commotion outside as the prisoner shouted. "Bank files! No problem, Rev! I can do it."

The Rev turned around to see the smiling face of a handcuffed Jimmy Brickhouse.

"What the hell is he talking about?" Susan Granger said as she looked out the doorway. "Who is that?"

"Yo! Lieutenant." The man in leg chains sounded like he had just walked into a bar. "It's me! Your man Brickhouse!"

"Get this clown out of—"

"I hate to tell you this, Susan," the Rev said, moving over to her, "but he *can* get into those files. And on your own computer here in your office."

The escort officer protested. "He's on his way to TDC, Lieutenant. Parole violation—in a church with a gun tonight. They're pulling the chain right now. Van's downstairs, waiting."

"'Pulling the chain'?" Cora Mae looked at Dorati.

"That's what they call it when the jail sends a group of prisoners to TDC—Texas Department of Correction. Pulling the chain—like on an old toilet." Dorati made a downward gesture over his head. "You pull the chain to flush 'em down the tubes."

"Thank you, Nicholas. I stand enlightened."

"Come on, Susan," Holt intervened. "I can explain the whole thing about him being at Sparks's church. And besides, even if you send him back, what's the difference where he does the next twenty-four hours—here or Huntsville?" The Rev knew she didn't have many options. But then, neither did he. It was a good sign that she pursed her lips and sighed.

"Damn. Bring him in here." She punched Brickhouse hard on the arm as she removed his cuffs. "If you're bullshittin' us, Brickhouse, and that chain goes without you for nothing, I will personally make sure with the warden that solitary confinement looks like luxury compared to where they put you."

Holt watched Brickhouse smile the smile of a man who had

gotten over one more time. The Rev enjoyed the hell out of seeing his Squad beat the system, if even for a night. It reminded him that authoritarians were not always authorities.

"Bring on the bug box," Brickhouse commanded with a grin.

Granger led him to a chair by the computer on her desk.

"Any coffee?" he requested.

"Don't push it, criminal," Granger hissed under her breath.

"You can have mine." Holt handed it to him as Granger scowled. He had seen the man work wonders in Huntsville. Like Babe Ruth pointing to the right field fence, he'd hit the home run and grin rounding the bases.

Jimmy Brickhouse laced his fingers and cracked his knuckles. He rubbed his fingertips together and blew on them as if he had the D.A.'s private safe in front of him—which he'd had at one time. Holt watched him glance at the clock to make sure he took long enough for the chain to pull without him.

"What's your account number, Miss Hartwig?"

She gave it to him with the date of the check and the bank.

"Everything I needed to know I learned in prison, to coin a phrase," Brickhouse mimicked as he quickly punched the keys, watched the results, punched more keys, and waited.

"They taught you this in computer class?" Granger said.

"Not exactly, Susan," Holt interrupted. "He learned this from a guy named Petey McGaskill who could access nearly anything in the world from his jail cell. And he only had a palmtop."

"It was swell," Brickhouse said, staring at the screen.

Susan Granger shook her head. "Well, has Petey's prime pupil come up with anything? Or do we need to call Petey?"

Brickhouse punched in several more commands. "McGaskill got out last month, Lieutenant. He's long gone by now, and all on other people's money, too. Quite a guy."

"Cut the crap, Brickhouse," Granger warned. "I can still get you on that chain."

"I don't think so, Lieutenant." Brickhouse pointed to a small subsection on the screen. "I think you'll be too busy checking out airports for late international flights tonight." He motioned them over.

"What's with all the numbers?" Holt asked, looking at the screen filled with eleven-digit codes.

"These tell us the routing of the check, Rev," Brickhouse proudly announced. "According to this number trail, it went directly from here to a bank in San Antonio—that's this number here. I don't pretend to know all the sequences listed, but most of them are big cities like New York and Miami."

"Bottom line?" Granger demanded.

"Bottom line," he said, pointing to the screen, "is that the money ended up in a bank in São Paulo, Brazil. I know that number because so many, uh, people use it. Or so Petey said."

"So we need to check flights to Brazil?" Cora Mae asked.

"Makes sense to me," Brickhouse said.

Granger ordered the escort officer. "Get on the phone to the airport. Tell them it's an emergency. Find out—"

"Wait a minute, Susan." Holt glanced at Brickhouse and raised his eyebrows. "Can you do it?"

"Give me a minute," Brickhouse said, clearing the screen.

Holt spoke to Granger. "He may be able to access that data for us right here."

"But this computer isn't hooked into that system," Granger protested.

"It wasn't hooked into the bank files, either," Holt replied for him. "Let him try it."

Granger dumped her coffee in the trash. "Shit."

"Susan, dear."

"Sorry, Cora Mae. Sometimes it's hell being on the right side of the law."

"It sure is," Holt added.

"How would you know?" Granger said.

Brickhouse punched keys like he was playing Chopin.

"We're in the SABRE system."

"He learned this in *prison*?" the lieutenant said.

"Isn't rehabilitation wonderful?" Cora Mae smiled.

Brickhouse kept typing. "I'm checking flights to South America, or ones ending up there, from Texas, Oklahoma, Louisiana, and New Mexico. He could have rented a small plane to take him to an outlying airport." He paused. "The names?"

Holt glanced at Dorati. "We just have one so far. Try this." He wrote out *Reinhardt*.

Brickhouse punched it in. "Checking." He paused and looked

at the screen. "Nope. Nobody by that name is leaving any of these states in the next seventy-two hours."

A deep voice came from the office doorway.

"That's because you're using the wrong system." A tall woman with black hair and red lipstick strode into the room, smoking a cigarette.

"Who the hell are you?" Granger asked, pointing to the ashtray. "And put that damned thing out."

"I don't know the name, but I know the scent," Cora Mae announced. "It was in Marie Wilkins's apartment."

The Rev walked up to her. Although he had only caught fleeting glimpses of her at the hospital Auxiliary dinner, he was certain this was the woman who had accompanied Truman Reinhardt and whisked out the door as Holt and Granger told Mrs. Gottig her son was murdered. What had Mrs. Gottig called her? The name came to him. "Ms. Pelham, I presume?"

"Another little surprise you've been holding back on me, Lucas?" Susan Granger advanced on the two.

Before he could answer, Cora Mae Hartwig responded, "Haven't I seen you at the Westlake Retirement Center?"

The tall woman flipped an ID in front of Granger's face.

"FBI, Lieutenant. Special Agent Pelham." She acknowledged Holt with a slight bow. "Helen Pelham."

Holt wondered what was going on here with this woman's sudden appearance. He also noted Nikky's odd reaction to her. Usually Dorati observed every move of new people, scoped them out to get a line on them, or see how he could use them. Why was he hanging back, staring at the screen more than Brickhouse?

The Special Agent continued. "I've been trailing Reinhardt—and his wife, Ida Tabor—around the country for five years. And yes, I have been living at the same retirement center he did. This is the closest I've gotten, and I'm not going to let go now."

Susan Granger checked the ID and moved toward Pelham. "So you expect to just barge in here and take over? On my jurisdiction? After we've spent all this time and effort to flush out the quail, you want to come in for the kill?" She was face to face with Pelham now. "I don't think so, lady."

The Rev smiled at Susan's defensiveness. He would remind her later that she was actually giving credit to the God Squad. He stepped beside her to intervene. "I believe the goal here, Susan, is to catch a murderer or two, right? So if this woman can help us, don't you think we ought to let her?"

"Wait a minute," Granger said to Pelham. "You're the reason BCI was stiffing me! You're why they were so cool about information on this guy, aren't you?"

The black-haired woman took a step back. "I regret that I could not let you or anyone else in on this undercover work, Lieutenant, but too much was at stake here."

Jimmy Brickhouse broke the tension. "I ran the other name through the system. No correlation there, either," he said.

The Rev spoke to Pelham. "Did you say he had to get into a different system?"

"Yes, I did." Pelham looked at Granger. "May I?"

Lucas touched Susan on the shoulder. "I want these people as bad as you do."

Granger nodded. "Do it. But I'm checking credentials," she said, picking up a phone.

Special Agent Pelham leaned over to Brickhouse. "Let me get into the master SABRE system. It's not well known, but it's called—"

"It's called XCALIBR," the prisoner announced smugly. "But not even Petey McGaskill knew the sequence codes."

"I'm glad to see our prisons are teaching useful skills." Helen Pelham moved to the machine. "I can get in, but I'm not sure how to access individual files. Can you do it from there?"

"Does a bear shit in the woods, lady?"

She took his place and, making sure his back was turned, punched in a series of numbers and commands. The computer beeped as though it had been burped after feeding.

"Ready," she said, moving from the chair. "Go for it."

Jimmy Brickhouse again sat, drank his coffee, and punched up different screens using different initials.

"Try using R.T. instead of T.R. for Reinhardt," Pelham said. "Simple reversal is the most common disguise."

"Where's Rod Serling when I need him?" Granger complained.

The Rev walked over to Nikky, who was leaning against a file cabinet. "What's going on with you?" he asked.

"Don't know what you're talking about, Rev."

"You only say that when you know exactly what I'm talking about." Lucas knew the door was shut, and there was no sense trying to break it down. Nikky would show only the cards he wanted to be known. "You'll tell me when it's time, right?"

"When you need to know," Dorati answered, and moved behind the computer where Brickhouse stared at the screen. The prisoner could move faster now that the chain had been pulled. Holt watched him punch a three-key sequence to speed up the search. Anything to control and manipulate. Just like the rest of us.

"Nothing in DFW Airport or Houston under any of the six possible combinations of R.T. and T.I. There are interesting initials but none of the ages match. Same with the other regional airports. Last try is San Antonio, but that's way too obvious. It's the closest one, other than Austin."

"Did you try Austin?" Holt asked.

"Didn't think there'd by any need to, Rev. That's the first place they know the cops would check."

"Run it next," Pelham said.

Brickhouse reluctantly typed in the numbers and squinted his eyes at the data scrolling past him. "Blank screen, Fed lady. Only hope is San Antone." He pulled up the flights and ran the initials through them. "Got some fun names, but only one matches perfectly." Brickhouse pointed to the screen as Lucas Holt looked over his shoulder. "But the flight leaves in an hour."

Helen Pelham leaned close and whispered something only Brickhouse could hear.

"Are you shittin' me?" he answered, grinning ear to ear as he turned to the keyboard.

"Did anyone in this room hear me give an order to this man?" Pelham asked and looked around. "Good. Then we had better hurry if we want to get to San Antonio before that plane leaves."

"Listen, lady," Dorati said. "Even if you let the Rev drive, you can't make that plane in an hour. San Antonio is ninety minutes away, at least."

Susan Granger hung up the phone. "FBI says you're legit and to do everything to cooperate." Her tone was reluctantly acquiescent. "We can get you there on time in a copter from Mueller Airport."

Helen Pelham thought a second. "Problem is I want to be as unobtrusive as possible. This couple is very savvy. They may be monitoring air activity as well as the police radio. I don't want to do anything to chase them underground now."

Holt spoke to her. "If we take an EMS copter from San Jacinto Hospital, we can radio we're life-flighting a patient back to Mexico from Austin via San Antonio."

"And there's no problem with the ride to San Antone, lady." Brickhouse swiveled to face them. "It seems there's suddenly been a ninety-minute delay in the departure time."

"Brickhouse?" Susan Granger began. "What the hell did you do?"

"Young man," Pelham said. "If you ever get out of jail, come see me for a job."

"Whatcha think, Lieutenant? 'Special Agent Brickhouse.' Got a nice ring to it, huh?"

"I think I'm going to puke."

"Susan, you'll have to call EMS and make this happen," Holt said cautiously. He wondered how cooperative she'd be after the intrusions from the God Squad, a returning prisoner, and the FBI.

"Just get them there." She picked up the phone. "Get me the chief," she growled into the receiver. "STAT."

"I'll drive to the hospital," the Rev said on his way to the door. "Meet me out front."

"I'll catch you guys later," Dorati said, standing to leave.

"You come with us, Dorati," Helen Pelham said. "You don't look like a cop, and from what I hear you can shoot straight."

"Do I have to?"

Holt knew Dorati hated heights and seldom flew in commercial jets, much less helicopters. "In a word: 'Yes,'" Holt answered, and vanished.

Pelham started out the door. "Lieutenant Granger, would you phone, not radio, the State Troopers to provide silent backup at the airport? And I mean I want them *invisible*."

"No problem." Susan Granger scowled.

"Be careful, Nicholas," Cora Mae Hartwig admonished.

"Tell that to the Rev," Dorati replied as he and Helen Pelham hurried from the office.

Lieutenant Granger hung up the phone. "I need a drink."

"So do I, dear," Cora Mae Hartwig agreed.

"Me, too," a voice echoed from in front of the CRT.

"Brickhouse, get away from that computer. What are you doing?"

"Just backing out of the system so no one can trace us, Lieutenant. It's like wiping off fingerprints. Give me another half minute." He continued and shut off the gray box. "Done."

"Officer Lindsey!" she yelled into the outer room, and a short, bearded man with glasses appeared. "Take the prisoner to his cell. And find out when the next chain's being pulled."

"Thank you for your help, Mr. Brickhouse." Cora Mae waved as he went out the door.

"Any time, ladies. My pleasure, I'm sure." He held his hands out to be cuffed by the officer.

Susan Granger plopped down in her chair as they left. "I'm exhausted. It's been a hell of a twenty-four hours."

"Now about that drink, dear?"

"What drink? I don't have anything here."

Cora Mae Hartwig reached into her purse. "A little brandy okay?" she said as she closed the office door.

The black-haired woman sat at a table overlooking the San Antonio Riverwalk and sipped a strawberry margarita. It was the nightly special at Dos Amigos, and it was her third in less than an hour. After the second one she had made a phone call that, despite the way he treated her, was the hardest thing she had ever done.

Ida Tabor watched the long, low boats full of tourists glide down the river; newlyweds celebrating their honeymoon, seniors spending their remaining time and money on vacation. Tears filled her eyes for the emptiness of her own future alone.

She finished the drink and signaled the waitress for one more. "For the road," Tabor said as she handed the young woman a fifty. "Keep the change. Spend it with somebody you trust."

That was, after all, the issue, wasn't it? He had betrayed her one too many times. And after all she had done for him. Well, two could play at that game. She had not told him of the one last contract she had taken, the one that would detain her one more day, the one that would prevent her meeting him on the plane in San Antonio tonight.

The chill of the evening overcame her tequilaed numbness and sent a shiver through her body. It was time to go back to the hotel room she had rented here when she abandoned the apartment in Austin. She would draw a hot bath and imagine events unfolding just a few miles away. She would not meet her husband of fifty-five years on the plane tonight. But, thanks to the call she had made, someone else would; someone who would change both of their lives forever.

Truman Reinhardt returned the car to the Gold Section. It was rented under one of several aliases he had acquired over the years, complete with credit cards. He pulled his small suitcase from the trunk, signed "Richard Tarpin," dropped the keys in the gold box, and walked quickly to the airline ticket counter.

"Flying first class today, Mr. Tarpin?" the agent said as though the man in front of him were a four-year-old and the agent were Mr. Greenjeans. "Destination São Paulo?" Without waiting for an answer, he continued. "It's one of our newest routes, and we think you'll find the service, well, superlative."

Truman Reinhardt was surprised the man didn't end the sentence with another question. "When does boarding begin?"

The agent hit a few keys. "Oh, there's been a delay."

Reinhardt's antennae went up, and he glanced around the terminal. "Is anything wrong?"

"No. When you're flying this distance and into foreign countries, there are often small delays due to weather." He squinted at the screen. "That's what this one says, in fact. Don't worry, it's only ninety minutes. You'll board in about forty minutes." He started to hand Reinhardt the ticket. "Wait a minute, Mr. Tarpin! Since you're first class, you have the pleasure of boarding early. You could go sit on the plane and have a drink while you wait. It's a new service we're offering on this route."

"I'll do that," Reinhardt said. Anything to get out of the mainstream of traffic. He would feel more secure on the plane, and a drink was just what he needed. "Thank you."

Minutes later "Richard Tarpin" settled comfortably into seat 4B of Flight 1179 from San Antonio to Buenos Aires, with through service to São Paulo. He had done it. They had done it. "What can I get you to drink, Mr. Tarpin?"

"Champagne, if you please." Reinhardt flashed the FDR smile that always got him what he wanted.

"Coming right up, sir."

It was too bad Ida wasn't here yet. But she would arrive soon enough, under a different name and in a different part of the cabin, of course. She had been testy the last few times they'd been together anyway. Maybe a couple of drinks would put him in a better mood to see her. Just what the doctor ordered, so to speak. The stewardess brought champagne. The sticky sweetness bubbled down his throat. Life was good. To a lifetime of luxury. To Ida—or maybe not to Ida. Maybe they had enough now to go their own ways. He was still attractive, still having occasional flings. Aging men had much more opportunity than aging women. Why would he want to tie himself down to Ida Tabor for the rest of his life?

He held his glass out to the stewardess to pour. Maybe Ida felt the same. That would account for her attitude lately. There was no way she could have known about the affairs he'd had.

He held his glass silently in the air. To the stewardess. To rich yuppie kids treating their parents like garbage. To parents taking their lives back into their own hands—at the expense of those same shitty rich kids.

He had realized a long time ago that he hated them all, the parents and their kids. He hated the greed that motivated them both, and the vengeance that wreaked death from parent to child, like some insane Abraham plotting the murder of Isaac and then putting the blame on the will of God. He hated it in the people that came to him, the people he used, and he hated it in himself for what he had done to his own offspring; ungrateful, manipulative shits that they were.

But he liked the money. He liked that very much. And since he figured, according to actuarial tables, that he had ten to fifteen good years left, he determined to live the hell out of them and spend every dollar they had acquired.

The stewardess filled his glass. His body grew soothingly warm.

After all, who was there to leave it to? His wife would outlive him, probably, barring unforeseen circumstances. When she died, the Mandala Foundation was directed to pay for them to be entombed together in the cemetery at Montmartre, near Sacré Coeur in Paris. The Foundation would then dissolve and distribute any remaining funds solely to that cathedral, which had been the favorite of their travels.

He closed his eyes and remembered their trek up the steps to the white domed church capping the hill overlooking Paris. Life was like going up those steps. Steep. Arduous. Yet the higher up you got, the more you saw. The further along the wiser, the more you knew. The steps seemed never ending, until you reached the last two and it was over too soon. You were at your destination and it was done. Maybe now that they were at the top of the steps, they had gone divergent ways, stood on opposite sides of the stairs with nothing left in common, looking at separate futures. Hell, maybe he'd give her one more try in Brazil. He could always change his mind.

He opened his eyes to see passengers queuing onto the plane. His glass refilled, he stared out the window. No sense making eye contact. You never knew who you could run into. He hoped nobody would sit in the seat beside him and try to make senseless conversation. Unless, of course, it was a gorgeous woman. He wouldn't mind that, even with Ida a few seats away.

Either the champagne had affected his vision, or he had just rubbed a lamp. A striking red-haired woman about ten years his junior put her bag in the overhead bin. As she lifted her arms, her skirt pulled up to the very bottom of her white silk panties.

"Those little things are hard to get into," she said as she sat down.

"They certainly are." Reinhardt smiled, meaning something entirely different. "Care to join me in some champagne?"

"I don't think we'll both fit in that little tiny glass, honey." The woman laughed, adjusting the low-cut front of her blouse. Reinhardt thought she knew he was looking and she liked it. "But I'll order some of my own."

The plane filled and the hatch door was about to be closed. The curtain was pulled separating first class and peon. A deep, stern voice sounded overhead.

"Ladies and gentlemen, this is the captain speaking."

"I hate it when they do that," the woman said. "Always means something's wrong."

"There's no problem with the aircraft and we'll be ready for departure in a matter of minutes if we can have your attention."

"One more glass of this and you can have all my attention you can handle, honey," the redhead said, lifting her glass to the speaker.

"This flight is overbooked and we need two volunteers to give up their seats to accommodate passengers. If you are willing to trade your reservation for the first flight out tomorrow morning we will compensate you with a $250 coupon good on any other ticket you purchase in the next year."

Truman Reinhardt looked at his companion. "Not enough money. They'll up it to $500 in a minute and get the people."

"Five hundred isn't enough money to get me off this flight. I'm spending inheritance money from my poor, deceased no-count husband who didn't even know I had insurance on him, and I can't wait to get to Brazil to do it."

"Three hundred fifty dollars," the captain said as again no hands went up. "Okay, folks, you win. Five hundred dollars."

Truman Reinhardt admired the view as the woman leaned over to get something from her purse on the floor. When he sat up, he felt cold steel at his temple.

"What the—?"

"This is our stop, honey. Five hundred did it. And please make a move. Please. Because there's nothing better I'd like to do right now than to air your friggin' skull out."

"Good job, Max," Lucas Holt said from the door of the cockpit, a gun in his hand. "Sit tight," he said to the other passengers in first. He saw they had trouble putting together his gun with his collar. "Special Agents." He winked at Max. "God Squad. We're out of here." He went ahead of the red-faced, startled Truman Reinhardt.

"You're not law enforcement officers," Reinhardt protested. "I don't have to go anywhere with you."

"And I don't have to stand trial for shooting an old fool like you," Max said. "We got deputized on the way down here. So shut up and walk."

"And if she won't shoot you, asshole, I will," Holt added angrily, nudging Reinhardt with the gun. "Move it."

"Ladies and gentlemen," the captain announced, "we have our volunteers. Flight attendants please prepare for departure."

The stewardess opened the first class curtain to reveal empty seats in 4A and B.

Helen Pelham met them at the end of the ramp, where she cuffed and Mirandaed Reinhardt.

"Where's Ida Tabor?" Holt asked. "She had a seat reserved in first class with you." He didn't really think Reinhardt would talk, but it was worth a try. Sometimes the collar conned people into public confessions.

"I don't know anyone by that name," Reinhardt replied.

Holt smirked. Sometimes a little competition worked. "Your loyalty may be misplaced, Truman. You notice who got busted tonight, don't you?" The Rev bit his lower lip. "Money in *both* your names, is it?"

"She'd never—"

"What was that, Reinhardt?" Helen Pelham said as she walked him through a cordon of plainclothes police.

The Rev glanced toward the next gate exit, outside of which a car waited with Nikky Dorati at the wheel. Instinctively, as if he were walking down a long cellblock corridor at night in the pen, he looked back over his shoulder into a darkened doorway. Why were the lights out in the men's john? He saw movement and pushed Max to the left, away from Truman Reinhardt. They had just passed the open entrance to the men's rest room when they heard the yell.

"Murderer!"

They turned in slow motion as a man fanned six shots into the jerking body of Truman Reinhardt.

Holt shielded Maxine as Pelham and others simultaneously crouched and fired, knocking the man backward with the exploding force of their bullets.

Dorati appeared at the door, gun in hand, thinking Reinhardt had killed Holt. "Shit I'm glad to see you!" he yelled to the Rev and went to help them up.

"Check all areas!" Pelham shouted as police scrambled to find other, nonexistent gunmen.

Nikky, Max, and the black-haired woman stood above the bloody body lying facedown on the bathroom floor.

"Who the hell is it?" Pelham said.

"'Was,'" Nikky corrected.

Holt knelt to turn him over, looked up at them, and said: "It's the grandpa of Lisa Enright's baby."

• Twelve •

Lucas Holt drove into his still unmarked parking space behind the church and gently closed the car door. He walked to Maxine's car and rolled up the window. It was unlike her to leave her car unlocked and open. She must have been in a hurry, probably rehashing last night's events at the San Antonio airport. He had done the same thing until a few hours ago, when exhaustion overcame him and let him sleep.

The Rev locked the door and smiled, knowing Max would think he was taking his time coming into the church, counting the seconds to predict his mood. Actually his mood was more relaxed, resolved, now that Truman Reinhardt was dead.

And J. D. Enright, too, quite frankly.

He knew it was unforgiving of him to feel gratified at their deaths, but it seemed one small step for justice as this world knows it. Not fairness, he thought as he crossed the parking lot back to the church; there was nothing fair about any of it, about life for that matter. But justice, maybe. More justice than he had seen in what was jokingly called the criminal justice system where "money talks and bullshit walks."

Both of the dead men were selfish and cruel; they used each other in ways that caused suffering to many others. No matter how well psychologists could explain and lawyers justify their behavior, the angry part of him was glad they were dead. The priest part of him trusted that Reinhardt, J.D., and himself would work this out in a very long, perhaps eternal, screaming match with God at the appropriate time. For now, he thought as he pulled open the huge brass and wood door, it was get into church or risk Maxine calling 911.

The red-haired ex-madam saw him coming and stood to hand him his mug of Earl Grey tea as he strode down the hallway to the office. Ironic that this was the first female face he had seen every morning for the last twenty years, with the same cup of tea in her hand. No wonder he felt attached to her. "Mornin', Max," he said, pecking her cheek. "Thank you very much. I need this."

"Mornin', Rev." She pecked him back in their usual ritual fashion. "You've got no idea how much you're gonna need it." She waved a sheaf of pink slips. "You have a zillion calls, with some good news and some bad news."

"Great," Holt said, leaning against the file cabinet. "Bad news first."

"Bad news is your computer file this morning says to remind you that you have to do twelve miles today and twenty tomorrow."

"Thanks," he said in feigned disinterest. "The good news?"

Max reached under her desk and handed him a cardboard box with a red ribbon around it that he could tell had been retied.

"This was sitting on my desk this morning addressed to you with a note from the Vestry." She handed him the paper.

"All it says is 'Isaiah 40.31.'"

"Which, of course, you can quote off the top of your head?" she said with a knowing smirk.

"That's why God made concordances." Bible passages were his worst area of expertise. "You looked it up for me, right?" he said hopefully.

"They shall run and not be weary," Max announced in her most austere voice.

"Drugs!" Holt said cheerily. "The Vestry bought me *drugs*!"

Maxine shook her head. "Not hardly, your reverendship."

Holt fingered the ribbon and narrowed his eyes at her. "You peeked?" he said in joking astonishment.

"Of course I peeked. What's a secretary for? I been peekin' since the pen. Shoot, I don't even *give* you half of it. Next time you come to my place remind me to show you the closet with all your stuff in it."

The Rev laughed. "Awright, awright. So what is it?"

Max untied the ribbon and handed him a bright yellow running headset.

"Dynamite!" Holt said, putting them on. He flicked the switch and country-western music blared into his ears.

"The sticky note said your old one couldn't be repaired."

"This is great! My other one wasn't digital. This one is preset to the local stations so I can avoid commercials."

"Who do you think preset it?"

"What?" he yelled, then took it off. "What?"

"I said I preset them myself this morning when I found it."

"Thanks," he replied. "Could you come home and do my VCR?" Holt picked up his mug and walked toward his office.

Maxine laughed and stuffed the pink slips back in his shirt pocket. "Don't forget these babies. And call the bishop first. Called four times before eight-thirty. The fifth time I told him you died and don't call back."

Holt grimaced. "My call will be a surprise, then?"

"Probably." Maxine winked and followed him into his office.

The Rev smiled. "I still think you'd make a great wife."

"Course I would. But nobody I know would make a great husband."

"What about Travis Layton?" he said, sitting at his desk and leafing through the messages. The image of the two of them together had some symmetry, as he pictured himself doing their wedding at St. Margaret's altar.

"Let you know after dinner this week."

There was a slight knock at the door. They turned to see Cora Mae Hartwig standing in her pink jogging suit, white Nikes, and purple fanny pack.

"I hope I'm not interrupting anything."

"Hi, Cora Mae. Not at all." The Rev was constantly amazed at how good she looked; healthy and vibrant and mentally alert in her eighties. He hoped he would be that energetic when he was her age. But seeing her was another reminder that he might not make her age; a reminder that Ida Tabor was still out there with a contract to make sure he *didn't* reach the age of Cora Mae Hartwig. The question was whether she would complete it.

"I know I don't have an appointment, Lucas, dear."

"Since when do you need an appointment for anything?" Max said, ushering her in. "You want some coffee or something?"

"That would be lovely, Maxine. I need to talk to Father Holt a minute about some, well, some personal things."

"I understand," Maxine said. "I have to do that sometimes, too." She disappeared and returned with coffee. "But Cora Mae, if you're havin' man trouble, you need to come talk to me."

"Thank you, dear. As soon as I do you'll be my first stop."

Maxine backed out of the office. "I'll just close the door and leave you two alone, real confessional-like."

"Thank you, Max," he said, coming around the desk to sit opposite Cora Mae in an overstuffed chair. He was curious about her coming to him like this. Usually their conversations were pleasant and heartfelt, but this time he sensed an urgency in her voice. Given her age, he hoped she wasn't going to announce the discovery of some fatal condition.

"First of all, how are Eddie and Omar?" Cora Mae sipped her coffee and set it down on the end table.

"'Treated and released' I believe is the official EMS language." How typically kind of her to begin with polite concern on her way to her own agenda. "Last report was they were well enough to go to the Buffalo for a nightcap with Max."

"Good." She put down her coffee and reached over to take the Rev's hand. "And can we safely assume that the other deal—that awful contract we set up on you—that it is done now that Reinhardt is dead?"

So that was it. She was having buyer's remorse. Holt smiled and put his other hand on hers. "Don't know yet, Cora. We'll have to talk to Nikky about that." He hoped it was off, but he knew that if Nikky had taken such a contract, it would be completed. That was why he drove a different way to work this morning. "Till then," he said, "I'll just have to be careful."

"Until this is settled, Lucas"—Cora Mae held his hand tighter—"I want you to lock yourself down in the crypt of the church, in the Treasury, where no one can get you."

"I love you, too, Cora Mae." He patted her hand and leaned back. "And I'll do the best I can." He wondered how hard it would be to train for the marathon in the crypt.

"Very well." The pink jogging suit relaxed into the chair. "Now, there is something I need to talk with you about of a confessional nature. Do you understand?"

"This conversation is sealed," Holt replied, a serious look on his face. It was unusual for this woman to come to him for ritual confession other than the usual Advent and Lent occasions. "What's happened?"

"Nothing has happened, Lucas. But, as you know, I have talked with Marie Wilkins."

"Yes. You said you called her at the prearranged number." Holt didn't get it. "And the problem is?"

"The problem is I know the last traceable number for her. She is or will be wanted for murder, won't she?"

"I haven't talked with Susan yet. I don't know what she'll do. I presume charges will be filed." But Holt knew it was one thing to file a charge, another to find the suspect, and quite another to get a conviction. "Even so, you could argue coercion from the man she thought was her new boyfriend."

"I hadn't even taken it that far, Lucas." Cora Mae held her coffee cup in both hands. "No, I was thinking that I could be an accomplice if I knew how to trace her, by having her last known number and not providing it to the police." She looked directly at the Rev. "Of course, I am not giving it up. Marie Wilkins and I have been friends since we were little girls." Cora Mae's eyes got teary. "And I just cannot, will not do it."

"Didn't you say Marie indicated she was moving from that place anyway, wherever it was?"

"Yes. But it would give the police somewhere to start."

The Rev sighed. She had a point. Two points, actually; a moral and a legal one. Or maybe not. He handed her the portable phone. "Go ahead and try the number now."

Cora Mae pulled a slip of paper from her fanny pack. She walked across the room to punch in the numbers. "No offense, Lucas." She waited, listened, then handed the phone to Holt. "What's it say?"

He listened to the recorded message. "It's the Spanish equivalent of 'no longer in use.'" He hung up the phone. "The police have no jurisdiction in a foreign country. You're absolved on both counts. The number is useless."

Tears welled over and Cora Mae put a lace handkerchief to her eyes. "It also means I'll never hear from her again."

The Rev held her as she cried. He wondered if he would have

lifelong friendships such as Cora Mae had had with Marie Wilkins? Eighty years of memories, a lifetime of shared experiences was incredible to him. And it resulted in moments like this, when one of the two was gone and the other was left in pain, hurting and empty because of the absence. Life was a setup for death; attachment inevitably meant loss. He sat Cora Mae down in the chair and watched as she blew her nose. She looked older now. Or maybe it was he who was older.

"There's nothing like a good cry—or a good bowel movement—to make you feel alive again." She reached for his hand and squeezed it. "Thank you, Lucas, dear."

Max's voice blared through the intercom. "Yo, Rev! Sorry to interrupt, but Nikky just called. He and the FBI lady and your favorite cop are on their way. ETA is fifteen minutes and they're bringing sandwiches and champagne compliments of the Feds. Guess I won't go out for lunch, huh?"

"Guess not," Holt said. "Send them in when they get here."

Cora Mae Hartwig stood up. "I need to use the ladies' room a minute, Lucas, dear." She opened the door. "But I'll be back for the bubbly, if that's okay with you."

Holt punched the intercom. "Max, get me Boom-Boom at the God Box."

"One Bishop, comin' up. Make sure you tell him Maxine sends him a big, wet, sloppy kiss."

Lucas took a deep breath and braced for the attack du jour.

Half an hour later the group was gathered in Holt's office.

"What did he say when he heard the cork pop?" Dorati said.

"Things unbecoming a bishop of the Episcopal Church." The Rev laughed.

"He wasn't happy with the extent of your deep community involvement?" Granger kidded.

"No." Holt shook his head. "He wasn't happy having a priest of the Diocese of Austin rumored to be involved with a bloody corpse in the San Antonio airport."

"How'd that rumor get started?" Dorati asked, smiling.

Helen Pelham spoke up. "Witnesses—other passengers—must have talked with reporters."

"This is still a very small state, grapevine wise," Holt added. "You sneeze in Lubbock and they bless you in Luling."

"He'd have been happier if the corpse had been your very own self," Max said, "with me beside you."

The mention of his dead body caused him to step away from the window and look at Cora Mae, who changed the subject for him.

"Thank you for the champagne, Helen," she said. "It's very, very good."

"If a bit premature," Granger replied, moving from the couch to the windowsill. "We don't have Ida Tabor in hand yet. They either had different plane arrangements, and she wasn't on any flight last night. She's vanished from the face of the earth."

Lucas Holt glanced at Nikky, then quickly away. "You've been chasing this couple for years, did you say, Helen?" The Rev was anxious to get Dorati alone, to hear what the Mafia Midget would recommend. If Nikky arranged the contract, could he cancel it as well? In the meantime, maybe they could get information from Helen Pelham that could help with the problem. "So everything we assumed about them is correct?" Holt asked.

"From what you've told me, yes. They make sure the 'clients,' as they call them, never use the same insurance company or attorney. Cashier's checks—with the exception of Cora Mae's personal check—are nearly always untraceable. They would enter a city, do just enough 'business' to raise suspicions, then vanish without a trace."

"Where had they been before Austin?" Cora Mae asked, with what the Rev thought was a bit too much feigned interest. They must avoid talking about the present and get everyone out so they could decide what to do next about Ida Tabor.

Helen Pelham continued. "I've chased them from Minneapolis to Kansas City to Cincinnati to Austin. This time I had to show myself to get close enough to Truman Reinhardt. Of course it helped that Ida Tabor looked a lot like me, so I figured he might be attracted enough eventually to spill the scam." She laughed and put down the champagne glass with bright red lipstick on it. "I got so close I think he was about to throw Ida Tabor over for me. At one point I almost had them both together—an unusual occurrence—but your friend Corinne Spellman got into difficulty with them and I had to bail her out. Her information was useful to me, though. She's not as out of it as everybody thinks."

"That's what I've always said, too, dear."

Lucas Holt passed the champagne. "I have what might be considered an indelicate question, Ms. Pelham." He was about to ask it when the phone rang. "I'll get it." He punched the speaker button. "St. Margaret's Church. This is Father Holt."

The voice of Travis Layton boomed through the phone. "Hell, you ain't no more a father than I am—that we know of anyway."

"Hey, Travis!" Holt began. "You're on the speak—"

"That reminds me," Layton charged ahead. "Did you hear Mickey and Minnie were getting divorced?"

"Travis, this is no—"

"And the judge says, 'You can't divorce her because she's crazy.' And Mickey says, 'I didn't say she was crazy! I said she was fuckin' Goofy!' "

The room broke up laughing.

"What the hell's that noise?" the old attorney scowled through the phone.

"I tried to tell you you're on the speakerphone."

"Shitdamn, boy! Why didn't you say so? Who's there?"

Holt listed them off, introducing them to Travis Layton.

"Well, hell's bells, I apologize to Maxine and Miss Hartwig. The rest of you, it don't matter."

"So why did you call?" Holt asked. Maybe there would be further leads to track Ida Tabor before she tracked him.

"Called to tell you about that Mandala Foundation."

"I'm particularly interested in it, Mr. Layton," Helen Pelham said. "I've seen the name in connection with this case but haven't been able to get very far."

"Turns out I know an old friend of the court who now resides in Geneva. I called him and he ran down some leads for me. The way it looks is this. Like the paper said this morning, old farts bumping off their kids for the insurance money."

"Mr. Layton?" Cora Mae said.

"Sorry. Old despicable unforgiving greedy hateful narrow-minded farts bumping off their ungrateful selfish shit-ass kids for the insurance money."

"Oh, that's much better," Holt said with a groan. "But not quite complete, is it, Susan?" He looked over at her.

"Right. It seems that Reinhardt's kids themselves woke up dead one morning, so it must have started there. The Reinhardts must have had some reason to hate their kids, needed the money, or just resented them and wanted what they thought was their investment back to spend on their own retirement years. Then, when the deed was done, they must have figured there would be others in the same boat; so they started a little business to help other people do what had worked so well for themselves—bump off their kids."

"There were certain guidelines,". Pelham added, setting down her glass. "The kids had to be despicable, have no offspring of their own, and make the parents the beneficiaries."

"And later on," Layton said, "the couples would find themselves making further payments to Mandala to keep it quiet."

Helen Pelham continued. "Each older couple changed their own wills to make the Mandala Foundation the final beneficiary, so the murderers not only got money up front, they got money deposited to their foundation when the old couple died."

"So as Travis said," Susan Granger added, "the killers then blackmailed the old people until they died, threatening them with exposure unless they continued to ante up."

"Rather a smart setup," Cora Mae said pensively.

"Except that they murdered a pregnant woman," Holt replied with an edge in his voice as he stood next to the wall to look out the window. "Which reminds me"—he turned to face them—"does anyone know how J.D. knew where to find Truman Reinhardt?"

"Gimme a break, Rev." Dorati stood up. "Don't you remember the hack we called 'Shoes'?"

Lucas Holt squinted his eyes. The picture of a particular guard appeared in his mind. "Shit. Why didn't I think of that?"

"You boys want to let the rest of us in on this?" Susan Granger asked sarcastically. "Or is it a man thing?"

The Rev remembered that it was one of the first cases the God Squad had cracked. "Shoes was a guard who was hit in a really obscure section of Houston. He'd been messing with the wrong woman—the common-law wife of an inmate—for a long time.

Nobody knew how the mechanic knew where to make the hit. Nikky thought the only way was that the guy's wife must have dropped a dime on him." Holt nodded at Dorati. "He was right."

"Ida Tabor dropped a dime on Reinhardt?" Granger said, walking over to sit next to Cora Mae.

" 'Dropped a dime'?" Cora Mae said.

"Made a phone call," the Rev said, realizing the old phrase hadn't caught up with the new price. "Turned him in. Gave him up. Called J.D. and told him the flight time and airport."

"But why?" Layton's voice asked. "It was a sweet deal."

Helen Pelham responded. "Because he was cheating on her."

Dorati looked up. "How do you know that?"

"Good undercover work." She raised her eyebrows.

"Anything else, Travis?" Holt asked.

"Nothin'. But call me later. We need to go over those renovation contracts before the next Vestry meeting."

"Right," Holt said and then remembered. "And thanks for the headset from the Vestry."

"You're welcome for whatever they did. Gotta run. *Adios*."

Lucas Holt punched off the phone and turned to face the black-haired woman. "Now, about that indelicate question?"

"Call me Helen. And when you get to be my age, not much is considered indelicate, I'll tell you."

"That's my point. How is it that someone of 'your age,' as you put it, is going around the country chasing bad guys? I thought the FBI had a retirement mandate, or at least they did when we were at the pen." He nodded toward Nikky, who had become noticeably silent. "Right, Nikky?"

"Yeah, I think so," Dorati mumbled.

"You talked about it in the copter last night, Lucas," Helen Pelham said. "About the aging of the population and the growing number of older people. That's where I fit in. I'm an old cop for old people's scams. Old people aren't getting any dumber with age—therefore there will be more need for someone their age to trip them up, human nature being what it is. The FBI is just trying to stay ahead of the curve, so to speak."

"I just don't think of older people as being the criminal type," Susan Granger said. "And that's even my business."

"The criminal type isn't based on age, Susan," Pelham offered.

"It's based on greed, vengeance, a quick fix, and the perception that life is so short it doesn't matter what they do."

Holt moved around the desk and put his drink down. "Besides," he said, "who's going to lock up a seventy-nine-year-old man dying of cancer or heart disease? And what's he going to get? Life?" He shrugged his shoulders. "So what?"

"What he'll get is three hots and a cot, free health care, free legal services, and maybe a free college degree," Susan Granger said sarcastically. "Not a bad way to retire, actually."

"Let me know when you sign up, Lieutenant," Nikky said, as if he finally had taken notice of something other than his glass.

"So, Helen, we know what you are and what you do." Cora Mae Hartwig looked her straight in the eye and smiled. "But isn't it about time you told us *who you are*?"

The special agent nodded as though she had met her match.

Dorati coughed champagne through his nose.

Holt and Granger looked at each other. The lieutenant put her hand on her weapon. "What the hell's going on here?"

Holt looked around the room. That there was something he obviously had not connected was not unusual. That Dorati missed it too was impossible.

"So you know, Cora Mae?" the special agent said.

The old woman nodded. "You'd have to be blind not to know."

"Know *what*?" Holt said, backing up and moving toward Cora Mae. "Susan, put the gun away," he ordered. "What are you two talking about?"

"You can work with me any time, Miss Hartwig," Helen Pelham said, lifting her glass. "More champagne?"

"Not until somebody tells me why I should holster my weapon," Granger said, worried that the pieces were coming together in her own head with lightning speed. She turned to Cora Mae. "Are you trying to tell us that this woman is, in fact, Ida Tabor?"

Cora Mae and Helen laughed out loud.

"Okay, guys." Nikky Dorati stood and put his arm around Helen Pelham. "Rev? Lieutenant? Let me introduce you to my *mom*."

"No!" Holt said as though someone had just invited him to meet Jesus in the chancel.

"You have a mother?" Granger said before she realized what words were leaving her mouth. "Oh, I'm sorry, Mrs. Pelham, or Dorati, or whatever your name is. I didn't mean—I meant—"

"It's okay, Lieutenant," Pelham said, wiping her eyes with a tissue. "This is the best time I've had in years."

"She's a disgrace to the family, Rev," Nikky said, pouring more champagne.

Holt was untypically stunned. Only Nikky Dorati could have pulled this off. "But how? What?"

"I ain't never seen you at a loss for words, Rev," Nikky smirked, motioning Holt back to a chair. "Park your keyster and I'll explain—if it's okay with Mother here?"

Pelham nodded.

Dorati rolled his eyes at her. Holt thought he looked as if he was twelve, which he would always be in his mother's presence.

"Mom was always a reluctant part of what the family did for a living. She tried to raise us with good values, which was like trying to serve ice cream in a sewer. I had been busted for years when Pop and the family finally bought it big time with the Jersey cops and the Feds. The only way out was for Mom to turn State's—she did it with the family's support by the way—and she did it so good the Feds offered her a job. Undercover, of course, so she could never see me in public on the short visits I made between stretches."

He turned to Helen Pelham. "How am I doin', Mom?"

"Not bad, but you've left my glass empty."

Dorati dutifully filled it and continued. "I ain't seen her all these years. So she turns up in Austin right under my nose."

"Why didn't you tell me?" Holt asked.

"Sorry, Rev. I was so stunned I didn't know what to do when I first saw her at the Westbank Retirement Center when I dropped off Cora Mae. I couldn't risk blowing her cover, even with you."

"Cora Mae," Pelham asked, "how did you know?"

"The family resemblance struck me from the very first, and then there was your *name*, dear."

Holt screwed up his face at the puzzle. "Pelham?"

"No, silly. Mrs. *Nicholas* Pelham." She turned back to the agent. "I decided it was your maiden name, but you kept your husband's first name for sentimental reasons. And if it was

Nicholas—then Nicholas Dorati would just be a junior step from there, so to speak."

Dorati laughed. "How else would I be able to do the deal with Ida Tabor?"

Everyone stopped in place; freeze framed.

"Oopsie," Cora Mae Hartwig said through the bubbles in her cerebellum. "I think you let the bag out of the cat, Nikky."

"You know where she is, Dorati?" Granger pounced toward him. "You know where this murderess Ida Tabor is and you haven't said anything?" She threw up her hands. "Mrs. Pelham—Helen—your son does this shit to me all the time. Where is she?"

"Why would you hold back that information, Nikky?" his mother asked sternly.

"He's not exactly holding back information." Holt jumped in. "It's more like he knew where she was, but he doesn't know now, so it really didn't make any difference." Nikky Dorati was more nervous than Holt had ever seen, and with good reason. Lucas was feeling pretty anxious himself. He trusted the God Squad to handle the problem better than the officials. If Susan and the Feds got involved, they would bring in more firepower than necessary and certainly botch it, let her escape, or get him killed. He hoped they could lie their way out of this and get to themselves, meet with the Squad and determine what to do.

"Rev's right. I don't know where she is, Mom. Thanks to you I knew how to contact her, and I did. But I have no idea where she is right this moment."

Holt tried again to divert the course. "I'm not sure this conversation is relevant to anything." He looked at his watch. "Max, don't we have something on our schedule for right now?"

Maxine looked at him, puzzled and a little tipsy. "No, I don't think so."

Holt glared at her.

"Oh! That!" She stood and looked at the calendar on his desk. "Yessir, there it is right there. I forgot about that important meeting with some dead person for their funeral."

"Great job," Holt said dejectedly.

"Knock it off, you two." Granger looked back at Cora Mae. "Now, do you have a little something to tell us?"

Cora Mae Hartwig looked up at Lucas, who nodded. "What the hell," he said, turning away. "Bag's out of the cat."

She began. "We were going to tell you before the day was out, weren't we, Lucas?"

"Yeah, sure. That was the plan all right."

"Perhaps you should do this, Lucas," Cora Mae said. "I may be a little unclear on the sequence of events." Holt knew she was giving him the chance to think up a better lie than she had.

"It turns out it was Cora Mae's idea," Holt began.

"I knew you shouldn't hang out with Dorati, Cora Mae," Granger admonished. "And I think she should tell this. That way we'll get more of the truth." She looked at the woman in the pink jogging suit. "Spill."

Holt's hopes for police noninvolvement vanished. Cora Mae was a lousy liar.

"Very well," the old woman said. "You all have been lamenting the fact that you haven't been able to find the mysterious Ida Tabor, Truman Reinhardt's wife. Well, you don't have to worry about finding her." She caught Dorati's eye. "We think that she'll come to us," she said proudly.

"Why—if I may be so bold as to ask?" Granger queried.

Dorati jumped in. "As soon as I found out Mom was workin' the case, I started pumpin' her for info. Eventually I learned Ida Tabor's name, and with the God Squad's tracking help, it was easy to find her. The next part is a little trickier."

"I'm dying to know what it is," the lieutenant said.

Holt and Dorati exchanged glances.

"That's sort of what it's about, Susan," Holt said.

"What?" Susan Granger looked like she was ready to shoot all of them but was afraid the champagne would foul her aim.

"Cora Mae met with Ida Tabor to put out a contract on her nasty, yuppified, ungrateful slimeball son," Dorati said meekly.

"But she doesn't have a—" Granger began. "Oh, shit."

"Wait a minute," Helen Pelham said seriously. "You two took out a contract on *him*?"

"That's the wild card," Holt replied. "We don't know if Ida Tabor has blown the whole thing off now that her husband is dead, or whether she can't leave Texas because she has one more contract to fulfill—on me."

Helen Pelham stood face-to-face with her son. "This was not a good idea, Nikky," she said. "That woman is as serious as a heart attack about her business. Dead husband or not, she will do her best to keep the contract. You should know that."

"No shit, Sherlock," Susan Granger said, her red face showing her incredulousness. "I cannot believe you did this. Especially you, Cora Mae."

Cora Mae spoke seriously. "It seemed like a good idea at the time, Susan. After all, you don't have much other evidence for a case, do you?"

"No, I don't, but I don't want to have another dead body on my hands and have to lock you two up for a contract murder."

Dorati interrupted and the Rev knew he would be defensive. "Actually this is not a problem, you know. We watched the Rev's back for twenty years at Huntsville when he was surrounded by people who'd have Ida Tabor for breakfast and not even burp." He sat down in the plush chair by the sofa. "Naw, all we gotta do is keep track of him and we catch her in the act."

The lieutenant shook her head. "Unless you catch her *after* the act, in which case Lucas Holt is dead and the rest of us are just sorry as hell about it."

Holt watched her pace the room and rave about their interference with police duties. He wondered if she was madder about the God Squad or about the possibility of him getting killed. In either case now was not the time to ask.

Susan continued. "Like I noticed how well you protected him when the bullets were flying last night."

Dorati defended. "We figured the cops and the friggin' FBI were watching him. If you can't do your job, then—"

"Watch it, Dorati," Granger snapped back. "Or I'll do my job and drag your butt downtown right now on about a dozen violations of your soon-to-be short-lived parole."

"Wait a minute. Wait a minute." Helen Pelham stood and walked between them. "Maybe it's not such a bad idea after all."

"Now I know where he gets it," Granger commented to Holt. "Unless she gets it from him."

"No, really," Pelham insisted. "Listen." She turned to her son. "The God Squad backs off, Nikky, or it's no bet. But we—APD and FBI—keep a tail on Lucas until we either get her or find out she's someplace where she can't get you."

Holt imagined himself walking down the aisle of St. Margaret's accompanied by acolytes with automatic weapons. "Forget it," he said. "Too intrusive. I have services to do and hospital visits to make." Besides, it would get in the way of the God Squad.

"You'd have to stay at your own place, too," Granger said disdainfully. "That'd be a real problem."

"Give me a break, Susan," Holt replied. She sounded as if this was the eighth grade and she had just found out he asked someone else to the dance.

"Alone," she continued. "With one of us in the house."

Holt could play eighth grade, too. "Is that a proposition?" He noted her face was a different color red this time.

"Not unless you have feelings for Officer Campbell, who will be in there with you."

It was no use. This was a losing battle. He would go along with the program and then do as he damned well pleased, as usual. Dorati and he would figure it out when everyone left. "And if I have other plans? Church work, for instance?"

"We'll accommodate you," Pelham said. "It won't be for that long, I can assure you. She has to act soon, Lucas, in the next day or so. If she's in the state, she'll be anxious to get out of here, now that she has all that pretty money to herself."

"So that will make her madder and more prone to mistakes," Granger added. "We hope." She turned to Dorati. "Where'd you get fifty G's for a down payment anyway?"

"What's the military say? 'Don't ask—don't tell?' You don't ask and I won't tell. Anyway, it's a good investment."

"How do you figure that?" Pelham asked.

"The National Insurance Alliance is offering a three-hundred-thousand reward for information leading. That'll help out the old retirement fund for you and me both, Mother dear."

"I hope your buddy here will live to see us spend it." She pointed to a quiet Lucas Holt, who seemed unconvinced.

"Your people will be everywhere?" Holt asked. Better to know where they weren't, so he'd know how to meet the Squad.

"Yes," Pelham and Granger agreed. "But don't do anything out of the ordinary, and check with us before you go anywhere."

"Sounds like the pen, Rev," Nikky said. "This should be easy for you." Dorati raised his glass to him, and Holt knew his back was covered. The Rev felt more secure with the God Squad's surveillance than with the cops. The Squad played by their wits, the cops by the rules. Wits were always better. Still, a couple of uniforms with guns couldn't hurt. Or could they? He looked at his watch and determined the first test.

"Okay, playmates, for openers, I've got a short run to do—five miles around the lake. Got anybody that can go that distance, Lieutenant?"

"You can do it at the Fitness Center and I'll go with you."

"You'll be the hit of the locker room."

She held her fingers at him like a gun. "Better the hit *of* the locker room than the hit *in* the locker room."

"I'll take you home, Cora Mae," Dorati offered. "I have to drop off Mom anyway."

"Thank you all for your cooperation," Helen Pelham said as they left the office.

"What cooperation?" Holt said. "Since when did cooperation have anything to do with this?"

The Rev told Maxine to take the rest of the day off, put the phone on the service, and get some rest. With all the funerals this week, they both needed it. As he picked up his running bag he hoped the next one wasn't his.

At six o'clock the next morning a phone call was placed from the bedroom of Lucas Holt's house to a room in the Alamo Hotel. The Rev knew the line was tapped, in case Tabor tried to contact him directly.

After a dozen rings, a sleepy voice answered. "What?"

"Nikky."

A long pause was followed by recognition. "Rev?"

"You remember Spider Webb?"

"What the hell are you talkin' about? What time is it?"

"Spider Webb."

Another pause while Dorati swallowed his breakfast rye, and coughed. "Yeah, I remember him."

"Good."

The line went dead.

At seven o'clock Officer J. L. Campbell woke abruptly fully dressed and stretched out on the couch in Lucas Holt's living room. The last thing he remembered was losing a sawbuck to Nikky Dorati in a poker game at three in the morning and turning on the movie channel as the short guy left to go home.

The smell of coffee lured him to the kitchen, where a black pot sat steaming under the white Krups. Assuming the Rev was asleep upstairs, Campbell yawned and poured himself a cup. It wasn't until he was halfway back to the living room to report in that he wondered who had made the coffee.

He put down the cup in the dining room and raced up the stairs. On the made-up bed was a note:

Campbell:

Good morning! Hope you like the coffee. It's from Whole Foods Groceries. All organic. Today's a long run day. Must do 16 to stay on schedule. Catch up with you later. Thanks for the wonderful night. Was it good for you? It was good for me. Maybe I should have a cop in the house all the time?

Later! Gotta run!
Lucas

Campbell stuck his hand under the covers, then ran down to his car radio. In an eternity he was patched through to Susan Granger at her home. "Lieutenant? By."

"Campbell? What happened?" Susan knew from experience. "When did you lose him? By."

"He can't be gone long because the bed's still warm, even though it's made up. I'd say fifteen minutes. By."

"Is his car there? By."

Campbell ran to look out the kitchen window at the garage.

"Car's not there. By."

"Shit. Then he could be anywhere. I remember he had a long run today. If he'd left the car we could assume he ran up to Camp Mabry or out of town to some Ranch Road, where he'd be relatively safe. But this way he could have parked anywhere to hit the

Town Lake Trail or just be wandering around the empty streets waiting for a bullet from Ida Tabor. By."

"What do you want me to do, Lieutenant? By."

"Haul ass to the Alamo Hotel and pick up Dorati. I'll get Maxine and Pelham and meet you at St. Margaret's. In the meantime, put out an APB on him. By."

"Ten-Four, Lieutenant. Campbell out."

Susan Granger threw on her clothes and hurried to her car. She turned on the siren and looked at her watch.

"Damn you, Lucas Holt," she said out loud. "It's too early to die."

• Thirteen •

Ida Tabor drove onto the MoPac Expressway just as a Missouri Pacific train chugged up the median strip dividing the north- and southbound lanes. She smiled at the symmetry of their simultaneous movement; the train headed north, her car south, passing each other like brush strokes on canvas. She enjoyed the connection and wondered how that happened, that seemingly random timing of events that produced such artistic intersections.

How was it that some convergences resulted in Mozart-like artistry, the harmony of form and emotion, while others, equally precise in their timing and confluence, produced disaster and death? Both were accidental, the random crossing of purposefully moving lines. Maybe both rainbows and midair collisions were things of equal beauty or equal senselessness, valueless in themselves, given value by our attachments to them.

She slowed to exit on Lake Austin Boulevard.

And what of the intersections of events and people that were not random, but planned with equal precision as natural convergences? Perhaps those were our way of taking charge of random events, of guiding the collisions of paper and ink, of sound and voice, of idea and dream so that, unlike rainbows and plane crashes, the outcome was known ahead, desired, and celebrated when achieved.

She waited for the light at the end of the exit ramp, gazing at its red color in the dark of the morning. Sometimes random events interfered with planned ones. This red light for instance, had she not allowed time for it so it did not matter, could throw off a whole series of subsequent events and result in the failure of a desired outcome.

She smiled to herself. The conversation in her head reminded her of college dorm discussions at Antioch. As a philosophy major she thought it sad that, after years of successful teaching, she was reduced to having them with herself. Truman had never been interested in that level of dialogue. His surgeon's mentality was practical, not speculative. One did not ponder over a hot appendix or a cancerous breast. "When in doubt, cut it out," was his motto. That was exactly what she had planned to do for the last year, but, like the red light now changing to green, random events had done that for her.

She had enjoyed the vengeance and the plotting the first few times their scheme had worked. But she saw how Truman, the insipid, self-centered doctor that he would always be, used the time apart for his own affairs—literally. He grew tired of her after forty years of marriage, bored and ungrateful even though it was her scheming that had bailed him out of the worst lawsuit of his career. She ignored his fooling around, lived separately from him most of the time as they managed their "business," and planned, ultimately, to leave him on his own when they had accumulated enough money.

This solo contract was the last one she needed to meet her financial goal. Like the others he had not known about, the proceeds would go into a separate fund of her own devising.

Once accomplished, she had planned simply not to meet her husband in São Paulo, but to vanish from him the way he had emotionally vanished from her years ago, to send him papers of a completed Brazilian divorce along with the statement of a severely diminished balance of the Mandala Foundation account.

But, like the train and the traffic light and now the drizzle that caused her to turn on the intermittent wipers, other intersecting lines had intervened with his to take him out of her life. Had the girl not been pregnant, Ida Tabor would have been on that plane with Truman Reinhardt last night, would have separated from him at the Caracas layover as originally planned. But the intersecting line of J. D. Enright had, with some guidance, crossed Truman's path with deadly impact.

Ida Tabor drove under the Amtrak trestle beyond Lamar Boulevard. She would park behind Zach Scott Theatre and walk to the trail from there, leaving a broader range of exits either by car or on foot if that route was blocked.

Even though she had enabled it to happen with her phone call, even though she had come to hate him for his narcissistic disloyalty, the initial news of her husband's death was surprisingly hard on her. She had cried when she opened the paper to read the front-page story of his violent murder, splayed out on the airport terminal floor; cried for the loss of him she had experienced years ago and for the relatively good moments together before that. But the tears were short-lived; there were so few left. Now the feeling sweeping over her was exhilaration, the freedom of no attachment, no need to worry about divesting herself of the albatross that Truman Reinhardt had become. The rest of her life awaited her with nothing to do but enjoy it. All she had to do was one small, and very easy, hit.

She parked the car in the dirt lot adjacent to the theater and took the lid off the coffee she had purchased on the way. The thick white cappuccino foam clung to her red lips, and she licked it away lasciviously. She looked in the visor mirror to adjust the scarf around her blond wig and dab her lipstick.

Her watch beeped and she took the coffee with her from the car, pressing the button on the small transmitter in her pocket that automatically locked the doors. Dressed in a gray warm-up suit with black jogging shoes, Ida Tabor casually strolled through the Zachery Scott Theatre complex to the trail by the Lamar Boulevard Bridge.

This convergence was carefully planned, the intersection of her own line with Lucas Holt's, the merging of Holt's random pattern of running with the careful order of her own design. Where the two lines met, an event of beauty would occur.

His schedule had not been easy to get. The hardheaded secretary at the church had to be convinced that major schedule changes depended on knowing the priest's availability on this particular day. She guarded his privacy like a pit bull, but she inadvertently mentioned that his availability revolved around the fact that this was a sixteen-mile run day. A few times watching revealed his pattern of parking at Deep Eddy Pool, picking up the trail and either crossing the First Street or Congress Avenue Bridge for the loop he needed to run. Long runs usually meant

First Street, but if his line randomly went to Congress, she would have just enough time to drive to the north side of the lake to accomplish her task.

She sat on a bench by the trail and drank her steaming coffee, nodding at the sporadic early-morning runners, touching, from time to time, the little transmitter in her pocket, holding it like a rosary whose prayer would end in the death of a priest.

Lucas Holt ran past Fiesta Gardens and sang along with Patsy Cline. It didn't get any better than this. The cool mist of the early morning felt great as mile five melted into his running watch. By now Campbell was up and Susan had her panties in a wad wondering where the hell he was. She would contact Nikky and Max. Max would eventually remember he was at Town Lake and not running around some Ranch Road in the middle of nowhere. In the meantime, no killer in their right mind would be out this early at this end of the trail. He glanced at the graffiti on the vacant buildings. This was far East Austin, where a gang would take her gun and shoot her with it but not bother joggers who could outrun them and carried mace if they couldn't.

This logic made perfect sense to him as the three cups of hightest, leaded, Ethyl, Whole Earth Columbian coffee percolated in his veins and the country-western songs blared through the headset the Vestry had given him. The sound was much clearer than on his old one and preset buttons meant no commercials. The coffee was another story. He'd switched to try the caffeine effect, and he needed to go back to Earl Grey. If he was any more wired he'd be invulnerable. He hoped the runner's high would replace the caffeine that made him overconfident.

But his bravado did have some basis in fact, he reasoned. The call to Nikky Dorati had initiated the Spider Web, from the inmate of the same name. William "Spider" Webb was the only member of the God Squad who would never leave the prison, unless he managed to live three lifetimes back to back. Society seemed to frown on killing people and eating them, and Spider's current body count was twenty-five. The Rev knew Dorati would remember, once he was awake, how they had used Spider's "recipe" to capture a killer in the pen: "Put out the bait. Watch and wait." Nikky would alert the Squad that the Web was set, and the Rev could assume that somewhere, unknown and unseen to him, the God Squad was near even if the cops weren't.

Instead of waiting for the killer to pick him off, Holt had decided to stop acting like a caged animal guarded by APD zoo-keepers and put this problem into the hands of people who understood it—ex-cons. Besides, all the rumination on his mortality had left him with the conclusion that life was too damned short to pussyfoot around in it. If he had learned anything in the last two weeks it was that death was inevitable, not optional, and those who feared it most lived it least. It was not so much that he no longer feared the possibility of death, but that he had begun to accept it as part of life. So rather than sit around waiting, he would be the bait and draw the killer out into the Spider Web of God Squad members, run up in her face, make her the hunted instead of the hunter.

He crossed the Tom Miller Dam and turned back west toward town. By the time he reached the IH 35 bridge, he'd have to decide whether to loop over Congress or First. First was farther and Congress would shorten the first half but make the last loop longer. He would cross at Congress. Light was coming up on the morning, and the drizzle would burn off to eighty-degree heat by the time he finished around nine o'clock. As the day cleared he would be a better target, if he was to be one at all.

Holt wasn't worried about being picked off on the trail. This was a woman's plan for murder, and they never used rifles. Women killed up close and personal, with a knife, a snub nose, or poison. He should be careful in elevators and movies, going to his car, or out to get the morning paper. He should not leave drinks unattended or eat at a restaurant. Men killed at a distance where they would not have to get involved; women wanted a relationship.

Lucas Holt relaxed into the music and the run. Between the odds and the Squad, he was convinced that they might get her, but there was no way she would get him this morning. No way at all.

Nikky Dorati poured another round of coffee for the people in the Rev's office. So far, the morning had gone as he predicted. Susan Granger, Max, and Mom met at St. Margaret's and worried while Max pulled up the running schedule. She guessed Lucas would run Town Lake instead of 360 or the Ranch Roads this morning. APD confirmed it by locating his car at Deep Eddy. That was the easy part. He had stalled them long enough to get the web of the God Squad in place, locate the Rev, and wait for the fly to circle. That was all Ida Tabor had to do—circle in close enough to slam her into the sticky trap from which she could not escape. Put out the bait. Watch and wait. But if anybody else shook the web, the prey would be suspicious, go away to come back another time. So Dorati had to deflect both Granger and Pelham and their thundering, web-shaking hordes. If he couldn't deflect them, he had to contain them, he thought as Helen Pelham hung up the phone.

"Plainclothes officers, FBI and APD, will be strategically placed around the trail within the half hour," Helen Pelham said.

"The problem is we don't know what to look for—or if Tabor's even going to do anything now," Susan Granger replied. "It's one thing to cover him, it's another to know what to cover him from." She looked over at Nikky Dorati. "Perhaps we should ask the expert?"

" 'Former' expert," his mother defended.

"Okay." Dorati stopped and pursed his lips. He saw no reason not to cooperate here. It took up time and might even be productive. While the Squad was looking for a killer, they also needed to have a method in mind. This might help narrow the possibilities, though he thought he pretty much knew them all. "If I were doin' this, I'd use a rifle with an electronic scope, one that makes you an Indian before you go to Nirvana." He explained: "The laser puts a red dot on your forehead before I pull the trigger."

"You're sicker than I thought," Granger said.

"That's my little boy." Agent Pelham raised her eyes at the lieutenant. "But a gun's too risky, too bulky for her to carry, too visible, and too distant. Besides, it's a man's weapon."

"She could be running the opposite direction on the trail and shoot him or knife him as he passes her," Maxine offered.

"Good thought, Max," Dorati said. "But remember her age. She'll be more discreet than that and arrange a better getaway. It'll be distant but personal, too." Nikky flashed on a memory. "Something like—I don't know—like a bomb."

"How would she know about that?" Maxine asked, bringing the pot around again.

Pelham opened the file on the chair. "Easy. She was big time into SDS as a college professor in the late sixties. People learned strange things in those times. Anyway, you can get the information from your local library."

"Not at Huntsville," Dorati added, checking his watch. The bomb idea had not occurred to him until now. If it was right, maybe he could use the forces at his disposal here to help.

"So what's she going to do, have him step on a land mine?" Granger said. "That's too uncertain. Too many people around."

Dorati saw his chance. "His car is personal—and easier." He turned to Susan Granger. "Can your people check it?"

She picked up her radio. "Granger to base. Have a commercial wrecker pull up by Holt's car as if they were going to tow it from Deep Eddy. Then have the driver—Mikeska from explosives is the best—check under the car for a device of some kind. By."

"You got it, Lieutenant. Ten-four. Out."

"I still don't think she'll do anything this morning while he's on the move." Dorati walked with his coffee cup to the window and looked out over Sixth Street. Maybe he could get them to call this off, or tone it down. "Why wouldn't she wait until he was seated at a meal, or at a movie or at home where he'd be less of a mobile target? Maybe all this is for nothing, and we ought to back off. I mean, don't your officers have other crooks to catch this morning?"

"Not as long as you're in my sight, Dorati."

"Pressure's on to do it and get out, Nikky," Helen Pelham responded to her son. "The longer she waits, the better our chance of catching her. She's more willing to risk a miss than risk getting nabbed. My guess is that if she doesn't make the hit today, she'll blow it off and leave. She's already got plenty of money and no husband to get in her way spending it."

"No," Granger said, joining Nikky by the window. "Her ego's involved here. She wants to do this one solo, either in spite of Reinhardt's death or to commemorate it." She glared at Dorati. "She has to make good on your little contract, and I think she's out there right now."

Nikky continued to stare at the street. Maybe he was being too protective. Maybe they did need some extra troops here. If the Rev got hit and it could have been prevented, Dorati would never forgive himself. On the other hand, they could really screw things up.

"Why can't we just assume it's going to happen while he's running and then figure out the options?" Maxine stood and raised her voice. "All this talk is driving me crazy. The Rev is out there bein' a movin' target so we can catch this crazy bitch. So let's *catch* her, for God's sake."

"Okay, Maxine." Dorati walked over and put his hand on her arm. "I'm with you. However she's gonna do it, it's personal. The car's ruled out, so we gotta think of other possibilities." He addressed the group. "What can she carry that's small enough not to be obvious, that is concealable under, say, a raincoat, that she can use and still make a clean getaway?"

"Hell, Dorati," Susan Granger commented, "you could get a *tank* under a raincoat. And you probably have."

Nikky suddenly had a new worry. What if the fly didn't have to land? What if the bait was also the weapon? He turned to his mother. "What if we're looking at the wrong person here? What if the method isn't something she's going to do *to* him, like a gun or a knife? What if it's something already *on* him, something he'd take for granted?"

Helen Pelham replied, mostly to herself. "That way she doesn't have to worry about hitting a moving target at a distance *or* up close." She sat on the corner of Holt's desk. "Max, Susan, you've seen his running outfit. What's he carry?"

"Running watch—that's out," Granger thought out loud.

"Small fanny pack," Max started. "Not much in it. Driver's license, a couple dollar bills, a quarter, tissues for T.P."

"Bingo!" Granger exclaimed. "She could poison his drink bottle." She reconsidered the picture. "Except that it's already poisoned. He mixes his own concoction of electrolytes, fruit juices, chocolate, Earl Grey, and Shiner Bock. It's awful stuff. And he does it just before he leaves to run. So she wouldn't have access to it."

"Anything else?" Pelham said.

"Not unless she blows up his shoes." Dorati imagined how that could be done and filed it away. You never knew. "Has he done anything different lately, Max, gotten something new or changed his routine?" Nikky got more nervous by the minute. This personal shit put a whole new light on things. Hell, she might not have to be there at all to kill him.

"No," Max said hastily. "Nothing new."

Dorati moved to Holt's desk and rummaged through the rubble.

"What are you looking for?" Max cried, coming to help.

Nikky looked at papers and tossed them. "Receipts, charge slips. Anything." He glanced at the cardboard in the trash can and picked it up. "What was in this box?"

"Oh, that was his headset. I took his old one to A and A last week for repair. But somebody on the Vestry must have discovered it couldn't be fixed. They surprised him with a new one. I found it on my desk with a nice note from them yesterday."

Dorati looked at Granger. "I don't think so," he said, his mind spinning. If this was what he thought it was, he would need all the help he could get. And fast. "That's why Travis Layton didn't know anything about it."

"Of course," Susan Granger said.

"You got the receipt from the repair shop?" Dorati asked as calmly as he could.

"Sure," Maxine said, running to her desk. "But why?" she said as she returned with a yellow slip of paper.

Susan Granger grabbed it from her and picked up the phone. She punched in the numbers and checked her watch. "It's after eight, somebody should be there."

Max punched the speaker button so they all could hear. The line rang and rang with no answer.

Finally: "A and A Appliance. Can I help you?"

"This is Susan Granger. I'm a friend of Father Holt's. I thought I'd stop by and pick up his headset if it's ready."

"It's sittin' right here on the counter waitin' for you."

"Thank you. I'll be there later today." Granger hung up and stared at the others.

"Shit," Dorati said, his worst fears confirmed. "The bomb's in the headset. She's going to blow his brains out."

He ran from the room.

• • •

Ida Tabor finished the cappuccino and walked from the trail to Lamar Bridge. If her calculations were correct, Lucas Holt should be heading in this direction, deciding which loop to take.

She removed the car alarm transmitter from her pocket and crossed to the east side of the bridge—the perfect spot because there were no obstacles to stop the signal. She had tested the distance with her car, and, when unobstructed, the signal opened and closed the door locks at two hundred yards. Standing on the sidewalk in the middle of the bridge, she could lean over the railing as if observing the lake and aim the transmitter with a clear shot to his headset as he jogged across the First Street Bridge.

This was much more interesting than simply shooting him as he left the church on his one late evening, as she had originally planned. Thanks to the pit-bull secretary, she had learned about the headset being repaired. As Ida Tabor was timing the approach to the church one afternoon, the red-haired woman was locking up the back door with the headset in her hand. Tabor had engaged her in conversation about the church but was brushed off with the excuse that the secretary had to get to the repair shop before it closed. From there it was a simple matter to follow her, ask about repair times, and provide the substitute "gift."

And now it was on his head.

A coffee vendor with a stainless steel cart and umbrella sold her another cappuccino as she left the trail. She must not be seen conspicuously standing in the middle of the bridge for a long time, but, along with other joggers resting and mothers sitting with their babies, she could find a spot on a bench at the far end, watching for him to round the corner before she stood to move to the center.

At eight-fifteen the trail became more populated with later risers still wanting to run before the sun burned through the morning haze. Wonderful, she thought. The more the merrier. The more, the more difficult to spot her. The more, the more confusion when the explosion occurred.

Nikky Dorati had used his car phone to wake Omar Dewan, who was now in the rear seat of the racing BMW. "Drop the seatback. It's a false compartment between the seat and the trunk."

"Slow down, man. I can hardly think straight, much less open the damned seat up."

"Can't slow down, Omar!" Dorati yelled. "Gotta cruise the bridges till we find her."

"Why the bridges?"

"They're the only places open enough for the signal to be clear and close enough to pull it off." He turned for the MoPac bridge. "Got it open?"

"Yeah," Dewan said, whistling. "This is some package!"

"Can you assemble it?"

"Is the Pope Catholic, man?" Omar Dewan bounced in the back seat, dropping gun parts, cursing, and locking them into place. "What you gonna shoot with this thing, Dorati, an elephant?"

"Bigger game than that, my main man. This chick's got a 300G bounty on her that you and I can split if we work it right."

Dewan smiled and carefully assembled the automatic rifle with the laser scope. "We'll work it right."

"She ain't on the MoPac overpass," Dorati announced. "Next stop's Lamar. Hang on." The Beemer shot down Barton Springs Road. The phone beeped and Dorati punched the speaker.

"Yo, Nikky. Eddie here. Doors and Valdez spotted the Rev at the dam. He's on his way back toward the bridges."

"Good. Cover him whatever you do."

"We're on him like stink on a skunk, man."

The speaker was silent when Nikky shouted, "Red light! Hold tight!" Dorati careened across the double yellow line into the left lane around two stopped cars and barely missed one turning in his direction. Horns honked. Tires squealed.

"It's together, but I'm not," Dewan said. "You damned near broke my neck." The car took a corner on two wheels. "Shiiiit."

Nikky slowed when he came to the light at the bridge. "Too many people out here." He frowned.

"Not if you know what you're lookin' for. All I saw in Nam was targets, no jungle." Dewan scanned both sides of the bridge. "Cross it slow. With that picture you got from FBI, man, she's mine."

Nikky hit 911. "This is Special Agent Dorati, FBI," he lied. "Patch me through to Lieutenant Susan Granger, STAT."

"What is your ID?"

"If the priest dies, you're roadkill, asshole. Patch me through."

Clicks came through the speaker.

"You really a special agent, Dorati?"

Nikky glanced back at him. "Just keep lookin', Dewan."

"Granger here. Where are you, Dorati?"

"Lamar Bridge. You got him yet?"

Susan's voice sounded panicked. "Spotter thought she saw him cross IH 35 to the south trail. Lost him then."

"My crew says he's headin' back to the bridges. You gotta get the damned headphones off him."

"I know it," the lieutenant replied desperately.

"I'm goin' to find the woman and take her out."

"Dorati, you can't do that."

Nikky made static sounds with his voice. "Bad connection, Lieutenant," he said barely audibly. "I'll get back to you."

Before he could disconnect, Dewan yelled: "There she is, Dorati—in the blond wig!"

"Shit!" Nikky punched the button. "Great work, Omar. Now we'll have a thousand cops to keep us company. They'll make the web feel like an earthquake. Double shit!"

"Sorry, Nikky, but that's her to my right on the bench."

Dorati controlled his emotions. This was no time to be pissed. "You got her," he said. "Now it's my turn."

As Nikky Dorati did a u-ey to park the car by the trail, Susan Granger yelled into her radio. "Suspect on Lamar Bridge in blond wig. All units go. No sirens! And watch her *hands*!"

Lucas Holt ran past the Hyatt up to the Congress Avenue Bridge. Halfway to the sidewalk he changed his mind and returned to the trail. He was feeling good after a couple swallows of his energy drink and the country-western station was on a nonstop KASE of Country—Twelve in a Row. The route over First Street Bridge would provide the mileage he needed to finish.

So far, so good. With no sign of Ida Tabor, and the web in place, he could relax. Three minutes to the bridge if he kept his current pace. He punched a button on the headset to change stations.

"And now for the Clint Black favorite from your KASE Country Twelve Pack: 'No Time to Kill.'"

The Rev cleared his throat to sing along.

The blonde in the gray jogging suit smiled sweetly at the mothers and sipped her coffee as she stood to stretch her back, arching it like a cat. She walked to the railing of the bridge and looked toward Congress Avenue. She was glad to see no sign of him there.

The intersecting of lines, his and hers, would happen momentarily. All was in symmetry. It would soon be over.

Susan Granger sped down Riverside Drive with her lights on and her siren off, weaving and dodging her way to First Street. She thought she caught a glimpse of Lucas by the Statesman Building as he ducked down to the trail by the Hyatt. If that was true, he would round the corner under First Street and head up to the top level of the bridge in less than a minute.

As she spun around the corner of Riverside and First, she saw him.

Nikky Dorati placed the blond wig in the intersecting crosshairs of the gunsight. All he needed was the red dot to appear on her forehead. If she would light for just one second he would take her off the count, do to her what she wanted to do to the Rev, blow her brains out her ass.

Omar Dewan had dropped him in the parking lot of Zachery Scott Theatre. From there Dorati had managed, with the help of his oversize raincoat, to cross to the dense stand of trees just below the end of the bridge. He knew the cops were tailing him, set on him by Susan Granger after she overheard their location.

Fifty yards to her right ear.

Piece of cake.

No problem. Keep the web intact. No movement.

His peripheral vision noticed them on the hill behind him. Plainclothes cops for sure. Just what he wanted.

If only she would stand still. Just once.

Lucas Holt came over the lower end of the bridge, running on the east side. Ida Tabor saw him, disappointed he was not on the west side, directly parallel to her where vehicles could not distort the signal. A possible minor delay. Random events intersecting her line, like the traffic light or the rain. She advanced to the center of Lamar Bridge. She would make do.

Susan Granger floored the blue-and-white up the middle of First and flipped her outside speaker on High.

"LUCAS HOLT! STOP! TOSS THE HEADSET!"

Vaguely aware of his name over the loud music, Lucas turned to see Susan motioning to him. Either she thought he was in danger and wanted him off the street, or they had found Ida Tabor and she wanted him to know. In the first instance she was shaking the damned web and screwing things up. In the second it was not worth stopping the run.

He waved her off.

He also pointed for her to be careful of the yellow moving van heading directly toward her.

Ida Tabor saw the racing police car, glanced behind her, and caught the telltale plastic earsets of FBI. On her chest she saw the red laser dot announce its target. She turned toward First Street and pressed the button.

The huge, yellow moving van passed between the signal and Holt, stopping it.

Nikky Dorati placed the red dot on her ear. He felt a steel circle on his own.

"Drop it or die!" the agent said. "*Now*!"

"Shitdamn." He grinned and squeezed the trigger.

Nothing happened.

Out of her car Granger dodged past the van and ran at full speed to the singing Lucas Holt. She pulled the headset off from behind and threw it over the side of the bridge as she tackled him to the pavement.

Lines converged.

Tabor pressed the button.

Midair, the set boomed into a fireball sending shrapnel in all directions.

People screamed and fell to the ground.

Bullets from the window of a screeching red car pommeled the body of Ida Tabor, doubled her over the railing, and she fell, silent as the explosion was loud.

In perfect synchrony, the body and shrapnel from opposite bridges touched the water together.

Helen Pelham jumped from the passenger seat and held her badge to the officers surrounding the red Celica. "You!" She pointed to a known agent. "Over the side and get that body."

"Yes, ma'am." He tossed her his wallet and gun and dived over the railing.

Swarms of blue uniformed officers contained the crowd.

"APD?" Pelham yelled to the woman at her right.

"Yes!"

"Get EMS back up for that agent and I mean now!"

"Yes, ma'am." She hollered into her shoulder radio for medics.

The small woman in a pink jogging suit still sat in the car.

"You can get out now," Pelham said as Cora Mae Hartwig exited the driver's side. "Great driving. I couldn't have both hands free and hold the wheel, too."

"Tell that to the DPS, Helen dear. They think I shouldn't be on the road at all, especially without my glasses."

"You wear glasses?"

"Mostly for reading, dear."

Two agents marched Nikky Dorati up to Special Agent Pelham.

"Hi, Mom."

"Damndest thing, Agent Pelham," the man said. "The guy was aiming this laser rifle at the suspect—but the thing wasn't loaded. I damned near killed him for it."

She looked at her son with pride. "Good job, Nikky. You diverted the cops for the seconds we needed to get close in."

"What?" the agent said.

"I'll explain later. Let him go. He's with us."

Reluctantly he uncuffed Dorati, and Nikky put an arm around Helen Pelham.

"I was the designated driver, Nicholas," Cora Mae said to him. "What were you doing with that big gun?"

Nikky Dorati grinned as if he'd just hit a grand slam home run. "Designated decoy."

Helen Pelham smooched him on the forehead, and the red lipstick matched the color of his face.

•   •   •

Susan Granger rolled off the back of Lucas Holt.

"You skinned my knees!" he yelled irately, dabbing his shirt on the trickles of blood.

"Yeah," she replied, brushing herself off. "And I wrecked your precious headset, too."

"What if I can't run now? Then what? After all this training?"

She offered him a hand up from the pavement. "Get up here, you idiot. I should have let her blow your brains out."

Reality set back in as Holt looked over the bridge at the burning debris below. Two hundred yards to the west, EMS divers carried the body of Ida Tabor to an ambulance. Three familiar forms waved from the First Street Bridge.

Susan nudged him. "Wave back, so they'll know you're okay."

"I'm not okay." He pointed down. "You skinned my knees."

"Wave or I'll shoot you."

Holt waved vigorously, and smiled. "Guess we got her, huh?"

"Who's *we,* white man? You were singing and ignoring me."

He was grateful for her, but annoyed that she hadn't let him do it his way. "I just wanted to see you work."

"Well, you did. And we worked pretty damned well."

"Yeah, for cops." He winked at her as they walked together to her car. Thinking he was being too harsh, he added: "You do good work, Lieutenant Granger, APD." When they got inside, he kissed her cheek. "Thanks for the rescue."

"That's all I get?" Her eyes were wide with feigned disbelief. "I saved your worthless *life* here."

"What more do you want?" Holt said, casting her a provocative sideways glance.

Granger paused. "Dinner with wine." She reconsidered. "Make that champagne."

"Done."

"And a movie."

"Fine."

"Of my choosing."

"No problem."

"With drinks and popcorn."

"Good."

"Not the cheap show."

"You're pushing it."

"And Kristen can't come along to chaperon." Susan started the car and drove toward downtown.

"Omigawd, Kristen."

"What about her?"

"She'll get this on the TV and think I'm dead."

"Not if there's a committee meeting."

"Susan—"

"I speak the truth and you know it, kemo sabe."

Holt did know it, but he didn't want to say it. Not now, anyway. "Can you drop me at my car? It's at Deep Eddy."

"I know where it is." She turned down west Sixth. "You going over there, to Kristen's?"

"Yep."

"Can I ask what for?"

"You can ask." But he probably wouldn't answer.

"What for?"

Lucas Holt looked straight ahead. He knew Susan was disappointed, but there was nothing he could do about it now. "I gotta talk to her, that's all."

They rode in silence to Deep Eddy Pool.

"Hope I didn't get blood on your car, ma'am," he said as he closed the door.

"No problem."

"I'll call you tomorrow."

"Sure."

"We'll set a time for dinner."

"Right."

Lucas Holt walked to her window. He leaned down and reached in, taking her chin in his hand. He kissed her hard on the lips.

"Thanks for saving my life, Susan."

Without speaking, she rolled up the window and drove off.

The couple sat opposite each other, immersed to their necks in the bubbling hot tub.

"This must be how the missionaries felt"—Lucas Holt laughed—"in all those old jungle movies."

"They did if they had a four-course dinner at the Belgian

Restaurant followed by passionate sex, Dom Perignon champagne, and a naked nightcap in a hot tub."

"I don't think the missionaries sat naked in anything, even a boiling pot."

"I knew there was something we forgot." Kristen Wade pouted.

"What's that?" The Rev lifted his glass from the deck.

"The missionary position." She stood and moved toward him, foam from the water clinging to her breasts. "Come here."

"Missionaries never do it standing up."

"Why not?"

Holt stood and embraced her. "They're afraid God will think they're dancing." He poured more champagne in their glasses.

"This is good, isn't it, Lucas?" Kristen said, pulling him down beside her.

He leaned his head back against the tub. "Yes, it is."

"I don't think it could possibly get better," she mused.

Holt was silent. He had thought about this a long time. "Couldn't it?"

"No, I don't think so. Why? Do you?"

He sat up and turned the knob to adjust the force of the jets. "I'd like it on slow simmer instead of rolling boil."

"This sounds serious." She kissed his ear. "Hope it's not."

"Depends on your definition of serious." He sipped the champagne. No amount of rehearsal had prepared him for this. He thought he knew what he wanted, but he wasn't sure how to say it without sounding pompous.

"Serious," Kristen said in a deep baritone voice, "is when you turn down the bubbles to talk like this." She slipped her hand underwater. "Don't do it, Lucas. Not now. Let's just play."

Holt smiled and kissed her. "We can still play in a minute."

"You sure?" she said, backing away.

"Positive," he lied. There was no telling how this would turn out. "Just listen to me."

"You said one minute." She looked at a nonexistent watch on her wrist. "Go."

"Okay." He sipped the champagne and looked at her. "It may have taken a bomb to knock all the jumblings in my head together into some sense, but I think I figured it out this morning."

"I hope so. Figured what out?"

"All this midlife stuff I've been talking about for so long."

"And?"

"And I've come to the conclusion that life is short."

"Really?" Kristen Wade stared at him. "Lucas, you already knew that. We both know it in ways that other people don't. That's one reason we're together, and one of the things that keeps us together. Life is too short not to do what we do. It's the best of all possible worlds."

"It's one of the possible worlds," he said solemnly.

Kristen smiled at his demeanor. "Not the best?"

"What I think I want is somebody to grow old with, Kristen."

Kristen laughed and pulled her lips over her teeth. "Can you thee uth ath an old couple, Lucath?"

Holt took her hand. He loved it when she made him laugh. "No. That's the problem. To be an old couple you have to have spent a lifetime—or some length of time—making memories together to look back on."

Kristen waved her glass over the tub. "So what's this? Duck soup?"

Lucas shook his head and laughed again. "Of course not. But it's a respite, an interlude from what we normally do."

"I thought it was what made the norm palatable, do-able. If I didn't have this with you, the State work would be impossible."

"I guess what I'm saying is I want more of this. I want time with you to be the norm, not the oddity, the rare occasion of closeness secondary to careers."

"So you're talking stability here?"

Holt nodded. "Nothing in life is stable. Things change constantly. I've done enough funerals in the last three weeks to reinforce that message. But continuity seems to make a difference. It's continuity that I see in old couples holding hands at the retirement Center, looking at each other like they're still twenty-five, even knowing one of them will die and leave the other behind."

"God, Lucas, I don't even want to think that far ahead. For me the future is the next election. Why can't we just keep going on and on the way we are right now?"

"To what? Death? And that's it?"

"Yes, that's it. I don't need to look back on a picture album to realize I've had a good time with you and with my career. And I can't believe you need that, either."

"I think I didn't used to want it, and I'm not sure that's exactly what I want now. But after all that's happened, I do know I want a life lived together, not alone together."

Kristen Wade poured more champagne. "And there's the rub in the tub. Because for me, at least from where I sit now, in the middle of bubbles and bubbly, it's okay to do it alone." She looked to see if his feelings were hurt. "I don't mean that harshly, Lucas. I want you in my life. I like you. I enjoy you."

Holt pointed to the animal lying in the yard. "So I'm sort of like Aspen over there. Nice to have around, but I could be replaced by a terrier."

"I don't do it doggie-style with Aspen." She grinned. "And that's not the way it is." She looked at her empty wrist. "I think your minute's up."

"Listen, Kristen, this is serious."

"No, it's not, Lucas. It's not serious at all. We've just reached a slight parting of the ways. You want commitment and continuity, and I want this—sporadic, uncommitted, convenient, and second to my career. At least that's what I want right now," Kristen replied.

"And later?"

"Later will get here when later gets here. No guarantees. Like you said, the only thing certain is change. I'm willing to wait and see what happens."

Holt spread the foam on the top of the water with both arms. "Moses parting the hot tub."

"Parting temporarily, maybe. Probably." She turned up the force of the jets and poured more champagne. "But please, baby, please, let's have this last na'ht together," she said in her best Texas twang.

"Why does this sound like a country-western song?" He sat back down in the tub. "All we need is a pickup, a train, and mama goin' to jail."

Kristen Wade pressed her body to his. "I'm not convinced it's as bad as a C and W song. I like you, Lucas Holt." Her hand disappeared again. "And I like you for more than that." She kissed him. "But right now I want my career and I want like crazy to be the U.S. Senator from the State of Texas, and who the hell knows after that? But for all I know, things could change tomorrow, and I'll want to cook and clean and have your babies." She raised her glass as Holt laughed at the image. "Keep your powder dry and your options open, darlin'."

"Here's looking at you, kid." He put his arms around her. "We'll always have Paris."

Kristen backed her head away. "We've never been to Paris."

"Oh." He grinned and kissed her. "Then I guess we'll have Lubbock."

She laughed and pulled him down into the hot bubbling water.

• Epilogue •

Lucas Holt stepped from the shower and looked at the green numbers on the digital clock. He dried off and went downstairs for his favorite mug, the one with the copulating bears on it, filled it with Earl Grey, and pulled on his lucky Texas Flag running shorts from the dryer.

This was what he had trained six months to do. His body was fit though somewhat battered from the mileage, not to mention the skinned knees he acquired from Susan Granger. And his mind was clear, committed, ready to go the distance.

There was special meaning for him in this race. Coincidentally merging his forty-third year with the issues of aging in his parish, and his near death on the First Street Bridge, it signaled the start of a different attitude, a feeling about his work and his life, a different view of relationships.

He poured more tea and hoped there would be ample Porta Pottis around Mile 15. He held up the T-shirt given to him by the God Squad for the race and put it on.

The front read: I'D RATHER BE— The back: AT TDC.

Ironic. While that would certainly be his sentiment at Mile 21, for the first time since he'd left the prison, it was no longer true for his life. He'd made the awkward transition to St. Margaret's and found—no, had made—a commitment there. Maybe his time with Kristen was the equally awkward transition to wherever he would find—and make—his emotional commitment.

He placed his fanny pack by the front door, where his ride should arrive any minute; beside it lay his visor and sunglasses. He went to the kitchen and mixed his energy drink, then set the jug aside and quickly glanced through the obits as he did every morning. The one for Marlane Enright reminded him he wanted to attend her funeral at First Baptist this afternoon, if he could walk okay. Obviously J.D. planned to die killing Reinhardt, and his remorse for what they had done led him to take his wife's life as well. Susan said the coroner believed J.D. had replaced insulin with saline in Marlane's medicine cabinet. The police had found her dead of diabetic shock when they went to the house to tell her of her husband's death. The Rev left the paper open to remind himself of the funeral time when he came home later.

His digital running watch read 6:05. Last night's carbo-loading manicotti and garlic bread suddenly wanted out.

A horn honked out front.

"Hang on!" he yelled out the door. "Last minute pit stop."

He returned from the bathroom to find Susan Granger in the kitchen. "Come in."

"I did. The least you can do is offer me coffee."

"Tea's in the Krups. Sorry."

"It's caffeine," she said sleepily. She took a go-cup from the drainboard and filled it. "Let's blow this pop stand. You don't want to be late for the insanity."

Lucas locked the door and dropped the key in his fanny pack. They were in the car when she noticed he didn't look right. "Forgot a little something, didn't we, Lucas?"

He glanced over himself, taking inventory. "What?"

Susan Granger cupped both hands to her ears.

"Princess Leia?"

"Get your headset, smartass, or you won't make mile three."

He returned with it in hand. The digital model was an exact duplicate of the one that had nearly killed him, but this one was personally supplied by the FBI as a gift for his assistance.

She started the car and headed for MoPac. "You're nuts, you know. But I admire your tenacity."

"Thanks. And thanks for picking me up. Nikky doesn't get up before noon if he can help it."

Granger watched for the exit to Jollyville Road. "Oh, thought you might want to know I talked with Dr. Welch last night at Archie Mac's. Garvin and Lavell were released yesterday. Minor smoke inhalation and shock. They're home already—in a motel actually."

"Probably stay there till Garvin hears for sure about the transfer," Lucas suggested.

"Probably. But guess who left town with no forwarding?"

"Helen Pelham?"

"Nope. She's sticking around to spend a little time with her son." Susan sipped the tea. "Señor and Señora Villalobos."

Holt was not surprised. "Makes sense, given their newfound wealth and their underworld contacts." He was sure their crime-family friends had whisked them off to a ranch in some obscure Mexican town. "They didn't answer the door when you knocked?"

"Not hardly. Turns out they left right after Al and Lisa's funeral. Went directly from the church to a plane for Mexico."

Holt thought a moment. "So there's nobody left to testify against Ida Tabor, assuming she lives."

"That's the other bad news," Granger said. "Ida Tabor's going to pull through after all."

"Long enough for a lethal injection?"

"I doubt she'll get that far, though I think she deserves it." Granger signaled a left turn. "No, with all her money—which is probably untouchable but which Helen Pelham asked IRS to investigate—she'll get the best justice money can buy."

Holt smirked at her. "'Blessed are the merciless, for they shall obtain lawyers'?"

"'Retain,'" she countered.

"Cynic."

"Realist." She laughed. "And another thing. Your criminal buddy Jimmy Brickhouse? Of computer fame?"

"Gone to TDC?"

"Not hardly. Seems while he was at the computer in my office he made a few minor adjustments to his booking record."

Holt laughed. "He's out?"

"Free as a jailbird. Charges dropped, or rather vanished."

"He's creative." He smiled. "You got to give him that."

"We'll see how creative he gets next time he sets foot in my building—which, of course, he will."

Before Holt could answer, the sound of a loudspeaker blared outside with race announcements. "There's the banner for the starting line." He pointed.

"How long will this take you?" Susan Granger pulled the car into the mall parking lot and turned off the engine.

"I'm slow. Five hours."

"Good." She exited the car with him. "You'll have time to figure out how to pay for dinner at the Emerald."

"Great. When we going?" the Rev asked hesitantly.

"Depends. How soon after the race will you be able to do stairs? It's two flights up to the restaurant."

"Today's Saturday." He pursed his lips. "Tuesday."

"Pick me up at seven." She handed him the headset with a knowing look on her face. "And don't make me save your life before then." She kissed him on the lips. "Give 'em hell."

"Heaven."

"Whatever."

The Rev disappeared in the mass of scantily clad bodies and lost track of Susan Granger. He was surprised by her kiss; more surprised at how much he wanted to return it. He passed through the pack of senior runners, some of whom were in their seventies, and silently vowed to be in that same group when he reached their age. Suddenly he saw a banner on the sideline to his right. It echoed his T-shirt.

I'D RATHER BE—AT TDC! GO REV!

He waved at the group holding it. Maxine, Omar, Eddie, Doors, Brickhouse, Helen Pelham, and a half-awake Nikky Dorati waved back.

Over the din of the loudspeaker he could barely hear Maxine yell, "Yo, Rev! You made it to the starting line!"

Lucas jumped up and down and hollered with the rest of the runners as the timer raised the gun in the air. He flipped on the headset. Country-western backbeat pounded with his heart.

To his left, Susan Granger appeared. He half heard her yell and half read her lips: "Meet you at the finish!" The gun fired and the massive wave of runners cheered across the line.

Maybe you will, he thought as he punched his watch and ran under the banner. Maybe you will.

For now, he had five hours to recall, one by one, the lives and deaths of the people he had buried these last weeks, friends and parishioners who had been torn from the tapestry of his life, and to begin to expunge the emotional pain and sadness stored up within him, to pound it, step by step, into twenty-six and two-tenths miles of Austin pavement.

He turned up the volume and quickened his pace. There was no time to kill.